ONE FORBIDDEN EVENING

A chill slipped under her skin and Cybelline shivered.

"You're cold?" asked Ferrin. He made to go the fire again, but Cybelline stopped him.

"No, it's nothing. The odd shiver. Do not trouble yourself." In spite of her words, she shivered again.

This time when Ferrin got to his feet he put himself directly in front of her. Without asking permission to do so, he placed the back of his hand against her forehead, then her cheek. His touch lingered in spite of his intention for it to be otherwise.

"I told you it is nothing." Cybelline's skin tingled under his fingertips. She did not ask him to remove his hand. How was it possible that he could evoke such a response from her? The merest brush with him arrested her heart. She glanced upward and saw the dark centers of his eyes were wider than before. She suspected it was the same for her.

"You feel it, don't you, Cybelline?"

She did not ask him to explain. She simply nodded.

He took one of her hands in each of his and raised her up. "It is like completing a circuit."

"Electricity," she said softly.

His mouth was gentle on hers, the tug of his lips infinitely soft. Opposites. Attraction. His words came back to her as he nudged her lips apart. The kiss was long and slow and deep, and when he raised his head she felt herself being pulled toward him . . .

D0954602

Books by Jo Goodman

The Captain's Lady
Crystal Passion
Seaswept Abandon
Velvet Night
Violet Fire
Scarlet Lies
Tempting Torment
Midnight Princess
Passion's Sweet Revenge
Sweet Fire
Wild Sweet Ecstasy
Rogue's Mistress
Forever in My Heart
Always in My Dreams
Only in My Arms
My Steadfast Heart
My Reckless Heart
With All My Heart
More Than You Know
More Than You Wished
Let Me Be the One
Everything I Ever Wanted
All I Ever Needed
Beyond a Wicked Kiss
A Season to Be Sinful
One Forbidden Evening

Published by Zebra Books

One
Forbidden
Evening

ZEBRA BOOKS
Kensington Publishing Corp.
www.kensingtonbooks.com

ZEBRA BOOKS are published by

Kensington Publishing Corp.
850 Third Avenue
New York, NY 10022

Copyright © 2006 by Joanne Dobrzanski

All Kensington titles, imprints, and distributed lines are available at special quantity discounts for bulk purchases for sales promotion, premiums, fund-raising, educational, or institutional use.

Special book excerpts or customized printings can also be created to fit specific needs. For details, write or phone the office of the Kensington Special Sales Manager: Attn. Special Sales Department, Kensington Publishing Corp., 850 Third Avenue, New York, NY 10022. Phone: 1-800-221-2647.

Zebra and the Z logo Reg. U.S. Pat. & TM Off.

First Printing: August 2006
10 9 8 7 6 5 4 3 2 1

Printed in the United States of America

Prologue

He was coming to bed. At last. She smiled sleepily and raised the quilt and coverlet just enough for him to slide in beside her. Her body conformed to the depression in the mattress, then again as he closed the distance between them. She could feel his warm breath on her face, the nearness of his mouth, a hint of whisky on his tongue as he kissed her.

"You work too hard," she whispered. "You have been gone an age."

"I'm here now."

"Mmm. Yes, you are."

Their kiss deepened. She felt him stirring against her, and she rocked her hips forward, cradling him. Her arms lifted, circled his shoulders. When he lifted his head she buried her face in the crook of his neck and breathed deeply. The hem of her nightgown grazed her calves and thighs as he raised it with his fingertips. His touch was light, intimate, and familiar. Her breasts swelled against his chest.

"I've missed you," she said against his mouth.

"It is the same for me."

Yes, she realized, it was the same for him. Sometimes she doubted it, but not just at this moment, not when his lips moved so sweetly across hers, not when the scent of him enveloped her and the weight of his body secured her.

"Of course it is the same for me," he said, just as if he knew there were times when uncertainty plagued her.

Her fingers mussed the curling ends of hair at his nape. She felt him shiver, and it made her smile. His response was most surely an invitation to do it again, so she did.

"Ahh."

She raised her head. It was too dark to see him clearly. She thought she could make out the fine line of his profile against the pillow, but perhaps it was just that she knew how sharply defined his features were. Of a sudden it seemed important that she see him. She could not explain it, understanding only that the fleeting desire had become need and she should not ignore it. She began to draw back, intending to sit up.

"No," he said, catching her by the arms. His thumbs massaged her flesh as his grip tightened a fraction. He pulled her back, his touch insistent but still more gentle than not. "Stay here. Stay . . . close."

Resistance, such as there was, dissolved. She allowed herself to be pulled back into his embrace. It was where she wanted to be, she told herself. Still, she said, "Permit me to light a candle."

He chuckled softly. "Do you think I don't know where to put my hands? That I cannot find my way around your body? I have not been gone so long as that, and my sense of direction has always been good."

She sucked in a breath sharply as he palmed her bottom and brought her in full intimate contact with him once again. "Yes," she said on a thread of sound. "Oh, yes."

His mouth was on hers, this time engaging her tongue. She felt a fullness in her breasts, another in her heart. How careful he was with her, even when his own need was great. The kiss took on a languid, leisurely quality, and she was reminded of a kiss shared out of doors when they were but newly married. The manor was some distance behind them, the lake close enough to hear the rhythmic lap of water. On that occasion there had been sunshine and ducks preening on an outcropping of rocks. She could hear the snap of the rug as he laid it down on the uneven tufts of grass. A pleasant aroma rose from the picnic basket: warm bread and cheese and a skin of red wine.

Perhaps she should have been shocked that he would want her in the full light of the afternoon, but she was not missish or shy and wanted exactly the same thing. She lay on the rug in just the same fashion as she lay on the bed, one arm flung over her head, the other resting on his shoulder. Her gown was bunched around her hips and he was settled between her raised knees. She felt him reach between their bodies and cup her mons. His fingers wandered with purpose.

She was wet. He teased her with his fingertips, dipping, stroking. Her hips jerked. Her body sought him out. There was no shame in wanting this man . . . her husband.

He shifted position, resting his weight on his forearms. His lips nudged hers. The kiss was no longer so sweet or soft. Hunger made it urgent, hard. This was all right as well. He could have bloodied her mouth in service of this kiss and she would have welcomed so much fierceness. He did not always have to be careful with her; she would not break under his touch. It was the lack of it that made her snappish and fragile, separation that made her less re-silient. She was a woman with a woman's needs, and there was no shame in that.

Her tongue touched the ridge of his teeth. It swept the interior of his mouth. She sipped on his lower lip, then the upper one. Through it all her eyes stayed open. Had there been candlelight, she thought, she would be darkly reflected in his eyes now, the wide pupils like black mirrors. She would see her own desire and not turn away from it.

"Shh," he said. "Shh."

At first she did not understand, then she heard her own whimpers. The sound was at the back of her throat, a soft mewling cry of need and satisfaction. She could not help it. Did he think she could? It was not possible to remain so quiet when his mouth was moving across the curve of her neck, then sipping the skin at the base of her throat. She would be marked there. In the morning there would be a purplish stain where his lips had been, proof that he had come to her, proof that he had been in her bed.

She whimpered again, this time because his mouth was stamping the high curve of her breast. He did not chastise her this time. Instead he made a damp spot in the batiste covering her aureole. He drew the flimsy fabric and the rosy tip of her nipple between his lips. He flicked it with his tongue, rolled it between his teeth.

Beneath him her body rose in a perfect arch. Even with his weight on her, the small of her back lifted from the bed. Her heels pressed hard into the mattress. She thought the bed shuddered slightly, but perhaps it was only that she did.

He pressed his entry. The fullness of his erection was so welcome to her that she almost sobbed with relief. Her thighs clutched his hips and in all ways she was open to him. She thrummed with pleasure as he seated himself inside her. His own quiet was unnerving. Did he not feel it, or was it only that he refused to give voice to it?

She was on the point of asking him what was wrong when she heard his soft groan. It was all right, then. *They* were all right. Fear of not being able to pleasure him was immediately forgotten.

"You are my heart."

Had she said it aloud or only thought it? Neither, she realized. The words had come from him. So right. So perfect. She had not known how much she needed to hear those words until they were said. How had he known? How did he always know?

"Please," she said softly.

"What is it?"

But she had no words to explain what she meant, only this one word and the hope that he would understand everything. "Please," she said again.

"Just so." He began to move in her, slowly, with long, sure strokes that she could match with the rise and fall of her hips. "Am I hurting you?"

She realized that he had wrested a cry from her. "No," she said quickly. Immediately she knew he was not convinced. His next thrust was not as forceful as his last. "No, truly you are not. It is good. All of it."

He stopped moving. Waited.

She was not proof against his patience. She was impulsive, occasionally reckless. He was the essence of fortitude. In a test of wills that involved forbearance, he would always be the victor.

"It is only that it has been so long," she said. "I have been waiting for you ever so long."

"You fit me as closely as a glove."

Unintentionally she contracted around him. "Yes."

"I'm afraid I will hurt—"

She did not let him finish. Even in the dark it was not difficult to find his mouth with hers. Against his lips, she whispered, "You cannot hurt me, not like this. It is only when you are gone from my bed, from my life, that I am hurt. Do not make me wait again."

"It's as if you're a virgin."

This made her laugh softly. "I'm not."

He sucked on her lower lip. There was a corresponding tightness within her. She squeezed him and he moaned, closing his eyes and releasing her. "God, but you will be my undoing."

She locked her hands around his neck. "If you mean to flatter me, then I will count that as a good thing." Her sigh was audible as he began to move again. Her bottom lifted, fell. She knew his rhythm and his strength. They had done it just this way many times, and familiarity heightened her arousal rather than diminished it. She knew what to expect and when. Her responses were as measured as his. Her breast filled the warm cup of his hand, and her nipple scraped the center of his palm. Her breathing sharpened.

And just when she thought he could not—or would not—surprise her, he withdrew suddenly and turned her on her stomach. He lifted her hips and positioned himself behind her. She rested her cheek against the pillow sham and reached for the bedhead, bracing herself. He came into her with a short thrust, then a deeper one. His hands kept her tightly joined to him while hers sought purchase.

"Yes?" he asked, his voice husky.

She nodded, then realized that in the dark it was no answer. Desire made her voice thick, the consonants sibilant. "Yes. Please, yes."

Between her thighs, he stroked her. Heat and wetness made her receptive. Just when his touch was so insistent as to make pleasure teeter on the edge of pain, he eased back, rubbing the hood of her clitoris and not the uncovered nub. She felt him gauge her breathing and her movement, marking when she was controlled and when she was on the cusp of having none.

How well he knew her body, but no better than she knew his. She was aware of even the small changes that had occurred in his absence. The weight of him was perhaps a stone heavier. The breadth of his shoulders was wider by a fraction, the muscles of his upper arms more taut. He did indeed work too hard. His labors had reshaped his frame, roughened the pads of his fingers and the heels of his hands. He still fit her exactly as she remembered, or mayhap it was that she fit him.

She had come to learn her own body in contrast to the planes and angles of his. She was not so curvaceous except when his palms were cupping her breasts or bottom, or when his hands were resting lightly on her hips. When he embraced her it seemed that her shoulders were no more broad than they should be, nor her waist too narrow. Her head fit snugly under his chin.

Elsewhere, it was he that was fit snugly. A faint smile touched her lips. She was rocked forward, then she did the rocking, this time backward, pressing into him with the full roundness of her bottom.

She felt changes in her body, a tightness under her skin, a ripple across her belly. Her eyelids fluttered closed, though she fought to keep them open. Her lips remained slightly parted. There was fierce heat where there had been only warmth and the first crests of pleasure where there had been only unhurried, rolling waves.

She cried out, though she wished she had not. He liked her to be silent, and she did not wish to be indifferent to what pleased him. She sucked in her lower lip and bit down hard enough to taste blood.

"No," he said. His mouth was against her ear, and he was spilling his seed into her. His hard frame spasmed, and his neck arched. "No," he said again.

She did not know what he said no to. Was he cautioning her not to cry or not to stop her cries? Or did he mean it as a warning to himself, a last effort not to have this pleasure end?

"No!"

This last shout shook her. It echoed painfully in her ears, each repetition louder, not softer, than the last. She clapped her hands over her ears and felt the weight of him leave her. The blankets were torn from her, and she understood that she was once again alone in the bed.

The shouting in her head stopped abruptly. The silence startled her. What frightened her was that she could no longer bring the sound of his voice to mind. How could that be? How could she have forgotten the sound of her husband's voice as if she'd never known it?

Her eyelids fluttered open in the same manner they had closed just a short time ago. The candle in the dish on her bedside table still flickered.

She had never been in the dark, only in her dreams.

The bedcovers were in disarray around her. Her nightshift was crumpled about her hips. One of her hands lay cupped under her breast, the other was tucked between her thighs. She removed it slowly, conscious of the dampness of her fingertips. The small friction of withdrawal was enough to prompt a contraction and a residual ripple of pleasure. Her hips moved once in helpless response. She jerked her other hand from under her naked breast and turned away from the candlelight, pressing her face into the pillow.

Tears welled in her eyes. She bit her lip and tasted blood quickly. So that part of her dream had been real, too.

Only he was not real. Her husband. She had betrayed him, she knew that now, for it was not her husband who had come to her bed. She had been alone, yet not. She had wanted it to be Nicholas who was with her, but how could he be? Nicholas was dead, and she had betrayed him with a stranger. She understood that it had happened only in her mind, that what pleasure she'd felt had been by her own hand, yet it still seemed like the worst sort of betrayal for even her dreams to have turned on her.

Five years ago today she had exchanged vows with Nicholas Caldwell. So it was on the anniversary of her marriage, not on the anniversary of his death, that she had allowed herself to entertain another lover.

At her sides her fists bunched and she wept in earnest. At last.

Chapter One

If it was possible to die of boredom, Ferrin was of the opinion he was not long for this earth. Only minutes ago he had been contemplating murder. Not seriously, of course. Perhaps if he had been contemplating the murder of someone other than his own mother, he reasoned, he might have been able to think the deed through to completion. But murder his mother? No, it was just not done. Not even in his own mind, no matter the provocation.

He could, however, cheerfully throttle Wynetta. The masquerade had been her idea and everyone—save him— had pronounced it a splendid notion. He would have pronounced it corkbrained, but since his views on such things were well known, no one considered it necessary to consult him.

There was never any doubt but that he would throw in his lot with the rest of them. He was ever the easy touch when it came to matters of family, though he knew this would surprise his society and many of his acquaintances. That was just as it should be, else what was the point of cultivating a reputation for not suffering fools?

"I say, Ferrin, you're a dark one, right enough. Are you going to make your play or merely scowl at your cards?"

One of Ferrin's dark eyebrows lifted in a perfect arch; the scowl remained unchanged. "Why cannot I do both?" He tossed a four of spades toward the other cards at the center of the table and took the trick with trump.

Across from Ferrin, Mr. Porter Wellsley returned to the contemplation of his own cards. "Don't know how you manage to do that," he said idly, rearranging his hand. "Damned if you do not always make the right play."

Ferrin led the next round with an ace of hearts. "Then count yourself fortunate that you are my partner."

"Oh, I wasn't complaining. Just don't know how you do it."

To the left of Ferrin, Mr. William Allworthy flicked his cards with the buffed nail of his index finger before choosing one. He didn't look up as he spoke. "Enough chatter, Wellsley. This ain't the ladies' table."

Wellsley was about to respond, but he caught Ferrin's deepening scowl and thought better of it. He threw off a card and sat back, waiting for their fourth to make his play.

Mr. Bennet Allworthy folded his cards, tapped one corner of the slim deck on the table, then fanned them out again. He studied them as carefully now as he had upon receiving them. He glanced repeatedly at the cards already thrown down as though they might have changed their spots while his attention was on his hand. He never looked at his cousin.

Ferrin placed two fingers on Bennet's wrist just as he was about to make his play. "Not the spade, Allworthy. Not when you still have a heart in your hand. You do not want to renege, do you? Wellsley might not be so generous of a nature as I and consider it a cardsharp's trick."

Bennet froze. Just above his carefully crafted neck-cloth the first evidence of a flush could be seen creeping toward the sharp point of his jaw. He did not raise his eyes from his cards, nor did he shake off Ferrin's light touch. "Is your lordship calling me a cheat?"

"Merely doing my part to make certain you don't become one. Wellsley is credited to be a decent enough shot."

Wellsley rubbed the underside of his chin with his knuckles. "Decent enough?" he asked. "Is that the best you can say about me, Ferrin? Damned by faint praise. That's what that is. I'd do better by you, you know."

Ferrin removed his fingers from Allworthy. He regarded his partner at cards from beneath his hooded glance. "That's because I'm better than a decent shot."

"What? Well, there is that."

"Indeed." Ferrin waved idly in Bennet Allworthy's direction. "Play the heart and have done with it."

For the space of a heartbeat three of the four players were aware of nothing so much as the music from the adjoining ballroom, the drone of too many guests crowded into the space, the flirtatious laughter of a few as new liaisons were made and old partners were dismissed. It was only in the card room that others seemed to sense a shift in the atmosphere. Voices dropped pitch to a whisper; glances shifted uncertainly toward the center table. No one made a play. For a moment, no one save the Earl of Ferrin breathed.

Mr. Bennet Allworthy dropped the ten of hearts on the table.

As simply as that, the natural order was restored. Ferrin collected the trick as if nothing untoward had taken place. Indeed, from his perspective, nothing had, except perhaps that for a few moments he had not been bored. He led trump, resuming play. It required only another minute to finish the set. He and Wellsley thoroughly trounced the Allworthy cousins. When it was done, no one suggested another go at whist. The cousins excused themselves and exited for the refreshment table in the ballroom, making rather too much of their parched throats by clearing them loudly and often.

"I shouldn't wonder if they don't trip over themselves in their haste to be gone," Wellsley said. He shuffled the cards absently. "You were rather hard on Bennet, don't you think? Playing trump out of turn might have been an honest mistake."

Ferrin shrugged. "If you thought that was so, you could have come to his defense."

"And pass on an opportunity to shoot someone?" He unbuttoned his frock coat and patted the pistol tucked into his breeches. "Not bloody likely."

"A pistol, Wellsley?"

"Part of the costume."

"What part? I don't recognize your intent. Save for that much abused hat you are wearing, you are dressed as you always are."

"I'm a highwayman. You did not notice the disreputable twist of my neckcloth?"

"Disreputable? I do not think it can properly be called that when your valet has merely failed to tie the mathematical." Ferrin's coolly colored glance dropped to the pistol. "Never say it is primed."

"Do you take me for a fool?" Wellsley immediately thought better of his question and held up one hand, palm out. "Pray, do not answer that. It's lowering enough that you did not take me for a highwayman. Mayhap I should have forsaken the highway for the high seas as you have. A pirate would have been just the thing. Which do you suppose the ladies find more dashing?"

"You are welcome to put that poser to them this evening."

"Don't tempt me, Ferrin. I might."

Ferrin merely grunted softly.

Wellsley cocked his head toward the ballroom. "You find all of this tiresome." It was not a question.

"It is obvious, then. Bother that. You will warn me, will you not, if some member of my family wanders in this direction?

They will take exception to my *ennui*, and I cannot watch the doorway easily from here."

"Indeed. You will get a crick in your neck."

Ferrin laid the flat of his hand against his nape and massaged the corded muscles. "I already possess the crick. I am hoping not to break the thing."

"Poor Ferrin. Your family is such a trial to you."

"Can you doubt it?"

Wellsley regarded his friend a moment longer before he spoke. The eyes that held his study were glacial, yet there was a hint of something that might have been amusement. "As a matter of fact," he said, "sometimes I can. It occurs on occasion that you could be naught but a fraud."

"Careful. I will not hesitate to run you through." Ferrin's hand dropped to his cutlass. "My sword trumps your unprimed popper."

Heads turned in their direction as Wellsley gave a bark of laughter. "Just so." He continued to shuffle the cards. "How did you know Bennet had a heart remaining in his hand?"

"Because he told his cousin."

"Told William? Are you quite certain, Ferrin? I didn't hear such an exchange."

"Because while you were contemplating my scowl, Bennet was tapping his cards on the table. One for hearts. Two for diamonds. Three for—"

"I get the gist of it."

"See? Perfectly discernible to even the meanest intelligence when one is not preoccupied."

"Did you just insult me?"

Now there was no mistaking the amusement in Ferrin's ice-blue glance. "If you are uncertain, then there is no harm done."

Grinning, Wellsley handed over the cards. "Do not be so sure. I am of a mind to get a little of my own back."

"By all means. You must do as you see fit." Ferrin began to deal the cards, setting up two dummy hands just to keep things interesting. When he was done, he fanned open his cards and examined them.

"What is to be done about the Allworthy cousins?" asked Wellsley.

"What do you mean, what is to be done?"

"They are cardsharps, Ferrin."

"They are dullards, and they are not so deep in the pockets that they can do much damage at the clubs."

"I am not sure the amount of the wagering matters. I was thinking that someone less forgiving than you will surely call the pair of them out. Do you want that on your conscience?"

Ferrin was uncertain how the consequence of the cousins' cheating had become his concern. "What would you have me do? Spread the tale of what was done here so they will become pariahs in the card rooms?"

"That would do nicely, yes. Save them from themselves."

"At considerable damage to their reputations. One or the other of them will call me out, and we shall be precisely at the juncture you are bent on avoiding, save *I* will be the one facing a pistol at twenty paces. If that is your plan for revenge, you are deuced good at it. I will choose my words more carefully when I am speaking of the meanest intelligence."

"Thank you, but I have some other revenge in mind for that slight. One with a more certain outcome than you and one of the Allworthys in a field at dawn." He held up his hand when Ferrin looked as if he intended to object that there would be any doubt about that outcome. "There is *always* doubt, Ferrin. Your opponent might turn too soon. Your pistol might misfire. Allworthy—whichever cousin throws the glove—might be on the side of the angels that day. When I cast about for revenge, I want complete assurance that there can be but one end."

"I believe you make me afraid, Wellsley."

Wellsley threw down a card in the manner a man might toss the gauntlet. "Good."

Chuckling, Ferrin turned over a card from one of the dummy decks, then laid his own card. "How many shepherdesses do you think are here tonight?"

"I counted six, one of them your sister Imogene. Will she be put out, do you think, that her costume is not at all original?"

"She is the only one carrying a crook with a blue bow. In her mind it is enough to set her apart from the rest of the flock. Besides, she is married and not set on making the same impression upon the guests as Wynetta. It is Netta's debut, after all. Or nearly so. She made her come out at the Calumet affair a few weeks ago."

"I danced a set with her, remember?"

Ferrin did not, but he didn't say so. "Good of you. She was frantic she would go unnoticed."

"Not possible. Your sister is quite lovely, a diamond really, though I suppose that's escaped your notice."

"Hardly. I admit that it surprises that you find her so."

"I will not inquire what that means. It's bound to be an uncomfortable conversation."

Ferrin nodded. This evening his sister was Cleopatra. A black wig covered her cornsilk-colored hair, and she'd darkened her brows and lined her eyes. The effect was as dramatic as she was. Never shy about holding court whether she had admirers or only her family around her, Netta was immediately taken with her role as queen. It did not matter in the least if they were young bucks in togas, Corinthians wearing armor, or gentleman courtiers from two centuries past, she gathered them to her like children to a bake-shop window. Early in the evening he'd stood with his stepfather and watched her effortlessly charm her company. In contrast to Sir Geoffrey, who nervously shifted his weight from one foot to the other, Ferrin was all admiration. The success of this sister, his stepsister really, meant that she would be off the marriage mart quickly and that he would have to suffer but a handful more of these occasions. Ian and Imogene, his stepfather's twins, were both married four years ago at twenty. If Wynetta accepted a proposal this Season, then it was left only to Restell, another stepbrother, to succumb to leg-shackling. Unfortunately, Restell was not as interested in the state of marriage as he was in the state of his affairs. For reasons that Ferrin could not entirely comprehend, Restell was determined to pattern his own life after Ferrin's, or rather what he imagined Ferrin's life to be. As Ferrin was still unmarried at two and thirty, it occurred to him that Restell would require rescue and intervention for years to come if he was not to bankrupt the family with his gaming or be at the center of a scandal with his paramours.

Ferrin wondered if settling his stepfather's four off-spring in good marriages was merely preparation for what lay ahead. At twelve and eight, his half-sisters Hannah and Portia were already twice the handful that Wynetta had ever been—or was likely to be. For all that Netta could have trod the boards at Drury Lane with her penchant for dramatic sighs and asides, she still was possessed of a keen mind and a sensible disposition. Hannah and Portia were not. His youngest sisters were intelligent, he supposed, but hadn't sense enough between them to find shelter in a rainstorm.

The fault for that lay at his own dear mother's feet. Sir Geoffrey Gardner had always impressed as practical, if somewhat romantic. Ferrin's mother, though, was a flibbertigibbet, and he could no longer ignore the signs that Hannah and Portia were strongly influenced by her. He was already calculating what it would cost in six years' time, and four years after that, to see that these sisters found decent partners who could take them in hand but not abuse their generous though silly natures.

A bloody fortune, he thought.

"What's that?" Wellsley asked, drawing another trick toward him. "Did you say something?"

"Did I?" Ferrin had not realized he might have spoken aloud.

"We're not making a wager here, are we? I thought you said something about a fortune."

"Can't imagine what you heard." Ferrin picked up his tumbler of whisky and sipped. "Your play. Go on."

Wellsley's dark glance drifted momentarily from his cards to a point past his friend's shoulder. He did not allow his eyes to linger on the doorway but applied himself to choosing a card and schooling his features. He placed a seven of spades on the table.

"Aha! So it is true! Lady Arbuthnot did not mistake the matter when she said I would find you here!"

Ferrin was about to make his play when every hair at the back of his neck stood at attention. Many a grown man so neatly caught out by his mother might have dropped the card he was holding over the table, but Ferrin managed to slip it back into his hand and set all the cards down as though nothing untoward was taking place. It was no good reminding Wellsley that he'd agreed to give him fair warning of any family members approaching. This had been done of a purpose. The look he speared his friend communicated that it would have been kinder to allow him to face the Allworthy cousins at daybreak than to have his mother bear down on him unaware.

"Enjoy your revenge, Wellsley," he said under his breath. He doubted he'd been heard. Wellsley was chuckling, in every way enjoying himself. With a last sour look in his friend's direction, Ferrin got to his feet as his mother came to stand beside his chair. "Mother. How good you are to make your way round to the card room. You will perhaps join the play?"

Lady Marianna Gardner, the former Countess of Ferrin, and now the wife of Sir Geoffrey, regarded her eldest child as if he had the sense of a bag of hair. She had to look a considerable distance upward, as she was a diminutive woman and he stood half a foot taller than most of the men of her acquaintance. This never mattered, of course, as she had once suckled him at her breast before being persuaded to give him over to a wet nurse. The bond that had been forged on that occasion was still very much intact, at least in her mind. "Join the play?" she asked in hushed accents. "Can you really have made such an outrageous utterance?"

"He did," Wellsley said. "I heard him."

Her ladyship turned a gimlet eye on Mr. Wellsley. "And you will not repeat it, for I have no doubt that it is your unseemly influence at work here. Did I not recently say as much to your grandmother? You are a scapegrace, Mr. Wellsley. I have always thought it unfortunate that I like you so well, but there you have it. I cannot account for it myself." Before that worthy could answer, her head swiveled sharply to her son. She was supremely unaware that Ferrin had to draw back to avoid being tickled by the long ostrich plume fixed in her turban.

"You do not mean to spend the whole of the evening in here, do you?" she asked pointedly. "It is not done. I cannot help but think you have forgotten you are the host."

"I believe I have provided a great deal of the ready as well as the location," Ferrin said dryly. "In every other way I am well out of it."

"Oh, this is too bad of you. What will people say? And your sister is working so hard to make a success of the evening. It will surely be noticed that you occupied yourself playing cards. Nero fiddled while Rome burned. People remember that."

"I will fetch my fiddle directly." Ferrin observed his mother beginning to push her lower lip forward. This was but the opening salvo. The weapons that she kept in her arsenal included the moue, the tear, the trembling pout, and the tremulous voice. These were generally more effective than her reasoning, which Ferrin found nonsensical and a trial to his gray matter. "You are looking quite splendid tonight. The plume is particularly charming."

"Thank you." She allowed the silver half mask she held over the upper portion of her face to fall away and reveal her full pleasure of the pretty compliment. "You will join us in the ballroom, will you not?"

"Of course, Mother."

"My friends delight in seeing you. I fear they do not know many rakes. They are quite fascinated by your manner."

"I see." He bent forward so there was no danger that he could be overheard. "May I roam freely or will you want to parade me on a leash?"

This time when her ladyship lowered her mask it was to snap it sharply against her son's forearm. "You are the very devil," she whispered.

Grinning, Ferrin straightened. "You are mistaken, Mother. Tonight I am a pirate." From beneath his tricornered hat, he pulled down a black silk patch and fixed it over his right eye. "See?"

"The very devil," she repeated. There was no censure in her tone, only affection. She touched his cheek and smiled, perfectly content with this outcome. Turning to go, her ladyship paused when she glimpsed Wellsley standing at attention on the other side of the table. "And you, Mr. Wellsley, you are of an eligible age, are you not? Well past it, I should think. As is Ferrin. Do not squander your inheritance in one sitting at the card table with my son when there are so many young women in the next room willing to relieve you of it over the course of a lifetime."

Before Wellsley could make a reply, Lady Gardner presented her back to him and made a grand exit for the ballroom. Wellsley sunk back into his chair and looked up at Ferrin. "I need libation."

Ferrin nodded, waving over one of the footmen. He

finished the last finger of whisky remaining in his tumbler and gave it over. "Two more of the same," he said. "None of the punch from the fountain, please." When the liveried servant was gone, Ferrin took measure of his friend. "Will you be all right? I cannot tell whether it is astonishment that put you back in your chair or relief."

"Both, I think." Wellsley tossed his hat on the table and used four fingers to rake back his hair. The effect was to lend him more in the way of a disreputable air than the disheveled neckcloth. "She said she likes me well enough, so that is something, I suppose."

"Well, of course she likes you. Why wouldn't she? You have £12,000 per annum, a townhouse in London, an estate in the North, a family with as few rascals as one can properly hope for, and a countenance that does not stop clocks. God's truth, Wellsley, I can't think why I haven't proposed."

Wellsley's staccato burst of laughter had heads turning in their direction again. He collected himself, straightening in his chair just as the drinks were brought to them. He raised the tumbler, saluted his friend, and drank deeply. "Dutch courage," he said, setting the glass down. "Mayhap Miss Wynetta will take another turn on the floor with me."

"The queen of the Nile? You will have to cut through the throng to get to her. Will you take my cutlass?"

"No. I do not think that will be necessary." He returned his hat to his head and relied on Ferrin's judgment to let him know when he'd achieved the proper roguish angle. With most of his bright-yellow hair covered, it was left to him to disguise his face. He withdrew a scarf from beneath the sleeve of his frock coat, folded it in a triangle, then used it to hide his nose, mouth, and squared-off chin. "Well?" he asked, getting to his feet. He removed the pistol and aimed it at Ferrin's chest. "Stand and deliver."

"Convincing. You will not credit it, but I am quaking in my boots."

"Good. Now let us see who—" Wellsley stopped, his attention caught by the figure who had stepped forward and was now framed in the open doorway.

Seeing his friend's gaze fixed on the threshold of the card room, Ferrin thought his mother had returned. "Never say she has brought reinforcements to drag us out."

Wellsley merely shook his head.

Seeing something akin to reverence in his friend's eyes, Ferrin was forced to turn and see what manner of creature could inspire it. He was aware of a niggling hope that it was Netta.

The queen standing at the threshold was not the woman-child Cleopatra, but she was immediately recognizable to him and every other man in the room. They were all staring at Boudicca come to life. The heavy mass of flame-red hair, the brightly dyed orange tunic and thick blue mantle, the twisted golden torc at her throat, and gold bracelets on her left wrist and arm proclaimed her as the fierce warrior queen of ancient Britain. Lest anyone doubt it, she carried a spear a head taller than she was.

Wellsley started to take a step forward, but Ferrin managed to rise and insert himself directly in his friend's path. "You do not even like redheads," Wellsley whispered from behind.

Over his shoulder, Ferrin said, "I am prepared to reevaluate. One must, you know, when presented with new evidence. It is in the nature of scientific inquiry. Do you know her?"

"If I did, I would go to my grave with it."

It was just as well, Ferrin decided. She was Boudicca, and more than that he didn't need to know. Like the torc at her throat, the brooch that held her mantle closed, and the bracelets on her wrist and arm, the mask that covered her upper face was hammered gold. Gold threads were woven into her tunic, and her bodice shimmered in the candlelight as she drew in a deep breath. Ferrin had the odd notion that she was steeling herself for battle. She had yet to hold the glance of any one man, but she had paused long enough on the threshold to examine all of them.

He stepped forward and closed the distance between them. "My queen," he said, making a courtly bow. "There is someone in particular you are seeking? A pirate, perhaps?"

She did not smile or incline her head to acknowledge the overture. Her posture was unyielding: shoulders back, head high, feet planted slightly apart so she would not be moved. "A shepherdess," she said.

Ferrin indicated the occupants of the card room with a wave of his hand, encouraging Boudicca to take a second look. "Knights Templar. Roman centurions. King Arthur. A highwayman. Two Harlequins. A king's executioner. Sir Francis Drake. A cardinal and a friar. Not a single shepherdess. Tell me, does she have ribbons on her crook?"

"Yes."

"Their color?"

"Green."

"I have only seen pink, blue, and yellow."

"That is what I have observed also."

"May I escort you through the squeeze in the ballroom? Mayhap with two pairs of eyes making the search, we shall find her." From behind her mask, Ferrin could make out the faint narrowing of her gaze. She was regarding him skeptically, her attention riveted on the black silk patch covering his right eye. "Three eyes are not as good as four," he said, "but they're half again as good as two."

She smiled a little then, not enough to show her teeth or brighten her eyes, but enough that he was encouraged.

"Will you take my arm?" he asked. When he saw her hesitate, he added, "We will make but one circle of the ballroom, and I will release you."

She raised her weapon slightly. "I am carrying a spear. Of course you will release me."

"Point taken."

"No, not yet you haven't," she said. "But I won't hesitate to see that you do."

Ferrin gave a shout of laughter, unwittingly making him the envy of every one of his guests within hearing of it. He saw she did not startle. Rather she held her ground and gripped her spear more tightly as if she might have use of it sooner than she'd thought. He held out his arm and waited patiently for her to accept it. "As pirates go, I am not considered a particularly ruthless one."

"Like Blackbeard."

"Far and away more ruthless than I."

"And Bluebeard?"

"I have yet to take a wife, let alone murder one." She took his arm and allowed him to lead her back into the ballroom. "Do you think I would be afraid if you had?"

He did not have to pause to think on his answer. "No. There is the spear, after all."

"Just so."

As soon as they stepped beyond the threshold they were swallowed in the crush inside the ballroom. Ferrin had the advantage of height and he immediately spied two crooks with pink streamers near the stringed orchestra. He steered Boudicca in the opposite direction, weaving her in and out of the conversational clutches that formed near the refreshment table and beside the fountain of cider punch. They skirted the drooping fronds of the potted plants that made a veritable jungle of one corner of the ballroom and drifted among the dancers as though they were taking a set themselves. Ferrin was quick to notice that their passage around the room was made easier because the guests parted for her, not him. The novelty of it amused him.

She was not the amazon that Queen Boudicca was alleged to have been, but she was taller than many women present, taller certainly than all of the shepherdesses he had seen thus far. Her bearing was in every way regal. She moved with a certain fluid grace among the guests but somehow remained apart from them. He wished he might know the shape of her nose better, but the mask defined it, not flesh and bone. The arch of her cheeks was also hidden and he could not quite make out the color of her eyes. Candlelight from the chandeliers and wall sconces glanced off the hammered gold and defied his best efforts to determine whether they were gray or green or even blue. Her mouth was the feature most openly revealed to him, and when she was engaged in looking over the crowd, he took the opportunity to mark the shape of it, noting the full bottom curve and the way her upper lip curled slightly each time she caught him out.

"You are staring," she said, not bothering to look at him this time. "We have not met before, my lord, so you should not apply yourself to divining my identity."

"But you know mine?"

"I would be a very shabby guest if I did not know the name of my host."

"Perhaps, but are you certain I am he?"

"You were pointed out to me earlier."

Ferrin wondered that he had not seen her before. He had obviously been too eager to quit the ballroom, though he was reminded now of all his reasons for wanting to be gone from it.

The room, in spite of being quite large, was too warm. The energy of the dancers, the milling of the onlookers, the occasional heated discussion, bursts of laughter, smoldering glances, and all of the incessant gossip combined to raise the temperature five degrees above what was comfortable. Guests spilled into the adjoining rooms so that revelers now occupied a drawing room, the gallery, and Ferrin's library. All of this was in addition to room he'd gladly given over to card play at the outset of the evening.

As they passed the refreshment table, Ferrin managed to lift two glasses of lemonade, though it meant releasing Boudicca's arm. She thanked him for the refreshment, but of necessity both hands were now occupied, one with her drink, the other with the spear. She hadn't an arm for him as they proceeded, a turn of events Ferrin regretted.

"Perhaps the library," he said. "Your shepherdess might have slipped inside in want of a good book."

"Unlikely."

He made to turn her away from the entrance to that room, but she shook her head and indicated they should look anyway. "You are thinking that there might be some other reason the shepherdess would be interested in the library? A tryst, perhaps?"

"Perhaps."

Ferrin wondered if he would know this shepherdess. Boudicca was not forthcoming, and he suspected it was because she did not want him to be able to identify her through her friend. He decided not to press. In truth, he was disappointed that she knew him. He would have liked to have remained a pirate to her this evening, not her host, certainly not the Earl of Ferrin.

He stepped to one side of the pocket doors and gestured to Boudicca to proceed. When she passed him his senses were teased by the light fragrance of lavender. A favorite scent of hers? he wondered. Or something she wore for this evening only, like the rest of her costume?

Ferrin followed her into the library and saw quickly that she would not find what she sought there. The musketeer on the chaise longue gave up trying to kiss his lady-in-waiting and eased his arms from around her shoulders. Ferrin's lips twitched. It seemed she would be a lady-in-waiting a bit longer.

"Something amuses?" Boudicca asked.

"Always." When she did not ask him to explain himself,

he had the impression she was drawing her own conclusion. "Your friend does not appear to be here, either."

"No, she doesn't."

"Shall we try the gallery?"

"You do not mind?"

"Not at all."

Ferrin pointed in the direction of the door that would lead them through to the gallery. Not many guests had stumbled upon this room, though the evening was hours yet from being at an end. Several couples were touring the room, some unattached females were exchanging the latest *on-dit*. There was not a single shepherdess.

He thought Boudicca would want to leave immediately, but she turned her attention to the paintings. "Would you like to view them?" he asked.

"I would."

He took her empty glass and set it on the entry table with his own, then he offered his arm again. She accepted his escort without pause this time, and he drew her toward the full length portrait of his great-grandfather. "This is George Howard Hollings," he told her. "The third Hollings to hold the title. Intimidating, is he not?"

"Impressive, I was thinking. You have his eyes."

"One of them."

She smiled again, this time more easily than before, then pointed to the painting to the right. "His father?" she asked.

"His grandfather. The first earl."

"He looks vaguely disreputable."

"You are putting it too mildly. He was wholly disreputable."

"How did he acquire the title?"

"A letter of mark. He preyed on Spanish galleons in the Americas. It was quite lucrative."

"Then he was a pirate . . . as you are."

"A privateer, I believe, is the proper term. A pirate has

no letter of mark from his queen. He served the interests of the Crown and he was rewarded with a title and lands."

"And considerable fortune."

"That is my understanding, yes."

"How was he called?"

"Captain Hollings, I imagine." He could not quite temper his amusement when Boudicca's splendid mouth flattened. So his queen did not suffer fools, either. It was a mark in her favor, though he kept his own counsel. He was quite certain she did not care for his opinion, good or otherwise. "He was called Christopher Charles Hollings."

"As you are."

"I am Christopher Andrew, but I think I see where you are going with your inquiry. If I lent him my patch we might be mistaken for twins. You are aware, I collect, that I am also disreputable."

"Wholly?"

"I never do anything in half measures, so yes, wholly disreputable. You should probably not be alone with me."

She purposefully looked to the fireplace where a Roman senator and a Greek goddess were admiring the large landscape hanging above the mantel. "We are hardly alone." Her chin lifted to indicate the clutch of young women still gathered in the center of the gallery. "Although I wish our chaperones were less inclined to titter."

"You do not titter?"

"No."

Another mark in her favor, Ferrin thought. "My sisters titter. All of them. My mother also."

"That must be a considerable cross to bear."

It was her dry-as-dust tone that raised one corner of his mouth. He answered in like accents. "You cannot imagine."

Boudicca returned to her study of the first earl. Ferrin could not summon the same interest in it. The resemblance was so profound it was rather like regarding his own face in a mirror, and he did little enough of that. What was the point, after all? Nothing could be changed. His brow would stand as high; his eyes would retain their peculiar heavy-lidded cast. A scar might draw attention away from the cut of his cheekbones and chin, but only a collision with a stone wall or a fist would flatten the aquiline shape of his nose. He had no particular desire to acquire either as pain was a consequence of both.

His mouth twitched slightly as Boudicca turned from the portrait to make the same study of his profile. "I am unused to such scrutiny. Most people remark on the likeness and have done with it."

"I beg your pardon. I fear I have been unconscionably rude. I did not mean to give you discomfort."

"Do I strike you as one so easily discomfited? It is more in the way of diverting." He paused a beat. "And curious. I am wondering if your study would be so open if you were not wearing the mask and the raiment of a queen. As Boudicca, you may say or do as you please."

Boudicca glanced at the spear she carried. "It does give one pause, I suppose."

"It certainly gives *me* pause." He glimpsed her faint smile again, this time recognizing the reluctance of that mien as it crossed her features. She did not want to be amused, or at least she did not want to be amused by him. The possibility that her disinclination was in some way personal intrigued Ferrin more than put him off. "Shall we go on?" he asked, indicating the next portrait. "Or have you seen enough? There is still the matter of your shepherdess."

"She will not leave me. I'd like to see more, but you are perfectly welcome to attend to your other guests. I can manage to navigate this room, indeed all of the rooms, on my own."

"I have already observed that is the case. Only Moses might be more effective at parting the sea of guests. However, you will be doing me a very great favor by allowing me to escort you. I am discharging my responsibilities as host and no longer in danger of expiring from boredom. Until you stood on the threshold of the card room, I wasn't at all hopeful that I could do the former without succumbing to the latter." Ferrin saw that she did not seem to be moved by his request. The damnable mask was not all that was keeping her expression shuttered from him. He suspected that she was as adept at confining her emotions as she was at confining her thoughts. "I understand that you have no reason to grant me such a kindness," he said rather stiffly. "All the benefits are undoubtedly mine."

"What a foolish thing to say."

Ferrin's dark brows lifted. "I beg your pardon."

"You tempt me to prick you with this, you know." She tilted her chin, indicating the spear. "It is you who have done me the favor. I am quite glad of your escort, but it is passing strange to me that you have invited so many guests and express so little interest in them."

"The invitation list is not my doing. That detail was left to my sister and my mother."

"But this is your residence. Surely they—"

He stopped her with a shake of his head. "They surely did not. Do not misunderstand. I gave them permission to act on my behalf, so I accept responsibility, but playing host at affairs of this nature is far and away more about duty than personal choice."

"You would rather be at your gentleman's club."

"That might suit."

"Playing cards and gaming."

"Perhaps."

"Discussing politics."

"That is done on occasion."

"Scheming."

He smiled slightly. "That is done more often."

She made no response to this last but allowed him to resume their tour of the gallery. The other couples in the room were moving on as well. The wizard Merlin entered not long afterward, accompanied by Pocahontas and a shepherdess.

"She is not the shepherdess I'm seeking," Boudicca said.

"I know. She's Mrs. Edward Branson, better known to me as my sister Imogene."

"I had not realized. I was introduced to her earlier, but I did not understand she was a relation."

"Then she is not the one who placed you on the invitation list."

Boudicca gave him a sidelong glance. "I think your lordship is fishing for my name. I will not take the bait, you know. I am finding anonymity to be in every way to my liking."

"As you wish."

She smiled a little then. "I did not expect you to give up quite so easily."

"Do I disappoint? The truth is I've never enjoyed fishing. You are aware, are you not, that there are worms involved. And fish. It's a messy business."

"I think you are teasing now."

"Am I?" When she did not reply, he wondered if he had finally disconcerted her into silence or if she was so certain she was in the right of it that no argument was necessary. She was quite correct in one assertion: He *had* been fishing.

They paused in front of another portrait that intrigued her, and while he gave her an account of his ancestor's accomplishments and missteps, he watched her out of the corner of his eye, searching for some feature that he would be able to identify at a later date. The flame-red hair would distinguish her, of course, if it were indeed her own. He was no longer confident that was the case. Skillfully woven, natural in every detail, Ferrin could imagine the wig—if indeed it was one—had cost a goodly sum. He wondered that anyone considered this one evening's entertainment to be worth such expense.

He did not voice this thought aloud. She would have found it more peculiar if he had. After all, he'd paid far more to provide tonight's entertainment, as she was likely to point out. He could explain it as fulfilling an obligation to his family, another responsibility of his station, yet duty was no factor in this night's work. A rake's reputation was never served, however, by admitting that there was little he would not do for his family. Netta, in particular, merely had to crook her finger and he would walk through fire. That he was so vulnerable to the whims of his mother and sisters, and only marginally less susceptible to the impulses of his stepfather and brothers, was not an element of his character that he wanted known. He would be exploited to distraction and very nearly helpless in the face of it.

"Why Boudicca?" he asked.

"I don't understand."

They began to walk again. "What I mean is, why not Cleopatra? A lady-in-waiting. Guinevere. Or even, Heaven help us, a shepherdess. How did you come to choose Boudicca?" She remained quiet so long that Ferrin thought she did not mean to answer. When she did, he was struck by the gravity of her response.

"I chose her for her ruthlessness."

"I see."

She smiled a little at that. "That cannot possibly be the case, for I am uncertain that I understand it myself."

"It is rather surprising."

"Yes."

"You admire ruthlessness?"

"It would be truer that I have come to respect the need for it."

"It has its place."

She nodded. "You are more than passingly familiar with it, I expect. A man of your reputation would have to be."

"Because I am a pirate?"

"Because you are accounted by the *ton* to be a rake."

Ferrin glanced sideways, marking her profile. What he could make out of her features appeared to be composed. She had not even the grace to flush at her own boldness. "Is it Boudicca that makes you daring or do you always speak so directly?"

"Did I misspeak? I wasn't aware. You cannot be unfamiliar with your reputation in society."

"You will allow, perhaps, that it is disconcerting to have it placed so plainly before me."

"I didn't realize. It was not my intention to cause you discomfort, indeed, I thought gentlemen were agreeably flattered by that reputation. Was I wrong?"

"Some gentlemen are, I suppose." Ferrin waited to see if she would pose the question to him. She did not, thereby saving him from the complication of a lie. "You are acquainted with a great many rakes?" he asked.

"No, not at all, else I would be more certain of my facts regarding their character."

He chuckled. They were almost upon another couple, so Ferrin slowed his step and pretended interest in the landscape above the mantelpiece. "Tell me more about a rake's character," he said. "I am frankly fascinated."

"I believe you are more amused than fascinated, but I will indulge you, nevertheless." She disengaged herself from his arm, though she did not turn to face him. "By the accepted definition, he is a libertine. A rakehell. Someone given to licentious behavior. It is not so much that he has disdain for the conventions of society, but that he is unrestrained by them."

"It is a fine distinction."

"Mayhap it is."

"You will have to say more about these conventions of society—the ones that do not restrain a rakehell."

"Now I know you are amused because you cannot be ignorant of them."

"There is always the possibility that I have restrained myself unnecessarily. I certainly hope that is not the way of it. I should very much like to hear your list."

"Freethinking," she said. "Libertines are by their nature freethinkers in matters of religion and morality."

"Yes, I can see how that could disturb the order of society."

"Drink."

"Pardon?"

"Rakes are given to excess in drink."

"Oh."

She glanced at him. "I do not think it was lemonade you were imbibing in the card room."

"You have me there. It was whisky. I am compelled to point out that I am not foxed."

"And I am compelled to counter that it is yet early in the evening, by your own admission boredom was upon you, and who is to say that my interruption has not saved you from an overindulgence of spirits?"

"As you are of the firmly held opinion that I am a libertine, I suppose you will not accept my word on the matter."

"It would be foolish of me to do so, would it not? Rakes cannot be relied upon to tell the truth, else how would they manage the seduction of so many females?"

Ferrin's brows lifted. "My, you do speak frankly, Boudicca."

"Perhaps you think that is only the province of men."

Ferrin recognized dangerous waters without having to

put his toe in. He chose his words carefully. "What I think is that convictions such as you are wont to espouse should have the support of fact, not fancy."

Her step faltered, and she held back, drawing Ferrin up short as well. "Then you are not, in fact, a rakehell?"

He turned slightly, facing her. His superior height and position drew her eyes upward. "A question first," he said. "Why is my answer of so much consequence to you?"

There was no hesitation, only a slight shift in the forward thrust of her small chin. "Because what I wish above all things this evening is that you will seduce me."

Chapter Two

Although Ferrin was certain he'd heard Boudicca correctly, he believed it was incumbent upon him to put this highly unusual disclosure before them again, lest there be a misunderstanding. "You are hoping to be seduced?"

"Yes."

"I cannot help but wonder if I am the candidate of your choosing or the candidate of your desperation."

"Will it wound your pride to know that you are the fourth rakehell I've put this matter to this evening?"

He laughed outright at that. "I would be devastated if there was a grain of truth in it. However, I am confident there are not three rakes in all of London who would refuse to grant you what you say you wish above all things. If someone turned aside your proposal, then it is either because he is not a libertine of the first stare or because he was struck dumb. Nothing else explains it."

"You are very sure of yourself," she said. There was no accusation in her tone; it was merely an observation.

No amount of inducement could have tempted Ferrin to admit he had never been put more off his stride. He wondered what was to be done about her, for clearly she was a danger to herself. It occurred to him that finding the shepherdess was perhaps where he needed to begin.

He was also very aware that Boudicca was waiting for an answer.

"You will appreciate, I think, that it will be difficult to seduce you when you seem to be agreeably inclined toward that end. It is in the nature of seduction that one participant is persuaded to engage in an activity that they might not typically consider to be prudent."

"I understand the definition. Perhaps I could seduce you, as you do not seem eager to go about the thing."

"It is timing," he said, "and opportunity. Neither are in our favor." Ferrin looked around the gallery. "You saw for yourself that the library is in use."

"Is that a usual place for seduction? I confess, I'd thought it would be better accomplished in a cupboard under the stairs."

"Not even if you were one of the housemaids," he said. "Deuced uncomfortable."

"You have familiarity, then."

"With the cupboard, not the housemaids. I was fourteen and not by any measure a practiced libertine. My companion—I will call her Lady M—was herself a freethinker and introduced me to the advantages of that state of mind. The cupboard, though, had no advantages. I doubt that's changed."

"I am persuaded you know best."

"Good." Having made a full circle of the gallery, Ferrin paused when they reached the doorway. They broke apart as a Viking with long pale hair filled the entrance from the other side with his broad shoulders. He clutched a horned helmet to his chest. "Have a care, Restell," Ferrin said, putting out his hand to stay his brother. "You'll gore yourself. Are you invading or fleeing?"

"Fleeing. I have never made the acquaintance of so many determined mamas in one evening, every one of them with a daughter they swear is a veritable diamond."

His attention shifted from Ferrin to his companion. He made a slight bow. "Queen Boudicca, your servant."

She nodded regally. "A Norseman. You are welcome here if it is your intent to slay the Romans."

"Romans. Dragons. Mothers. You have but to point to whatever offends you, my queen, and I shall slay it. Is it your command that I begin with this scurvy-ridden, half-blind buccaneer?"

Boudicca was long in responding, making clear her intent was to carefully consider the suggestion.

Restell laughed when he observed Ferrin give her an arch look. "Oh, I believe she is baiting you, Kit. This is a good turn." He glanced over his shoulder, saw a determined mother approaching, and excused himself hurriedly. "I am for my longboat," he said.

Ferrin and Boudicca turned as one to watch him go. His long-legged stride made short work of the length of the gallery. He disappeared through a paneled door set into the wainscoting.

"I wonder where he keeps his longboat," Boudicca said.

"Unless I miss my guess, he's headed for the wine cellar."

"That is rather presumptuous of him, is it not, to pillage your wine cellar?"

"That was Restell." When she regarded him blankly, he realized the name meant nothing to her. "My brother. My stepbrother, actually. Netta's older brother."

"Is he a rake?"

"He certainly aspires to be one."

"You disapprove of him following in your footsteps?"

There she had him. He reminded himself that he would have to be cautious not merely with what he said but also how he said it. Boudicca was a clever one for hearing the fine nuances of his tone. "One rakehell in a family is generally considered quite sufficient," he told her.

"I had not realized."

"It is a matter of the family marshaling its resources to manage a scandal and quell the gossip. There is bound to be a nine days' wonder now and again, but no family, not even an eccentric one, tolerates abusing their good graces."

"And since you are the oldest . . ." Her voice trailed off thoughtfully.

"That's right. I am the designated rakehell."

"A title. A fortune. And a reputation. It rather takes one's breath."

He caught her by the arm and escorted her back into the ballroom. "I have not noticed it taking yours, at least in any way that it affects your speech. You never seem to be at a loss for a rejoinder."

"You are not the first to remark on it."

Ferrin kept a firm link with Boudicca's arm as they wended their way through the crush yet again. He inclined his head politely whenever one of his guests caught his eye, but he did not linger for conversation. He observed that Wynetta was looking flushed and happy to be taking a set on the dance floor with a wizard. Wellsley, he noted, did not look particularly pleased to be watching from the perimeter of the room. Imogene had collected several other shepherdesses to her side—though none with green ribbons on the crook—and was engaged in animated conversation. Her husband stood nearby, patiently awaiting her pleasure. Ian, Imogene's twin, was partnering his wife in the set, and Sir Geoffrey was at his most persuasive, urging his wife to join him in the steps.

"Do you see your friend?" Ferrin asked.

"No. Perhaps the wine cellar."

"Let us hope not. She will not be at all glad to make Restell's acquaintance there. Perhaps the garden."

"The garden? I had not considered she might step outside."

"Then you have not found it as warm as I have. It is not unreasonable to suppose hothouse flowers would thrive in here. Come. This way. It will not take long. The garden is not large." He led her to the entranceway and through the drawing room to the rear of his town residence. "Unless you intend to skewer your friend, mayhap you will want to leave your spear on this side of the door."

Boudicca's glance shifted to the spear. One corner of her mouth lifted, shaping her lips in a mildly scornful smile. "Of course." She leaned the spear against the doorjamb.

"Where did you find that weapon?" Ferrin asked, opening the door for her. His nostrils flared as the introduction of the cooler air lifted the scent of lavender in her hair. "It looks as if it might be an artifact."

"It is. I took it from my—" She stopped, looking up at him. "I think you are fishing again. It doesn't really matter about the spear, does it?"

"I don't suppose that it does, no. Unless you stole it from a museum."

"No."

"Then I agree, it doesn't matter." He led her to the narrow marble balustrade. "You will have noticed that we are alone."

"Yes."

Ferrin turned a little to the side, maneuvering Boudicca so she was cornered by the curve of the rail and his body. When she pivoted to look up at him, he had her neatly confined between his arms. He did not miss her shiver, but he chose to misinterpret it. Without asking permission, Ferrin pulled her blue wool cloak more securely about her shoulders and refastened the brooch. She made no move to stop him, even when his knuckles brushed the soft upper curve of her breast.

"You are no longer armed," he said.

"It was clever of you to encourage me to leave my weapon behind."

"Damnably sharp-witted." He cupped her chin in his hand, raising her face another fraction toward him. Moonlight glanced off her hammered gold mask. His gaze fell to her mouth, and he used the pad of his thumb to trace her bottom lip. He felt the slight parting, the moist warmth of the sensitive underside. For a moment he thought she might touch the tip of her tongue to his thumb; her mouth trembled instead. His own reaction to that was something more than he could have predicted.

Ferrin released her face and bent his head. He kissed her, pressing his mouth to hers without regard for tenderness or reserve. Passion is what he felt and what he showed her. The sudden surge of it ran hot in his blood and settled hard and heavily in his groin. An involuntary thrust of his hips brought him flush against her and pushed the backs of her thighs against the rail. She would have to be singularly naive to mistake his response for anything but what it was.

Boudicca was not naive.

He plunged his tongue into her mouth, and she answered immediately in kind. She sucked, drawing him in, then teasing him. He groaned, the sound torn from the back of his throat, reluctance and relief mingling to make the whole of it deeply felt.

He reached beneath her cloak and grasped her by the upper arms. Under one hand he felt taut, warm flesh; under the other was one of the wide metal bracelets. He could make out the intricate scrollwork under his palm, ancient symbols raised above the delicately beaten gold. He jerked her to him hard, eliminating what had been only a small space between them. She would have come up on her toes, but he held her down, responding to some perverse need to keep her still and answerable to him. She did not struggle or insist that it be different. She was both lithe and pliant, at her ease taking his direction.

It was not precisely surrender that he sensed in her, but something akin to it, an acceptance that he would have the upper hand and that she would allow it. What she might permit him to do made him fear for her, but what he wanted to do frightened him more.

Breathing hard, he drew back suddenly. She rocked forward on the balls of her feet, and he set her from him. He saw her seek purchase against the marble rail behind her, her elegantly tapered fingers curling around the polished stone.

"Are you married?" he asked abruptly.

"What?"

"Is there a husband you are wont to make a cuckold?"

"No."

"Then a lover? A fiancé?"

"No." There was uncertainty in her voice. "Neither."

"Then it is my honor you wish to impugn?" He thought he saw her blink behind her mask, but he could not be sure. "There is a brother waiting in the shrubbery, perhaps. A father. Three male cousins who box for sport. Can I expect to be called out?"

"How am I impugning your honor? You have chosen a damnably inconvenient time to discover that you are in possession of certain scruples."

"It is not the scruples," he said somewhat harshly. "It is the trap."

"What trap? You are speaking nonsense."

Ferrin drew himself up stiffly. He was unused to being addressed in such a manner. The fact that he might indeed be speaking nonsense did nothing to improve his mood. "Then Restell is paying you dearly for this charade. You are one of his paramours."

She shook her head. "I never met your brother before this evening."

"Wellsley, then."

"I don't know any Wellsley. Is he another brother?"

"A friend."

"You entertain peculiar notions of what tricks your family and your friends will get up to. If you are so suspicious of some trap being laid, it might be more the thing to look to your enemies."

That she was making sense and he was not was the end of enough. The urge was upon him to shake her, but only because he could not shake himself. What he did was draw a steadying breath and release it slowly. Except for the light strains of music coming from the house, quiet settled around them. He was aware of her stillness. Her fingers still held the rail at her back. The length of her slim throat remained exposed to him as she had never once dropped her chin or tried to look away in the face of his accusations.

"I have no enemies," he said at length.

"Everyone has enemies, though if you are the exception to the rule, perhaps you should cultivate some. They might be less apt to play false with you than either your brother or this Wellsley person."

"I did not say Restell or my friend ever played me false."

"You charged them with entertaining themselves at your expense, and you named them with unseemly haste. I think that speaks to what you think of their character."

"They are both possessed of good character."

"And yet," she said, "you do not trust them."

"No, that is not it at all." Ferrin regarded her upturned face closely, trying to see behind the mask. "I don't trust you."

"That is altogether different. At least you have begun to make sense."

"Have I?" He was not so sure. That kiss—and it was the only explanation for what followed—had turned his brain to pudding. His chest rose and fell as he released another long breath. "I was thinking that if you had retained your spear I could impale myself upon it." He watched the curve of her smile appear slowly. "I take it you approve."

"Let us say, it's difficult to make any argument against it."

Ferrin discovered that he had not entirely lost his sense of humor. A chuckle rippled through him, releasing tension in its wake. "I could prostrate myself at your feet, I suppose. Would that suffice?"

"Suffice for what?"

"An apology."

"For what? For asking if I was married or betrothed? It was not an unreasonable question, though the timing of it was ill-considered." She held up one hand when he would have spoken, cutting him off. When he fell silent, she did not let her arm fall away but rather placed her palm squarely against his chest. "You cannot wish to apologize to me for the accusations you made against your brother or your friend. That would be better done with them, if you are ever of a mind to tell them what has passed this night. I will not. And finally, would you apologize for saying that you do not trust me when I have given you no reason that you should?"

"I was thinking I would apologize for making a cake of myself."

"Well, there you have me." She glanced down. "You will not want to lie at my feet long. I think the stone will be quite cold."

He drew her close instead, kissing her with more gentleness this time. Her hand remained between them, but she didn't push him away. Her fingertips nudged the top button of his waistcoat. Her mouth opened under his, and she allowed him to drink from her. He thought her lips trembled under his, then thought the tremble might have begun in him. The kiss was long and slow and sweet. He could not quite get enough of her when it seemed she was always willing to give more. Her mouth was warm. He tasted the sweet-tart tang of the lemonade they'd drunk earlier. It was precisely how she should taste, he thought, both sweet and tart with kisses made liquid by desire.

When he raised his head he noticed that her fingers were no longer trapped between them. Instead, both hands were clutching the sleeves of his frock coat. It was

the first indication that she was not so steady on her feet
as he'd thought. It was fitting, then, because he was in
danger of rocking backward. They teetered a moment,
weight and counterweight, before a tenuous balance was
achieved.

His voice, when he found it, was not much above a
husky whisper. "It does not mean that I trust you."

"I understand." Her fingers did not relax their grip.
"But know this: I mean you no harm."

"I believe you. I wonder, though, whether it matters
what your intentions are. Harm will be done."

She shook her head. "No. That is not—"

Ferrin placed one finger firmly against her lips. "I
didn't say I minded, merely that I expect it. Do not be
contrary."

"I'm afraid it is in my nature."

No surprise there. "Does anyone, save me, know what
it is you wish for above all things this evening?"

"To be seduced, you mean?"

His eyebrows kicked up in tandem. "If you have some
other wish, I should like to hear it before I proceed grant-
ing this one." He thought he heard her breath catch. What he
knew with certainty was that she was again unsteady on
her feet. The moment quickly passed, and she was Boudicca once more: determined, ruthless warrior.

He remembered thinking that she was a danger to herself and wondered if he was merely choosing to ignore
that aspect, or if he was in the right of it when he sensed
the greater danger would be to allow her to leave him.

"You are thinking again," she whispered.

"Guilty."

"It cannot be good for you. A rake should not entertain
so many qualms."

"You will scarcely credit it, but I've never had my
qualms put to such a test before."

"Perhaps if you kiss me again." Hesitating, she bit her

lower lip and worried it for the span of a heartbeat. "Or does that merely qualm the waters?"

Ferrin literally took her in hand, ignoring her light laugh, which he thought sounded suspiciously like a titter. He drew her back into the house, not pausing long enough in the doorway for her to retrieve her spear. The hand she flung out for it came away empty.

"This way," he said, brooking no refusal. "This way" was through a deserted second parlor and into a dimly lighted stairwell. He drew her up eighteen steeply winding steps before he stopped on the small landing. An explanation was hardly required, but he gave her one anyway. "Servants' passage."

"It is almost as good as a cupboard."

"Better, in fact. The servants are busy everywhere below stairs, not above. There's no reason for one of them to come this way."

"Then we will not be disturbed."

"That is the idea." He regarded her, trying to make out her thoughts from a shadowed expression that gave nothing away. "At least that was my idea. It is not part of your wish that we are observed, is it?" He was gratified to see this caused a reaction he could finally interpret. She was properly shocked at the notion of being watched. "Is it all you hoped for?"

Boudicca glanced about the close quarters. "It is . . . cozy."

He smiled. "It is roomier than a cupboard."

"My. I hadn't realized."

Ferrin never thought she was in the habit of making propositions like the one she had tonight. Still, he was gratified to have it confirmed. "You weren't in anticipation of a bed, were you?"

"No. Oh, no. That would seem calculating rather than precipitous."

He could have pointed out that throughout this

encounter she had demonstrated more in the way of strategy than Napoleon had upon escaping Elba. He said nothing, however. Apparently she was taken with the notion of a chance meeting and reckless abandon. He was in favor of both those things, but they had nothing at all to do with this night's work.

Ferrin observed that she was still looking around. He wondered if she was having second thoughts and how he felt about it if that were so. "Have you changed your mind?" he asked.

She shook her head. Her flame-red hair, so brilliant in the ballroom, had faded to burnt umber in the constricted space of the stairwell. A lock of it fell forward over her shoulders. Before she could push it back, he did it for her.

"I thought it was a wig," he said.

Boudicca made no reply to that. What she said was, "Will you extinguish the lamps?"

"If you wish."

"I do."

Ferrin was disappointed but not surprised. She'd made it clear at the outset that she wanted to preserve her anonymity. He was the one exposed here, with or without candlelight. "Very well," he said. It did not take him long to blow out the lamp below them, then climb to the second landing and extinguish that flame as well. His returning descent was slowed by the complete darkness. When he reached what he thought was the last step, he felt her hand brush his sleeve and knew then that he had arrived.

It was not that she was waiting for him with open arms, but that she went so easily into his. The fit was perfect. As soon as he kissed her, he knew she was no longer wearing her mask. Darkness had freed her. His hands came up and cupped her face. He let his thumbs pass lightly across the arch of her cheekbones. She was more finely made than he'd imagined the raw-boned queen of Britain had been. This Boudicca's features were elegantly contoured, the symmetry just shy of perfection. He used his index finger to trace the pared line of her nose. No break or bump altered the intended shape of it. His fingers slipped under her heavy fall of hair, threading behind her head to support her as he deepened the kiss.

She was working the buttons of his frock coat, her movements not so practiced that they weren't a bit tentative and clumsy. When she released the last one she began on his waistcoat, then pulled his shirt free of his breeches. He sucked in a breath when her hands lay flat against his chest.

"Cold?" she asked, beginning to pull away.

"Hot," he said, drawing her back. His mouth covered hers again, harder this time, insistent. He pushed her against the wall and swallowed her moan. Her hands slid around his back until her fingers met at his spine. Her nails lightly scored the length of it from his nape to where it disappeared beneath his waistband. Her breasts flattened against his chest, but he was so sensitive to her touch that the twin buds of her nipples seemed to score him much as her nails did. He lifted his lips, then placed them at the curve of her neck just below her ear.

His breath was hot and humid, and he whispered what he wanted from her, what he wanted to do to her. She strained against him and clutched him tighter. He sipped her skin, knowing he would leave a mark there. She knew it too. Her hands and fingers stilled and she stiffened, then the moment passed and she was yielding to his mouth again, no longer caring that he was placing his stamp upon her.

The golden torc she wore fit closely. He kissed her at the opening, above the base of her throat. He felt her tremble.

They lowered each other to the landing, neither of them consciously taking the lead. It was surprisingly simple. At one moment they were standing, in another they were not.

He found the brooch that fastened her cloak. "Be still," he said, "else I will stick one of us with this. I would rather it not be me."

"You are not at all gallant."

"Rakes rarely are. Or rather they can be when it serves their purpose." His chuckle rose deep from the back of his throat when she pushed his hands aside and managed the brooch herself. She let him remove the cloak from her shoulders. He folded it so that it made a pillow for her head, then he bore her down on it.

Her tunic fell to her thighs when he raised her knees and settled himself between them. Neither of them moved at first, becoming acquainted with this new intimacy. Of necessity there were adjustments to be made. Her head bumped the lip of an upper step. His knee caught the lip of a lower one. The landing afforded them not much more space than an armoire, and they turned and twisted until they had an arrangement that suited them both.

"Aren't you pleased I talked you out of the cupboard?" he asked.

"You cannot imagine." She raised her head just enough to brush his lips with hers. The tip of her tongue wet his lower lip. "Shall I help you with your flies?"

If the mask had made her bold before, darkness made her bolder. "I can manage. Do you need help with your shift?"

"I can manage."

There was no mistaking that he was ready for her, but Ferrin was not as certain the reverse was true. Reckless and impassioned they might be, he reasoned there was time enough yet to lay siege to all of her senses. To that end, he began in precisely the same place he had stopped when they had slid to the floor. The hollow of her throat was still damp from his last kiss. Her pulse thrummed beneath his lips.

He moved lower, finding the edge of her tunic with his teeth and tugging. He used his fingers to slip it over one of her shoulders, then traced the line of her collarbone. He retraced it with his lips. She arched a little under him, raising her breasts. He pulled the tunic lower until it was her flesh he felt under his palm and the sweet thorny point of her nipple against his thumb.

She filled his hand. He bent his head and suckled her. She cried out, and he was forced to stop. He placed his mouth near her own and whispered that she must accept quietly what was done to her, else they would arouse the curiosity of the housemaids and footmen. He felt her nod and smiled because she would not for anything risk a single word in reply.

This time when he took her nipple in his mouth she merely whimpered. The sound of that tight little gasp made his blood surge again. He was achingly hard. He ground his hips against her, and he rolled the tip of her breast between his lips, touching her ever so lightly with the ridge of his teeth. He felt the hand she'd laid on his shoulder lift, then heard her muffled cry and knew she'd jammed her fist against her mouth.

When she shifted under him he realized she meant for him to show the same delicate attention to her other breast. He did. She was so responsive to his touch that he found himself holding back, gentling her as though she might break apart in his hands. She would have none of it, or none of it for long. When his reserve became too much for her, the fragile foreplay a torture in itself, she caught his face between her hands and kissed him hard enough to bruise their lips.

As an invitation it could not have been clearer. Ferrin released his erection from his breeches, then slipped his hands under her bottom and lifted. He felt her draw her knees higher, opening for him, then clasping him. He did not go gently now but thrust forward so that she reared up and for a moment seemed as if she would stop him. The fists that he thought might pummel him when they pressed against his shoulders slowly uncurled. Her fingers fluttered, then were still.

He waited her out, another adjustment to be made as her body stretched to accommodate his entry. Her breathing was quick and shallow, the response to a heart racing so hard it threatened to burst her chest. He was quiet, patient. That would change, but for now he could be patient.

"Please," she whispered. "I want . . ." But she did not say what she wanted. "Please," she said again instead.

They fit so tightly that the cramped space they occupied was without consequence. He moved slowly at first, long, sure strokes that helped her find his rhythm and take him so deeply he thought he might die with the pleasure of it. He didn't, but he would not have minded if he had.

He set about making certain that she felt the very same. Releasing her abruptly, he turned her over and folded her forward on her knees. Her forearms braced on one of the steps above; the curve of her bottom was raised toward him. He palmed her buttocks, finding her cleft, then entered her again, this time from behind. He sensed her ducking her head and realized she was protecting her nose and chin from a collision with one of the upper steps. He swore softly, in way of apology, then leaned forward and kissed her shoulder to punctuate it.

"All is well?" he asked.

"Yes." He began to move in her again. "Oh, yes," she said.

One of his hands left her hip and sought the wet, slippery folds of flesh beneath her mons. He ran a finger between them, flicking the hooded bud with the tip of his nail. Her entire body quivered. The cadence of her breathing changed again, this time coming more irregularly as she caught, then held, a sip of air at the back of her throat.

In the ballroom a waltz was being played. The lilting three-quarter time insinuated itself into the dark passage. The vibration of so many dancers taking to the floor could be felt in the stairwell. Occasionally a servant moved below and then they would quiet, only the harshness of their breathing hinting at the mixture of anticipation and excitement they held at bay. Each brief respite served to heighten pleasure already spiraling in a dizzying arc.

He didn't know what she did to keep from screaming, but when she shuddered violently in his arms he had little doubt it was what she had wanted to do. His own climax came as hard: short, shallow strokes followed by one that buried him so deeply that he touched her womb.

They could not linger in the aftermath, of course. Neither of them tried. They separated, though not too quickly as to be unseemly. He helped her turn and get her knees under her but did not hold her in his arms. When he tried to assist her with righting her tunic, she gently pushed his hands away.

"Will you permit me to light one of the lamps?" he asked. It seemed unlikely that she would and, indeed, she firmly turned him down. He addressed the sorry condition of his own clothes. His tricornered hat was crushed, forcing him to beat it against his knee and press each side to return it to some semblance of its former shape. It was not so important that his stock was loosened. That was in no way out of keeping with his costume. He touched the eye patch to make certain it was still in place and refastened his breeches, waistcoat, and frock coat, then ran one hand down the front to judge his success with matching the buttons to the proper hole.

She was already standing when he got to his feet. "Have you your cloak?" he asked, brushing himself off. "The brooch? Do you require help with it?"

"No help, thank you. I have done the thing myself."

He never doubted that she was that most thorny of all females to manipulate: independent *and* managing. He set his hat on his head, adjusted the angle, and inquired if she had her mask.

"Yes, of course."

"Then will you want to return first to the ballroom or should I?"

"I'd like to go."

"As you wish."

She hesitated. "You will not . . . that is . . . you will not . . ."

He waited. Even on short acquaintance he knew it was not her way to leave a thought unfinished. When it was clear to him that she would not, *could not*, complete her sentence, he rescued her. "No, I will not. Whatever it is that you hope I will not do, know that I will not do it."

"Thank you."

"Shall I escort you down the stairs?"

"That will not be necessary."

"Have a care, then; they're steep."

"Yes, I remember."

"Very well, Boudicca."

There was an awkward silence—at least Ferrin found it so—then he felt her brush past him and begin her descent. He waited there on the landing for what he calculated was the better part of ten minutes, a decent enough interval for her to rejoin the party and perhaps even find her friend. Better yet, time enough for her to make her escape. It was this last that Ferrin anticipated she would do. The shepherdess, the one with the green ribbons on her crook, most likely had never existed but merely served as a ploy to engage his interest and activity. It had worked, though he'd never been very determined to resist it.

He started down the steps slowly, wondering what he would make of this extraordinary encounter in the morning or at any other time in the future. It was difficult to predict because he certainly did not know what to make of it now. Although his own motives were rather straightforward, hers defied him. He'd thought he'd hit upon her reasoning for seeking him out when he had suggested there might be a husband or fiancé she wanted to betray. Boudicca's denial had seemed most sincere, and since no one had burst in upon them, it would appear she'd been honest in that regard.

He could even acquit Restell and Wellsley of playing him some trick. If either was so fortunate to know a woman as clever and diverting as Boudicca, he would have kept her to himself. Neither his brother nor his friend had given any indication that they recognized her. Indeed, Wellsley had hoped to make her acquaintance first. Restell was too preoccupied escaping marriage-minded mamas to pause for an introduction. And what would have been the point of serving him up a courtesan or opera dancer when he could fill his own plate as he wished?

No, it was neither about betrayal nor sport. Boudicca was a woman outside his experience, something he had not thought possible at the age of two and thirty. The puzzle that she was intrigued him, and he acknowledged that this was probably the worst of all outcomes for her.

Whenever he set his mind to inquiry, there was little he was not able to discover.

Cybelline Louisa Caldwell, née Grantham, wanted more than anything to have a lie-in. She wanted to fit herself comfortably in the warm depression she'd made in the mattress during the night and remain there, perhaps with the coverlet over her head or the drapes drawn. She wanted to pull a pillow about her ears so she could ignore what would surely come next: a scratching at the door and the subsequent well-intentioned questions regard-

ing the state of her health. She wanted to refuse breakfast, refuse tea, and refuse visitors.

She would not do it, of course. Cybelline was not a
petulant child, and she did not surrender to her wants.

Except that last night she had.

That thought was all that was required to propel her out
of bed. She would not find respite from herself by remaining alone in her room. What was needed was activity and
companionship, and she knew where to find both.

Cybelline rang for her personal maid. Miss Sarah
Webb had been with her since Cybelline was sixteen and
could be relied upon to observe everything and say
almost nothing. She was in no circumstance a confidante,
but Cybelline found her quiet, competent presence a
comfort more often than not.

Webb assisted Cybelline with her ablutions and attire,
then dressed her hair, scraping it back against her scalp,
then securing it in a tight coil. The whole of it was hidden
under a white linen cap.

"You don't approve," Cybelline said, catching Webb's
rather grim reflection in the mirror.

"It's not for me to say."

Cybelline did not press. Webb, who possessed a handsome countenance, if not a delicate one, looked as if she
would put her teeth through her tongue before she'd offer
an opinion about the condition of her mistress's hair. "I'm
going to take my breakfast with Anna."

Webb set the comb aside. "I'll tell Cook."

The nursery was on the floor above her bedchamber.
Cybelline climbed the stairs, lifting the hem of her dove-
gray day dress just high enough to avoid a tumble. She
passed through Nanny Baker's room before coming upon
the nursery. Crossing the threshold, her mood was immediately lighter.

"Mama!" Anna wriggled out of Nanny's plump arms
and toddled full tilt toward her mother.

Cybelline bent down and scooped her soft, warm, and freshly scrubbed daughter into her arms. She rubbed her face against Anna's downy cheek and hair. "So sweet," she said. "I want to eat you up!"

Predictably, Anna giggled. "Eat you! Eat you!" She gnashed the tiny pearls of her teeth together to emphasize her intent.

"My, but you're a fierce one, darling." Cybelline looked past her daughter to where Nanny Baker was rising to her feet. "Is that another tooth I'm seeing, Nanny? One in the back?"

"Yes, ma'am, it is. It broke through yesterday."

Cybelline regarded her daughter again but spoke to Nanny. "Did she fret?"

"Not overmuch. She rubbed her cheek a bit, which is how I knew something was amiss. I gave her some sweet cloves for her gums, and she liked that well enough."

Anna was now tapping her teeth together, quite aware the conversation had everything to do with her. "You minx," Cybelline teased. "You cannot imagine a world in which you are not the center of everything." She kissed her daughter's brow. "And that is quite as it should be."

Anna buried her face in the curve of her mother's neck and shoulder and snuggled. This surfeit of affection squeezed Cybelline's heart to the point where drawing a breath was painful. For a moment her eyes welled. Turning so that Nanny might not see them, she rapidly blinked back tears.

"I am having my breakfast here with Anna this morning, Nanny Baker. There's no need for you to stay."

"Will you want me to finish dressing her?"

"I'll do that. Anna will help me, won't you, darling?"

Anna's head came up abruptly. Her damp, red-gold curls fluttered around her ears and forehead. "No!"

"Really?" Cybelline asked, untroubled by this refusal. Her daughter was possessed of that singular independence common to two-year-olds, or so she was given to understand. She was perhaps more indulgent regarding this expression of individualism than Nanny Baker, but she did not let it rule her. "Because I was going to tell you a story, but I need your help first."

"Story!"

"Help."

"No!"

Cybelline merely smiled and waited Anna out. "You can go, Nanny Baker. I'll manage here."

"I can't say that I like it when she speaks to you like that, ma'am."

"I'm not particularly fond of it, either, but didn't you tell me it will pass?"

"I did, and so it will, but she's especially headstrong for one that just had her second birthday."

"Is that so?" She tapped her daughter on the mutinous line of her lips. "I cannot imagine where she comes by that. Her father was a most agreeable gentleman."

Nanny Baker snorted softly, pursing her lips together in disapproval. "I'll be in the servants' hall," she said, excusing herself.

When Cybelline heard the heavy fall of Nanny's retreating footsteps in the stairwell, she finally gave in to the urge to laugh. "Nanny takes herself—and us—a bit too seriously, doesn't she? She thinks I don't know that you are in every way my daughter. It is true that your father was most agreeable. I, in perfect contrast, have rarely been."

Mimicking Cybelline's good humor, Anna giggled.

Cybelline gave Anna a little bounce. The giggle changed pitch, causing Anna's blue eyes to widen as she realized the wavering sound came from her. Cybelline bounced her again to the same effect, and they carried on in such a manner until one of the younger housemaids arrived carrying their breakfast tray.

"Not there," Cybelline said when the girl moved toward the round cherry wood table near the fireplace. "Put it on Anna's tea table. I'll sit in one of her chairs." The maid did as she was directed while Cybelline turned her attention back to her daughter. "You like it when I sit perched like a bird on one of your tiny chairs, don't you?"

Anna looked around, caught by the part of her mother's sentence that she understood best. "Bird? Where bird?"

"Oh, dear, now I've done it." She carried Anna to the window where the drapes had already been tied back. The morning was overcast, but there was a break in the distant clouds that held the promise of sunshine. Cybelline opened the window and allowed Anna to poke her head out.

"Bird?" Fortunately, there were several plump pigeons on parade. They were strutting along the lip of the neighbor's roof, perfectly content to be the object of so much admiration from across the way. "Bird! There bird!"

"Indeed." Cybelline squeezed her daughter, making small cooing noises that were not unlike the conversation going on between the pigeons. It was only when Anna flapped her arms that the birds objected. They scattered so quickly that Anna was startled. Her small head snapped back, catching Cybelline on the chin.

"Oooh!" They said it in unison.

Cybelline rubbed the back of her child's head, forgoing the urge to massage her own chin. She kissed the injured spot for good measure and to keep Anna's face from crumpling, she pointed to her chin and said, "Kiss Mama here."

Anna pursed her dewy lips and followed her mother's finger. There was a rather loud smacking noise and a bit of drool, but the sentiment was clear.

"How I love you," Cybelline whispered, her heart in her throat. "There are no words."

* * *

Lady Rivendale set down her cup as Cybelline entered the breakfast room. "I was not certain I would see you this morning. I thought you might enjoy a lie-in. You returned quite late, I noticed."

Instead of responding to this overture, Cybelline went to the sideboard and served herself from the plate of eggs and sliced tomatoes. "Good morning, Aunt Georgia."

Georgia Pendleton, Countess of Rivendale, was in point of fact no blood relation to Cybelline, nor even the wife of a blood relation. Those who might offer the homily that blood was thicker than water failed to measure the viscosity of the relationship that Lady Rivendale had nurtured over a score of years with her godson and his younger sister.

The countess, being the dearest friend of Cybelline's mother, had been named godmother to Alexander Henry Grantham at his baptism. Eight years later, when Cybelline had had the same rite performed on her, Lady Rivendale was touring the Continent, and no one was named to that position of responsibility. It was just as well, Cybelline had come to realize, for Lady Rivendale would have cheerfully removed the competition.

When Cybelline's parents perished in a fire it was the countess who came to take her and her brother in hand. There had been an uncle who was named guardian, but Lady Rivendale and her solicitor made short work of that. It was not as if the uncle had tried very hard to keep them. She was not long out of the nursery and her brother—now the Viscount Sheridan—was still at Eton. They must have seemed singularly uninteresting persons to their uncle, she thought, but to Lady Rivendale they were fascinating—in a bug-in-a-jar fashion.

"You are smiling," Lady Rivendale said as Cybelline

turned away from the sideboard. "Am I right to count that as a happy turn?"

"I believe it is a good thing, yes." She took her seat beside the countess and picked up her fork. "I was remembering your timely rescue of me and Sherry from our uncle's home. Do you know that he called us brats at the funeral of our parents?"

"I knew it. I didn't realize you did."

"I overheard him, the same as Sherry."

"You trod on the man's tocs, I hope."

"No, but I sobbed until I made myself sick—at his feet."

"A perfectly elegant solution. I have always been impressed with your ability to rise to the occasion, Cybelline."

"Thank you . . . I think." She relieved her discomfort by taking a bite of shirred egg. "Did you sleep well? I have not inquired as to your health this morning, though you are looking fit."

"You mean you have not inquired as to when I intend to quit your home."

Cybelline waggled her fork at Lady Rivendale. "I meant nothing of the sort. It is very bad of you to put words in my mouth." She returned to her meal. "I should very much like to hear how you fare."

"I slept very well, thank you. I do not know the cause of the plaguey stomach ailment that has confined me here these last three days, but I am pleased to report it seems to have vanished last night." She indicated her plate. "You can see for yourself that my appetite has returned. I am fit enough to travel and I will be making arrangements for doing so this morning."

Cybelline kept her smile in check. The distance to the countess's residence was no greater than a mile, but to hear her speak of traveling there one could be forgiven for thinking she lived in Cornwall. When she took ill suddenly during an afternoon visit, there was no question but that she would stay. Although Lady Rivendale might have been more comfortable in her own bed, ordering around her own servants, Cybelline suspected that she truly did not want to be alone while she made a drama of her recovery. It was easier to uproot the countess's servants and bring them to Cybelline's than it was to distress the countess.

"You know I was delighted to have you stay here, though you must not think I am happy that it was illness that forced your hand. Anna enjoys your visits, as do I."

"Still, I was a bother."

Now Cybelline let her smile surface. "I am never certain what the politic response is. Is it more important that I agree with you, thereby sustaining the notion that you are always in the right of things, or is the better strategy to argue that in this instance you could not be more wrong? I should like you to advise me how to proceed."

Lady Rivendale picked up her coffee cup and shrewdly regarded Cybelline over the rim before she sipped from it. The tactic gave her time to digest the whole of Cybelline's question. "I declare, you are even more accomplished at disarming me than your brother—and Sherry is excellent."

"No one disarms you, Aunt Georgia. If you do not fire back a volley, it is only because you are choosing your battles, not because you have been relieved of your weapons."

The countess nodded appreciatively. "A very pretty compliment, one I shall cherish." She set her cup in the saucer again and touched her chin thoughtfully, still regarding Cybelline but without her earlier intensity. "What is that on your cap?" she asked. "On the ruffle."

Cybelline touched the front of her cap and felt a sticky globule of something she could not immediately identify. She carefully removed it with a fingertip and examined it. She chuckled when she saw what it was. "Porridge. Anna lobbed a spoonful of porridge at me. I'm afraid I didn't eat much myself, which is why I came—" She stopped because Lady Rivendale's gaze was riveted on the cap again. Her hands flew to it. "What is it? What—"

The countess stood and quickly rounded the table to Cybelline's side. Without communicating her intention, she plucked the cap from Cybelline's head. Her sharp intake of breath was perfectly audible. She abandoned the dramatic gesture of placing one hand on her heart and chose instead to sink slowly back into her chair. It was also effective.

Although the question was largely superfluous, Lady Rivendale felt compelled to ask it anyway. "Bloody hell, Cybelline, what have you done to your hair?"

Chapter Three

Cybelline calmly held out her hand for her linen cap. Lady Rivendale gave it over immediately. Crumpled as it was, Cybelline returned it to her head and carefully tucked away all evidence that her hair was now fiery red. "I am sorry it offends you, Aunt Georgia."

"Offends me? Why, it caused me to swear, and you know I have been trying to set a better example for the scoundrels."

"Then it is good they are not here." The scoundrels were her brother's three wards. Sherry had plucked the young ruffians from the streets of Holborn, giving the matter as much thought as one might have for plucking feathers from a chicken. Pinch, Dash, and Midge—names from the streets that had not yet been put to rest—were a considerable trial as well as a source of great joy. Lily, Sherry's wife, remarked more fondly than not that they were like puppies in want of proper training: There were bound to be accidents. There had been noticeably fewer mishaps since Lily gave birth. The presence of a baby in the home had quieted them but in no way quelled their spirit. "I will tell them about your slip, of course. You can depend on it. You will have to add a shilling to their collection jar. It's only fair since you set the rules."

Lady Rivendale's generously full mouth flattened, and she harrumphed softly. "I disapprove of tattling, you know."

Cybelline merely smiled.

"Though I might be tempted to tell Sherry and Lily what you've done to your hair."

Cybelline's smile faltered.

"Hah!" The countess possessed a remarkably smooth countenance for one in her fifty-fourth year. This was a consequence of a nightly regimen of creams and lemon juice and avoidance of the sun. Lines such as she had— at the corners of her mouth and eyes—did not overly concern her, as she believed they were righteously earned by love and laughter and surviving the vagaries of life. Her face crinkled now, amusement deepening twin creases between her eyebrows. "So you do not want your brother to know. Nor Lily either, though I imagine she would come to understand your actions much more quickly than Sherry. I wonder, however, if she will understand more quickly than I."

The threat was subtle but clear, and Cybelline did not miss it. Some explanation was expected. She was not hopeful that she could stray far from the truth and stand up to Lady Rivendale's scrutiny. It was never comforting to have that steely, sharp-as-a-razor glance turn in her direction. Sherry had always been better at ducking his godmother's inspection, and he would be the first to admit he suffered it far more often than was his wish.

"It was you, Aunt Georgia, who suggested that some change might be in order." It was a good beginning, Cybelline thought, reminding the countess of her own words. "You cannot have forgotten our conversation."

"No, indeed, but I think I remember it differently than you. We were speaking of your taking up residence at

Penwyckham. I suggested that you consider spending a few months there with Anna. It was a change of scenery that I had in mind and well you know it."

"We were discussing change," Cybelline said. "I was thinking of it in another manner."

"I doubt you were thinking at all. That is a most unfortunate shade of red you have acquired. There is not so much orange in it as to be carroty, but neither does it have the richness of auburn. You were right to cover it. I shouldn't wonder if Anna might think you have burst into flame."

Somewhat self-consciously, Cybelline adjusted her cap again. She smoothed the ruffle where it had crumpled against her ear. "It is merely henna. I admit I thought it would be darker, but I do not think Webb mixed it to the proportions suggested by the chemist. However, I do not blame her. She disapproved, though naturally she would not fail to assist me."

"Undoubtedly because she determined you were set on the matter with or without her help."

"I'm certain you're right."

"It's a blessing, I suppose, that you did not go out like that last night. I cannot imagine what comments it would inspire—even at a masquerade. Forgive me for speaking frankly," Lady Rivendale said as though it were not a common occurrence, "but it is a color more suited to a cyprian."

"That is precisely why I wore a wig."

"So you *did* do this yesterday?" Now the countess placed one hand over her heart and regarded Cybelline with astonishment. "*Before* you departed?"

"I certainly did not do it after I returned. You noted quite correctly that it was late when I arrived home." Cybelline leaned forward in her chair and extended one arm toward the countess. "You must calm yourself. No harm has been done. I showed you the powdered wig, remember?"

"Yes, but not when you were wearing it. I was sleeping

when you left, and you had not the good sense to wake me." She let her hand drop away from her heart and took up Cybelline's, squeezing it lightly. "Tell me, was your costume a great success?"

"I think that is fair to say. I was the only shepherdess there with green streamers on her crook."

It took Lady Rivendale a moment to hear the meaning behind Cybelline's words. She frowned. "The only shepherdess with green streamers? Pray, how many shepherdesses were there?"

"I counted seven. One blue, three pink, two yellow, and my green."

"So you were one of seven. Oh, but that is unfair. They were not all cut from the same cloth, I hope."

"Panniers. White leggings. Lace trim on the underskirts. Bows on every tier of fabric. Perfectly coiffed white wigs in the French fashion."

"Beauty marks?"

"Yes. I suspect we took our inspiration from the same painting."

The countess was having none of that explanation. "I suspect someone took their inspiration from me. I was the one who sat with the dressmaker while she put my ideas to paper. She said it was a complete original. I selected the fabric, the lace, the bows, and the streamers. Must I remind you that the painting hangs in *my* home?"

"And you have noted that it is oft admired by your friends. Perhaps you should be flattered that they considered it so worthy of imitation."

"I cannot be flattered when I feel sorely abused."

Cybelline gave her a disbelieving look. "Aunt Georgia, you are making rather too much of it. I would prefer it if you returned to scolding me for my hair. I certainly was delighted to be in such esteemed company. Mrs. Edward Branson was one of the shepherdesses. Blue ribbons, I believe. I had not made her acquaintance before last night. She was everything gracious."

"Of course she was. She was wearing *your* costume."

Cybelline ignored that. As a rule, Lady Rivendale was not given to being disagreeable. Some tolerance was in order. "She is Lady Gardner's stepdaughter. I did not make that connection before."

"I do not know her. She was married and gone from home when I made the acquaintance of Sir Geoffrey and Lady Gardner. She has a twin brother, I believe. I suppose he was present, given that the masque was in Miss Wynetta's honor."

"Yes, though I cannot say I met him. He was pointed out to me."

"He was not also a shepherdess, I hope."

Cybelline smiled. Lady Rivendale was recovering her sense of humor, albeit tinged with sarcasm. "One of the Knights Templar. There were enough of them present to mount a crusade, I can tell you that."

"And Miss Wynetta?"

"An exotic-looking Cleopatra. Indeed, her admirers were thick around her, which was the point of it all, I suppose."

"Then I was not wrong to insist you go without me?"

There was but one way Cybelline could respond to that poser. It was difficult not to look away as she spoke. "No, you were not wrong."

"Does that mean you are prepared to rejoin society, Cybelline?" the countess asked gently. "I wish beyond everything that is so."

Cybelline removed her hand from under Lady Rivendale's and sat back in her chair. "I am prepared, I believe, to enter a smaller society, Aunt. You will scarcely credit it, but I have been considering your offer of the house at Penwyckham. I would like to accept it. Last night's entertainment convinced me that I am not yet comfortable with the crush. I did not find the conversation easy, nor of particular interest. There was gossip, of course, but I could not restrain the thought that sooner or later I would hear Nicholas's name."

"Oh, my dear girl, that you should have suffered those thoughts. It has been over a year since . . . since his passing."

"Since he killed himself," Cybelline said firmly. "It is better to say it plainly, I think, than to speak of it as if he merely slipped away. Almost seventeen months, Aunt Georgia. Sometimes I mark the days since I held him in my arms. It was four hundred eighty when I recorded it last. I dream of him. I cannot seem to help myself."

"I know," Lady Rivendale said quietly. "It is why I thought it was time for you to leave this house and embrace the possibility of meeting someone."

Cybelline flushed a little. "I should not have told you about that dream."

"Stuff! Who better to confide in? I have not lived my life under a rock. I have experiences that make me the perfect confidante—and I am family. You can trust it will go no further." She pitched her voice lower so there was no chance she could be heard beyond the breakfast room by a passing servant. "I believe it is quite unexceptional to dream of one's husband after he has passed. Oh, shush, do not make me dwell on the fact that Mr. Caldwell killed himself. I am still out of patience with him for that." She saw Cybelline's mouth snap shut in surprise. "Good. Now, as I was saying, it is within the bounds of reason to suppose that from time to time those dreams would be about your most intimate moments. I cannot think how it could be otherwise. I thought the same when it happened to me—though I will say that Lord Rivendale was a better lover dead than he was alive—and I have not heard anything from you that persuades me your dreams are at all unusual. I am uncertain how I can be more clear that you are not at fault for the nature of your mind when it is in the throes of Morpheus."

Cybelline required a moment to consider all that had been said. Putting aside the rather surprising revelation about Lord Rivendale's lovemaking, the remainder of the countess's speech was something Cybelline had heard before. She remained unconvinced.

There was something terribly wrong with her, something dark and lowering, something wholly reprehensible. It could not be in the nature of what was decent that of late her husband's face was obscured by shadow so that she could only pretend he was the one coming to her bed. She had never told Lady Rivendale that she'd woken up to discover that she'd pleasured herself. It still shamed her when she thought of it.

But not so much, it seemed, that it hadn't happened a second time. And a third.

So last night she had invited a man to do the same. It had been what she wished for above all things, to submit herself to a man's touch again, to engage in an act of moral and carnal prostitution, selling what was left of her soul and all of her body to a man who would not ask why she had chosen him or why she despised herself.

The Earl of Ferrin had proved in the end that he was just such a man.

Thinking of him now, Cybelline felt another rush of heat flush her cheeks. She was aware that Lady Rivendale's gaze had narrowed again and that she was the subject of further study. "I'm sorry," she said, looking down for a moment. "You can appreciate, I think, that I am embarrassed to discuss these things. You believe my dreams to be unexceptional. They do not seem so to me. I agreed to attend last evening's entertainment, but it has left me knowing that I want a different experience than parties and social circles and the *ton* during the Season. Sherry and Lily have invited me many times to Granville Hall, yet I cannot bring myself to spend more than a few days in their company when they are in town. They are so happy that my presence makes them feel guilty for it."

"That is nonsense."

"No, it's not. They would deny it, of course, as you do, but I can feel there is always some strain. If it is not with them, then it is with me. The pretense of trying not to grieve openly is wearing, Aunt Georgia. It is enough for me that I must do it in Anna's presence. I love my brother and do not wish him any unhappiness, so it is beyond everything I understand that I can resent him for having in his life what I no longer do. I do not think you can appreciate how deeply it hurts me to admit that aloud, or how it tears at my heart when it intrudes upon my thoughts and I remain silent. I cannot put Nicholas's suicide in the past because I am as angry with him as I am sorry for myself. Sometimes I am frightened that it will never change. How shall I go on, then? What will I say to Anna that will ease her when I find no ease?"

Lady Rivendale used the serviette lying on her lap to dab at her damp eyes. "How I wish I could take this burden of yours upon my own shoulders. I have grieved, true, but little enough of it has been for Mr. Caldwell. I grieve for you, Cybelline, for the ache that has permanent residency in your heart."

"I know you do," Cybelline said quietly. "And I am sorry for that, though I do not know how it can be different. It is why I am prepared to accept your gracious offer. As you have remarked to me more than once, leaving London is just the thing. I should have done it months ago." When the letters began to arrive, she told herself. She knew better than to share this last thought. It was odd that it was far easier to speak to her aunt about the dreams than it was to even hint at the letters. Removing herself from her momentary reverie, Cybelline added earnestly, "You have been everything patient to wait me out and not force my hand."

Although the countess's eyes no longer glistened with tears, her smile was a trifle watery. "I could hardly order you to go, now could I?"

"I trust that is a rhetorical question, because you certainly have been that managing before."

"It has always worked better with your brother. He permits it, you know, to humor me. You do not."

Cybelline nodded. "Sherry indulges me as well. He is the best of all of us, I think." She took a small, steadying breath when tears threatened. "I will write to him, of course. I will even tell him what I have done to my hair. There was an invitation to spend Christmas at Granville. I did not know how I might graciously refuse it, but I think he will understand when I tell him that I mean to set up in your home at Penwyckham. If my explanation does not serve to allay his concerns for me, I hope you will help him understand."

"I will do my best."

"I have never doubted that, Aunt Georgia. You have always been our rock."

"A pebble in your shoe, mayhap."

"When you had to be."

Lady Rivendale chuckled. "I should have expected that you would agree." She replaced her serviette in her lap and absently smoothed the creases. "When will you want to leave?"

Cybelline wanted to tell her that tomorrow would not be soon enough, or even better, that she should have left before the masque. "It will not take long to arrange our departure. I was thinking that all could be made ready in three days."

"Three days! That is no time at all. The house has been neglected, Cybelline. I thought I explained that. There is only Mr. and Mrs. Henley from the village who look after the property. I have not been there in four years. I cannot say that I even recall how many rooms you shall have use of."

"More than enough, I should think," Cybelline said confidently. "Can you not know that the home's neglect is one of the attractions for me? Of course you do, you sly puss. That is why you suggested it and not one of your other properties. I will take such servants as I think I need and keep the Henleys on. There cannot be so much work in Penwyckham that I will have difficulty hiring gardeners and grooms should I have need of them."

Lady Rivendale lifted one hand and massaged her temple with her fingertips. "This is not unfolding in quite the manner I had envisioned." She raised her fingers and indicated the silver threads of hair. "Have I more? I do believe that I have more. It is astonishing to me that I will go to my bed tonight with more silver in my hair than I had upon rising from it this morning."

"I highly recommend the henna."

The countess's humor asserted itself. She had a full-throated, husky laugh that filled the small breakfast room. Cybelline was immediately warmed by it.

"You are too clever by half," Lady Rivendale said, still smiling. "You will always have the better of me. Very well. What is to be done, then? Shall I send a missive to the Henleys and hope it arrives before you do? It will give them perhaps as much as a day or two to prepare. The journey will require some three or four days of travel, much of it on roads that rarely do not cause a mishap. Penwyckham is not on the other side of the earth, but close enough."

"Warning the Henleys of my imminent arrival is only fair to them. It is my experience that such surprises are generally unwelcome. I will be relying on them to assist my own servants and provide such information as I require about the village and the locals. They will be invaluable if I need to hire more help. You are satisfied, I collect, with their quarterly reports to you?"

"Yes. What repairs they have suggested have always

seemed reasonable, though I have entertained fears they err on the side of doing too little. It was why you will be doing me a very great favor by going there."

"Surely you've had your steward visit from time to time."

The countess shook her head. "Matters at Rivendale keep him occupied. There is also the property at Trent and the one near Nottingham. I have stewards for each. The house at Penwyckham is not part of an estate that requires overseeing tenants and lands, collecting rents and the like. I hope I have not misled you in that regard. I have to trust that the Henleys were as they presented themselves to me when I engaged them. I encourage you to write to me and inform me if I was wrong."

"I suspect I will write to you about all manner of things, though I doubt any one of them will be about your making an error of judgment."

Lady Rivendale gave her a skeptical look. "Is it that you don't think I can make such an error or that you shy from confronting me?"

"There is no answer to that poser that will not put me in Dutch with you."

"Not if you tell the truth, there is not. Lying, however, will put you in my good graces."

Cybelline laughed. She picked up a triangle of toast, now stone cold, and bit it delicately. "Why have you not visited Penwyckham yourself, Aunt?"

"The house was left to me by my own aunt, my father's sister. I could scarcely abide her. Upon reflection, it is more truthful to say I was afraid of her. I spent summers with her as a child when my parents were abroad. Her heart was hard—that is what I remember thinking as a child. Bitter, I would say now. I conceived the notion that she didn't like me. Certainly she had no use for me. I don't think I saw her more than a score of times in all of the summers I resided there. She spent a great many hours in the drawing room reading from her Bible. She took her meals alone and suffered my presence only when a melancholia was upon her."

"She was unmarried?"

"Yes. And childless. Friendless, too, I think. It should not have been so surprising that she named me the foremost beneficiary in her will. I was a logical choice since I was her closest blood relative, yet I remember being shocked when I learned of it. The Sharpe house was mine along with a tidy sum for its upkeep. I thought at first I would sell it, but upon going there, I found I could not. Whatever the source of melancholia, it was not reflected in the house she kept. The rooms were bright and cheerful, and I remember that she was never tightfisted with candles or wood for the fires. The furniture was in good order, polished and freshly upholstered. The linens were all of fine quality. Still, while I could not bring myself to sell, neither could I remain there overlong."

Lady Rivendale sighed. "I have told you perhaps more than you wanted to know, but there you have it. I fear I have not been a good steward of the property by leaving it for so long in the hands of others. The Henleys are not the first to care for the house and grounds. There was a Mr. Younger and a Mrs. Ayres before them. They were excused from service when I last journeyed to Penwyckham. It is putting it too mildly to say that the home came to a sad state while in their care. I promised myself that I would not allow it to suffer neglect a second time, yet I have done little to ensure that hasn't come to pass."

"Anna and I will set your mind at ease. After we have settled and made ourselves happy there, you will come to the country and see for yourself that the Sharpe house has all the light and life one might wish for."

Lady Rivendale looked at Cybelline with some surprise. "I believe you mean it."

"You doubt me?"

The countess was long in responding. She finally waggled one hand to indicate that what she was going to say was no longer of any consequence. "I have been possessed by the oddest thought since you told me you are ready to quit London."

"Oh?"

"You will think me ridiculous since I have been encouraging you to leave for the country for well on five months now. It is only that I cannot rid myself of the notion that you are bolting."

Cybelline's features remained perfectly unchanged until a small smile reshaped her mouth. "You are right once again, Aunt Georgia."

"Then you *are* bolting?"

"No, you're right that I think you are ridiculous."

Viscount Sheridan set his quill aside as the door to his study opened. That this breach of his sanctuary occurred without a warning knock was enough to indicate who would be there when he lifted his eyes. He smiled warmly, inviting the interruption to continue.

"Forgive me, Sherry," Lily said, "but the post has arrived and I knew you would want this immediately." She held up a letter between her thumb and index finger, waving it gently. "And I knew you would want to share its contents with me, so I have saved you the bother of hunting for me."

"That was very good of you, though I like the hunt well enough."

"Do not raise that eyebrow at me, my lord. I am able to understand your meaning without having it underscored in that particular manner."

Chuckling, he lowered the offending eyebrow. The last time he'd hunted for his wife, he had finally run her to ground in a hayrick. She'd burrowed deep, and he'd burrowed deeper. All things considered, it had been a lovely way to spend the afternoon. But that was yesterday. Apparently Lily had other thoughts to occupy her for the nonce.

"Allow me to see what you have there," he said, extending his hand. "Is Rosie napping?"

Lily laid the letter in Sherry's palm. "Rose," she said deliberately, "was playing with her toes when last I looked, and Nurse Pinter was sleeping. It seemed to satisfy them both."

Sherry nodded absently. He was already looking at the elegant copperplate handwriting. "It's from Cybelline."

"Yes."

He took a knife from his desk and slit the seal. "Will you not sit, Lily? Or would you prefer to read over my shoulder?"

"Do not tempt me." Her smile held a hint of mischief that was reflected in her green eyes. She sat, taking the delicate Queen Anne chair on the opposite side of Sherry's desk. Sherry, she saw, was already skimming the letter. A crease had appeared between his dark eyebrows, and he was tapping the knife tip against the edge of the paper, rattling it. Her heart sank a little. "She is not coming to visit, is she? What does she say, Sherry? Pray, do not keep me on tenterhooks."

"I have not gotten so far. She says first that she is well. Anna also. Aunt Georgia is enjoying better health, having recently recovered from a stomach ailment. It seems she—Aunt Georgia, that is—was unable to attend the masque given by Sir Geoffrey and Lady Gardner in honor of their daughter's debut. You will not credit it, but Cybelline attended."

Lily did not credit it. "Are you certain you have not mistaken what she's written?"

Sherry read it again. "She is quite clear. She attended without Aunt Georgia."

"Even more extraordinary." Lily pointed to Sherry's

knife. "Do put that down. I am in fear that it will slip, and you will do me grievous injury."

He frowned. "I am more likely to do injury to—" He stopped, glancing down to where the knife was certain to meet the sticking place squarely between his legs. "Oh, yes, I see. That would be too bad for you." He carefully set the knife aside and ran one hand through his dark cocoa-colored hair. His attention returned to the missive. "She writes that Aunt Georgia was adamant that she should attend, and since it was a masquerade, Cybelline persuaded herself that she had the courage to do so."

"It was her come-out, then," Lily said. "After a fashion."

"She writes the very same." Sherry turned the first page over and continued to read. "A shepherdess. That was her costume. Again, Aunt Georgia's fine hand at work. Cybelline was gratified to see so many other shepherdesses present, though when Aunt Georgia learned of it she was understandably less than pleased. Apparently Aunt thought her idea a complete original."

Lily pressed three fingers to her lips to tamp her smile. She noticed that Sherry was smiling as well. It was not difficult for either of them to imagine Lady Rivendale being most put out to discover her original idea was so common. "Go on. What does she say about the evening? Did all go well?"

Sherry reported all of Lily's observations about the masque, then mused aloud, "She seems to have enjoyed the anonymity. I wonder that no one recognized her."

"She has rarely been about in society since Nicholas's death. Perhaps if she had accompanied Lady Rivendale someone would have guessed her identity. Your aunt merely has to laugh, and she would make herself known to the assembly. Cybelline would be caught out for the company she keeps."

Sherry considered that. "You are most likely right."

"And then there was the costume. If Cybelline was the

shepherdess from the Gainsborough hanging in your aunt's London home, even you might have passed over her for all the flounces and furbelows."

"I think I would know my own sister."

"Do not underestimate your aunt's design. The fact that there were so many there of a similar mode could have confused you."

"I would know you in any manner of costume."

"I think you flatter your powers of observation. I could fool you. In fact, you have forgotten that I did. On the occasion of our first meeting you mistook me for a lad."

"I would not make the same error again."

Lily did not argue the point. She indicated the letter. "Please go on. What has she to say about joining us for Christmas?"

"I am not come to that yet. She writes that she made an unfortunate decision before the masquerade to wash her hair with henna." Sherry's eyes widened, and he read the passage a second time. "Henna. That is what she says. What could she have been thinking?"

"Mayhap she did not wish to wear a powdered wig." Lily fingered her own penny-copper hair. "Or mayhap she wished to copy my own coloring—and the disposition that accompanies it."

"God's truth, I hope not."

Both of Lily's eyebrows lifted. "It is just that sort of thinking that you will want to keep to yourself if you expect to find me in your bed this evening."

Sherry was uncertain if he was being teased or warned. He decided to tread carefully. "I only meant that your sweet temperament cannot be forced by trying to capture the rare beauty of your hair. I would have thought Cybelline would know that."

"Prettily said. You recover quickly from your missteps."

"The scoundrels' influence."

Lily was certain there was some truth in that. She smiled. "Does Cybelline say how the henna worked?"

"Since she tells us at the outset that it was an unfortunate decision, I think it is safe to say it did not work well." He read on. "The color, she says, prompted Anna to throw porridge at her, Webb to cluck her tongue many times over, and Aunt Georgia to make unflattering comparisons to a cyprian."

"Oh my. It must have been ghastly."

"She mentions here that it was the red-orange of a popping ember."

"Goodness."

Sherry withheld comment and continued to read. "I gather the henna is coming out with repeated scrubbing, and there will be a return to her honey-colored tresses within a sennight."

"Then no permanent harm has been done."

"Apparently, that is the case." He began the second page of Cybelline's letter, and it was here that his frown deepened. "She is going to Penwyckham. I cannot believe it." Looking up, he saw that Lily was not following. "Penwyckham is several days' journey northeast of London, still south of Norfolk. It's a village—a hamlet, actually, if that is the smaller. Aunt Georgia inherited a home there years ago. It was her aunt's, Lady Beatrice Sharpe. Aunt Georgia never spent any significant time there, though I've always understood her to care for it."

"Care for it? How do you mean?"

"What? Oh, I see. I was ambiguous. She cared for it in the sense of hiring people to keep it in decent repair and tend the garden. She has never, I believe, had any special affection for the house. At least she has not intimated as much to me."

"But why is Cybelline going there?"

Sherry regarded his sister's handwriting again and read on quickly. "She writes that remaining in London gives her no peace. She wishes to retire to the country and set up a house for herself and Anna. She will stay the winter there, perhaps longer. Cybelline believes Penwyckham will offer what she has not had in town: solitude."

"Solitude? But she is often alone there."

"No," Sherry said softly, shaking his head. "She lives with Nicholas. I do not think she is ever by herself."

"Oh, Sherry." Lily's shoulders sagged. "Is there nothing we can do?"

"I don't think so. It seems she is set on the matter, I have never been able to persuade her to do anything different than what she will. Once turned in a particular direction, Cybelline is single-minded to a fault."

"Then there will be no inducement that will bring her to Granville at Christmas."

"Not Rosie, not the scoundrels. Certainly not you or me."

Lily heard something in her husband's voice that gave her pause. How hard it was for him to accept that Cybelline did not come immediately to his side. Until her marriage, Sherry was the man his sister put before all others. She still asked for his opinion about a political interest or looked to him for guidance in matters of finance, but nothing was as it ever had been. Nicholas Caldwell had absorbed most of Sherry's critical responsibilities when he married Cybelline, then abandoned them when he put a pistol to his head.

"She loves us, you know," Lily said. "Her decision to go to Penwyckham is not because she does not love us, you above all."

"I know." He had to work the words past the lump in his throat. Sherry could not quite meet his wife's eye. "God forgive me, Lily, but I find a measure of relief knowing she will not come here—and a greater measure of guilt because I am relieved. Will there ever be a time when any of us is unburdened with regret and pain and guilt?" His voice dropped to a strained whisper. "Cybelline most of all."

"Yes, there will be such a time." Lily felt Sherry's gaze shift to her. He wanted to believe what she was saying; she could sense the hopefulness of his expression. "I don't know when, Sherry, or how it will come about, but each of us will make peace with what happened. Perhaps you and I cannot do so because Cybelline has not found it yet. I know it is what we both wish for her."

"Above everything."

"Yes, above everything. If Nicholas's death had been in the course of an illness, an accident, mayhap even foul play, all of us would not be at the loose ends that we are now. But it was a suicide, and we both know, Sherry, while Cybelline does not, what profound consequences that has had for you."

Sherry laid his sister's letter on the desktop. He stood and crossed the room to the small drinks cabinet, where he selected a decanter of whisky. "Will you take something with me?" he asked, pouring two fingers for himself. He glanced in Lily's direction and saw her refusal. It was only when his first swallow settled in the pit of his stomach that he spoke.

"I know better than anyone how a man might be persuaded to kill himself. I also know how it can be arranged to look like one thing while the reality is quite another."

Lily nodded, though she said nothing.

"I could find no evidence that either of these things was true, and I cannot say whether I would be better or worse for knowing. If I accept that Nicholas's suicide was precisely as it appeared, then the why of it troubles me as it does Cybelline. You have reason to know that he was a most amiable fellow. He doted on Cybelline and was elated at the birth of his daughter. He was a man with varied interests and a true scholar of antiquities. He provided more than adequately for his family. He did not gamble, keep a mistress, or entertain himself with whores. How did it escape us, then, that he was possessed of demons?"

Sherry took another short swallow of whiskey. "I made a point to learn all I could about Mr. Caldwell before he married my sister. It is not something I would admit to anyone save you, but I am not ashamed of it, either."

"Do you think Cybelline would really be surprised to learn you made inquiries about her betrothed? I am certain she knows how seriously you take your responsibilities toward her. And if she thought scruples would restrain you from doing such a thing, she would not acquit Lady Rivendale of having the same."

Sherry returned to his desk but not his chair. He hitched one hip on the edge closest to Lily and rolled the tumbler of whisky between his palms as he considered what she'd said. "If you are right, then Cybelline depended on me not to allow her to make a mistake, and—"

Lily interrupted. "I did not say she depended on you. I said she would not be surprised by your actions. It is not the same thing at all."

He went on as if she had not spoken. "And it does not relieve me from the knowledge that my inquiry failed to bring something dark in Nicholas's past to light."

"Why do you think it must have been in his past? Could circumstances not change after his marriage? It might have been something in his present that troubled him enough to kill himself. How can you expect that you should have known that? Or warned Cybelline? Or prevented it? I love you, Sherry, and have thought upon occasion that the sun rises and sets by your pocket watch, but you are *not* all knowing." She paused and under her breath added, "Your pocket watch is not even always accurate."

Sherry blinked. After a moment, one corner of his mouth twitched. "You are damnably good at taking me down a peg. Two pegs in this instance. To discover that I am no visionary *and* my pocket watch is off the mark, well, it is most definitely lowering."

Lily stood and stepped into the vee made by Sherry's splayed legs. She took the tumbler from him and finished it before setting it aside. Taking his wrists, she drew his arms around her waist in a loose embrace. She felt his hands lock behind her and his double fist rest against the small of her back. Lily leaned forward just enough to brush his lips with hers.

"Cybelline is fortunate, indeed, to have you for her brother. You are in every way a good man, no matter that you do not always believe it. This strain will not last. I think her journey to Penwyckham is a first step in ending it. When you favor her with a reply, tell her that we miss her and Anna, that we wish her peace and joy of the season, and that we understand her decision to leave London. Write to her of what is in your heart, Sherry. She will find relief there, not more pain. I have to trust that you will find the same."

Sherry lifted his head just enough to rest his cheek against Lily's hair. She fit herself more closely to him, and he closed his eyes. "It is good advice," he said quietly.

"I have not overstepped?"

"No. No, not at all. I cannot tell Cybelline what is in my heart without telling her of you. There is no part of you that is separate from it."

She placed her palm over his chest and felt the steady beat. "It is no different for me," she said. "No different at all."

Restell Gardner regarded his brother from his half re-cline on the chaise longue. "I say, Kit, you have been in a dark mood of late. I don't believe you've been attend-ing me at all."

Ferrin did not turn away from the shelf of books he was

studying. "Good for you, Restell. I am *not* attending you. In fact, I am ignoring you. I believe you are bright enough to understand it is of a purpose."

"I stand corrected," Restell said. "It is not a dark mood. It is a black one."

Porter Wellsley, sitting in the wing chair turned toward the fire, chuckled appreciatively. "You would do better to relate all of the particulars of your adventure to me and not attempt to include Ferrin. He is lost to us, I'm afraid, when he is engaged in matters of scientific inquiry."

"Is that what he's doing? Science?"

"Just so, though I don't pretend to understand it. He's a deep one, is your brother. It was the same at Cambridge. The darling of the dons and the bane of all of us with less talented upperworks. He was at his most content in one of the fusty old laboratories or the library. I was not the only one who despaired he would come to a bad end, blow up some damn fool thing or another. That's what was in the wagering books, with substantial winnings to be earned by predicting what part of his anatomy he would lose to his experiments."

"He has all his fingers and toes."

"More's the pity," Wellsley said. "I wagered on the left pinky. I was his friend, you see, and I felt that making money from the loss of a larger appendage was rather beyond the pale."

Ferrin made his selection from among the titles he was perusing and finally turned. "You would have wagered on the loss of my left bullock, Wellsley, if you thought I would be that careless."

Wellsley shrugged. The grin he cast in Restell's direction was somewhat sheepish. "He's right. It was not misgivings that prevented me from making the wager but some understanding of your brother's meticulous work habits."

Restell laughed outright. "I am glad that I was sent to Oxford, then. Under no circumstances could I be mistaken for the darling of the dons. It would have been too much to follow in Ferrin's footsteps at Cambridge. It is deuced difficult now, and I am only trying to secure a reputation as a gentleman about town."

Ferrin looked up from his book long enough to roll his eyes.

Wellsley scratched his chin thoughtfully. "Mayhap you are too determined in the matter. Ferrin is two and thirty and has been at it for a time. There are those—Lady Gardner, for one—who would say he's been at it too long. If you want to cultivate a rep such as your brother enjoys, you must not be so quick to avoid the clutches of all those females with marriage on their mind. Ferrin has always been careful to allow those young things and their mamas to hope that he can be caught. At least that is what I have observed as the trick of it. He is fascinating to them because he permits them to think he might be changed. I fear it is more of a balancing feat than I am able to manage. I am quite ready to be changed, while your brother is peculiarly content to remain a rascal."

"I want to be a rascal," Restell said feelingly.

"What do you mean you are ready to be changed?" Ferrin asked at the same time.

Restell, realizing that in his self-absorption he had missed something of import, echoed his brother. "Yes, Wellsley, what do you mean by that?"

"It means what it means," Wellsley explained stoutly, if inadequately. When he saw that this was not going to pass muster with either Ferrin or Restell, he reluctantly elaborated. "I am all for the comforts of a married state. I think I will like to share the breakfast table with my wife."

"Yes, but will you share the newspaper?" asked Ferrin.

Ignoring that, Wellsley went on. The broad planes of his face softened and a smile played at the corners of his mouth. His eyes, while in no way remote, were certainly engaged in seeing something as if from a distance. "I will enjoy the tricks wives get up to: planning parties when their allowance is insufficient; buying parasols and ribbons for no reason except they are struck by a mood; flirting with other gentlemen to lead their husbands about by the nose. It has been on my mind lately that there is nothing at all disagreeable about it."

Ferrin dropped his book. Although it was done of a purpose and fell only so far as his desktop, the thump was considerable and had the desired effect: Wellsley jumped as though shot through the heart.

"What?" he asked, glaring at Ferrin. "What was that in aid of?"

It was Restell who offered the explanation. "You were speaking such nonsense as to be perfectly objectionable."

"Was I?" He looked to his friend for confirmation.

Ferrin's mouth pulled slightly to one side, and he offered a nod reluctantly. "I'm afraid so."

"Oh, dear." Wellsley sighed. "I am over the moon, then."

"I think that might be understating it," Ferrin said dryly. He skirted his desk until he came to stand in front of it, then he leaned back and folded his arms across his chest. "Might we inquire as to the name of the female who has put you there?"

The tips of Wellsley's ears reddened. "I have not declared myself to her. You will understand, then, my reluctance to give you her name."

Restell chose a small embroidered pillow from the chaise and pitched it at Wellsley's head. "He might understand, but I do not. Are you afraid we will let it about? That's not very trusting of you. I know how to keep a secret."

"So do I," Wellsley said, tossing the pillow back. "And that is by keeping it to myself. Is that not right, Ferrin?"

"That's right." Ferrin was prepared to say more on the subject for Restell's benefit, but a commotion in the adjoining drawing room put a period to the half-formed moral lesson. Restell might have preferred it, Ferrin thought, to what surely was coming. "It is Mother," he said unnecessarily. Restell was abandoning his negligent posture on the chaise for something more like a military bearing, while Wellsley was already on his feet.

Lady Gardner swept through the door thrown open to her by the butler and demanded, "Ferrin, is that rascal—. Never mind, I can see that he is." Her eyes bored into her stepson.

"Take heart, Restell," Ferrin said. "Mother thinks you are a rascal." Ignoring Restell's unamused glance, Ferrin pushed away from his desk and stepped forward to greet his mother. He took both her hands and kissed her cheek. "You are looking in the very pink of health, Mother."

"Frankly, I am overset."

"But you are in fine color."

Lady Gardner removed her hands from Ferrin's and patted her cheeks. "They are not too flushed?"

"No."

"It is no thanks to Restell."

"I am sure it is not."

She looked around her son's broad shoulders to dart a sharp glance at her stepson. He was standing stiffly beside the chaise. "He said he could not escort me to either Bond Street or the bookseller's because he was calling upon Miss Martha Hopkins this afternoon. He knew I would approve of that. She is to have a dowry of six thousand pounds and shall come into a trust established by her late grandmother when she is twenty-five."

"I am sure you do not mean to be mercenary."

"Mercenary? Of course not. I mean to be practical. One must plan, you know, and I am credited with being able to see the long view. Restell's prospects are not the same as yours, are they?"

"He will not be an earl," Ferrin said cautiously.

She waved that aside. "That is the least of it. He will not have thirty thousand pounds a year. He will not have homes in town and in the country. He will not have lands in abundance nor tenants to work them. There will be no rents to collect or profits to be made from cattle and crops and investments."

Restell's weight shifted. He cleared his throat and made what he hoped was an acceptable offer. "I shall put a bullet to my head at once."

Lady Gardner stepped around Ferrin and pointed a finger at Restell. "That is not at all amusing. Do you know with whom I spent the afternoon when you would not escort me?" She did not give him time to answer and neither Ferrin nor Wellsley—who thought himself well out of it—ventured a guess. "Lady Rivendale. I met her at Barkley's and had tea with her. Mr. Nicholas Caldwell was her niece's husband." Restell's blank look did not put him in her good graces. She speared Wellsley with her glance. "I suppose you do not know who that is, either?"

"I believe Mr. Caldwell killed himself with a pistol ball to the head," Wellsley said. "That was the *on-dit* at the time, though I have never speculated as to the truth or falseness of the rumor."

"You do not often impress me, Mr. Wellsley," Lady Gardner said. "But it is excellent that you have done so now." She smiled at him warmly, further evidence of her approbation. This evidence vanished when she returned her attention to Restell. "Mr. Wellsley is quite right not to engage in rumor. I know it from Lady Rivendale herself that what was alleged was true. I can assure you that no one in that family finds anything diverting about it. Mrs. Caldwell was at your sister's masquerade. It was one of only a handful of public appearances that she's made since her husband's death. Imagine how she would have reacted to hearing you speak so cavalierly about putting a pistol to your head."

Ferrin watched Restell take his mother's harangue on the chin. A lock of pale yellow hair fell over his brother's brow, but except to shake it back, he did not move. The lecture was undeserved, but it was good of Restell not to try to defend himself. He had to realize that if he had provided an escort rather than shirking the responsibility, she would not be put out with him now.

"In fairness to Restell," Ferrin said, "the subject did not come up at the masque."

She rounded on him. "The subject did not come up now, either. He plucked it out of the air." She touched her cheeks again. "I will have a drop of sherry, Ferrin, to calm my nerves." Accepting Wellsley's escort, Lady Gardner took the chair he had previously occupied and fanned herself lightly. "How would any of us know if we had said something untoward?" she asked. "Mrs. Caldwell is unknown to me even when she is not dressed as a Gainsborough shepherdess."

Ferrin paused in pouring his mother the drink she requested. "A shepherdess?" he asked with considerably more casualness than he felt. "That does not narrow it at all, does it? Pray, what color were the ribbons on her crook?"

"Green," Lady Gardner said. "I asked Lady Rivendale the very same question. I was assured they were green."

Chapter Four

Boudicca's spear stood in the corner of Ferrin's study. He'd wondered earlier if Wellsley, Restell, or especially his mother, whose eyes were as sharp as a peregrine falcon's, would notice it. None of them had. He suspected they were distracted by the absurdity of their own conversation, and for once he did not regret his presence or participation in it.

He had learned something valuable and unexpected: Mrs. Nicholas Caldwell was the friend for whom Boudicca had been searching. Ferrin picked up the spear, turning it over in his hand. It was every bit as old as he had suspected. He'd had that confirmed by taking it to one of his former professors who'd made a study of such things. It was from Sir Richard Settle that he heard the name Nicholas Caldwell for the first time. Caldwell was a student—some would say scholar, but not Sir Richard—of the Iceni people. Boudicca was their queen.

It did not stretch the imagination to suppose that Mrs. Caldwell had permitted her friend to borrow the spear, the torc, the brooch, and the bracelets to lend authenticity to Boudicca's costume. Ferrin wondered how Boudicca would explain the loss of the spear. Mrs. Caldwell could not have anticipated her friend would be careless with an

item whose value was better measured in terms sentimen-
tal and historical rather than financial.

He considered calling upon Mrs. Caldwell to return the
spear but was uncertain this was the best course of action.
She might not be willing to tell him anything about her
friend, especially once the artifact was in her possession.
Gratitude would not necessarily guarantee her cooperation. He also had questions as to what Mrs. Caldwell
might know about her friend's behavior. It was difficult to
believe Boudicca would have spoken of their encounter to
anyone, even a friend considered to be a confidante. Presenting his card at Mrs. Caldwell's might raise questions
that he was most definitely not prepared to answer.

Ferrin was acquainted with Lady Rivendale and had
known before this afternoon that she was a friend to his
mother. His own introduction to her had come some six
years earlier in Lord Hardcourt's card room. She was an
accomplished player, one of the few women invited to sit
at Lord Hardcourt's table and make wagers. Her participation did not occasion notoriety as it would have a
woman of less stature in society. The wags had it that
the Countess of Rivendale was merely eccentric. It was
Ferrin's observation of the great lady that she'd rather
have been notorious.

Ferrin could not recall anyone closely resembling the
countess in form or feature at the masquerade. When he
mentioned this to his mother, she confirmed that Lady
Rivendale had not been present. A stomach ailment had
kept her confined to her bed, and she had been most unhappy about it. According to his mother, Mrs. Caldwell
had been encouraged by the countess to attend the masque
in any event and had arrived unescorted.

Ferrin did not gainsay his mother on this point. Indeed,
he could not be certain it wasn't true, but Boudicca had
expended some effort in looking for her friend, and it
begged the question: Had they, in fact, arrived together?

Given that Mrs. Caldwell was no longer often about in society, Boudicca was likely concerned that her friend had bolted. It did not present Boudicca in a flattering light that she had been so willing to set consideration for Mrs. Caldwell aside and seek her own pleasure first. But then, Ferrin recalled, Boudicca had not only taken on the mantel of a queen, she had cloaked herself in ruthlessness as well.

Ferrin replaced the spear in the corner. He had several such artifacts at his country estate in Norfolk. They were occasionally found by the tenant farmers turning over the ground in preparation of spring planting and always brought to him for inspection. Because his estate was situated in and around the same environs that Queen Boudicca and her people had once occupied, it was not difficult for him to make an educated identification. More Roman weapons were found than those belonging to the Iceni, but that was because in the end, by sheer force of numbers, the Romans had emerged as victors.

Not knowing the origin of the spear Boudicca had carried to the masquerade was what prompted Ferrin to seek Sir Richard's expertise. That meeting had turned out favorably in two ways: the spear was identified as a weapon forged and used by the Iceni, and the name Caldwell had been brought to his attention.

Ferrin returned to his desk and sat down. He made a steeple of his fingers and rested his chin on the tips as he contemplated his next step. When information came to him from two unrelated sources and carried certain commonalities, he could not dismiss it as coincidence. Still, he knew himself reluctant to approach Mrs. Caldwell. It was quite enough dealing with his mother when she was overset; he did not want to provoke the same state of nerves in a widow who rarely left her home.

It seemed to Ferrin that Lady Rivendale was the answer to his every question, and a smile played about his mouth as a plan began to take form. He knew precisely how to engage her interest.

Cybelline gave a small start, waking suddenly as the carriage jolted. She observed that her fellow passengers were not affected in the same way. Nanny Baker was snoring softly, her head turned at an uncomfortably sharp angle toward the window. Anna did not stir in Cybelline's lap. The rolling and swaying carriage had turned out to be superior to the rocker in the nursery for lulling the little girl to sleep.

It was nearing nightfall on their third day. Cybelline lifted the blind just enough to gauge the onset of darkness and saw at once they would have to secure lodging soon. She had hoped to reach Penwyckham today, but the countess had greatly underestimated the length of the journey. Her driver had tried to tell her the trip could easily require as long as a sennight, but she had misunderstood, thinking he meant to prepare her for the inevitability of a mishap with an axle, a wheel, or a horse coming up lame. Thus far, they had experienced no larger mishap than Nanny Baker becoming as sick as a midshipman on his first tour of duty, and still they were little more than halfway to their destination.

Nicholas had traveled some of these same roads on his way to Suffolk and Norfolk Broads, but she could not recall him complaining of either the length of the journey or of the lack of decent accommodations along the way. In truth, her husband was not one to complain, especially about things that could not be changed. What she did remember quite clearly was how excited he was at the outset of each excursion. Nicholas was unfailingly optimistic about where each journey would lead. "You will see, Cyb," he'd tell her. "This time I will find a piece worthy of the Royal Society's interest."

Often, he did. Nicholas's scholarly study was not limited to the Iceni, of which there were precious few artifacts to be uncovered. He also had an interest in the East Anglia kingdoms of the sixth and seventh centuries. Shrewd investments in shipping, particularly the China trade, supported Nicholas's intellectual pursuits. It was in his role as barrister that he supported his family.

Cybelline's thoughts wandered, as they had since the masquerade, to the problem of the missing spear. A rare find, one that Nicholas had been most enthusiastic about, the spearhead was in excellent condition as it had been protected from the elements for almost two thousand years by an unusual formation of stone around it. Cybelline knew she had acted unconscionably by removing it from the house. Nicholas had intended to sell it to a collector who would preserve it as well as the stone had, but he had not been able to bring himself to part with it. Now she wondered at her motives for taking it.

At the time she'd told herself that it lent authenticity to her costume and gave her the courage she needed to become Boudicca. That was true as far as it went, but as a complete explanation it fell far short of the mark. Was she really so angry at Nicholas for abandoning her that removing the spear—then leaving it behind—was an act of spite? Or was it because every glance at it reminded her painfully that Nicholas would never share his joy of discovery again?

Cybelline rested her head back against the plump leather squabs and closed her eyes. She had been but halfway home from the masquerade when she realized she'd left the spear behind. She considered returning for it, but she'd already changed into the shepherdess costume in the event that Lady Rivendale was waiting up for her. More important in her decision was her fear that Ferrin would not allow her to leave so easily a second time. He would find out easily enough that she had never been properly introduced to his sister Imogene, nor had she made the acquaintance of his mother. She had been careful to excuse herself from any group of guests that lingered on the subject of identifying one another. Her conversational contributions were small; she did not offer an opinion except when she was asked directly. To refuse on such occasions would have caused more comment than a simple response.

What would Lord Ferrin do with the spear? she wondered. It occurred to Cybelline that he would want to return it. It was hardly the sort of thing one kept as a memento of a lover's tryst, and the earl seemed oddly honorable in spite of the fact that he often flouted the rules and mores of the *ton*. She had not expected to find him . . . well, to find him *likable*. That he was, in point of fact, so damnably congenial had almost caused her to abandon her plan.

She feared complications from a man who dismissed polite society but embraced a civil manner.

How hard would he try to find the owner of the spear? In the stairwell he made her a promise without knowing what she was asking of him. She hadn't been able to finish her sentence because she hadn't been able to complete the thought. She hardly knew what she was asking him herself. Not to speak of their encounter? Not to search for her? Not to remember what words had been exchanged?

And if he found the widow Caldwell, would he know he'd found Boudicca?

Cybelline could barely suppress the involuntary moan that came to her lips. She pressed a knuckle to her mouth and held it there. The ridge of her upper teeth marked her skin. She glanced at Nanny Baker. The woman remained slumped and sleeping, insensible to her distress. Anna's tiny bow mouth was parted around a dewy bubble that came and went with each soft breath.

"Anna." It was little more than a whisper from Cybelline, but Anna burrowed against her mother and both of them were comforted.

The card room in Ferrin's home was arranged for twelve players. Three tables were set equidistant from one another, like the points of a triangle. For those attending the supper and entertainment who did not wish to play at cards, two chairs and an upholstered bench had been added to the room's complement of furniture.

Wynetta played the pianoforte, though not with such resonance that it distracted those who were drawn to the cards and conversation. Ian's wife sat on the bench beside her and turned the sheets of music. Ian and Imogene were partners at one of the tables, playing opposite the Allworthy cousins. Ferrin had already warned his brother and sister that the Allworthys might get up to more tricks than were strictly available for the taking. The twins understood immediately and were prepared to make short work of the cousins. Sir Geoffrey and Lady Gardner sat at a second table, but in the interest of preserving a happy marriage they were not partners at whist. Lady Gardner partnered her longtime friend, Mrs. Samuel Franklin, while Sir Geoffrey sat across the table from Mr. Gordon Sawyer.

Ferrin had carefully selected his guests and maneuvered the choosing of partners so that he might at the very least sit at the same table as Lady Rivendale. He was pleased that it had all come about as he'd hoped, even better, since the countess was his partner, not merely one at the table. Restell and Porter Wellsley had the remaining seats. Wellsley, Ferrin noted, was frequently guilty of looking more often in Wynetta's direction than at his own cards. His play was not up to his usual thoughtfulness and Restell, always a fierce competitor, was not enjoying being trounced.

"That would be my trick," Lady Rivendale said. She laid her hand gently over Wellsley's when he would have moved to sweep the cards off the table for his side. "My diamond. That's trump this round."

The tips of Wellsley's ears reddened, and he begged her pardon while studiously avoiding Restell's glare. "So it is. You are good to remind me."

"I reminded you," Restell said, "twice."

"Yes, but you were mean."

Ferrin chuckled when his brother's mouth snapped shut. Sometimes Wellsley hit a thing so squarely that no reply was possible. Ferrin saw that Lady Rivendale was also amused. He waited for her and Wellsley to make their plays, then followed suit. After Restell tossed his card on the table, the countess once again gathered the cards to her side.

"I am fortunate, indeed," Ferrin said, "to have you as my partner this evening."

"I hope you will acquit me of being immodest when I say that you certainly are. I am having a good run with the cards."

"Then I regret even more that you were unable to attend the masquerade. I played several hands with a highwayman whose concern for the fold of his neckcloth was nearly our undoing."

"Oh, that is too bad," Lady Rivendale said. "Good card play requires one's full attention, at least I find it so. Tell me, Lord Ferrin, was the highwayman Mr. Gardner on my right or Mr. Wellsley on my left?"

Restell answered as he idly rearranged his cards. "I was a Viking warrior, my lady."

She cast a sideways glance at Wellsley. "Pray, Mr. Wellsley, what was wrong with your neckcloth?"

"Wasn't properly disheveled," he said.

"Yes, that would be a bother." She laid another card down and watched their plays carefully before taking the trick. "What about you, Lord Ferrin? A highwayman also?"

"High seas. I was a pirate."

"Always a good choice."

"And what personage did we miss when you did not attend? Queen Titania?"

"A very nice compliment," she said. "Shakespeare was my inspiration, but I was drawn to Lady Macbeth."

Ferrin grinned. "An excellent selection. She most certainly was not present that night. Cordelia. Ophelia. Juliet and Viola. They were all accounted for, but no Lady Macbeth."

"It is gratifying to hear that *one* of my ideas was an original." In deference to Imogene, who had been a shepherdess, albeit with blue ribbons, Lady Rivendale's voice dropped to a confidential whisper. "I was disappointed to learn there were seven shepherdesses, my dear niece among them."

Ferrin affected mild interest. "Your niece? I do not remember making her acquaintance, or perhaps it is only she did not remark on the connection."

Restell took the last trick of the hand and recorded the score. "Don't you recall, Ferrin? Mother mentioned that Mrs. Caldwell was there."

Restraining the urge to kick Restell, as it would serve nothing except to make him yelp like a wounded puppy, Ferrin pretended to think about a conversation he had, in fact, not been able to put out of his mind. "Mrs. Caldwell. Yes. Yes, of course. I remember. Mother said she had green ribbons."

Lady Rivendale smiled, satisfied that her creation had been unique in at least one regard. "She informed me that she was in very good company, your sister being among the flock."

"Indeed," Ferrin said. He picked up the deck and

began to shuffle. "Do you know, I believe I met a friend of Mrs. Caldwell's."

"Oh?"

Ferrin had hoped for something more than this polite inquiry. "I cannot say beyond doubt that she was a friend, just that she engaged me in looking for Mrs. Caldwell—or rather a shepherdess with green ribbons—and I assumed they were friends."

"Perhaps they were." Lady Rivendale looked pointedly at the cards in Ferrin's hands. "You mean to deal, do you not?"

He smiled. "Forgive me." He slid the deck to Wellsley to make the cut, then began to distribute the cards.

Wellsley picked up his cards as they were dealt. "Are you speaking of Queen Boudicca, Ferrin?"

Before Ferrin could answer, Restell said, "Never say you did not acquire the fair Boudicca's name?"

"I did not say that."

Restell grinned impishly. "But you didn't, did you? She wouldn't tell you."

Ferrin no longer desired to kick his brother. He was once again contemplating the murder of a family member. "It was a masquerade," he said calmly. "Anonymity is part of its charm."

Lady Rivendale quickly struck at the heart of the matter. "If you wish me to identify her, you will have to offer something more . . . and you will have to finish the deal."

Ferrin realized he was holding what was left of the deck as if he intended to shuffle it again. He quickly dealt the remaining cards and concentrated on the hand he had given himself. He had hoped to be less transparent in his desire to learn Boudicca's name. Wellsley and Restell clearly could not be counted on for subtlety.

After the bidding, Restell led. Ferrin restrained himself from being the first to mention Boudicca again. He did not think he would have to wait overlong.

"She disappeared before I returned from the wine cellar," Restell said.

"Who?" Wellsley said.

"God's truth, Wellsley, you cannot follow the conversation tonight any better than you can follow the cards. What is it that keeps drawing your attention?" He glanced over his shoulder and saw Wynetta and his sister-in-law at the piano. He winced as his sister stumbled badly over a passage. Leaning forward and indicating that Wellsley should do the same, Restell whispered, "She has been practicing that piece all of a week now and still does not have the fingering mastered. Still, we must encourage her efforts, not stare at her as if we'd like to steal her sheet music." Having said his piece, Restell straightened and fanned open his cards. "Now, we were speaking of Boudicca."

Ferrin decided his brother was a blockhead but refrained from telling him so. He noticed, too, that the countess was smiling to herself, evidently thinking much the same thing. For Wellsley's part, that poor worthy looked as if the tips of his ears might burst into flame. Concentrating on his cards, Restell was supremely unaware that he had missed the forest for the trees.

"Boudicca, yes," Wellsley said weakly. "She left while you were in the wine cellar. Why should that arouse comment?"

"It did not arouse comment. Or rather it was only *my* comment."

Wellsley rallied, trying to get a little of his own back. "I should think that hiding out in the wine cellar would have aroused comment."

Lady Rivendale folded her cards and sharply tapped the table, drawing attention to her at once. "Have done," she said pleasantly. "Give me the particulars so that this matter might be laid to rest. What manner of costume was she wearing?"

"A blue cloak, I think," Wellsley said.

"An orange shift," Restell said. "Though it might have been red. Like her hair. Splendid hair, really. Was it a wig, I wonder? What say you, Ferrin? You seemed to have spent the most time in her company."

"I couldn't say about her hair." He lied without compunction. It was surprisingly easy to recall the silky texture of it between his fingertips. "It was the spear that intrigued me. I wondered how she came by it, though she would not tell me that, either. I thought it might be an artifact."

"Genuine, you mean?" Lady Rivendale asked, one eyebrow lifting skeptically. "Are you saying the spear might have been from Boudicca's time?"

"I doubt it was from ancient times," Ferrin said. Determined to give nothing away, he carefully schooled his features and watched the countess for any sign that would hint that she knew something. "But to my eyes, at least, it appeared to be quite old."

"It strikes me as an unusual accoutrement."

"I was carrying a pistol," Wellsley said. "Not primed, naturally. And Ferrin had a sword."

Not to be outdone, Restell pointed to his head and added, "One Viking helmet. Two dangerous horns."

Lady Rivendale laughed. "So there were weapons in abundance."

Restell nodded. "Every Cavalier, Musketeer, and Hospitalier."

"Goodness." She fanned herself with her cards. "The guests might have laid siege to your castle."

"I feared the shepherdesses most," Ferrin said. "The crooks, you know."

The countess smiled. "Oh, yes. They were most fierce, I am sure." She opened and closed her cards, thumbing them with her nail. "I do not think I shall be able to help you. I cannot recall that my niece mentioned any one of her friends attending the masque as Boudicca."

"Perhaps if you told her about the jewelry," Wellsley said to Ferrin. "I recall a golden torc and some unusual bracelets."

Restell nodded. "The mask looked as if it was made of hammered gold."

"Gold leaf," Ferrin said. "I could not say what sort of metal it covered."

Lady Rivendale's head tilted as she regarded Ferrin with interest. "Are you a collector, my lord? I was not aware."

"Not a collector. Not a serious collector. I have an interest but not a passion."

"I see. Then it is not your intention to acquire some of the pieces Boudicca was wearing? Or that spear, perhaps? I was beginning to think it might be otherwise."

Ferrin pretended to be caught out. "Am I so easily read? I find that maddening, you know. One is allowed so few secrets these days, I fear I have surrendered another one. You are quite right, my lady. I have been entertaining the notion of making Boudicca an offer."

Restell frowned. "I cannot say I like hearing it this way. Didn't know you were in the market for some old baubles. I know someone who can—"

Ferrin's raised eyebrows stopped his brother from speaking another word. "It is the spear, Restell. I was frankly intrigued and wanted to know more about its provenance. Boudicca was not inclined to answer my questions."

"She might not have known the answers," Lady Rivendale said. "If none of the pieces were her own, say, then it is unlikely she would have been familiar with their history."

"Borrowed the lot of it?" Restell asked. "Is that what you mean?"

"Precisely." Lady Rivendale studied her cards and chose one to lead, placing it at the center of the table. "Perhaps a generous friend allowed her to borrow all the appropriate accessories for this one evening."

"Most generous," Ferrin said. After Wellsley made his play, he followed. "Is Mrs. Caldwell so generous?"

"Generous, not foolish. Not that it matters a whit. My niece has no redheaded friends nor jewelry as you have described. She certainly is not in possession of this spear that has piqued your interest."

Ferrin knew this last statement was true. The spear remained safely hidden in his study. "So Mrs. Caldwell could not have lent these items. That is unfortunate. I have nowhere else to turn."

Lady Rivendale shrugged as she took in another trick. "Have you considered placing a notice in the *Gazette* of your interest? You never know, it might lead to a response from Boudicca."

"An excellent suggestion." Ferrin smiled warmly at her. "I will do precisely that on the morrow. I wonder, though, if you will inquire of Mrs. Caldwell for me in the event she might know some detail that will be helpful."

"Certainly," the countess said, her own smile firmly in place. "I regret to inform you that it will require some time. My niece is no longer in town."

"Oh?"

"She's gone to the country. I shall have to write to her. You must not be in expectation of a reply before a fortnight has passed." She selected another card to play, laying it down carefully.

"There is no urgency to the matter," Ferrin said. "It is entirely possible I will have that spear in my possession long before your correspondence reaches her." He grimaced slightly as he was forced to trump his partner's trick. "Her country home is to the north?"

"She has no country home of her own. Her brother is at Granville, but she is not going there. I've offered her use of one of my homes. Are you familiar with Penwyckham?"

"No."

Wellsley's eyebrows lifted. "In Suffolk?"

Ferrin did not miss Lady Rivendale's quickly shuttered surprise. He was certain she had offered the name of the place thinking it would be unknown to him or anyone at the table. He watched her bring her cards protectively toward her bosom and hold them there. She hardly seemed cognizant of how she appeared to be shielding herself. He had been aware almost from the outset that she was not sharing everything she knew. If there was nothing to hide, surely she would have mentioned that Mrs. Caldwell's husband had made a study of the type of artifacts they were discussing. That she had not was as telling as holding her cards close to her chest.

Ferrin was cautious about demonstrating too much curiosity. In somewhat bored accents, he asked, "How is it you know the place, Wellsley?"

"My grandmother's family is from Suffolk."

From beneath his hooded glance, Ferrin observed that Lady Rivendale was interested in spite of her best efforts not to be. He waited to see if she would take the bait Wellsley had unknowingly dangled. It was not in any way a test of his patience.

"Is that right, Mr. Wellsley? Who is your grandmother?"

"The Viscountess Bellingham."

"Lady Clarice Bellingham? Why is this the first time I am hearing of it? Can the world really be so small? You are the scapegrace, then."

Wellsley glanced at Lady Gardner across the way and saw she was looking directly at him. He had no doubt she had overheard the countess's comment. Though her mouth was hidden by her fan of cards, he was sure she was smiling smugly behind it. "So I have been given to understand," he said. His eyes narrowed warningly on Restell when it seemed as if he might contribute to the conversation. "You did not realize her family hailed from Suffolk?"

"No, indeed not. It is quite possible your grandmother

knew of my aunt, though Penwyckham is small enough to escape notice. I shall have to inquire."

"I hope you will," Wellsley said. "She enjoys discussing those halcyon days. Your aunt is still living and resides elsewhere, or is it that she's deceased?"

"The latter. Years ago. Lady Beatrice Sharpe, she was called. Her house is mine now. My niece is going to take it all in hand, which I count as excellent since I have neglected the property."

"It is always pleasant to find commonalities and refine upon them," Restell said. "I would like to point out, however, that there are no cards in the middle of the table."

Lady Rivendale nodded. "Quite right you are. It is my lead, is it not? Yes, of course it is." She reviewed her cards and made a selection. The others followed, and in short order the trick was hers. Satisfied with her play, she smiled at Ferrin. "There, we are returned in good form with no harm done."

Ferrin's eyes darted toward his brother. "I believe Restell is disappointed that we have won the point."

The countess was at once solicitous. "I propose a change of partners following this hand. Mr. Wellsley and I—in celebration of our newly discovered commonality—will challenge you and your brother. How does that suit?"

"Very well," Restell said, struggling to contain his eagerness. "Though it is only fair to warn you that Ferrin and I are accounted to be unbeatable when we are paired."

"I believe that is about to change," Ferrin said wryly. "Unless I am badly misreading Lady Rivendale's designs for us, Restell, we are about to be trounced."

And so they were.

Cybelline's arrival at the Sharpe house on the outskirts of Penwyckham came about late in the afternoon. With the days being so short of light now, it was already night-fall when the carriage finally stopped.

Looking out the window, Cybelline saw at first glance that there was no one to welcome them. The house was dark. There were no fires laid, nor any candlelight. What she could see was courtesy of moonshine and the carriage lanterns, and she thought it was perhaps a better introduction to her new home than if she had come upon it in the full light of day.

The house was much larger than she had envisioned. She counted ten windows on the ground floor, five on either side of a wide oaken door. There appeared to be a like number on the first story, though it was difficult to know with the profusion of ivy growing up the sides and across the shutters. It was also not possible to know the color of the bricks, though she suspected it was ochre that had long since gone to a dull, muddy brown. The path leading to the front door was in wont of crushed stone to make it a smooth entrance. Cybelline had to pick her way carefully across a series of ruts before she reached the steps. There were only two leading up to the house, and as soon as she stood on the first, she knew it to be badly listing.

Behind her, she heard Nanny Baker's footfalls. She turned to make certain Nanny did not misstep on the uneven ground. Anna had her small arms wrapped about Nanny's neck. "Perhaps attention has been paid to the inside," Cybelline said.

"That would be a mercy." Nanny Baker did not indulge herself or her mistress in being hopeful. The square, broad planes of her face were set obdurately even when she was not in expectation of unpleasantness. Comfort and such encouragement as she was moved to give were saved for her young charge. "A pure mercy."

Cybelline sighed. "You are certainly in the right of it there." She took another step up and placed her hand on the door. Glancing over her shoulder, she saw that the servants were moving quickly to join her with Webb leading the charge. It was Mr. Kins, the driver of her carriage, who stepped up to join her at the door.

"If I might be so bold as to make a suggestion, ma'am," he said, "it might be better if I was to go first. See the lay of the land." He held up the lantern he was carrying. "Leastwise, you don't want to go in without this."

"What we will do, Mr. Kins, is to proceed together. The door is certainly wide enough to accommodate our entrance."

He grinned, showing a gap between his front teeth. "It is that." He nodded to her, indicating she should give the door a nudge.

Cybelline was surprised to find that the door swung open quietly. Lady Rivendale's caretakers evidently kept the hinges oiled, and she allowed herself to believe this was a good omen. In point of fact, it signified nothing.

The house was every bit as cold as she imagined it to be. None of them dared removed their outerwear until fires had been laid in the drawing room, servants' hall, and the kitchen. This necessitated requiring the youngest, and more important, the slimmest of the grooms accompanying them, to perform the services of a sweep and unblock the flues. It was not in any way to his liking, but he had the sweet encouragement of one of the maids and the threat of Mr. Kins boxing his ears to spur him on.

Cybelline had had the foresight to list candles among the things she wanted to be packed. They used what they brought until they found a drawer filled with tapers of middling quality in the dining room. Someone stumbled upon the lamp room and at long last there was light sufficient for a more thorough inspection of the home's interior.

Cybelline's first order then was to establish a nursery for Anna and adjoining accommodations for Nanny. A charming room on the uppermost floor was located, or at least Cybelline believed it had the potential to be charming once the walls were repainted and morning sunlight lent its own cheer. The furniture was too large for Anna, but Cybelline was hopeful that she could commission a carpenter in Penwyckham or other nearby village to craft a bed, table, and chairs more in keeping with her daughter's diminutive size. The armoire was perfectly satisfactory and the appointments in Nanny's room were sufficient to her needs and comfort. Once a fire was laid and clean linens were placed on the beds, Cybelline arranged for supper to be brought to Anna and Nanny. As the larder possessed few supplies and they had little left in their own hampers, porridge was the best that could be managed. Anna was infinitely more agreeable to this than Nanny Baker.

It was quite late when Cybelline slipped into her own bed. Webb had warmed some bricks and placed them at the foot of the mattress. Cybelline had begged her not to bother and encouraged her to seek her own bed, but Webb ignored her, and for once Cybelline was glad that she had. Stretching, Cybelline cautiously pointed her toes toward the source of the heat and snuggled more deeply under the covers. The bedding was not as fresh as she would have wished, and tomorrow all of it would be stripped and dragged outside for a proper airing.

Upon leaving London, Cybelline understood that her small entourage would not be adequate to care for the home at Penwyckham. Though she wished she might be able to report otherwise, Lady Rivendale's confidence in the Henleys was indeed misplaced. On the morrow, Cybelline decided she would send out Mr. Kins with notices that she was hiring a cook and housekeeper immediately. At least one more housemaid would be required and perhaps a footman. She would rely upon Mr. Kins to tell her how many would be needed to manage the cattle and grounds.

Thoughts of all that remained to be accomplished clattered around in her head like so many marbles, rolling first one way, then the other, ricocheting with such force that there was always the danger one would escape her

notice. There were menus to be planned and the most
basic foodstuffs to be purchased. They would need a cow
for milking and hens for laying. She did not even know
if Penwyckham had a mill or how far someone would be
required to travel to buy grain. There was no store of
winter vegetables or cured meats. Clearly, the Henleys
had not received Lady Rivendale's correspondence, or
they had chosen to ignore it.

In spite of what was to be done, Cybelline did not lack
confidence in her ability to organize and oversee the accomplishment of every task. What she doubted, or perhaps
feared, was that it would make no difference.

This was the thought she could not bear to entertain,
thus she was able to fall asleep counting all the labors
still confronting her and avoid reflection on the one thing
that would have given her no rest.

Mr. Wellsley stood at the window of the gentleman's
club he frequented and regarded the passersby on the
walk below. He held a glass of port in one hand but had
not sipped from it since it was presented to him. He had
already turned down an invitation to play cards and one
to join a political discussion in one of the salons. He was
not at all in a frame of mind to enjoy company. Some
might question his decision to set out for the club when
he was not interested in participating in any activity, but
he knew one was never so alone as when one stood in opposition to the expectations of others.

He emitted a soft grunt, unconsciously punctuating his
disagreeable thoughts.

"What's that you say, Wellsley?" asked Ferrin.

Wellsley pivoted sharply to find that his friend had
been standing just off to one side. "How long have you
been there?"

"Long enough to know that you are nursing a black mood. What is toward?"

"Has it occurred to you that I do not wish to be cheered?"

"I am gratified to hear it. I wouldn't have the slightest notion how to go about the thing. I am all for drink at such times, but you do not seem to be of a similar persuasion. I do not believe you've touched your port."

Wellsley regarded the glass in his hand as if he did not know how it had come to be there. "What? Oh, you know I do not care for this stuff. I should have a whisky. Why do I not have a whisky?"

Ferrin gingerly removed Wellsley's drink and replaced it with his own tumbler of whisky. "There," he said. "It is all the same to me."

Wellsley knocked back a mouthful without tasting it. "Go away." He waved Ferrin off and returned to his contemplation of the pedestrian traffic.

Ferrin stepped closer and regarded the same view as his friend. "Is that Miss Washington with her mama stepping out of the milliner's?"

"You will not be moved, will you?"

"I don't believe so, no. It is a large enough window to support two perspectives. I will take the sunny view as you are already in full possession of doom and gloom. I fancy that Miss Washington's new bonnet looks like an iced cake."

"It is a ridiculous confection."

"And over there," Ferrin said, pointing to two men alighting from a hack. "They are sporting matching yellow waistcoats. How would you call that shade? Dandelion? Daffodil?"

"Jaundice."

One of Ferrin's dark eyebrows lifted in appreciation. "You are very good at this. What a pity you are not more often burdened by such stormy, weighty thoughts. It becomes you." Out of the corner of his eye he glimpsed Wellsley's mouth twitch. He proceeded cautiously, uncertain if it signified a favorable shift in his friend's humor or was merely evidence that the whisky had finally settled pleasantly in his stomach. "Look at the parade of lovely ladybirds leaving the booksellers, every one of them a picture to look upon."

"That picture hangs above the mantel in my study," Wellsley said. "Duck hunting."

Knowing the painting well, Ferrin gave a shout of laughter. There was indeed some similarity between the vee formation of the young women now crossing the street and the flock of ducks taking to the air in Wellsley's painting. "I am reluctant to drink my port, Wellsley, lest you make me choke on it." He paused a beat. "Would that brighten your mood, I wonder?"

The taut set of Wellsley's mouth softened a little. "I am all for finding out."

Chuckling appreciatively, Ferrin nodded. "I am certain that is the case today. Have I done something for which I must make amends?"

Wellsley's sideways glance was sharp. "No. My black humor has nothing at all to do with you."

"I am glad to hear it." He did not press further, but neither did he surrender his position. He waited for Wellsley to capitulate and share the nature of what was troubling him.

"It is Grandmother," Wellsley said at length. "She is determined that I should marry soon and present her with an heir."

"Surely this is not the first time you have heard her lecture on your duty. What has changed?"

"She has chosen my bride."

"Oh. That is a bit sticky. Who does she wish to see you marry?"

"Do you know Miss Clementina Fordham? The Fordhams reside in Wynterbury in Essex. Miss Clementina was presented last year and had several offers, I understand, though none that was accepted."

"She has some prospects, then, that she can afford to be particular. I cannot say that I recall the girl. She is an only daughter?"

"Yes. There are two brothers, I believe. Both older."

"Her parents are not necessarily eager to see her settled, mayhap."

"No, they are desirous of a good match for her."

"Is she in any way objectionable?"

"To marriage?"

"To *you*."

Wellsley frowned slightly. "I do not recall her well. She is pretty enough as I think on it. And accomplished in the same manner most young women are who are fresh from the schoolroom."

"Then . . . ?" Ferrin let the word hang there as a question.

"Bloody hell, Ferrin, I don't love her. What does any of the rest of it matter? I am in love with someone else."

That was certainly plain enough. "Have you told Lady Bellingham the same?"

"No."

"I see. I am forced to inquire why that is."

"For the same reason I would not tell you or Restell. I have not yet declared myself to the young lady."

"Again, why?"

Wellsley's square jaw became rigid as he clenched his teeth. A muscle jumped in his cheek. "For all the reasons a man does not usually declare himself: cowardice, inadequacy, impoverished wit in the female's presence."

Very much afraid that he would laugh, Ferrin chose silence as his best recourse until he could respond in a more solemn vein. "Devil take it, Wellsley, but you *are* in love."

Wellsley snorted. "Was I unclear before?"

"No, but—" He stopped because his friend was turning away and downing what remained of his whisky.

Wellsley raised his empty glass and garnered the attention of one of the footmen. "I am all for getting foxed. Hadn't thought about that end when I came here, but I believe it is just the thing for me."

Ferrin had not planned on spending more than an hour at the club. Indeed, he had come in search of Wellsley to beg a favor. After seeing his friend in such a pitiful state, and now so determinedly on a course toward complete inebriation, he knew he could not abandon him. "Let us sit, shall we? If we are to end up facedown on the carpet, then it should not be from so great a height as we are now."

"Good thinking. You will see me home, won't you? I walked."

"I will deliver you there myself."

"Excellent." Wellsley was now in possession of another whisky. He made a point of waiting until they were seated before he drank.

Ferrin leaned back into the deep leather armchair and stretched his legs before him. Fragrances peculiar to all the clubs were captured in the leather: tobacco smoke, fine brandy, man sweat, old cards, and cologne. The high standards of a gentleman's hygiene as promulgated by Brummell were not yet widely practiced. When they were, Ferrin thought, the chairs would have to go.

He raised his glass of port. "Shall we drink to something? A woman's penchant for changing her mind, perhaps."

"If you are thinking that my grandmother is one of those women, then you are sadly out of it." He shrugged. "Though it could not hurt to salute the possibility, could it?"

"Indeed not." Ferrin matched Wellsley's salute and they both drank, though Ferrin did not do so deeply. "Tell me, this woman you are in love with, is her family in any way an impediment to your making a match?"

"Don't know. Sometimes I think yes, other times no. The father likes me well enough, I believe, and would not oppose my suit. Whether the mother would countenance a match is more difficult to know."

"Mayhap she is the one you need to impress."

"Do not think I haven't tried. You will not credit it, but it seems I am damned by the company I keep."

"But you keep my company. Oh, I see what you are saying. This mama does not care for me. Have I offended her?"

"I shouldn't think so. It is just that you are accounted by society to be a rogue. As you are unmarried yourself, it should not be of such import, but I am painted with the same brush."

"But you are unmarried also."

"Yes, but I am not of a mind to continue in that wise." Wellsley took another swallow and was hit with inspiration. "Do you know what I think the answer is?"

"Did I miss something? I have not heard a question."

"There is no question. It is a problem I have, not a question."

Ferrin thought he probably should not be so amused by Wellsley's earnestness. If his friend would just admit that it was Wynetta he loved, all would be resolved. Of course, Ferrin was not certain that his sister *was* that young woman, and he was reluctant to embarrass either of them by acting on that assumption. "Pray, do not make me wait. If you have arrived at a solution, I should like to hear it."

Wellsley finished his whisky and indicated he would have another. "You will have to marry."

"*I* will have to marry? That is not what you said, is it? I cannot have heard that."

Afraid he was slurring his words, Wellsley repeated his statement, enunciating carefully. "You-will-have-to-marry. Don't you see? It is perfect. Even you can be redeemed by marriage. Standing in the ideal light that you cannot help but cast about you, I will look very good indeed for having a friend with such sound judgment."

"It is my judgment that excessive drinking has disordered your mind."

"My thoughts have never been so ordered."

"Then I am foxed."

"Is there no one, Ferrin?" Wellsley asked. "I cannot believe there has been no one to engage your interest since Miss Lewis left your protection. By my reckoning, that was six months ago."

"There was never any discussion of marriage with Miss Lewis, Wellsley. She was a diversion and set up nicely to be one."

"Miss Gaylord? She is from a good family."

Ferrin shook his head.

"Miss Scott? You were seen taking rides in the park with Miss Scott."

"No."

"What of Lady Hathaway?"

"Emma or Evangeline?"

"Either. Both. They are the daughters of a marquess, for heaven's sake. What can be objectionable about marrying the daughters of a marquess?"

"Even you must understand that I cannot marry both, and no man should be asked to choose between them."

"That is a good point." It did not take him long to find another candidate. "There is Lady Jane Appley."

"Too green for my tastes."

"Miss Knightly."

"An ape-leader."

"Lady Amelia Bents."

"Too silly."

Wellsley heaved a sigh. "Yet you have flattered and cajoled and been attentive to all of them."

"Hence my reputation as a rake." When Wellsley remained quiet for a time, Ferrin thought his friend had put the thing to rest and was heartily relieved by it. He failed to recognize that drink had merely slowed Wellsley's thoughts, not put a period to them. He blinked, startled, when Wellsley snapped his fingers.

"I know," Wellsley said, lifting his glass again. "I should have thought of it from the first. You must find Boudicca."

something that appeared to trouble the minister, stirred
rather. What then, would she do for food?

"I believe I should like to eat," she said. "I'll eat
slowly, nonetheless." I offered him the fork. "You must find
out how..."

Chapter Five

Cybelline nodded politely to Mrs. Meeder as they
passed outside Foster's notions shop. Mrs. Meeder had
been one of the first villagers to make a point to visit and
welcome Cybelline to Penwyckham. Cybelline recognized quickly that the older woman was not disposed
toward friendliness, rather she was insatiably curious
about her new neighbor. It occurred to Cybelline that
what answers she provided would be repeated with considerable relish, if not embellishment, to everyone Mrs.
Meeder henceforth called upon. At one point Cybelline
wondered if Mrs. Meeder were perhaps not an emissary
sent by the villagers to determine what sort of treatment
they might expect from her.

From Mrs. Meeder, Cybelline learned that neither of
her assumptions about the Henleys was accurate. The villagers knew she was Lady Rivendale's niece because the
Henleys had received the countess's correspondence and
discussed the imminent arrival. The couple also had not
ignored Lady Rivendale's instructions to make the house
ready. Mr. Henley had fallen while making repairs to the
countess's roof almost six months earlier. Mrs. Henley
had all she could do to care for her husband and her own
home. With two badly broken legs, cracked ribs, a dislo-

cated shoulder, and a head injury that thankfully kept Mr. Henley insensible to his own pain, Mrs. Henley was left to fend for both of them. There was help from their neighbors, but no one had time enough to spare for a home that had been unoccupied for more than four years.

Mr. Henley had been too proud to inform Lady Rivendale of his ignominious fall from her roof, and he promised his wife he would divorce her—no matter that the church did not sanction it—if she took it upon herself to write. The money the countess sent quarterly arrived but was not spent, even as the Henleys' own needs became greater with each passing month.

When Cybelline heard all of this from her visitor, she put herself on the Henleys' doorstep that very day. Mrs. Henley produced the money at once, certain that was the purpose of Cybelline's visit, and did not extend an invitation to come inside. It required all of Cybelline's persuasive powers to convince Mrs. Henley that she meant to take her and her husband back to the Sharpe house and see that they both were made comfortable there. They were still employed by the countess, she told Mrs. Henley, and, therefore, their welfare was now her responsibility, and she had no intention of shirking it.

Recalling that afternoon, Cybelline smiled to herself as she entered the notions shop. Mrs. Henley had been difficult to convince, but her husband would hear none of it. Seeing the futility of argument, Cybelline had simply ordered Mr. Kins and one of the grooms to put Mr. Henley on a litter and transport him to the waiting carriage. She was surprised by her own high-handedness, but Mr. Henley had no words for it. He did not speak during the entire journey. Mrs. Henley confided later that she could not recollect that such a thing had ever happened before, not in twenty-five years of marriage. She was also not unhappy about it.

"Good day, Mr. Foster," Cybelline said. The shop's

owner was standing on a stepladder rearranging bolts of fabric. She saw him grab the shelf to steady himself. "Forgive me. I did not mean to startle you."

He turned and smiled broadly when he saw who it was. "Ah, Mrs. Caldwell. It is always good to see you. You received my message, then, that your threads have arrived."

"Yes. My maid told me. She enjoys coming here, Mr. Foster, as you have an excellent selection of fabrics and patterns. Miss Webb is not easily impressed." She saw him blush at this bit of intelligence. Cybelline was amused that they had not been in residence much beyond a fortnight and Webb had made a conquest. "I am going to embroider pillows for my daughter's room."

Mr. Foster stepped off the ladder and ducked behind the counter. When he reappeared, he was holding a parcel wrapped with string. "Would you like to examine them before you go? I would be most distressed if you left and then discovered they were not precisely what you wanted."

Cybelline nodded and indicated that he should loosen the string. She unwrapped the parcel herself. The floss was of a superior quality and in the exact shades she had described to him. "All of it is perfect," she said. "You realize, Mr. Foster, that were you located on Bond Street there would be a steady stream of fashionable young ladies in your establishment."

"You are very kind to say so," he said modestly.

"I am speaking the truth, though if I hear that you are planning to leave Penwyckham I will not forgive myself."

Mr. Foster chuckled. He folded the fabric wrapping around the threads and retied the string, then slid the parcel toward her. "I have marked the price on it," he said.

"I see. I believe I have that much with me." She opened her reticule and found the proper coins. "It has been a pleasure, Mr. Foster."

"The pleasure is mine." He glanced past her shoulder to the window of his shop. The sky was markedly more gray than it had been when last he looked. "Did you walk all the way from the Sharpe house, Mrs. Caldwell?"

"I did. The distance is not so great. It cannot be more than six miles." She looked over her shoulder in the direction of the shopkeeper's gaze. "Do you anticipate it will snow? Is that what concerns you?"

"The answer to both your questions is yes. Will you allow me to find someone who can take you home? Mr. Harding has a wagon. Mr. and Mrs. Winslow own a carriage, though Mrs. Meeder reports the axle is broken and has not yet been repaired. Apparently it is a source of heated discussion at the Winslow cottage."

Cybelline quickly dispelled the idea of requiring help. "I would not want to be the cause of raising that subject with the Winslows, and while I am certain Mr. Harding's wagon would be just the thing, I could not ask it of him."

"I will ask him. I doubt it will be any hardship."

"No, please, do not trouble yourself or him. I will walk. The air is bracing but not too cold for my tastes. I am certain to be home before the ground is blanketed."

"Then allow me to escort you."

"It is a very kind offer, but I assure you that it is unnecessary." She collected her parcel, slipping it under her arm. "I am all for a brisk walk, and the challenge of arriving home before the storm is all I need to motivate me. Thank you, Mr. Foster, and good day."

Mr. Foster came around the counter quickly and walked Cybelline to the door. "Promise me that if you cannot win your race with the snow you will seek shelter. The Pembroke cottage is on your way. Do you know the place I mean?"

"Yes. Someone pointed it out to me on one of my earliest trips into the village. I had no idea that anyone lived there."

"Mr. and Mrs. Lowell have the run of the property now that Mathias Pembroke's passed on. He left the place to them, and they take boarders from time to time since there's no inn close by. It sits nicely back from the road, but not so far as you can miss it from a passing coach. On foot, though, you'll have to look carefully. I've heard the cottage was once a hunting lodge connected to the Sharpe estate. That would have been long ago, before my time, if you can credit it."

Inclining her head politely, Cybelline made small protesting sounds in response to Mr. Foster's self-deprecating remark about his age. She tried not to glance out the window again, but she was anxious to be off. If Mr. Foster kept her much longer, she would be forced to accept his escort, and while he was not the least objectionable, she simply did not want the company. It was to temporarily escape all the activity and interruptions at the Sharpe house that she had decided to walk to Penwyckham. No one was pleased that she ventured out alone, but there was no one in a position to stop her.

"Mrs. Meeder is of the opinion that it is Lady Bellingham's grandson who has taken possession of the cottage, leastwise that's what she's been able to learn from Mrs. Lowell. Such connections are of interest to her. It makes him a personage of some importance in these parts." Mr. Foster's ears reddened. "Like yourself, Mrs. Caldwell."

"I believe you mean that as a kindness, Mr. Foster, but"—here Cybelline pointed to the increasingly overcast sky—"I will have to be apprised of the details regarding the grandson at some later time. I must be off. You said so yourself."

"Oh, yes. Yes, of course. I have chattered on shamelessly. You will think me as great a gossip as Mrs. Meeder."

"Gossip? I would not call her such. When a village has no newspaper, one depends upon a town crier."

"The town crier. Yes, that is certainly the way of it." He chuckled appreciatively and opened the door for her. Cold air eddied into the shop. He shivered. "Have a care how you go now, Mrs. Caldwell. I will be inquiring after you when I next see someone from the Sharpe house."

"I am appreciative of your concern, Mr. Foster. It will go a long way to keeping me warm." She stepped outside. Once she was off the protective shelter of the stoop, the wind pressed sharply against her pelisse. She reconsidered Mr. Foster's offer to secure her a conveyance. Mr. Harding's wagon might be just the thing to get her home safely. It was Mr. Harding of whom she was less certain. He had been one of the first villagers interviewed, in this case for a position as a groundskeeper, but Mr. Kins reported smelling liquor on his breath and was of the opinion that Harding was a rough sort, too ill-tempered to accept direction from his superiors. Cybelline allowed that Mr. Kins knew best, and she had never met Mr. Harding. She did not think she wanted to now, not in circumstances where she would be alone with him.

Waving gamely at Mr. Foster through the shop window, Cybelline ducked her head against a fresh blast of wind and began walking. She stopped once on the edge of the village to secure the uppermost frog on her pelisse and turn up the fur collar. Icy fingers of wind slipped under her bonnet and tried to carry it away. The ribbons held, but they tightened uncomfortably on the underside of her chin. She wondered if it were possible to be hanged by one's own hat and what Mrs. Meeder might have to report to the villagers should that come to pass.

The road to the Sharpe house followed a meandering brook. It began to snow before Cybelline reached the first wide curve. When she turned to glance back at the village, the view was blurred by falling snow. The ground was already hard and cold enough at this time of year to keep the snow from melting. The road was quickly covered, though it remained visible to her because of the grass that bordered either side. When the snow became deep enough to hide the grass there was still the shrubbery, and farther back, the woods with the winding brook in their midst. She could hear the rush of water in the brook and thought that as long as she kept that sound within her hearing she would be able to find her way home. The brook ran along one side of the property, and the Sharpe house, rising as it did above everything save a few of the tallest trees, was easily visible from that distance.

It remained only for Cybelline to put one foot in front of the other, a manner of living she had perfected since her husband's death. It would serve her now in the most literal sense.

Cybelline stopped once more to open her pelisse and tuck the parcel inside. Her hands, though gloved, were clumsy with cold, and it took her far longer than was her wont to secure the fasteners again. She was shaking by the time she resumed walking.

There was nothing for it but to go on. The pace she set for herself helped to keep her warm, for thoughts of Mr. Foster's concern had long since vanished. Her boots were practical enough for the trek in dry conditions, but melting snow was seeping through the leather. Her stockings went from uncomfortably damp to sopping wet. She was not at all certain she could feel her toes any longer, though she worked at wiggling them from time to time.

Cybelline could not say precisely how far she had walked when she realized that she had lost all sense of where the road lay. The snow was slightly more than ankle deep and only tufts of the tallest grass were still visible to her, and then only when she was directly upon them. The curtain of snow was so opaque that the trees up ahead were no longer visible. Those off to her right she could still see, and she set herself on a path toward them. There was some shelter from the snow here also. Where there were pines, their boughs formed a protective canopy above her. The going was decidedly slower, though, with Cybelline having to pick her way through thickets of holly and over rocky inclines. The edges of the brook were heavily frosted with snow, but the water ran clear and loud, and she was in no danger of losing her way a second time.

Cybelline had never seriously considered seeking refuge at the Pembroke cottage, but she had also not anticipated the slip that put her in the drink. She counted it as something of a tribute to her hoyden youth that she was able to avoid falling squarely in the midst of the rushing water. Her brother would have been proud of her athleticism in avoiding a certain dunking.

This did not mean, however, that there were no consequences to her initial misstep. Her pelisse, gown, and underskirts were wet halfway to her knees, and her feet felt like iced stumps. She was immediately cognizant of the danger but with no options except to keep forging ahead.

If she had been looking for the Pembroke cottage, she would have missed it. What guided Cybelline to that place was the sweet smell of wood smoke rising from the chimney. The scent of it was carried on the back of the wind and made her pick up her head and take stock of it the same way a hound was alert to the first whiff of a fox.

She came upon the old hunting lodge soon after catching the fragrance of the smoke and stumbled around it, hammering ineffectually on the sides of the structure until she found the door. She pounded with both fists, calling out at the same time. It was only when the door swung open that she allowed herself the luxury of collapse.

The man answering the cries for help was knocked sideways by the body that hurtled into the room on its way to the floor. He managed to recover his balance enough to catch it but was unable to sustain the high ground for long. He and his bedraggled bundle lurched badly to the floor.

"Mr. Lowell! Here! I have need of you." He was not yet finished calling for help when it arrived.

Mr. Lowell, with his wife following closely in his wake, hovered over the tangle of bodies. The unexpected visitor had bested their distinguished lodger in the very first round.

"I do believe it's Mrs. Caldwell," Emily Lowell whispered. "I am certain that pelisse is from a London modiste. No one in Penwyckham has anything so fine."

Lowell grunted, a sound that could have a number of different meanings depending on pitch and vigor but on this occasion signified agreement. Bending, he slipped his arms under Mrs. Caldwell's and peeled her away. She was as limp as a hen whose neck had been wrung but many times heavier. He was a bull of a man, used to physical labor, but it was still a struggle to lift her.

"Put her in front of the fire, Mr. Lowell," his wife ordered. She quickly stepped back to clear the way. "I'll fetch blankets and start the kettle." She paused long enough to dart a sideways look at her boarder. He had risen to his feet but remained hunched over, straightening only as he dusted himself off. "Do you need assistance, Mr. Wellsley?"

He shook his head, for clearly the question had been an afterthought and rightly so. There was no fault assigned to Mrs. Lowell for considering his needs second to those of their guest. "Carry on, Mrs. Lowell."

She regarded him oddly. "She knocked the wind out of you, didn't she? Bowled you over and took your breath. And here I thought you cared far too much for the cut of your clothes. Do you see, Mr. Lowell? Mr. Wellsley has taken a hard spill."

Mr. Lowell grunted heavily and his wife scurried off to fetch the blankets as promised. He set his sodden bundle in the ladder-back chair where she promptly pitched forward. She might have broken her nose on the stone apron at the hearth, but Mr. Lowell caught her fur collar in his meaty fist and was able to lower her gently to the floor.

"Perhaps if we make a pallet for her here."

Mr. Lowell was startled to find Mr. Wellsley standing over him. The man had a silent tread that unnerved the hosteler. There was nothing natural about one body sneaking up on another the way he did. It would make even the most God-fearing creature wonder if he was suspected of some misdeed.

Rather than grunting, Mr. Lowell cleared his throat and nodded his approval of the suggestion. His wife saved him from actual conversation by appearing with an armload of blankets. She looked questioningly at their boarder.

"I suggested a pallet here, since she cannot sit up in a chair."

"Very good, Mr. Wellsley, but she must be moved back from the fire. Her clothes and the blankets will scorch." She dropped the blankets on the chair and chose two to spread out on the floor where she wanted the men to put Mrs. Caldwell. When that was accomplished, she folded a third so that it could be placed under her head. "You men will absent yourselves while I make Mrs. Caldwell comfortable." She gave her husband a significant look lest he mistake her meaning. She was depending on him to remove their lodger from the room, as he did not look inclined to go. Mrs. Lowell did not know what passed for modesty in London these days, but in Penwyckham, a woman, even an unconscious one with feet like blocks of ice, did not reveal her naked limbs like the veriest tart. "Go on now. Shoo."

Mr. Lowell backed away, then turned and headed for the rear of the cottage. Mr. Wellsley followed suit, though the caretaker doubted it was because he feared Mrs. Lowell's censure.

Mrs. Lowell wasted neither time nor movement stripping off Mrs. Caldwell's clothes. Only the short cotton shift was dry and, therefore, allowed to remain. Once the last of the blankets was securely tucked around Mrs.

Caldwell's shoulders and torso, Mrs. Lowell briskly massaged the younger woman's feet, infusing them with warmth from her own palms.

"That's just the thing, isn't it?" Mrs. Lowell chattered as she worked. "You'll feel the blood flowing soon enough. Sharp as pins and needles it will be but with no ill effects. Can't imagine what you were thinking going out today, though I suppose your parcel explains some of it. Most anyone around here could have told you it wasn't walking weather. And with you having your own carriage, it seems rather foolhardy. But don't take mind of my scolding, it's not my place to say anything, especially not to quality."

She continued to rub Mrs. Caldwell's feet while freely sharing all manner of advice that she frequently remarked was not her place to give. When she judged the feet to be sufficiently warmed and the urge to continue her scold had passed, Mrs. Lowell drew the blankets down, tucked them, and began to gather the clothes. She stuffed the shoes with dry rags and placed them closer to the fireplace. The stockings were laid carefully over the back of one of the chairs, and she wrung out the underskirts and wet drawers. Droplets of water sizzled on the hot stone apron when they fell in that direction.

"Mr. Lowell. Mr. Wellsley. I have need of you now." They responded quickly and were given the task of wringing out the heavy gown and pelisse. These items were removed to the tidy kitchen and draped over chairs that were pushed toward the hearth. At his wife's request, Mr. Lowell prepared tea.

"How can I be of assistance, Mrs. Lowell? I assure you, I am unused to doing nothing."

Mrs. Lowell regarded Mr. Wellsley with some skepticism. "I probably should not say so, but I have heard it somewhat differently."

"Oh?"

"Oh, dear. I have upset you. It's no good denying it. Mr.

Lowell says I am too forthcoming, but I have always thought it was because he will not come forth at all. I very well understand that you cannot like that there has been communication regarding you, but we are all interested when someone like you arrives in our village."

"Someone like me?"

"Why, quality, of course. You are the grandson of the Viscountess Bellingham. I have not mistaken the matter, have I? You *did* write of such when you arranged to take this lodging."

"By way of introduction. And what is that you've heard, Mrs. Lowell?"

"Scapegrace," Mrs. Lowell intimated delicately. "I've heard you called such."

"I'm sure." He hunkered down beside their guest. "She is shivering. Tell me what I must do."

"There's no harm in shivering. Keeps a body warm. But go on, take her hands and place them in yours. That will help."

He lifted her hands as instructed. "Are you quite certain this is Mrs. Caldwell?"

"Oh, yes. I've never met her, you understand. She hasn't been living at the Sharpe house for much longer than a fortnight, but other than you and the servants she brought from London, there are no strangers about."

"Mighten she be one of the servants?"

"Wearing that pelisse? It strains the imagination."

"She could have let one of the maids borrow it for the trek into the village."

"Do you see that?" asked Mrs. Lowell, pointing to the parcel she had placed on the caned seat of the chair. "It has her name on it in Mr. Foster's neat script. I should know. I've received enough goods like it from him over the years."

"She could have sent a maid to collect it."

"My, you are in want of convincing, aren't you? Well,

if I must speak frankly, I will. There's her intimate things that tell the tale. Mrs. Caldwell might be moved to lend her velvet pelisse to a servant doing an errand for her, but I doubt her generosity extends to permitting the same servant to wear her fine linen drawers."

"I see."

Mrs. Lowell studied him. "I thought that would put you to a blush, but you are made of sterner stuff than my own dear husband. Your grandmother is indeed in the right of it to name you a scapegrace."

"Lady Bellingham is frequently in the right of things." He continued to gently rub Mrs. Caldwell's hands. "She is not wearing a ring."

"She is a widow. I cannot know if that explains it or not."

"You say she is only recently come to Penwyckham?"

"That's right. We rarely have visitors from London, and now we have two at the same time. I can tell you without fear of being contradicted that it has created quite the stir."

Mr. Lowell arrived with the tea and held out the cup and saucer to his wife. She pointed to Mr. Wellsley, as she was occupied with wringing more water out of an underskirt.

"See if you can get her to take some of it," Mrs. Lowell said. "Bring it close to her nose and don't be surprised when it brings her around. A good cup of tea has restorative powers."

"A bit of whisky wouldn't be amiss, either."

Mr. Lowell snorted lightly and passed the brew.

Mrs. Lowell smiled. "He's already put it in there, Mr. Wellsley."

"Is that what he said?"

"More or less. Be mindful you don't splash her with it."

He sat on the floor and carefully slipped his free arm under Mrs. Caldwell's shoulders, raising her just enough to effect the proper angle for taking the tea. Doing as Mrs. Lowell suggested, he passed the cup beneath Mrs.

Caldwell's nose and observed that Mrs. Lowell was right: The brew had the efficacy of smelling salts.

Cybelline's nose twitched, then she blinked. Her lashes fluttered several more times before her vision focused enough to make out the features of the man looking down his aquiline nose at her. Shock held her silent. Her understanding of her situation did not improve when the gentleman holding her said, "Do not be alarmed, Mrs. Caldwell. I am Mr. Porter Wellsley, and these fine people are Mr. and Mrs. Lowell, the caretaker and the proprietors of this lodge."

Cybelline had no idea if he was telling the truth about Mr. and Mrs. Lowell, but she was absolutely certain he was lying about his own identity. She did not know any gentleman named Mr. Porter Wellsley, but she recalled the Earl of Ferrin in every detail.

This was he.

She opened her mouth to speak only to have the teacup pressed against her lower lip. She jerked her head backward and might have had the cup upended on her face if Ferrin had not drawn it away so quickly.

"It is too hot," he told Mr. Lowell, raising it up for him to take. "Bring me a glass of sherry."

"Oh, there's none of that around," Mrs. Lowell said. "There's only the whisky."

"Then bring me some of that," he said, directing his order to Mr. Lowell. "We will have the tea when it cools a bit."

Mrs. Lowell watched her husband return to the kitchen, where the spirits were kept, and offered an aside. "I suspect he thought adding the whisky would make it cool enough to drink. He's not the sort to do harm to anyone. Can't bear to witness another's suffering."

"Allow me to sit up," Cybelline said. She struggled to rise but Ferrin held her firmly in place, and Mrs. Lowell came to his rescue.

"There now, Mrs. Caldwell, you don't want to sit up yet. I've got the blankets all tucked around you and your clothes are on this side of them, if you take my meaning."

Cybelline did. Her eyes widened in alarm, and she could not look at Ferrin. Had he recognized her? He gave no indication of it, and he had called her Mrs. Caldwell. Still, *she* knew that this was the second time she was only partially clothed in his presence, and she had neither darkness nor Boudicca's mask to hide behind. She slipped her hands under the blankets and was only slightly relieved to find that she was still wearing her short shift. It barely reached as far as her fingertips when she was standing up. It certainly was not adequately covering her nether parts in her current position.

Ferrin could not find it in himself to be sympathetic to her alarm, not when it gave him the first clear view of her splendid eyes. They were a steely shade of blue-gray that made him think of flint about to spark or a finely honed blade caught in a beam of sunlight. He had spent an unseemly amount of time wondering about them, and now he knew. He was also aware that this discovery was not at all anticlimactic, as he had supposed it might be. When he had time to consider what that meant, he would decide if that necessarily boded well.

Mr. Lowell appeared with the whisky. Ferrin accepted it and raised the glass. "Will you take some of this?" he asked. When she nodded, he placed it against her lower lip and tipped it back. Her teeth chattered lightly against the glass, but she continued to sip the liquor without any indication that she disliked or appreciated it. He suspected that now that her initial surprise had worn off, and she had come to terms with her dishabille, she was not going to give much of her thoughts away. Her mask had slipped once; it was not likely to do so again.

When the glass was empty, Ferrin returned it to the caretaker and lowered Mrs. Caldwell's head to the folded blanket that was her pillow. "You are still shivering," he said. "Do you wish to be closer to the fire?"

"I wish to be in the fire."

"I do not recommend it."

"Then I shall remain where I am, Mr. Wellsley."

Though he did not reveal it by so much as a twitch of his lips, Ferrin was amused that she had called him Wellsley. He wondered if she would, or if she would admit that she knew him to be Ferrin. She must be entertaining some doubt that he was aware that she was his Boudicca. It was a delicious conundrum for her. If she owned that she knew he was the Earl of Ferrin, then she would surrender herself. The only way she could hope to secure her secret was not to reveal that she knew his.

"I am Mrs. Caldwell, but then you know that already." She frowned slightly. "You said so at the outset. How do you know me?"

"I don't know you," Ferrin said easily. "I know your name. As to that, Mrs. Lowell discovered it. It is printed on the parcel you collected from Mr. Foster. Apparently she is familiar with his handwriting also. I do not think there is much that escapes Mrs. Lowell." He looked up to find her smiling broadly. "Is that right, Mrs. Lowell?"

"There are those who say it's so."

"You see, Mrs. Caldwell, I am one of many who say it's so. Mr. Lowell? I think the lady will have that tea now." He supported her shoulders again and took the cup when it was held out to him. "You are in no danger of being burned by it."

Nodding, she accepted his help and took a large swallow before indicating it was enough. "There is rather more whisky in it than tea, I think."

"That explains its restorative powers." He glanced at Mr. and Mrs. Lowell, both of whom merely shrugged. "How long ago did you leave the village?"

"I could not say. I was not yet at the village's edge

when the snow began to fly. I thought I could not lose my way on the road, so I went on." She made a small grimace. "I was wrong."

Mrs. Lowell clucked her tongue, only narrowly restraining herself from delivering a full scold. "Your pelisse and gown, indeed all of your underskirts, are wet through and through. Did you take a tumble in a snow bank?"

"In the brook. When I lost my way I went toward the water. I knew I could find the Sharpe house if I stayed on the water's path."

"And walked a goodly distance out of your way," Mrs. Lowell said. "The brook meanders far and wide. I would venture to say it is slightly more than two hours since you left Penwyckham."

Cybelline immediately tried to sit up. She glared at Ferrin when he removed his arm from under her and placed one hand firmly on her shoulder to restrain her. "You do not understand. They will all be worried. I must get back. It is likely Mr. Kins is already searching for me."

"Mr. Kins?" asked Ferrin.

"He is my head groom and driver. He is the most logical person to have set out. If he makes it to the village he will discover that I left. It will cause a stir, all the while I am here safe and sound. I must make my way back."

"There is sense to what she's saying," Mrs. Lowell said. "Mark my words, there will be a search made for her." Her glance out the window drew everyone's attention in that direction. Snow was still falling wet and heavily, lining the skeletal branches of the deciduous trees and weighing down the pine boughs with a thick coat of frosting. "And it will be dark soon. Nothing good can come of this, I'm afraid."

Cybelline was unable to hide her distress. Her breath caught and then was expelled as a tiny moan. Ferrin gave Mrs. Lowell a look meant to quell her. She was oblivious to it. Mr. Lowell snorted.

"I will ride to the Sharpe house," Ferrin said, "and inform them you are quite safe. If I learn that Mr. Kins or some other person has been sent to find you, I will return this way and go on to the village. If there is a search party already formed, I am certain to come across it."

"Permit me to accompany you," Cybelline said. "If no one from my home has left in search of me, then I will be safely returned and no longer a bother to you."

"No." Ferrin's tone did not allow for argument. "You have not yet recovered from your first adventure. It would be unwise to support you in another."

"But you are only recently arrived here. You do not even know where you are going."

"The Sharpe house is due east of here, is it not?" He looked at Mr. Lowell for confirmation and received a firm nod. "There, you see? I will find it."

"It will be dark soon. You cannot hope to find your way without help."

"I will take the help I need with me, and you will remain here."

Mrs. Lowell paused in wringing out one of the damp petticoats. "I pray you'll forgive me for being forward, Mr. Wellsley, but I don't know that I like the idea of Mr. Lowell venturing out in this weather. Not that he wouldn't do it, but he's got a touch of the rheumatism and the cold makes his leg ache so."

Ferrin interpreted Mr. Lowell's rumbling growl as a directive that his wife should cease to speak immediately. When Mrs. Lowell's mouth snapped closed, he realized he was beginning to understand the nuances of Mr. Lowell's language. "I appreciate your concern, Mrs. Lowell, and it is a fitting one for a wife to have for her good husband; however, it was not my intention to ask Mr. Lowell to lend his assistance. I have in my possession a compass that I have used on previous occasions and found to be wholly reliable."

"A compass." Mrs. Lowell's tone indicated she was suitably impressed. "Why, aren't you the clever gentleman. And wholly reliable, you say. If it will take you directly to the Sharpe house, then I am all for it."

Finding it difficult to keep his amusement in check, Ferrin realized he was making some noises at the back of his throat that sounded rather like Mr. Lowell. He dared not look at the hosteler, afraid the man's expression would be so telling of his own suffering that Ferrin would howl with laughter. "It is gratifying to learn that you approve, Mrs. Lowell. I must inform you, though, that the compass will not take me directly to Mrs. Caldwell's home but guide me in that easterly direction."

"I'm sure you know all about it, Mr. Wellsley," she said confidently. "Shall I get your greatcoat?"

"In a moment." Barely suppressing his grin, he regarded Mrs. Caldwell. "I think we should discuss how best to situate you. There are but two bedrooms above stairs. Naturally, Mr. and Mrs. Lowell occupy one. The other is the one I have let for the time being. I think you will be infinitely more comfortable there."

"In your bed?"

He thought she sounded as if she might choke on the words. "Yes," he said with perfect ease. "It is the practical solution. Mrs. Lowell will prepare the warming pan and lay the fire. I believe you will find the room to your liking. Certainly there is privacy that you cannot be afforded here."

"It is good of you to wish to see to my comfort," she said carefully. "But I want the privacy of my own room and the comfort of my own bed."

"Then I regret that I must refuse you. It is not the most auspicious beginning for new neighbors, but I suppose it cannot be helped. We are of different opinions, you and I, and on this occasion I believe I shall have my way."

Ferrin stood. He set the teacup aside and addressed Mrs. Lowell. "I will have my coat now."

Mr. Lowell followed his wife, retrieved his own coat and hat, and left the cottage to make Ferrin's mount ready for the journey. Ferrin joined him minutes later turned out in a Carrick coat eminently suited for the bad weather, leather gloves, Hessians, and a top hat that rode low over his brow. The cinnamon-colored gelding, an Irish thoroughbred sixteen hands high, stood patiently while Mr. Lowell made the last adjustments to his bridle.

Ferrin accepted the leg up to mount Newton, gave the hosteler final instructions regarding the care and welfare of their patient, then was off. Newton didn't shy from the blizzard conditions, and Ferrin was forced to hold him back to make certain the horse did not come up lame. They picked their way through the trees in the general direction of the road. Ferrin carried a lantern that allowed him to make out the face of the compass as darkness settled.

He was riding directly into the face of the storm. Many leagues distant, the North Sea was churning water into an icy froth that smashed wave after wave against the East Anglia coast. Farther inland, the storm surge lent its powerful winds to driving the snow at the ground with such fury that Ferrin's vision was limited to the tip of Newton's nose.

The conditions caused Ferrin to wonder how Mrs. Caldwell's retainers would respond to her absence. So much depended on what they determined was her best judgment. Did they believe she was safely in the village because she would not risk making the return journey? Or were they aware of some reason that would compel her to set out for the Sharpe house regardless of what danger the weather presented? Did they comprehend that their mistress had a decidedly tenacious disposition that presented a danger to herself when not challenged by reason?

Ferrin's slight smile held no humor. Even when challenged by reason, he recalled, Mrs. Caldwell was likely to stay her course. This understanding kept him alert to the possibility that he would come upon someone who had set out from the Sharpe house. If Mrs. Caldwell's retainers were not inspired to rely on her good judgment, Ferrin believed they were probably inspired by loyalty. For better or worse, it seemed to him that she was a woman who could stir that emotion. In that manner, also, she was not so different from Boudicca.

Although the distance to the Sharpe house was only a few miles, the time it required to travel was not much improved for all that Ferrin was on horseback. When he finally arrived at his destination, it was without any chance encounters along the way. His heavy coat, even with its capes and deep collar, was not adequate for preventing the bitterly cold wind from slipping inside and climbing up his back. There was a frosting of ice in his hair and eyelashes and a frozen grimace on his face.

Ferrin sheltered Newton on the lee side of the house, then returned to the entrance and knocked loudly on the door with a gloved fist. He did not have to announce his presence with a second round of pounding; the door opened almost immediately.

The woman on the other side put him in mind of Mrs. Lowell. She had the same chin: gently rounded but thrust forward like a doorknob. The ruffled cap she wore emphasized ears that, if not precisely set at right angles to her head, could only be politely referred to as prominent. Her nose tilted upward, and her eyes were widely set. She was small of stature but held herself in a broad stance, arms akimbo, shoulders back, and feet planted so firmly they were taking root.

"I have come from the Pembroke cottage," Ferrin said. "I have news about Mrs. Caldwell."

"Oh!" Her hands moved from her hips to her mouth as she covered the open *O* it had become. "Of course. Come in. Come in." She stepped to one side and extended her hand to accept the hat he was removing from his head.

Ferrin did not hand her the hat. He merely snapped it once against his side to remove a clump of snow and ice from the brim. He set the lantern he was carrying on the floor beside the door. "I cannot stay. You are the housekeeper?"

"Yes. Forgive me. It has been such a night. I am Mrs. Henley."

"I am Mr. Wellsley. I have engaged lodging at the Pembroke cottage." He could not say whether this news in any way surprised her.

"It is good that you have come. Will you not let me take your coat? Please, at least warm yourself by the fire in the drawing room. We have been in such a state wondering after the mistress."

Ferrin did allow himself to be moved. "I am here only long enough to deliver my news. Mrs. Caldwell is quite safe. She is at the cottage and will remain there until it is safe to travel. Perhaps on the morrow. She was most particular that no one was sent—" He stopped. A man on crutches hobbled forward, having appeared suddenly in one of the doorways off to the side.

"Oh, Mr. Henley. Come. This is Mr. Wellsley, the new lodger at Pembroke cottage. He has arrived with good news about the mistress."

"Is that right?"

Ferrin observed that Mr. Henley leaned heavily on the crutches, but his progress was steady. Muscles in the man's shoulders and arms bunched with the effort. His left foot dragged on the parquet floor, while his right leg seemed to do most of the hard work. Ferrin nodded politely as the man drew himself up stiffly beside his wife.

"We've been anxious for some good news," Mr. Henley said. "There was talk of searching for her."

"She feared just such an end," Ferrin told him. "I was

just telling your wife that Mrs. Caldwell was most particularly concerned that others might put themselves at risk on her behalf."

Mr. Henley nodded. "Aye, that was my concern also. My wife and I owe a debt to the mistress that can never be repaid, but we had to trust that she would not set out from the village in these conditions. Mr. Kins and Miss Webb—they came with Mrs. Caldwell from London—were inclined to think otherwise."

"They were right. She did set out and was caught unprepared. However, she arrived at the cottage and is now being looked after by the most agreeable couple who own it." Ferrin's attention swiveled to Mrs. Henley. "I cannot persuade myself that you are not some relation to Mrs. Lowell. Are you also from Penwyckham?"

"Emily is my cousin."

"Mrs. Lowell did not mention that you were here at the Sharpe house."

"I doubt that she knows yet. The change in our circumstances happened very quickly. She would have learned of it only upon going to the village. Mr. Lowell might know, but he is not—" She paused, searching for the right description.

Ferrin offered it to her. "Forthcoming?"

"Precisely. I never met a man more taciturn than Mr. Lowell."

Ferrin thought that Mr. Henley looked as if he'd like to offer an observation about Mrs. Lowell's loquaciousness, but the man wisely held his tongue. He was not entirely steady on his feet, and his wife had the look of one who could blow a wind strong enough to knock him over. "What can I report to Mrs. Caldwell?" Ferrin asked. "All is satisfactory with the household? Is there any assistance I can lend before I take myself off?"

"You can tell her that all is well and that we were heartily glad to hear that she is safe. Has she need of anything?"

Ferrin realized it was a question he should have put to Mrs. Caldwell before he left. "If you will be so kind as to pack a valise, I think she would like to have a change of clothes. Boots, also. A nightgown would not be amiss."

Mrs. Henley nodded. "I will have it done right away. But you must wait by the fire and warm yourself. Mr. Henley, show Mr. Wellsley to the drawing room." She hurried in the direction of the stairs, leaving her husband to manage the responsibilities of hospitality.

"The drawing room's this way," he said, pivoting carefully on his sticks. "The fire's been laid in here in preparation of the mistress's return."

Ferrin followed, studying Henley's halting progress. The crutches the man was using were not helping him support his weight. They steadied him but did little to assist him move forward. Watching how Henley used the sticks, Ferrin was struck by a way of improving them.

Once they arrived in the drawing room, Ferrin went directly to the fireplace. He removed his gloves and held out his hands to warm them. In moments he was also removing his coat and hat. He laid the coat carefully over a sofa and balanced the hat and gloves on top.

Henley stood just inside the doorway. "How else can I serve you, sir? Something hot to drink or something that will warm you from the inside out?"

"Nothing," Ferrin said. "I imagine your wife will have the valise packed very soon, and I will be on my way. If the wind and snow have not covered my tracks, my return trip will take half as much time."

"How did you manage it, sir, if you don't mind me inquiring? I had a devil of a time convincing Mr. Kins that it was madness to leave the house, yet here you are, looking none the worse for it."

"A compass." He searched one of the interior pockets of his greatcoat and held it out for inspection. Henley hobbled forward and examined the object in Ferrin's open palm.

"Never thought I'd see the use of such a thing here. Clever of you to think of it, sir. Do you always keep it with you?"

"No. You'll understand that it is not much use in a London card room, but in the country I have often found it helpful."

"There's a shop that sells such things in London?"

"There is, along with the finest chronometers, sextons, and telescopes. But this particular compass, I made myself."

"Made it?" Henley regarded the compass even more closely. "It's a fine piece of workmanship, sir."

"Thank you. Would you like to hold it?"

Henley immediately refused, shaking his head quite firmly. "Oh, no, sir. These ham hands of mine might crush the thing."

"It has taken more abuse than that this night, Mr. Henley, and it is as large as a gentleman's timepiece." Ferrin pushed his hand forward. "I insist."

Still reluctant but unable to refuse Ferrin or his own curiosity, Henley carefully took the compass and let it rest in the center of his own palm. The needle jiggled slightly, then was still. "I thought it would be pointing north," he said, puzzled.

"It is. You have to turn the compass to reflect that direction."

Henley did that, marveling that the needle did not move. "I see. And you made this yourself?"

"Yes."

"You have an interest in scientific things, then."

"I like to tinker," Ferrin said modestly. "I am of the opinion that most things can be improved upon."

"My wife would say that I am one of those things."

Ferrin chuckled. "I imagine that there are many wives who share that view of their husbands."

Henley returned the compass. "I'll poke at the fire, sir.

You might as well be warm as possible before you set off again."

Ferrin watched Henley advance on the fireplace, making the best use he could of his crutches. "I hope you will not consider this remark misplaced, Henley, but I believe your sticks are something I can improve upon."

Henley drew himself upright, bracing himself with the crutches as if he were coming to attention. "I manage, sir," he said. "These do fine for me."

It had not been Ferrin's intention to prick the man's pride, but neither was he used to having to choose his words so carefully. He *was* the Earl of Ferrin, after all. It was his experience that people were glad of his attention; many sought out his favor. The fact that he had introduced himself as Mr. Wellsley did not explain the whole of Henley's stiff-necked response. Wellsley was a gentleman through and through and did not deserve to have his offer spurned out of hand.

Ferrin realized he was offended, not only for himself, but on behalf of Wellsley as well. Before he had an opportunity to determine when he had become so high in the instep, the unmistakable cry of a young child from somewhere beyond the drawing room caught his attention. His brows lifted, and he regarded Mr. Henley with an inquiring expression.

"The little one's been distressed since the mistress left," Henley explained. "No one's been able to tease her out of it." He cocked his head to one side and listened to the sound of two distinctly different sets of footsteps pattering and pounding down the stairs. "I do not think I mistake the matter, sir, but she's escaped the nursery and the nanny."

Ferrin turned on his heel just as a little girl skidded to a halt in the open doorway. Coming to such an abrupt full stop, she teetered on unsteady feet. Wisps of bright, red-gold hair fluttered around her head, and her mouth opened in a perfect *O* of surprise. Ferrin thought her expression mirrored something of his own shock, and seconds later, when surprise gave way to tears, he realized it was true.

Christopher Andrew Hollings, the Honorable Earl of Ferrin, felt very much like indulging in a tantrum of his own.

Chapter Six

Mrs. Lowell roused herself from napping at the fireside when Ferrin returned. She hurried to the door and relieved him of his outerwear and the valise he'd carried with him from the Sharpe house. Before he had shaken off all the snow, she presented him with a cup of tea liberally laced with whisky. Mr. Lowell nodded once in passing as he left to care for Newton.

Ferrin glanced at the empty space in front of the fire. The blankets were all folded and piled on one of the chairs. "She is abed?" he asked.

The housekeeper nodded. "Sleeping soundly. There was a protest about taking your room after you were gone, but we solved it by giving Mrs. Caldwell ours. You shall have yours, of course, and Mr. Lowell and I will sleep here. Do not think it is a hardship. There's a good feather tick in the linen closet that will do fine for us. Sometimes in the heat of the summer we have stayed down here and found it much to our liking."

"Very well done, Mrs. Lowell." Ferrin crossed the room to the fireplace and stood at the edge of the apron. He sipped his tea. "I was astonished to see your near-twin at the Sharpe house."

"Harriet." Mrs. Lowell smiled. "I didn't know she was

there until Mrs. Caldwell remarked on my resemblance to her own housekeeper. I was certainly glad to learn of it. She and Mr. Henley have had their share of troubles since he took a spill from the countess's roof. I urged Harriet to write Lady Rivendale and explain their reduced circumstances, but Mr. Henley would not hear of it, and she would not gainsay him. It was difficult to persuade him to accept the goodwill of his neighbors while he convalesced. He is a charitable man, though he will accept none of it for himself. Mr. Lowell and I did what we could, but the Sharpe house needed more attention than we could properly provide. This small property is enough to manage when one must meet the exacting standards of our best lodgers."

"Indeed." Ferrin felt that some comment was in order, but the single word was all he could muster. He was appreciating that Mrs. Lowell could rattle on at length with very little in the way of provocation. He massaged the back of his neck, which was still cramped with cold.

"Shall I fetch a hot compress?"

"Pardon? Oh, no. It is nothing." He let his hand fall away. "I cannot recall a more bitter wind." As if to punctuate this observation, the cottage windows rattled and the chimney whistled loudly with the force of the swirling air currents. He finished his tea and set the cup and saucer on the mantel. "I think I am for my own bed, Mrs. Lowell."

"As you wish, sir. You must be worn to the bone by your journey. It was very good of you to make the trip. Mrs. Caldwell was most appreciative."

Ferrin doubted that was true, but he did not say so. If Mrs. Lowell wished to make him think their guest was grateful, he would not argue. He suspected that she was thanking him in her own fashion for not insisting that her husband take to the road. "Goodnight," he said, nodding curtly in Mrs. Lowell's direction.

At the top of the stairs, Ferrin paused outside the bed-chamber where Mrs. Caldwell slept. He was tempted to enter, shake her awake, and demand to know what sort of woman she called herself. Harlot. Whore. Courtesan. Mother. Her behavior was outside his comprehension. He had considered there might be a husband, a lover, a fiancé that she meant to cuckold. He had thought a brother, cousin, or father might call him out. Never once had it occurred to him that there was a child.

The identity of the little girl at the Sharpe house was never a question in his mind. Except for the blue-gray eyes, she did not resemble her mother in any particular manner. The hair was too pale and too fine; the mouth did not have the same generous line. The eyes, as he thought about it, were more blue than gray and the face altogether too round. Yet Ferrin knew she was undeniably Mrs. Caldwell's daughter. It was not in the shape of the face, but in the obstinate set of the features and the tilt of the head that he recognized the mother.

She was introduced to him as Anna. He had only to say her name and she stopped crying. Curiosity overwhelmed caution and she had stepped forward when he hunkered down to make her acquaintance eye to eye. She flirted with him shamelessly, but he appreciated that it was the way of little girls even if he had no liking for the same deportment in their mothers.

Ferrin stood at the bedchamber door a moment longer, then moved on. In his own room, he prepared for bed. The decision to travel without the services of his valet, or any other servant, had been predicated on Wellsley's caution that any lodging he found in or around Penwyckham would not accommodate his usual entourage.

In truth, the cottage was more spacious than he had allowed himself to hope. In addition to the kitchen and drawing room, there was a substantially large study and an open area with a long table for dining. According to

Mrs. Lowell, before the lodge was parceled out and sold to Mathias Pembroke, it was used to entertain guests who came for the hunt on Sharpe property. The paucity of bedchambers suggested very few were invited to stay.

It was only after Ferrin secured the place for himself that he understood Wellsley had never visited Penwyckham and was getting a little of his own back. How the scapegrace must be enjoying himself in London, Ferrin thought, knowing that he would have to manage without anyone to help him in or out of his frock coat. Ferrin decided he would allow Wellsley to suppose it was a good trick. In point of fact, Ferrin had little regard for the way he was turned out and would not miss the attentions of his valet. That he gave the matter of his attire as much thought as he did had everything to do with sustaining his carefully cultivated reputation.

Mrs. Lowell had already turned down the bed. The sheets were warm when Ferrin slid between them. He lay on his back for a time, contemplating the ceiling, then turned on his side and contemplated the fire. As fatigued as he was from his journey through the snow, he was unused to falling asleep without reading. This change in his routine was infinitely more troublesome than managing without his valet.

It was not as irksome, however, as Mrs. Caldwell's presence in the bedchamber next to his. His resolve to leave her alone sorely tested, Ferrin reached for the slim scientific journal he'd been reading the night before. It wasn't there.

Although he had arrived at the Pembroke cottage without servants, he had not neglected to bring essays and journals to read. He had recently reacquainted himself with an investigation published a few years earlier by Berzelius, *The Theory of Chemical Proportions and the Chemical Action of Electricity*. Fascinating, really. The applications of such knowledge were extraordinary. Here was an understanding of molecules that the alchemists of the Dark Ages had hoped to conquer and never had. Not that Berzelius, or Ferrin for that matter, was interested in the transmutation of base metals into gold, but the introduction of electricity to molecules might permit one to understand the whole as well as the sum of its parts.

Ferrin turned on his back again and cradled his head in his hands. He considered some of the finer points of Berzelius's theory and wondered if the man might be engaged in correspondence regarding his work. Ferrin had been contemplating mapping the molecular weights of chemical compounds for some time. The Swedish chemist might be interested in his work thus far. Excited by this prospect, and gratified to be temporarily relieved of all uncharitable thoughts pertaining to Mrs. Caldwell, Ferrin rose from the bed and shrugged into his robe and leather slippers.

Berzelius's account, he remembered of a sudden, was on the table in the drawing room. He'd been warmly situated in one of the wing chairs reading it when Mrs. Caldwell had arrived. It was yet another reason to be out of sorts with her.

Ferrin opened the door and stepped into the hallway. He had not yet removed his fingers from the handle when Mrs. Caldwell joined him. The candlestick she was carrying almost flew from her hand when she realized she was not alone. Hot wax fell on the ball of her thumb. She winced but did not make a sound.

Leaning one shoulder against the door frame, looking for all the world as if finding her here was not in any way remarkable, Ferrin showed her he intended to stay his ground.

"You are in want of an explanation, I collect," Cybelline said.

"Did I say so?" Ferrin observed that she was not dressed to leave the cottage, though he did not acquit her of attempting to go below stairs to retrieve her clothes.

He judged the nightgown she was wearing to be one belonging to Mrs. Lowell, as it barely reached the midway point of her calves and seemed to be half again as wide as she was. The shawl thrown around her shoulders was one he recognized that Mrs. Lowell had been wearing earlier in the day.

"I heard you stirring," she told him. Her free hand closed around the knot in the shawl just above her breasts. The candle cast her features in pale golden light. "I wanted to speak to you when you returned, but I fell asleep. I was going to wait until morning, but when I realized you were up, I thought I—" One of Ferrin's dark eyebrows lifted, and her throat tightened. With some difficulty, she pressed on. "I thought I would ask if we might talk."

"Talk, Mrs. Caldwell?"

"You must know that I have questions."

"Must I?"

"Well, yes, Mr. Wellsley. How can you doubt it?"

Although he did not flinch, Ferrin felt as if he'd taken a blow to his midsection. He had very much mistaken the matter. Seeing her so unexpectedly caused his thoughts to veer off course. He'd allowed himself to believe she meant to confide that she knew very well he was Kit Hollings, Earl of Ferrin. It would be the same as confessing that she was Boudicca.

That was not the way of it, though. She was apparently determined to go on as she had and not surrender so much as an inch to him.

Ferrin straightened and indicated his room by raising one hand in that direction. "Shall we?"

Cybelline pressed her lips together, revealing her uncertainty.

"Or would you prefer your room?" he asked. When she made no immediate response, he explained, "We cannot speak here. We will wake the Lowells, who are sleeping below." At precisely that moment, an eardrum-crushing snore vibrated the very air around them. "We would not want to disturb that slumber. It seems he has found his rhythm."

Still doubtful, but amused in spite of it, Cybelline felt the corners of her mouth lift ever so slightly. "Very well."

Since she had not indicated a preference, Ferrin opened the door to his room. He stepped aside to allow her to precede him. She went directly to the fireplace while he remained near the door. He observed her shivering but could manage no sympathy. She might have comfortably remained deep under the covers in her own bedchamber, yet she had chosen this course. He watched her inch her bare toes as close to the fire as she dared.

"Have a care," he said. "You will singe that shift. I cannot imagine that Mrs. Lowell has many like it."

Nodding somewhat jerkily, Cybelline set her candlestick on the mantel and backed away. She turned toward Ferrin and hugged herself for warmth. The action was not sufficient to keep her teeth from chattering.

"Wait here," Ferrin said abruptly. Without offering any explanation, he quit the room.

Cybelline stared after him, wondering at his game now. She had been able to discover precious little from Mrs. Lowell after Ferrin departed for the Sharpe house. Nothing the housekeeper told her pointed to any comprehension that Mr. Wellsley was not precisely as he presented himself. Cybelline learned a great deal about the Viscountess Bellingham's grandson, and nothing at all about the Earl of Ferrin.

Upon his return, Ferrin saw that she was exactly as he'd left her. He set the valise on a table just inside the door and opened it. Rummaging through the articles that Mrs. Henley had packed, he found a pair of slippers. "These will help," he said, holding them out to her.

Cybelline hurried closer and accepted them gratefully. "I didn't know you'd brought me anything. It was good of you to think of it. Mrs. Lowell seemed to believe you would, but I was—" She stopped, consciously suppressing the unkind thought.

"Uncertain?" Ferrin said, finishing the sentence she would not. "Have I given you some reason to judge that I am uncaring of your welfare?"

"No. Oh, no. Not in any measure." She flushed lightly as he continued to regard her, clearly wanting more in the way of justification. "It is only that my own husband, a man accounted to be among the most solicitous of gentleman, would not have thought to ask for my belongings."

Ferrin kept his expression carefully neutral. "Then you are married," he said. "I was given to understand from Mrs. Lowell that you are a widow."

All color left Cybelline's face. "I am a widow," she said quietly. "Sometimes I—"

This time Ferrin did not attempt to finish her sentence. He had only a glimpse of her pain before her expression was shuttered, yet it was enough to know that it was deep and abiding. She made herself vulnerable by permitting him to see, if only for a moment, her open wound. His gaze dropped to the slippers she was still clutching to her chest. "Will you not put those on?" he asked. "You are trembling with cold."

Cybelline followed the path of his eyes. Her knuckles were white against the dark red leather slippers. Nodding faintly, she eased her fists open and set the slippers on the floor. She did not resist the hand he placed under her elbow to steady her as she stepped into them. "Thank you," she said, her voice not much above a whisper.

Ferrin's hand dropped away. He gestured toward the twin chairs in front of the fire. "Won't you sit? There is no robe in the valise, but there is a rug in the chest at the foot of the bed that will serve."

Cybelline did as he encouraged her. She drew her feet

up and smoothed Mrs. Lowell's shift over her knees, then permitted Ferrin to tuck a heavy blanket around her.

"It would be wrong of me," Ferrin said, "not to inform you that your instincts were correct."

Watching him take the wing chair opposite her, Cybelline frowned ever so slightly.

Ferrin continued. "Left to my own devices, I would not have asked your housekeeper for any articles of clothing or personal items. She is the one who thought of it. I merely had sense enough to know it was a good idea."

Cybelline's frown faded. "There is something to be said for having sense enough."

He smiled. "Yes. I am gratified, however, that Mrs. Lowell credited me with more foresight. I was not certain she could be persuaded that I have any sound judgment. It seems she has occasionally been privy to certain confidences and is of the opinion that I have not yet amounted to much."

"Scapegrace is the word she used, I believe."

"So you have heard it, too." He sighed. "Do you think it is at all affectionately meant, or am I being upbraided?"

Had they been speaking of the Earl of Ferrin, Cybelline knew the answer. But Mr. Wellsley? She suspected that if such a man truly existed, then "scapegrace" was a grandmother's term of endearment. "It is most likely the former, though I strongly advise that you make an apology for all slights, real or imagined. Mrs. Lowell will approve and your grandmother will be heartened."

Ferrin saw that she was more at her ease now. A bit of color had returned to her cheeks and the shivering had subsided. "I believe you have some questions, Mrs. Caldwell?"

She nodded. "I am anxious to learn how everyone fares at the Sharpe house."

"Your housekeeper indicated they were all well."

"All?"

"Yes, I believe that her meaning was to include everyone

in the household. You are perhaps inquiring after someone in particular?" He waited to see if she would take the opportunity presented to tell him about her daughter.

Cybelline merely said, "It is good to know there have been no mishaps. No one left the house in search of me, then."

"Mr. Henley reported that it was a narrow thing. The servant you mentioned before . . . your driver, I believe—"

"Mr. Kins."

"Yes. Mr. Kins. Apparently it was difficult to persuade him to remain at the house when you did not return."

"He has been in my employ for many years."

"You make it sound nothing short of a lifetime. You cannot be so old."

"I am four and twenty. Mr. Kins has been with me since before my parents died. Sherry retained his services, and when I married, he joined my staff."

"Sherry?" Ferrin asked without indicating any alarm. In truth, the hairs at the back of his neck were standing at attention. "Are you speaking of the Viscount Sheridan?"

"Yes. Sherry is my brother. Do you know him?"

Ferrin tried to remember if Lady Rivendale had spoken of Sherry. He recalled some mention of a brother in the country, but nothing else. He hadn't thought to make further inquiries. There was a rumor that had circulated the *ton* perhaps two years back that Sheridan was connected in some fashion to a murder. Ferrin rarely paid attention to the gossipmongers, but even he could not avoid hearing the talk. The details of it, though, were not fixed in his mind. He had gone out of his way not to learn them.

"I have had the pleasure of being introduced to him," Ferrin said, speaking for Wellsley. That was true enough. Ferrin had been the one to make the introductions. Sheridan was no more than an acquaintance, but they had been paired at cards one evening years ago and struck an easy discourse. It was rare that they saw each other following that occasion. They belonged to different clubs, had no friends in common, and pursued different interests, yet that evening at the card table had stayed in Ferrin's mind. He'd thought many times about Sheridan's well-ordered life, his partiality for manner and method, his disposition for routine. Ferrin found much to admire in the viscount's ease with himself. His public face and his private demeanor did not seem at all incongruous.

This last was what made the rumor about Sheridan so unsettling and kept it in circulation long past the usual nine days' wonder.

"He no longer frequents town, I believe," Ferrin said. "Do I recall correctly that he married?"

"Yes. I can scarcely credit that it has been two years. He is often in the country, which he vastly prefers to London."

It was another point he had in common with the viscount, Ferrin thought, though he had little enough opportunity to act on it. He could now recollect Lady Rivendale mentioning an estate at Granville. He wished he would have connected the pieces then, although he could not say how things might have been changed for it. What he knew with certainty was that if Boudicca had identified herself as the sister of Viscount Sheridan, he would have joined Restell in the wine cellar.

"The country has much to recommend it," Ferrin said politely. He managed to suggest that his thoughts were exactly the opposite of his words.

"You do not believe that," she said. "Mrs. Lowell says you are in the thick of society."

"That would be my grandmother's opinion. Mrs. Lowell cannot know the truth of it herself. Tell me, Mrs. Caldwell, are you acquainted with my grandmother?"

"I have never met her, but I believe she is a friend to Lady Rivendale."

"Yes, that is my understanding also. I have heard her speak of the countess. She is the owner of the Sharpe house, isn't that so?"

Cybelline nodded. It was her sense that this conversation had more traps than a poacher with six mouths to feed might set in the woods, yet she could not recognize each one of them. It was still unclear to her whether he knew her to be Boudicca and was merely enjoying playing cat to her mouse, or whether he was still in want of confirmation. "Lady Rivendale is my aunt," she said. "It is a relationship defined by great affection, not blood. She was my mother's best friend and is godmother to my brother. I have been fortunate that she assumed responsibility for me as well."

Ferrin thought he could have been forgiven if he had howled with derisive laughter. There was much that was lacking in Lady Rivendale's manner of assuming responsibility. Mrs. Caldwell might be a woman full grown but clearly she required a keeper more vigilant than the countess. He offered none of what he was thinking and stifled his scornful snort by clearing his throat.

"I beg your pardon," he said, indicating the base of his throat.

"I hope you are not sickening for something."

He thought it was good of her to evince so much in the way of concern when she probably wished he would contract the plague. "It is nothing."

"You were gone a long time."

"You were outside far longer with much less protection, and I did not fall in the brook. I am fine." He noted that if she was disappointed, she hid it well. "So Lady Rivendale has given you the Sharpe house."

"She has let me have the use of it." Cybelline wanted no further questions regarding the house. They would inevitably lead to why she left London. Instead, she baldly put that question to Ferrin. "I am curious as to why you have come to Penwyckham, Mr. Wellsley, though I will not be offended if you tell me I have overstepped myself."

"It is no secret," he said, "at least in light of all the

other things that are known about me. I am surprised Mrs. Lowell did not inform you."

"She didn't know." It was an admission that she had inquired, but Cybelline did not apologize for it.

"My grandmother and I are at loggerheads. We had words. I am banished, you see, and fallen so far from her good graces that I have landed in Penwyckham."

"It is not one of the circles of hell, you know."

"I didn't know, but thank you. It is a relief to learn."

Cybelline did not wish to encourage him, but she could not help herself: She smiled. "There must have been other places you could have stayed."

"London seemed very small of a sudden," he told her. "Grandmother has conceived the notion that I must be leg-shackled, and she has chosen the young lady. It seemed infinitely more prudent to leave town than try to avoid my grandmother *and* the young lady."

Ferrin had no reservations about sharing Wellsley's plight. His grandmother did indeed think he was in Suffolk for the nonce, as he had informed her it was his intention to seek sanctuary in the country and consider his future. The Viscountess Bellingham had not been entirely pleased with the notion of him running off. She was anxious to have the matter of his engagement settled but allowed that distance from his social obligations might improve his perspective on marriage, or Miss Clementina Fordham, or both. Wellsley believed he was up to the task of such subterfuge as was necessary to send Ferrin to Penwyckham while he worked up the courage to make himself known to the young woman he loved.

Of course Wellsley was also still possessed of the corkbrained conviction that his problems might be solved by Ferrin proposing marriage to Boudicca. Even when he'd sobered, Wellsley could not be persuaded otherwise. There was nothing for it but that Ferrin drink to excess.

"You are hiding," Cybelline said. His story amused her.

Ferrin had given a great deal of thought to his portrayal of Mr. Wellsley. It made her curious about the other man. She decided he must indeed exist, else it meant that Mr. and Mrs. Lowell were engaged in the ruse. It was not outside the realm of possibility, she supposed, but it was also a simple matter to uncover. Lady Rivendale could be induced to inquire of her friend Lady Bellingham and all would be answered. "I did not think gentlemen were so afraid of their grandmothers that they must hide themselves away."

"We are. Our mothers also. Our sisters. All females unnerve us."

"I hadn't realized."

"You might ask your brother."

"Sherry is not afraid of anyone." The corners of her mouth lifted, and she added, "Save for Aunt Georgia, his wife, his daughter, and me."

Ferrin chuckled. "My point precisely."

"Although it might be more accurate that he is afraid *for* us."

"I understand that also."

"What of your mother? And sisters?"

Ferrin came within a hairsbreadth of answering for himself, not Wellsley. She was clever, was Mrs. Caldwell. Like a siren she had lulled, then lured him dangerously close to rocky shores. "My mother died in childbirth. I have no sisters. No brothers, either. Grandmother took me in after my father accepted a commission and departed for India. He remarried that same year and has never returned."

Cybelline felt certain she had almost made him stumble, but then he had gone on smoothly, and she began to doubt herself. She was hoping for some incongruent detail that she might drop casually in conversation with Mrs. Lowell. If the housekeeper became suspicious that the visitor to the cottage was not Lady Bellingham's grandson, mayhap

Ferrin could be convinced to leave Penwyckham before the villagers ran at him with pitchforks and rakes. She could not, however, simply give up what she knew to be true without sacrificing her own identity. Ferrin would know there was but one way she could be privy to any particular about him and that was because she was Boudicca.

"The viscountess's desire to see you wed becomes more clear to me," Cybelline told him. "She is your mother's mother, is she not?"

"Yes."

"Then she is desirous that her line not end with you."

"So she has told me."

"I imagine they are some of the more pertinent words you exchanged with her."

"You understand it very well."

Cybelline shrugged. "Sherry exchanged similar words with Aunt Georgia." She inclined her head a tad, a gesture that admitted her own role in the conversation. "And with me," she said.

"You said your brother was married. I believe you also mentioned a daughter." He watched her carefully, but there was no indication that she was thinking of her own child. In some ways, the fact that she had not revealed she had a daughter was telling. No doubt she thought she had ample reason not to share this information with the Earl of Ferrin, but there was no reason that he knew of not to share the same with Mr. Wellsley. He wondered how he might use this to his advantage. "Sheridan is either a dutiful godson and brother, or he met the woman who made him think that marriage and children was in no way objectionable."

"Sherry is dutiful. I cannot say otherwise about him, but in this instance, it is the latter. Lily is his heart."

He saw a shadow pass quickly across her features. It seemed her breath caught, then was eased slowly out of her. Had she been thinking of her own husband? he wondered. Ferrin tried to imagine the sort of man the late Mr.

Caldwell had been to recommend him to this woman. All he knew was that Caldwell had made a study of the same type of artifacts that interested Sir Richard Settle at Cambridge and that he'd put a pistol to his head. It was so little in the way of intelligence that Ferrin cautioned himself about making any assumptions regarding the man's character. Had he suspected that upon meeting Mrs. Caldwell he would end his search for Boudicca, he would have taken the time to learn more about her husband.

Cybelline stood suddenly. The rug fell away from her lap. She stooped to pick it up and folded it as she straightened. "I fear I have been ill-mannered in the extreme." She pointed to the journal she had seen him carry into the room with her valise. "I see that you meant to read this evening, and I have kept you from that pleasure and the comfort of your bed. I only meant to determine if all was well at the Sharpe house and know for myself that you were safely returned."

Ferrin came to his feet. "I had no objections to passing the time in such a fashion, but mayhap you have some regrets."

Oddly enough, she had none. "No, Mr. Wellsley, I do not." She placed the blanket on the chair behind her. When she turned it was to find Ferrin making a study of her. Unprepared for his close regard and more than a little afraid of what he might discover, Cybelline hurried to the door. She picked up the valise and held it front of her like a shield. "I wish you a pleasant night. I am certain I will be gone from your house in the morning."

He did not raise an objection to this, though he doubted it was true. She had badly miscalculated the fury of the storm. He had passed through snowdrifts several feet high on his return. It was unlikely she could leave without assistance from him.

"Goodnight, Mrs. Caldwell."

She nodded once, opening the door. "Thank you again."

Ferrin watched her go. The door clicked into place, and he was alone. It had been on the tip of his tongue to tell her that he had a goodnight message from her daughter, but the cruelty of it stayed him. She would have to inform him that there was a child. It was not something that could be kept secret. Perhaps she would realize by morning that she had made a mistake by not telling him already. He would probably let it pass. The stranger truth of the evening was that he *had* enjoyed himself in her company.

He did not yet know what to make of it.

Ferrin picked up Berzelius's work and turned it over in his hands. He doubted it could hold his interest now, not when the chemical action of a different sort of electricity was pooling all the blood from his head to his groin.

Cybelline was drinking tea with Mrs. Lowell when Ferrin came downstairs in the morning. She was wearing the clothes he had brought back from the Sharpe house: a practical wool serge gown suitable for riding, heavy woolen stockings, and brown leather boots. When she saw his eyes drift to her feet, she pulled them back modestly and tucked them under the hem of her dress.

Mrs. Lowell rose to her feet upon Ferrin entering the kitchen. "It's the smell of baking bread that woke you, I'll wager. I'm not giving away a secret when I say it's just the thing to lure a man from his bed."

"Indeed," Ferrin said dryly.

"Will you have some tea, sir? There's porridge in the pot, and I'll give you a thick slice of the bread, toasted if you like. The storm made the hens skittish. Mr. Lowell couldn't find but two eggs this morning, and I'll need them for my special custard."

"I will eat anything you put before me," Ferrin said, meaning it. He was inordinately hungry. "You have broken your fast?"

"Hours ago," Mrs. Lowell said, unaware he had directed his inquiry to Mrs. Caldwell. "She's been waiting patiently for you to rouse yourself so she might return home."

Ferrin pulled out a chair and sat at the table. "I believe I am being admonished for lying abed."

Cybelline had her teacup halfway to her mouth. She regarded it rather than look directly at Ferrin. "I have not been up so long as that, but I am often an early riser."

"And this morning you hoped to be gone at first light."

Nodding, she made no attempt to hide her disappointment. "I had no idea how deep the snow had become. Mr. Lowell walked through a drift waist high to get to the henhouse."

Ferrin glanced around. He could not see to every corner of the lodge, but he had an expansive view from the kitchen, and Mr. Lowell was nowhere in sight. "Where is the man of very few words this morning?"

It was Mrs. Lowell who answered, her voice oddly distorted as she bent over the porridge pot. "He's shoveling a path to the necessary and another to the curing shed. Then he means to feed the cattle."

Remembering what Mrs. Lowell had said about her husband's rheumatism, Ferrin wondered that the hosteler could manage to labor long out of doors. He started to rise just as Mrs. Lowell turned away from the hearth.

"Where are you going, sir?"

"It occurs to me that Mr. Lowell could use an extra pair of hands."

"Sure, but he's had his breakfast, hasn't he? It's no help at all if you're facedown in a drift and have to be carted back here."

One of Ferrin's eyebrows kicked up. It was indicative of admonishment, and blessed silence usually followed. Mrs. Lowell, he noted, was perfectly oblivious to this communication. She chattered on as she set the bowl of porridge before him and while she busied herself toasting the bread. She did not seem to tire of the sound of her own voice. When he glanced sideways at Mrs. Caldwell, he saw she was unable to hide her amusement. The edges of her mouth were lifted above the rim of the teacup. He slowly sat.

"Sherry has an expression such as yours," Cybelline said. "One eyebrow lifted in that same perfect arch, though I believe he favors the right one, while you seem partial to the left."

Ferrin's tone was wry. "I am always willing to accept direction in these matters. Is the right eyebrow more effective, do you think?"

"I believe either has its limits. The scoundrels, for instance, are immune."

"The scoundrels?"

"Mmmm." Cybelline set down her cup and offered to pour for Ferrin. "The scoundrels are my brother's wards. Milk? Sugar?" At his double nod, she gave him some of each. "Pinch, Dash, and Midge, if you can credit it. There is considerable debate about finding more suitable appellations, but nothing has been decided. Beowulf has been mentioned, I believe."

"I understand the problem, then."

She smiled. "They are dear boys. Holborn's castoffs. All of them using their rum daddles to become boman prigs. It remains a question whether Sherry rescued them or the other way around, but they have been in his care for several years now."

Ferrin picked up his spoon and plunged it into the thick porridge. "Rum daddles?"

Cybelline held up her hands and wiggled her fingers. "Skilled hands. A boman prig is an adept at thievery."

"I had no idea that Sheridan was a social reformer."

"He is not, and he is always pleased to inform me of all the ways he is not. Yet I entertain no doubts that he has reformed the society of those three young ruffians. They will say the same."

"His wife has no quarrel with three boys living under their roof?"

Cybelline shook her head, and her flint-colored eyes took on a distant, secretive aspect. "No," she said, smiling faintly. "Lily has no quarrel."

Ferrin did not press for more information. He sensed that she had said as much on the matter as she would. Indeed, her offering seemed out of character. Perhaps the raised eyebrow had been used to good effect after all. He tucked into his porridge. He had not had the like since he was in short pants, and he found an appreciation of the the taste and the memories.

Mrs. Lowell set a thick slice of toast before him, richly spread with raspberry jam. The tea was hot and sweetened just to his liking, and Ferrin had the thought that following Mrs. Caldwell to Penwyckham might have been one of Wellsley's truly inspired ideas.

Cybelline folded her palms around her warm cup. Her hands and feet still felt chilled and sometimes one shiver chased another along the length of her spine. She was eager to go home and could think of nothing else to do but say so. "I am exceedingly aware of the great kindness you have already shown me, but I must press for another favor, Mr. Wellsley."

"You have only to ask, Mrs. Caldwell." He held up one hand, staying her request a moment longer. "However, if it is your wish that I escort you back to the Sharpe house, then you need not ask at all. It will be my pleasure to do so when I have finished."

"That is good of you, but I was only going to ask that you will permit me to borrow one of the horses. I would not ask for yours, of course, but Mr. Lowell informed me there are two others stabled here that he uses for the wagon and turning over the garden. He says both have gentle natures. I thought I might take one of them."

"I see." He was mildly surprised she hadn't made off with one of the animals already. Clearly she did not want him to accompany her home. "I don't think I like you setting off alone, Mrs. Caldwell. I could not forgive myself if you didn't arrive safely."

"That's what I told her," Mrs. Lowell said. She clucked her tongue to emphasize this point. "Mr. Lowell told her she would have to defer to your good judgment, as you made the trek once yourself."

Ferrin glanced at Cybelline for confirmation. "He said all that?"

"More or less." She thought about it. "Mostly less."

The housekeeper removed the porridge pot from the hearth and began scraping it clean with a large wooden spoon. "Some days I don't know what goes through that man's mind."

"I imagine he was depending upon me to stay her," Ferrin said. "He could not bring himself to tell her no, so it has fallen to me."

Mrs. Lowell looked up from the bowels of the iron pot. "You might be in the right of it there, Mr. Wellsley. Mr. Lowell does have a tender heart. A man has to when he doesn't say more than six words of a morning."

Six words? Ferrin had never heard so many strung together. He addressed Mrs. Caldwell. "We will look at the animals and determine which is the more suitable for you to ride. You will not go alone, however. The toll for leaving today is that you accept my escort."

Cybelline nodded once. "Then I shall be glad to have it."

Ferrin observed her fingertips pressing whitely against her cup, though he could not say if the action gave lie to her words or whether she was thinking of what else must be said. In a moment he had his answer.

"I think you will appreciate my urgency, Mr. Wellsley,

when I explain that it is for my daughter's sake that I must return."

At best it was a partial truth, Ferrin thought. It was not only for her daughter's sake that she wished to leave quickly, but for her own as well. "You did not mention her yesterday."

"No." She hesitated. "I did not think it would influence your objections to me returning, but today is a different matter. The sun is out, and while it is still bitterly cold and travel will be difficult, I am determined to go. I must know my daughter is all of a piece."

Ferrin was aware that Mrs. Lowell was scraping the pot with less industry than she'd previously applied to the task. He chose his words carefully. "Did you not believe me when I told you all was well at the Sharpe house?"

"I . . . of course I believed you."

"I had that information from your housekeeper. We can assume, can we not, that *all* was inclusive of your daughter?"

"It is not the same as seeing for myself."

"You might have inquired about her." It had not occurred to him that he would see the same vague shadow of pain crossing her features as when memories of her husband intruded, yet he knew he was not mistaken. He watched her quickly raise the teacup to her lips as she collected herself.

"I have learned to embrace privacy as my right, Mr. Wellsley. Not every aspect of one's life needs to be laid open for public inspection."

She showed a remarkable economy of words in delivering a set down, Ferrin thought. She had also managed to capture the high ground. He knew this because he'd been figuratively flattened. A glance at Mrs. Lowell confirmed that she, too, was impressed. All that was left for him to do was try to rise and dust himself off.

"I thought that might be the way of it," he said, oddly

pleased to discover a talent for putting forth the bold lie. "When you did not inquire after your daughter's welfare last evening, I assumed it was because you meant no one to know that she was in residence."

"No, that is, it's—"

"Then you meant that I shouldn't know." Ferrin was glad to be on his feet again. "I cannot imagine why that is, Mrs. Caldwell."

She set her cup down so firmly the saucer rattled. "Because it should be of no importance to anyone save me. I do not know you, Mr. Wellsley, and while you have shown me every manner of charity, you are no part of what is private in my life."

Ferrin realized he was not as steady on his feet as he'd thought. Mrs. Lowell's attention had gone from mild interest to avidly curious. He would shock her into apoplexy if he answered Mrs. Caldwell more honestly than she had him. He was part of her private life, her most secret life, and he need only remind her of how she had come in his arms to drive that point home.

Ferrin said nothing, however, nor did he give her any reason to suspect what he was thinking. For now he merely accepted what she served up, knowing full well there would be a reckoning. And he intended that it should be a most private affair.

Newton and a dappled mare named Divinity were waiting for Ferrin and Cybelline at the back door of the cottage. Mr. Lowell delivered the reins to each of them in turn and helped them mount, then strapped Cybelline's valise behind the mare's saddle.

The path Ferrin took the previous night had vanished under drifts of snow, but he had marked his way through the trees and knew the easiest route to reach what passed for the road. Cybelline turned up the chinchilla collar of her pelisse and followed in his wake. She was a competent rider, though not accomplished, and was glad that her mare was brought so easily around after a brief test of wills. Divinity was perfectly content to accept the gelding's lead. Perhaps she realized, Cybelline thought, that Newton was doing the hard work, pushing through deep crests of snow as if they were no more than a nuisance.

Occasionally Ferrin turned to satisfy himself that she was still in her saddle and not upended in a drift as tall as she was. Cybelline always nodded in recognition of his concern, but he offered nothing in return. His expression remained one of complete indifference. She did not think he would have been pleased to find her sprawled on the ground but that he wouldn't have cared. He seemed equally unimpressed that she remained in her seat.

She was supremely aware that there was much that was unsettled between them. She could own now that she had erred in not telling him about Anna at the outset, though even he must allow that there was little opportunity to do so when she first arrived. He had departed for the Sharpe house so quickly that she hadn't had time to reflect on what was in her best interests to say to him. Her decision to seek him out last night was prompted by her need to know if he had learned of Anna's existence. She was relieved in some measure when he made no mention of her daughter and decided then that she would not say more. In the event that he discovered she was Boudicca, she did not want him to be able to use her own child as leverage for whatever demands he might make.

Cybelline's thinking had changed when Ferrin insisted upon accompanying her home. There was nothing for it but that she tell him, else he would wonder why she had not done so. Her secret was from Ferrin, not Mr. Wellsley. It troubled her that he had adopted a certain air of indignation when she disclosed Anna's existence, and obviously believed he had the right to question her. It raised her hackles to be asked to provide answers in so preemptory a fashion, as if he were her brother . . . or her husband.

She had meant only to set him back on his heels, but perhaps she had succeeded in knocking him down. He had grown quite still, revealing nothing save for the fact that he was a patient man. Cybelline wondered then, as she wondered now, if she had reason to be afraid.

She abandoned that notion when the Sharpe house appeared before her. Her heart lightened, and she lifted her head in spite of the icy air that greeted her. The structure looked rather grand for something that had been sadly neglected these past six months. Snow covered the patching on the roof that Mr. Henley had never been able to complete, and icicles hung all along the eaves so the chipped paint was not the first detail one noticed. Heavy dollops of snow lay across the boxwoods and shrubbery. The evidence that all of it was wildly uneven and badly in need of trimming was not to be found.

The steps had been swept, but they were all that was uncovered. Snow had even been driven into the mortar between the ochre bricks. It veiled the windows and capped the lintels. It crested on the lip of the roof and mounded around the chimneys. Cybelline found herself enchanted by what she saw and wondered if Lady Beatrice Sharpe had ever known the same feeling of contentment upon coming home.

"Mrs. Caldwell?"

Cybelline was belatedly aware that Ferrin was standing beside the mare, waiting to assist her dismount. She could not say how long he had been there or what he thought about her daydreaming. He was as still as he'd been at the kitchen table, a man in expectation of something she did not properly understand.

"Your hand, if you will."

Cybelline had to smile to herself. She understood that well enough. She placed her gloved hand in his and did her best to ignore the frisson of awareness that crept up her spine.

Ferrin helped her down from the saddle and pressed the upturned collar of her pelisse against her cheeks. "You are cold, Mrs. Caldwell. Go inside. Quickly."

She didn't move. Couldn't. He did not seem to be aware that his hands remained on her collar. The fur pressed warmly against her cheeks, but it was as if his palms were there. She knew what it was to have his hands on her face. In the dark stairwell, his fingers had traced the shape of her nose and fluttered across her eyebrows. He had placed his thumb on her bottom lip and separated it from her upper one. Her tongue had touched the pad of his thumb. She recalled that he had shivered then, just as she shivered now.

Ferrin's hands dropped away suddenly. He stepped to one side and began to unstrap the valise. Cybelline knew she was supposed to take advantage of his apparent preoccupation, but like the statuary in the park, she stayed just as she was, frozen in place.

"Go!"

Cybelline jerked. He had fairly growled the command, but it had taken all of that to move her. She hurried away, not daring to look back. The door opened under the pressure she applied and she disappeared into the entrance hall.

Out of the corner of his eye, Ferrin watched her go. If he'd had Boudicca's spear with him, he would have gladly thrown himself on the sharp end of it. Just now it seemed as good a solution as any to what he faced.

Then it occurred to him to wonder if perhaps Nicholas Caldwell had once felt the very same.

Chapter Seven

"Come away from the door, Miss Anna." Nanny Baker delivered the instruction firmly, with every expectation that she would be obeyed. When the little girl continued to tug at the door handle, Nanny picked her up and gave her a direct scold. "Your mother is ill, Miss Anna, too ill to receive visitors. Come, we will go to the kitchen and see if Mrs. Minty has a treat for you."

Listening from her bed on the other side of the door, Cybelline could not make out her daughter's reply. Anna's voice did not carry into the room in the same manner that Nanny Baker's did. She strained to hear more but caught only Nanny's retreating footfalls. Cybelline had managed only to throw back the covers and sit up during that time. She hadn't been able to put her legs over the side.

She collapsed back on the bed, exhausted by this small effort. It was just as well that she hadn't left the bed. She could not have traveled the distance to the sitting room without assistance. Her breath was ragged and rough from what little she had done. Her heart raced. She lay quietly, unmoving, trying to calm both.

She had given instructions that Anna must not visit her, so she could not fault Nanny Baker for carrying them out, yet when her child was removed from the door, it seemed more punishment than protection. Cybelline had no hope that Anna could be made to understand why she was being kept away. No child could grasp the danger of being in the same room with a mother who was as ill as she was.

The physician concurred with her decision upon his first visit and had not changed his mind. He had come again this morning, listened to her lungs and heart, and announced that she must be bled again. Cybelline offered a mild protest that the treatment was not improving her health, but Dr. Epping explained that in cases such as hers it was not unusual to require a dozen treatments to release all the bad humors from the blood. She gave over her arm to the procedure and watched her blood pool in the bowl under her elbow with hardly any sense that she was the donor.

Cybelline pulled the covers up to her neck again and turned carefully on her side. Webb had been there, she remembered, standing stoically at the bedside while the doctor inserted the sharpened glass straw to begin the blood flow. She could not say whether Webb watched, but when the doctor departed, Cybelline noted that Webb's countenance no longer held any color. It begged the question as to which one of them was bled.

The door to the bedchamber opened and Webb appeared carrying a tray with the post on it. She brought it to the bedside table and set it down. She stood over the bed, regarding her mistress.

"I was thinking of you, Webb," Cybelline said. It was a strain to speak loudly enough to be understood. Laryngitis had claimed her voice not three days earlier. Dr. Epping had suggested tea with honey and a dram of whisky and a warm compress to place across her throat. Like every other aspect of her illness, her voice had not improved. "Thinking of you and you have come. Perhaps I am developing powers of the mind to compensate for having no corporeal strength. Did you feel me will you here?"

"What a lot of nonsense," Webb said. "As if I hold with such. And you should not be speaking. Resting your voice is what's called for."

"You sound like Nanny Baker scolding Anna."

"God's truth, I hope not. But it must be said that you are as willful as your daughter. Can you not remain quiet?"

Cybelline found strength enough to smile. "You should not ask questions then." She closed her eyes. A moment later she felt a warm, damp flannel pressed against her forehead. Light fingers brushed her hair back; the flannel touched her cheeks, the underside of her chin, and was wiped gently down her throat. "You are good to me, Webb."

"I'd do better by you if I could keep you from talking." She removed the flannel. "Shall I brush your hair?" The maid added quickly, "You've only to nod or shake your head."

Cybelline nodded.

Webb retrieved Cybelline's brush from the adjoining dressing room, then helped her sit up. She crawled onto the bed behind her mistress and employed the brush with a steady hand. "It's a nest for birds," Webb said, carefully working out the tangles. "All your lovely hair come to this. And after what we did to get all that devil's red out. There's a shame."

"Mmm."

Cybelline's eyes remained closed while Webb worked. A languor spread across her shoulders and limbs that was entirely different from the fatigue she'd experienced earlier. She could have submitted to this particular treatment for hours yet, so she was disappointed when the sense of contentment vanished as Webb became more hesitant in the application of the brush. "What is it, Webb? You have something to say. I can tell." Behind her, she heard her maid take a deep breath as though bracing herself for some unpleasantness. When Webb remained quiet, Cybelline used a threat to achieve results. "I shall recite the entire "Quality of Mercy" speech from *The Merchant of Venice* if you do not—"

"Stop!" Webb underscored this uncharacteristic sharp tone with a hard tug of the brush. "Please, Mrs. Caldwell, you will have no voice to use at all."

Cybelline was not unaware of the depth of her maid's distress. She remained quiet and waited her out.

"I have it in my mind that I should take it upon myself to write to your aunt and brother. I know you have expressly forbidden it, but I cannot help but think it is wrong for you to do so. It seems to me that they will want to know that you are ill. It has been a fortnight since you took to your bed, and I am not—"

Cybelline had heard quite enough. Without conscious thought, she touched her throat with her fingertips as though in support of her voice. "I have corresponded with both of them. You know I have. You posted the letters yourself."

"I suppose I might as well be hanged for a sheep as a lamb." Webb squared her narrow shoulders and went on. "I know you've written but not what you've written, and this last seems to be the important thing. It's my opinion that one or other of your family would have arrived already if you'd told them the truth, and since you will not permit me to write to them, I think you have not been honest."

"I take it you are not alone in this opinion."

"I haven't discussed it with anyone. It's not my place."

"But you hear things."

"No, I don't. I make it a point *not* to hear things." Webb gathered up her skirts and moved off the bed. "Please, will you not at least write to Lord Sheridan?"

"After Christmas. If I am not improved by Christmas,

I will inform him." Cybelline saw Webb's mouth thin disapprovingly, but her brief nod suggested she accepted this decision. "And you will not write, either, Webb. I am set on this matter."

Webb's lips were now pressed so tightly together that her mouth disappeared.

"The quality of mercy is not strained, it droppeth—"

Webb capitulated. "Enough. It will be as you wish. You know I will not disobey you."

Cybelline nodded and reached for Webb's hand. She missed on her first attempt, and her maid had to step closer to the bed and take up the hand when Cybelline tried again. "I rely on you, Webb. Perhaps too much. Am I such a great burden?"

"No, m'lady. Nothing of the kind."

Cybelline felt a heaviness steal over her limbs again. The hand that Webb held went limp. She found her voice, but it was little more than a thread of sound now. "I think I will lie down."

"Of course." Webb released Cybelline's hand and supported her shoulders, helping her lie back. She eased one pillow from under Cybelline's head, plumped it, then replaced it. Even after Cybelline's eyes closed, she did not leave her side. "He was here again this morning," she said quietly, "not long after Dr. Epping left. Mrs. Henley told him that you would not see him, that you were ill. I don't think he believed her."

Cybelline nodded faintly. "Mr. Wellsley has a suspicious nature."

Webb had to lean close to make out her mistress's words. She straightened slowly, shaking her head. "I think it is something more. He comes every other day. Mrs. Henley is finding it more difficult to turn him away; he is most insistent. He brought crutches for Mr. Henley, if you can believe it. I think he made them himself, or perhaps Mr. Lowell crafted them and they were Mr. Wellsley's design. I do not know all the particulars, but I could see for myself that Mr. Henley is getting around ever so much better than before."

Webb drew a breath to say more, then held her tongue. Cybelline's breathing was labored and harsh, but she was sleeping. Webb laid the back of her hand against her mistress's forehead. She was warm to the touch, and Webb sensed another fever would soon be upon her.

"Forgive me, m'lady," Webb whispered, withdrawing her hand, "but I cannot allow you to go so easily as he did."

It was nightfall when Ferrin arrived at the Sharpe house for the second time that day. This trip was by invitation, though not by the mistress of the house. Webb had dispatched Mr. Kins to the Pembroke cottage to fetch him. Mrs. Lowell quickly packed a valise for him, and Mr. Lowell offered to bring the rest of his things by wagon in the morning, as Ferrin would accept no delay in departing.

An unexpected spell of warm weather, highly unusual in December, had melted much of the snow since the storm. The road was passable, even bare in some places, and only where trees closely bordered it and blocked the sun was there still evidence of the drifts that had impeded travel.

In expectation of Ferrin's arrival, Mrs. Henley watched from the window in the front drawing room. As soon as she spied him breaking through the trees on his great Irish beast, she hurried to the door and threw it open. One of the grooms ran from the stable to assist Ferrin and take his horse.

Inside, Ferrin handed over his hat, gloves, and crop to Mrs. Henley. "Is she up there?" he asked, lifting his chin toward the stairs.

"Yes, sir. I'll take you right away, sir."

Webb appeared at the top of the steps. "Do not trouble yourself, Mrs. Henley. This way, Mr. Wellsley. I'll show you to her room."

Ferrin did not bother to remove his coat. He unbuttoned it as he climbed the stairs. When he reached the top it was to discover that the maid had placed herself squarely in the middle of the hallway. Ferrin towered over her, but she was unmoved by the disparity in their heights. One hand rested on her hip; the other held a candlestick. She raised it slightly, while she gave as good as she got, studying him as if she meant to have him for dinner if she did not approve of what she saw or heard.

"You are Miss Webb," he said. She could be no other. Ferrin had read that on the grass plains of Africa such fierce protectiveness could be found in a lioness for her cubs. In society, one had to look no further than a lady's maid for evidence of the same. "Mr. Kins said you are the one who requested that I come." Though he was out of all patience for civility, he inclined his head. He judged it was to his advantage to win this woman over. "I am Mr. Wellsley."

She curtseyed but did not give ground. "I fear you will find me impertinent, Mr. Wellsley, but I cannot apologize for it. My mistress is very ill, and I will do whatever is necessary to make certain she regains her health. She will not permit me to send word to either her aunt or her brother, and neither will she put the truth of her condition to paper."

"But surely a physician has been summoned."

"Yes. Dr. Epping from Bell's Folly. There is no one else. He is the same doctor who treated Mr. Henley after his fall."

Far from inspiring confidence, this intelligence made Ferrin want to pick up Miss Webb and put her out of his way. "Then you will show me to Mrs. Caldwell immediately." This was apparently the response she was hoping for, because she turned on her heel and began walking away. Ferrin followed her through a series of connecting sitting and sleeping rooms until she came to a door left slightly ajar. She placed her hand on one of the raised panels and held it there, glancing at him over her shoulder. He could see clearly that her handsome features were sharpened by concern. Whether it was doubt she harbored about him or some question about her own course of action, he couldn't say. He judged that she was most likely only a few years older than he, yet it was difficult to know given the finely etched creases at her eyes and the corners of her mouth.

"She will not want you here," Webb said, her eyes anxious.

"I know." He removed his greatcoat and folded it over his arm. "You have done right by your mistress, Webb. Go on. Open the door."

Nodding, Webb gave it a slight push. She stepped aside to permit Ferrin to precede her.

He passed her his coat and went straightaway to the bed. He thought he had adequately prepared himself for what he would find. He had not been able to imagine this.

She had dropped a stone's weight, and that was a kind estimate. The bones of her face stood out sharply. There were defined hollows in her cheeks and the same at her temples. Her great abundance of honey-colored hair was scraped back from her forehead in such a fashion that it gave clear form to the shape of her skull. Even the candlelight at her bedside could not lend color to her face. Her skin was very nearly translucent. Just above the neat fold of the quilt that covered her torso, he could make out the thrust of her collarbone through her thin cotton shift. One of her arms rested outside the blankets. He regarded the fragile overturned wrist and the starkly outlined webbing of blue veins.

He gestured Webb over to the bed. She placed his coat across the back of one of the chairs and joined him. "How is she called by her family?" he asked.

"Cybelline, sir."

Cybelline. He hadn't known. Ferrin circled Cybelline's wrist with his thumb and forefinger and raised it slightly. With his other hand, he pushed up the sleeve of her night-gown so that he could examine her elbow. "Bring the light closer."

Webb stretched forward and held the candlestick steady.

"How many times has she been bled?" he asked. "I count at least three scars."

"The doctor does it every time he comes and he's been here five times."

Ferrin rolled the sleeve down and reached under the covers for Cybelline's other arm. He made the same ex-amination of it. "Two more. It is a wonder that she has not been exsanguinated."

"I beg your pardon, sir?"

"Bled dry."

Webb shuddered as much at the darkness of his tone as the import of the words themselves. "It did seem rather like a lot of blood to me. My own mother was bled, so I know the efficacy of the treatment, but my poor lady, she never seemed to recover the way a body should."

Ferrin suppressed his own shudder. The more he read in the medical journals, the more he doubted that bleed-ing had anything to support it. If patients recovered, it was because they had a constitution capable of surviving the treatment, not because the treatment itself was proven. He was acquainted with several physicians who no longer practiced it and cautioned others against it. They were rad-icals, according to many of their colleagues, especially since they had no certain course of treatment to replace it, and their thinking had not gained wide favor.

"I beg your pardon?" he said, coming late to the real-ization that Webb was asking him something. "I did not hear your question."

"I said I was given to understand that you know things, sir. Uncommon things. Not like what the rest of us know. I wondered if that was true."

One of Ferrin's eyebrows lifted, but he continued to study Cybelline. "Will you bring me a basin, Webb? I will also require a pitcher of water, not cold, mind you. And a bottle of spirits. Whatever is in the drinks cabinet will serve."

"Yes, sir." She rang for help and requested the spirits, but she brought everything else to Ferrin from the dressing room.

He made room for the basin on the bedside table and indicated Webb should pour some water into it. "How did you learn that I know uncommon things, as you called them?"

"From Mr. Foster. Is it true?"

"Ah, yes, Mr. Foster. He and I have exchanged pleasantries. He owns the notions shop, I believe, or have I mistaken him for another?"

"No, that's Mr. Foster."

"He also owns a telescope." Ferrin wrung out the wet flannel and applied it gently to Cybelline's brow. "Did you know that?"

"I didn't, sir. It seems a might peculiar. What does he need one for?"

"To gaze at the heavens, one would presume."

"What a thing to do," Webb said. "And him with a shop to keep."

"It is my opinion that a man's livelihood should not dictate all of his interests."

Webb considered this as she watched him work. He was using the damp flannel just as she had earlier, though this time Cybelline was insensible to it. "Have you looked through a telescope, Mr. Wellsley?"

"I have."

"Do you own one?"

"No, I made a present to my father of the one I made."

She blinked. "You made a telescope?"

Ferrin nodded. "It was a number of years ago. More than six, now that I think on it." He turned down Cybelline's quilt another fold and pressed the flannel to the opening at the neck of her gown. She did not stir at all, and this alarmed him more than the look of her. "When the spirits arrive, Webb, ask for a bath to be drawn. The water must be warm but not hot. And have the tub placed as close to the fire as possible. If there are towels in the dressing room, stack them near the fire now so they'll be warm when we have need of them."

Webb disappeared again and returned in moment with an armload of towels. She divided them into two piles and placed one on the seat of a chair and the other on the footstool. She had not yet returned to the bed when one of the maids arrived with a decanter of whisky. Webb held it up for Ferrin to see.

"Is there no more? It's only two-thirds full."

Webb turned to the maid. "Ask everyone in the house if they have any spirits hidden away. It is a pity Mr. Kins did not hire that Harding fellow. He looked as if he knew the taste of the stuff well enough." She stopped the maid from leaving and told her, "And inform Mrs. Henley that Mr. Wellsley requires a bath to be drawn for the mistress. The tub will go in this room." The maid bobbed her head several times before she hurried off. Webb rejoined Ferrin. "Where shall I put this?"

"Pour a third of it into the basin."

She did as instructed, then stoppered the decanter and set it on the floor. She watched him wet the flannel again and wring it out. "Will it pull the fever from her, do you think?"

"That is my hope."

"Have you done the like before?"

"No. But I have read about it."

She made no attempt to hide her misgivings or her disbelief. "That is all? You've read about it?"

"It is how one acquires knowledge of uncommon things, Webb."

"But, Mr. Wellsley, she is—"

"Shh. You are a distraction now. Find a glass for me. A tumbler will be sufficient, but something taller would be better. Not a wineglass, though. That will not work."

Webb obeyed because she didn't know what else to do with herself. There was no glass in the dressing room, only a heavy stoneware mug and a tin cup. She used the servants' staircase at the rear of the house to reach the dining room.

Ferrin threw back the covers completely and raised the hem of Cybelline's nightgown as far as the tops of her thighs. He wiped down her legs from hip to ankle with the spirit-soaked flannel, working quickly to avoid Webb's scold in the event she returned. He replaced the covers up to her waist, then lifted the neck of her gown and slipped his hand beneath it so he could wash her chest. He finished just as the rustle of Webb's skirts signaled her approach. When the maid entered the room he was applying the cloth to Cybelline's limp forearm.

"She hasn't awakened?" asked Webb.

"No. How long has it been since she's spoken to anyone?"

"She stirred some not long before you came, but she didn't open her eyes or say anything." Webb bit her lower lip and worried it while she thought. "I suppose the last time she spoke was before I sent Mr. Kins for you. It's been several hours." She looked at her mistress; tears glazed her eyes. "She's not merely sleeping, is she, Mr. Wellsley?"

There was no point in denying what the maid knew to be true. Webb had the evidence before her, though she sorely wanted to deny it. "No, Webb. She's not." He glanced at the glass she held and put out his hand. "May

I?" Webb gave it over. "Help me turn her onto her stomach." When that was efficiently accomplished, Ferrin directed the maid to remove the pillows so Cybelline would not smother herself in them. Webb gently turned her mistress's face to one side while Ferrin resettled the blankets at the small of Cybelline's back.

He placed the overturned glass against her upper back to the left of her spine, then bent over and laid his ear to the solid end of the glass. Her heartbeat was neither as strong nor as steady as he could have wished. "Has she suffered any illnesses as a child? Scarlet fever? Rheumatic fever?"

"No." Webb shook her head. "That is, I've never heard her say so. I have only been with her since she was a young lady, before her come-out. I know that she enjoyed the best of health until—" Webb stopped suddenly, biting off the thought so deliberately that her teeth clicked together.

"Until?" Ferrin asked. "Until childbirth? Did she have a difficult delivery, some complication that could have—" Now it was he who stopped as he realized what it was that Webb would not say. "Until her husband died. Is that it, Webb? Mrs. Caldwell has not enjoyed good health since her husband died?"

"It is not that she has been sickly," Webb said. "But that she has been sick at heart." She looked away, clearly troubled. "I cannot say more."

"You certainly can." Ferrin straightened and employed both his superior height and superior station to his advantage. "And you will, Webb." He gave the maid full marks for not cowering, but it took only a moment before she caved.

"She's been troubled of late. There have been dreams, you see. And letters. I'm not supposed to know of either, but I've heard her weeping at night. Sometimes it is the same after the post comes. I can tell she's not anxious to read it. She picks through it carefully, and if she sees something she doesn't like, I have to take the entire tray away. She reads it all later, though. I know she does because it disappears."

"Have you never asked her about the letters?"

"Oh, no, sir. I couldn't."

"And the dreams?"

"She never speaks of them to me, though I think she told Lady Rivendale about them. I overheard them talking in London once during one of the countess's visits. I didn't listen, sir. I only heard a few words here and there, and because she weeps so at night, I thought I might know what they were talking about."

"I see."

"Can it not be good that she decided to come to Penwyckham? Change isn't always bad, is it, sir? To be away from London . . . from the house . . . it seemed like it would be for the better."

Ferrin nodded, encouraging her to go on. He wondered if she would mention Cybelline's decision to attend Wynetta's masquerade, or even if Webb was privy to any part of what had occurred there. He thought that Webb was mulling over what she might say next, but then two maids arrived carrying buckets of water, and his hope of continuing the conversation was ended. "Tend to the bath, Webb. I will finish here."

He moved the glass to different locations on Cybelline's back and listened at each one. Her every breath was accompanied by an unusual rattling sound that he thought might be fluid in her lungs. He raised the glass and turned it over, found the decanter, and poured himself a finger of whisky. He merely raised one dark eyebrow when he saw Webb regard him disapprovingly.

The whisky went down smoothly and put a satisfying heat in his blood. He continued to attend to Cybelline while the maids carried a tub from the dressing room and began to fill it in front of the fire. They worked under the watchful eye of Webb and Mrs. Henley, who came bearing a bottle of gin and another of whisky. There was some discussion among women as to where the spirits were found, but Ferrin gave it no heed.

He stopped what he was doing only once so that he could test the temperature of the bath. He bid them add another kettle of hot water before he pronounced himself satisfied. "Leave," Ferrin told them.

"But, sir, you cannot—" Webb actually took a step backward at what she saw in his glacial expression.

"It's not proper," Mrs. Henley said, then she, too, retreated a step.

The maids did not offer any objection, though their mouths hung open.

"Leave," Ferrin said, "or I will." He turned away, not waiting to see if they would obey or wait him out. They could not know he was lying; his own mother would not have been able to catch him out this time. It was only when he heard the door being closed behind him that he released the breath he'd been holding.

"Well, Mrs. Caldwell, it appears you have been abandoned to my tender mercies. Let us see what we shall make of it." There was no response of any kind, and he had not anticipated there would be. Ferrin had no use for idle chatter of the sort that Mrs. Lowell often practiced, but he spoke as he worked, hoping that the steadiness of his voice would give Cybelline comfort or draw her out.

He added the decanter of whisky to the bath water, cooling it slightly, then he removed his frock coat and waistcoat, and rolled up his shirt sleeves to the elbow. He loosened his stock as he returned to the bed. After drawing off Cybelline's blankets, Ferrin turned her and slipped one arm under her shoulders and the other under her knees. He lifted her carefully but was unable to cradle her head. It fell backward, exposing the long line of her throat. Her breath rattled. She was dead weight in his arms, but he was hardly aware of it.

She was as insubstantial as a wraith, and he carried her to the tub and set her gently in it. Her shift billowed around her, floating on the surface of the water for a moment before it sank.

Ferrin took one of the warm towels, folded it, and made a pillow so that she might rest her head against it. She was so limp that he was afraid she would slip under the water if he didn't hold her up. He positioned her feet against one end of the tub, wedging her in place long enough for him to retrieve the flannel and the bottle of gin.

Beads of sweat broke out on his forehead from the proximity of the fire. The task he set for himself with Cybelline was to keep her from becoming chilled while he drew the heat from her skin. He had never seen anyone with a fever who was not flushed. Her colorless complexion, the near translucency of her closed eyelids, alarmed him.

He applied the gin-soaked flannel to her forehead and added hot water from the kettle as the bath cooled. When it seemed that her chest with constricting with the effort to breathe, Ferrin leaned her forward against his arm and with his other hand tapped her back with his cupped hand, trying to loosen the phlegm when she could not cough for herself. After several attempts, and little success, he realized he needed much more in the way of cooperation from her.

Had she surrendered? he wondered. It was not what he would have anticipated from her, yet he freely acknowledged that on such a short and highly unusual acquaintance, he was in no position to assess what she might do.

"Did you love him so much," he asked aloud, "that you would follow him to his grave? When King Prasutagas died, his queen raised an army to keep what he'd meant for her to have. Did you know that when you chose to become Boudicca? Or did it mean nothing that you were queen to the Iceni people? You told me you selected her for her ruthlessness. Do you recall? It was a quality of character that you had come to admire, I thought. You cannot be ruthless and surrender so easily."

Ferrin watched her face carefully, looking for the slightest alteration in her features that would indicate she heard him. There was nothing.

"What of your child? What of Anna? She has lost one parent. Can you also leave her behind? She will never know her father unless you are there to answer her questions and tell her what sort of man he was. You cannot let his death define his character. The man who killed himself was not the man you loved. I cannot believe that and neither should your daughter."

Ferrin continued in this vein, his voice low, insistent. The last time he had used such a tone with her, his mouth had been at her ear and one of his hands had cupped her naked breast. What he had said on that occasion could not have been more different than what he was saying to her now, but he had learned that the manner in which something was said was often more important than the words themselves.

"Do you think he did not love you?" asked Ferrin. "I cannot conceive such was the case. I would argue that he loved you too well and himself too little. A man who puts a pistol to his head knows despair such as few of us experience. Have you been so despairing, then? I didn't sense that when you came to the cottage. You beat so hard against the door that the windows shook. That was not a woman who was eager to give up. That was a woman who fights. That was Boudicca."

Ferrin lifted Cybelline from the tub. Water cascaded from her sodden nightgown. Her head lolled to one side. He carried her to the bed, laid her down, then called for Webb. He was not wrong in assuming Cybelline's personal maid was close at hand. She hurried through the door from the sitting room with Mrs. Henley at her heels.

"The warm towels, please, and a fresh nightgown." He

stayed with Cybelline until the things were brought to the bed. "I will wait in the sitting room while you dry Mrs. Caldwell and change her gown. The linens will have to be changed afterward. Call for me when you are prepared to strip the bed, and I will lift her."

The women said nothing, but Ferrin felt their eyes boring into the back of his head as he exited the room. He did not know what they had expected him to do, nor could he take their expectations into account. Every decision he made, every action he took, had to be the result of his own best judgment. In the end, the responsibility—and the fault, if it should come to that—would rest squarely on his shoulders.

Ferrin sprawled on the damask-covered window bench, raising one knee toward his chest while the other stretched at an angle to the floor. He leaned back against one side of the alcove and turned his head toward the window. What he saw was naught but his own reflection in the dark glass. Looking past his own shoulder, he saw the interior of the room, the tasteful appointments, the artful and practical arrangements of the chaise and chairs and table so that conversation might be comfortably engaged when guests were invited to sit here. The sewing basket and embroidery hoop on the chaise made him think she enjoyed the room for its privacy, then his eyes fell on a cloth ball and wooden pull toy under a footstool and he thought he might know who was permitted to breach her sanctuary.

Ferrin was not given to fancies, so it surprised him when he had the sense of an abiding melancholia existing in this room. Casting about for an explanation, he settled on the fact that he was viewing the room through the darkly reflective glass. He turned his head, anticipating that he would shake the sensation of deep sadness, but not only was there no shift, the despair was edged with apprehension. Was it what he felt? he wondered. Or what he imagined Cybelline felt?

Of a sudden he felt the need for great draughts of fresh air, the colder, the better. Rising up on his knees, Ferrin threw out the window and leaned into the opening. A gust of wind beat hard against his face, and he was forced to close his eyes. He sucked in a lungful of air and held it, releasing it just as the wind took its own pause. He sat back slowly, closed the window all but a crack, and massaged his throbbing temples.

Bloody hell, but what was he doing here? He was no physician. What he knew was what he had gleaned from reading journals and medical accounts of surgeries on the battlefields and in the hospital wards, from studying anatomy and the physics of the body. He had never tried to apply that knowledge to the practice of treatment. Improving the efficiency of a pair of crutches, refining the design of a telescope, making a better compass, all of that required only that he think beyond what had already been imagined. Prompted by curiosity, blessed with cleverness, he had an imagination that had seen what could be while his hands made the vision possible.

Ferrin was uncertain that imagination had any place here or that his hands were skilled enough for healing. Still, there was something he could do. He clasped his fingers together and bowed his head. Imagination begat faith, and faith begat prayer.

Webb opened the door to the sitting room. What she observed caused her to pause on the threshold, then quietly back out of it.

"What is it?" Mrs. Henley asked. "He said to summon him when we were finished."

Webb shook her head. "In a moment." She took a handkerchief from under her sleeve and dabbed at her eyes. "Let us give him another moment. There can be no harm; only good can come of waiting."

The housekeeper frowned, but she said nothing and waited until Miss Webb gauged sufficient time had passed. Instead of opening the door without announcing herself on this occasion, the maid called out for Mr. Wellsley as she had been instructed to do. Mrs. Henley found it all rather queer, but she supposed she had a great deal to learn about quality and Londoners.

Ferrin entered the bedchamber armed with an idea he had not considered before. "When did she last eat, Webb?"

"I brought her a tray this morning before the doctor came."

"That is not what I asked. When did you last observe her eating?"

"Last night?" It was a question, not an answer. She looked at Mrs. Henley for help. "Do you recall if she ate anything on her tray? I did not stay; she wouldn't allow me to stay."

"Mrs. Minty remarked that it was untouched when Becky returned it to the kitchen."

Stricken by this news, Webb flushed and could not meet Ferrin's eyes. "Then it was as long ago as yesterday morning that she ate. I know she did not take anything in the afternoon save for tea. She told me she had her fill at breakfast."

"Then I want a cup of warm broth prepared for her. I will need bread also. It doesn't matter if it's stale. It's only to soak up the broth."

It was Mrs. Henley who nodded and left to relay the request.

Ferrin addressed Miss Webb. "Will you bring Anna here?"

"The child? Oh, no, Mr. Wellsley, I could not. And Nanny Baker will not permit it. My lady gave the strictest orders that Anna could not visit."

"Is the child sickly?"

"No. You could pluck roses from that girl's cheeks."

"Then I do not believe it is a great risk to the child, and

the benefit to her mother might be enormous. I will not keep her here long, and if it distresses her overmuch I will gladly allow her to leave."

"Will Nanny be permitted to stay? She's very protective of Anna. She doesn't allow the child out of her sight except when she's with her mother. "

Ferrin glanced toward the bed. He tried to imagine the nanny's reaction at seeing her mistress in such a state of ill health. What fears Nanny Baker might entertain would surely be the cause of more harm than help to Anna. "No," he said firmly. "She can't stay. It will be me and the child. I shall manage it well enough. I have never found children to be so very terrifying." He thought Webb might have snorted, but she did so with such delicacy that he wasn't certain.

Anna arrived before the broth did. Ferrin met her in the sitting room where she hid behind Webb's skirts while she took his measure. As he had on the occasion of their first meeting, he hunkered down and spoke to her in a voice that had always captured the attention of his youngest sisters when they were no older than she.

"Do you know the story of the sleeping princess?" he asked.

Webb felt the small fists tugging on her skirt open suddenly and release their hold. Looking down at her side, she watched Anna step boldly to the front and announce importantly that she knew the story very well. Webb backed out of the room then, certain now that Cybelline's daughter was in skilled hands.

Anna clambered onto her mother's bed, using the bed rail for a stepstool, then grabbing the quilt for purchase. Ferrin had offered her a leg up, but Anna refused him with something very much like disdain. Standing back, his hands raised in an attitude of surrender, he let her go and observed that her climbing was a practiced skill.

"Mama?" Anna inched closer to where Cybelline lay. She looked up at Ferrin. "She's sleeping princess?"

He nodded. "She's been sleeping for a very long time."

"Wake her."

"Soon. She wants to hear a story. Will you tell her one?" He sat at the foot of the bed and turned toward Anna. The child looked properly skeptical of his suggestion. "Go on. She will be able to hear you." He hoped it was true. What mother didn't know her child's voice and respond to it? Even his own mother, who rarely frequented the nursery, swore she knew the individual cries of each one of her infant children and precisely what was meant. He suspected that Cybelline was a more attentive mother to her child than Lady Gardner had been. *You only became interesting at eight,* she'd told him once, *and then it was time to send you to school.* "Shall I begin it, Miss Anna?" he asked.

"No. I do." She sidled closer to where the curve of the blankets defined her mother's waist and hip and laid her small hand on Cybelline's abdomen. "Once upon time . . ."

Ferrin remained silent while Anna wove the story. It was a rather convoluted tale as she told it, and acquired elements that were not part of the story as he remembered it, but it was charmingly, and most sincerely, related.

The broth came as Anna was arriving at the part where the troll fought the dragon. Ferrin thought it was a particularly compelling element to the story. He dismissed the maid at the door and brought the cup of broth and bread to the bedside. He encouraged Anna to continue while he sopped a bit of bread in the broth and put it to Cybelline's lips and pushed it in.

Beside him, he sensed Anna was waiting to see if her mother would spit it out. She was not alone. Ferrin touched Cybelline's throat and watched her swallow reflexively. He grinned at Anna, and she returned the smile just as if she understood the import of what had occurred.

When Anna reached the end of the story, or at least the end that satisfied her, the mug held less than a third of the broth Ferrin had been given. He deemed Cybelline had taken her fill and set the mug aside.

"Mama wake now?"

"Soon," he said. He did not expect that to satisfy Miss Anna, and he wasn't wrong. She puckered her lips and made a great smacking sound, communicating clearly what her expectations were. "A kiss?" he asked, though he knew the answer well enough.

"Wake her."

"In the morning. It is a morning kiss that wakes the princess. A kiss at night puts her to sleep." Ferrin waited to see if this logic would satisfy Anna. He thought it was inspired, but the face she pulled as she considered it made him think she was less impressed by his cleverness than he was. She surprised him when she nodded sagely and proffered her own cheek for a buss. "It's a night kiss," he reminded her. "It will put you to sleep."

She nodded. "Like Mama."

"Very well." He bent forward and kissed Anna's soft cheek. She smiled beatifically and lay down beside her mother, finding the curve of Cybelline's arm and shoulder to nest against. Ferrin expected her to close her eyes as part of the game she was playing, but he did not expect that she would keep them closed for long. In the short time it took him to remove the bread and broth tray to the sitting room and add wood to the fire, she was sleeping.

Ferrin was loath to disturb Anna by removing her from the bed so soon after she had fallen asleep. He decided she could remain there while he investigated what had become of his own belongings.

Webb responded promptly to his ring and showed Ferrin to the bedchamber he was invited to use. Ferrin thanked her for seeing to his comfort, but he didn't linger. He removed two pamphlets from the bottom of his valise, returned to Cybelline's room, and took up a chair at her bedside.

He read for the better part of an hour, then put the glass to his patient's chest again and listened to her breathing. As he expected, the rales were still present in the lower lobes of her lungs. He considered what he understood about the anatomy and how to position Cybelline to help her purge the fluid. In light of what he must do, he decided the time had come to remove the sleeping Anna.

She opened her eyes when he lifted her from the bed, then she gave him a sleepy smile and promptly snuggled in his arms. Perhaps it would have been better, he thought, if he had been more terrified of children. Had someone pressed a glass to his own heart just then, Ferrin felt certain it could be heard turning over.

Webb was happy to take Anna back to the nursery and happier still to see the child sleeping so soundly. "Nanny Baker has despaired of her sleeping through the night. Mayhap it will be different this evening. Poor thing has had such terrors that it breaks your heart to hear her cry."

In light of Ferrin's recent experience, he understood precisely what she meant. "Did Mrs. Caldwell know?"

Webb shook her head. "There was nothing she could do save feel all the worse for it. If there's blame to be meted out, then it's mine. I could not think how it would help her to know. It cost her peace of mind to keep Anna away; she feared for her so."

"I am not casting about to find fault," Ferrin said. "I cannot say what I would have done."

Webb flushed a little. "You are good to say so. It's never easy to know what the consequences will be." She hefted Anna in her arms. "I'll be back directly to sit with Mrs. Caldwell."

"That won't be necessary."

"But—"

The cast of Ferrin's features did not invite argument.

"Very well," she said grudgingly. "I'll be available if you have need of me."

"I know you will be." Ferrin waited until Webb exited the sitting room before he returned to Cybelline.

Turning her on her right side, he began the percussion on her back with his cupped hand as he had done earlier. He was rewarded this time by a weak cough. Ferrin kept up the steady beat, firm but not painful, and had success at last when Cybelline coughed hard enough to dislodge mucus into the basin he had ready for her. He repeated the treatment after turning her to the other side. This time her coughing was stronger and he collected more of the viscous fluid that made it so difficult for her to breathe.

Ferrin laid Cybelline gently on her back and tucked the blankets around her. He removed the basin, cleaned it, then took up the chair by the bed again. He started to pick up one of the pamphlets, when his eyes fell on the tray of letters on the nightstand. He had seen the post earlier, but he had tried to avoid thinking about it. Webb's words came back to him now: *She's been troubled of late. There have been dreams, you see. And letters.*

Ferrin's hand curled around the tray, and he lifted it slowly. The consequences of reading her private correspondence were enormous, regardless of whether his actions ever came to light. He would know of matters that were intended for her alone, matters that she might consider insignificant or grave, but were hers to share as she thought fit. Did he want to have knowledge that was not freely given?

He spread the letters out on the tray. There were four in all, none of them addressed by the same hand. There was a bold scrawl that he thought was probably Sheridan's and another that bore the wax seal of Lady Rivendale. The writing on the third was done by a careful hand, the letters formed with great attention to detail. He smiled, remembering how painstakingly he had made his letters when he wanted to impress his mother with his industry. This was a child's hand and the stamp matched Sheridan's. One of the scoundrels Cybelline told him about? he wondered. The fourth letter was not franked, nor was the stamp similar to the others. The address was scripted in a hand that was not quite steady, though each letter seemed to be formed as meticulously as the child's writing.

There was nothing he could learn without opening the post, and Ferrin knew he would not go so far as that. His decision had nothing to do with the possibility that what letters troubled Cybelline might not be among those on this tray, and everything to do with not allowing curiosity to overshadow his judgment.

He set the tray down, arranged the post exactly as it had been, then returned to his chair. He tipped it back on the two rear legs and rested his feet on the bed rail. The pamphlets were forgotten as he applied himself to the larger problem of earning the trust of a woman who had no single reason to give it to him and many reasons not to.

Ferrin did not recall drifting off to sleep. In one moment he had been awake, in the next, he was not. He was uncertain now what brought him suddenly back to consciousness. The chair was on all four legs again, but he didn't think it was an abrupt drop to the floor that prompted him to come to such sharp attention. He stood, rubbing the back of his neck and stepped closer to the bed.

It did not appear to him that Cybelline had moved, yet something had most definitely changed. He picked up the stub of the candle on the nightstand and held it over her. Her finely etched profile was still as pale as the lace sham it lay against, and her eyes remained closed. One arm lay outside the blankets; the other was folded under the pillow. Her lips were parted around a softly indrawn breath and—

Ferrin bent his head close to hers and listened. This

was what had woken him, he realized: the sound of her silence. The harsh, labored breaths were absent, and she drew air as sweetly as if she were sipping it.

He sat on the edge of the bed and touched her cheek with the back of his hand. His thumb brushed her ear. Did she shiver? He thought he felt the smallest tremor beneath the blankets. He held his breath, waiting.

"You work too hard," she whispered. "You have been gone an age."

Ferrin had to lean toward her to catch the hoarsely spoken words. He did not know how to respond and settled on, "I'm here now."

"Mmm. Yes, you are."

Cybelline turned and raised her head, then sought his mouth with her own.

Chapter Eight

A fortnight passed, and the memory of what she had done still embarrassed Cybelline. She did not speak of it, and neither did he. There were moments when she wished he would put aside his gentleman's manners. A rake as seasoned as the Earl of Ferrin should confront her, she thought, or treat her with less respect and make his own expectations clear. He had never done so, not once. He had been unfailingly polite, even solicitous.

But then, for reasons she could not comprehend, he was engaged in his own masquerade. He had won over her staff and made himself a comfortable and invaluable presence in her home, and no one suspected that it was Lord Ferrin who was underfoot. She remained alone in her knowledge that he was not Mr. Porter Wellsley.

Cybelline leaned her shoulder against the window and tilted her head to one side to rest it there also. The upholstered bench in her sitting room was a welcome change from the confines of her bed. In the earliest days of her recovery, Ferrin had carried her to this place. Now she could make the distance on her own and not become short of breath or overtired. At night, when she was certain everyone was sleeping, she sometimes walked the length of the house several times, moving from room to room until she reached the stairs. She was not so brave—or foolhardy—that she thought she could navigate more than a few of the steps without assistance, but that time was rapidly approaching. She could feel herself becoming stronger daily and shared her thoughts on it frequently.

The pity was, she reflected, no one paid her any heed. It was not that she was not given due attention. It was simply that what she said about her own health no longer held any sway. Webb and Mrs. Henley, even the maids who came to change the linens, listened politely and nodded their agreement occasionally, but they made no alterations to her routine or care unless it was sanctioned by Ferrin.

Maddening did not begin to describe what Cybelline thought about his lordship's behavior.

She plucked absently at some misplaced scarlet threads on the embroidery piece in her lap. When she asked for her sewing basket this afternoon, she'd hoped that some industry with her hands would better occupy her mind than reading had done. What she was coming to realize was that it did not matter what task she set for herself, other thoughts would always intrude unless they were confronted openly.

As it seemed Ferrin could not be depended upon to broach the subject that troubled her, the onerous task fell on her shoulders. That was not entirely unfair, she reminded herself, as she was the one who had behaved most precipitously. She could tell herself that she had been dreaming, that she had been sick, that turning to him had been the act of someone both desperate and disordered, but none of those excuses cleared her conscience. What must be said, had to be said to him.

Not for the first time, Cybelline wondered if she could find the resolve.

"Mama!" Anna slithered out from under the sofa, where she had squeezed herself, and rose to her knees.

"Look!" She raised her right hand to show off her prize. Her doll dangled awkwardly from her tiny fist.

Cybelline smiled. "Yes, darling. How clever you are to find it there. Come. Bring it here, and allow me to see if your poor baby is all of a piece."

Anna scrambled to her feet and rushed forward at full speed. She thrust the doll at her mother and tried to climb onto the seat beside her.

"Just a moment, Anna, while Mama makes room for you." Cybelline set aside her embroidery hoop and rearranged the blanket tucked about her legs, then she reached over and lifted her daughter onto her lap. "Oooh, are you really getting so big, or is it that I have not yet recovered my strength?"

"Might I be permitted to offer my opinion?"

Cybelline started at the sound of Ferrin's voice. Her head swiveled around, and she saw he had come to stand in the open doorway. As was often his habit, he stood with one shoulder resting on the jamb, giving the impression that he was not only at ease but also that he had been so for some time. It was this casual posture that she associated with the rakehell and not with the gentleman of manners. She felt quite certain that Mr. Wellsley, scapegrace though he was reputed to be, did not stand about in so familiar and easy a fashion as the rogue lord did.

"Misterlee! Misterlee!" In contrast to her mother's reserve, Anna welcomed Ferrin's interruption with a bright smile.

"Mis-ter Wells-ley," Cybelline enunciated. "Wells-ley."

"Wez-ley!"

Ferrin chuckled. "I think I prefer Misterlee."

"Will you join us?" Cybelline framed the question in polite accents but without enthusiasm. She wished she had not just been thinking of him. It was as if his physical intrusion went far deeper than into this room.

In a move that Cybelline could define only as traitorous,

Anna squirmed off her lap and raced to Ferrin. He scooped her up in one arm and placed her on his shoulder. Anna laughed delightedly. She begged to be put down but only so she could demand to be taken up again. Ferrin obliged several times before he called a halt, pleading exhaustion and placing a hand dramatically over his heart.

Anna accepted this without argument and returned to her mother. When Cybelline reached for her again, she was aided in the lift by Ferrin.

"Thank you," Cybelline said. She put the doll in Anna's hands and noticed that her daughter held it in the same fashion she was being held. It made her smile, this desire to practice motherhood at so early an age. She rubbed her chin against the crown of Anna's silky red-gold hair, then placed a kiss where her daughter's soft spot had been. Anna mimicked the behavior perfectly.

Observing the same thing from a slightly different perspective, Ferrin also found himself smiling, though he wasn't certain he was as comfortable with his reaction as Cybelline seemed to be with hers. He felt slightly restless and unsettled, while she appeared perfectly content.

Cybelline raised her eyes to Ferrin. "You had some opinion that you felt compelled to share, I believe." When he merely stared at her, she prompted, "Regarding my daughter's size and my strength—or lack of the same."

"Let us go on as if it's all been said," he told her. "I'm quite sure you are able to divine my thoughts on the matter."

"Indeed." Cybelline thought Ferrin might take up one of the chairs, or better still, quit the room, but he put himself at the opposite end of the window seat so that her feet were mere inches from his thigh. If she stretched her toes she would be able to touch him. To remove the temptation, she drew her knees forward and shifted Anna in the cradle of her lap. "You have come with some purpose in mind?" she asked.

Ferrin tempered his amusement. She was prickly this

afternoon. Upon consideration of all the signs that would point toward her regaining her health, he counted Cybelline's vexation with him as one of the important ones. "No purpose but to gauge your wellness this afternoon."

"I fear it is not much improved since you gauged it this morning. It occurs to me that if you were to absent yourself for a period of time, then you would be better able to note my progress."

Ferrin pretended to consider her suggestion. "When you say a period of time, you are perhaps thinking of something longer than a few hours?"

"Longer than a day, actually."

"A sennight?"

"At least a fortnight."

His dark eyebrows rose faintly. "Is distance also a consideration? You would prefer I absent myself from your home?"

"I hope you will not take offense when I say I would prefer that you absent yourself all the way to London."

Ferrin grinned openly now. "Offended? How can I be when you say it so prettily?"

She wished he would not be amused or amusing. It was completely comprehensible to her how he had managed to charm her staff. Even the redoubtable Webb was now in his thrall. The Henleys were anxious to seek his advice on matters regarding repair to the house. Mr. Kins admired his horse. The maids admired the cut of his figure. Nanny Baker was sufficiently moved by what she observed in his manner to compliment his treatment of Anna. The footmen and grooms were in awe of his athleticism. Mrs. Minty had been overheard to say that she appreciated his excellent appetite.

And Anna clearly was captivated by him.

Cybelline's own feelings were considerably more confused. "Anna, will you ring for Nanny, please? It's time for your nap." Although Anna did not generally protest going down for her nap, Cybelline thought that Ferrin's presence might tempt her to argue now. She wasn't entirely surprised when her daughter didn't move.

"She's gone down herself," Ferrin said, nodding at the little girl.

"What?" Cybelline tilted her head to one side to better see her child's face. Anna's long lashes lay still against her cheeks. "So she has."

"Shall I ring for Nanny?"

"Please."

Ferrin did as requested, then offered to take Anna from Cybelline's lap until Nanny arrived. Cybelline hesitated, then agreed because Anna's sturdy little body was pressing uncomfortably against her thigh. She was afraid that if her leg went numb, her daughter would simply slide from her lap.

"Thank you," she said, helping him take Anna up.

Ferrin merely nodded. He did not move away from Cybelline's side until Nanny Baker arrived. When she and Anna were gone, he did not return to the window seat, but took up a sentinel position to one side of the mantelpiece.

Observing his rather stiff carriage and reserved manner, Cybelline said, "I fear I have indeed offended you."

He did not deny it. "Are you saying that such was not your intent?"

"No. I mean yes, it was not my intent. I hesitated to give you Anna because I did not want to surrender her, not because I didn't want you to have her. It is not the same thing at all. The greatest hardship of my illness has been being separated from from my daughter. I find I am reluctant to turn her over, even to Nanny."

"I wondered if you were perhaps jealous of her attentions toward me."

"Of course I am," she said. "I freely admit it, but I hope I am sufficiently mature not to be mean-spirited. Anna is a flirt, Mr. Wellsley, and she must have everyone's heart. It does not follow that I do not have hers."

"Then I apologize for mistaking your motives. She has my heart, as you have already observed. It struck me as unkind that you had misgivings about me taking her."

"I have misgivings but not about that."

"Oh?"

Cybelline thought she was immune to that single raised eyebrow, having been on the receiving end of it for so many years from Sherry, so she was disappointed that Ferrin was able to put her off her stride with it. She had to take a deep breath and exhale slowly before she was able to continue. "I am prepared to speak to you of what is painfully embarrassing to me. Pray, do not make it more difficult."

Intrigued now, Ferrin stepped away from the fireplace. "It is not my wish to distress you, Mrs. Caldwell, or to provoke you to distress yourself."

"Then stay where you are. I know I would prefer it."

Ferrin obliged, hitching his hip on the arm of the sofa instead of taking a single step past it. He folded his arms across his chest and waited.

Cybelline was not eased in the least. She could not rid herself of the disquieting sense that she was being baited. "I hope you will know that I speak from the heart when I say I am so very grateful for your intervention. That you answered my maid's summons speaks well of you. You had no reason to come here save for your own sense of charity. I think you know also that the staff is grateful for what you have done for me. Indeed, for all of us."

"It has been remarked upon," he said.

"To me it certainly has. I was less sure they had said as much to you."

"Mrs. Caldwell, I am unclear if thanking me is what you find to be so painfully embarrassing, but I can assure you that I find it so. Please, have done with it."

She flushed. "Thanking you is but a first step," she said. "I do not know how else to go about the thing."

"You might put it before me plainly. I seem to be able to grasp most particulars in that fashion."

Cybelline realized she was worrying the inside of her lip and released it. Her chin came up, and she forced herself to meet his glacial blue eyes directly. "I believe you are due an apology for my untoward behavior."

Ferrin said nothing. He realized he was holding his breath and released it slowly, imperceptibly, waiting to hear what she would say next.

Now that Cybelline was healthy enough to have color in her cheeks, that color deepened to a dark rose. "I should not have tried to kiss you. In my defense, which you might well think is of no consequence, I must tell you that I was neither awake nor dreaming, but in a state which I can only describe as twilight."

"Twilight." Ferrin feared he might be entering that state himself.

"Yes. I am aware it does not satisfy as an explanation, but it is all I can offer. You were right to take offense of my actions."

"Offense?"

"I do not misremember your reaction. You were patently horrified."

"I'm afraid you do misremember. I was startled, not horrified. I hope you recall there was no kiss."

"That was because you were horrified."

"That was because your aim was not true."

Without thinking, Cybelline dropped her eyes to his mouth. The faintly amused curl of Ferrin's lips had her lifting them quickly. She could not think what to say.

"Mrs. Caldwell," Ferrin said gently, "I know better than you do how ill you were the night I was summoned. Anything you might have done—or said—is of no account, and it never has been. I wish that you would not—"

She interrupted him. "Said?" she asked. "What did I say?"

"You don't recall?"

Cybelline's fingers curled around the embroidery hoop, and she raised it in front of her as she shook her head. "I remember what I did," she said. "Or at least what I thought I did, but I have no recollection of saying anything."

He frowned slightly, wondering how much he might tell her. "You said, 'You work too hard.'" He watched Cybelline's grip on the hoop tighten until her knuckles lost their color. "And, 'You've been gone an age.'"

She nodded once. Her stomach turned over, and she thought she might be sick. She pressed the hoop against her midriff when she sensed there was still more to come. Although she did not want to know the answer, she forced herself to ask, "Is there something else?"

"I wasn't certain what I should say in response. I think I confirmed that I was here now."

Yes, she thought, that was also in her dream.

"And you agreed with me," he said.

Cybelline watched him closely and wondered if she could be satisfied it was all that passed between them. "And then I tried to kiss you." It was the smallest of hesitations, and if she had not been searching his face for it, she would have missed it. "Tell me the whole of it," she said. "What did I say before I tried to kiss you?"

"You do not want to know."

"I do," she lied. "In fact, I insist upon it."

"Very well," he said at last. The reckoning was upon them because she insisted it should be. "You thought I was someone else."

She closed her eyes a moment, then said weakly, "My husband, you mean. I called you Nicholas."

It would have been so comfortable to agree that she was in the right of things. He felt certain she would have appreciated the falsehood for a time but come to hate him for it in the end. He also had to acknowledge that it might come to that in any event.

"No," he said, holding her eyes with his own. "You said *my* name. You called me Ferrin."

She thought she might faint. Hearing him confirm her worst fear was like taking a blow. The hoop that she held so tightly against her abdomen offered no protection. It dropped from her nerveless fingers and fell to the floor. Neither one of them made any move to retrieve it.

"Cybelline?"

It was the first time she had ever heard him use her name, yet it seemed to come easily to his lips. She tried to hide her fear of this intimacy behind an icy attention to what was proper. "I've never given you leave to address me so familiarly."

"No," he said. "You have not. Shall I tell you how I addressed you in my mind before coming to Penwyckham?"

She almost put her hands over her ears. That he would taunt her for such childishness stayed her.

"You were Boudicca. Always Boudicca."

The effort not to cry made Cybelline's throat ache. The pressure at the back of her eyes was almost unbearable.

"I've known since your arrival at the cottage, Cybelline," Ferrin said quietly. "You will perhaps wish I had said so from the first. I do not know if that would have been the better way, but you also said nothing, and I know you recognized me as well. How could you not? I was merely wearing an eye patch at Wynetta's come-out, while I had to penetrate not only your golden mask but your magnificent mane of red hair as well."

Cybelline self-consciously lifted trembling fingers to touch her hair.

"I prefer what is you," he said, "though I imagine you think I have no right to say so."

A tear spilled over the lower rim of her lashes. Impatient with herself, she dashed it away. It was followed by another, then another. She turned her face toward the window. The landscape, white again after another snowfall, blurred so that the horizon disappeared. The lowering clouds lay seamlessly against distant trees.

She felt her wrist being taken, and a handkerchief was thrust into her hand. She had not heard Ferrin's approach, nor did she hear him back away. Her first indication that he had done so was when his voice came to her from his position at the sofa.

"I did not come to Penwyckham because I thought I would find Boudicca here," he said. "I thought I would find Boudicca's friend."

Cybelline pressed the handkerchief to each eye in turn, then glanced back at him. Her voice was husky with the thickening that persisted in her throat. "What do you mean?"

"Boudicca had a friend at the masque. Or so I was given to believe. Perhaps you recall that Boudicca was searching for a shepherdess with green ribbons on her crook. I learned from my mother, who had it from Lady Rivendale herself, that you were that shepherdess." Ferrin watched Cybelline ease herself around slightly. She was regaining a measure of her color. Her eyes, though, remained luminous with tears she kept at bay by sheer force of her will. "It was the spear, you see, that led me here. You left it behind."

She nodded, then said on a thread of sound, "But you promised . . ."

"I know." He thought she would say something then, but she remained silent. She seemed more resigned than angry. "I learned from my mother you were at the masque. It was only mentioned in passing, but it meant something to me because I had already heard the name Caldwell in connection to the spear. I'd shown it to a man who used to teach at Cambridge in the hope of find—"

"Sir Richard Settle."

"Yes. How do you know him?"

"He was an adviser to my husband."

"Adviser?"

"I do not know what other word applies. Mentor, perhaps. He did not consider Nicholas a colleague because my husband never made a formal study the way Sir Richard had. He was more than an acquaintance but less than a friend. It seemed to me that he was always willing to help my husband and that Nicholas was grateful for his attention and his advice."

"I did not receive the impression from Sir Richard that they were so well acquainted."

"I cannot say how Sir Richard would characterize their association. I only know how I thought of it." She bent now and picked up the hoop, putting it to one side. "I suppose Sir Richard told you the spear belonged to my husband."

"He thought it might have, yes."

"Tell me, how did you know of Sir Richard's interest in Roman and Celtic artifacts?"

"I was at Cambridge. He was one of my professors."

"Then it was not even difficult for you, was it?"

"No."

Her short laugh held no humor. She put her legs over the side of the window seat, removed the blanket, and stood, smoothing her gown as she did so. "Will you take tea with me, my lord?"

"Yes," he said. "I should like that."

Cybelline went to the table, where the service had been set out. The pot was still warm, and she poured tea for both of them. She was glad to see that her hand was steady as she passed the cup to Ferrin. "Who is Mr. Wellsley?" she asked, choosing one of the chairs to sit in. "Other than being a scapegrace, I mean."

Ferrin removed himself from the arm of the sofa and sat on one of the cushions. His smile was properly chagrined.

"Porter Wellsley is my good friend. Do you think I have sorely abused his name?"

"No. I have had it from everyone who's come to know Mr. Wellsley that he is a model of excellence."

"A paragon. Oh, I surely hope not. He no longer wants to be an incorrigible rascal, but I think he will find it a burden to be in so lofty a position as a paragon."

"You needn't worry that I will put the thing about," she said in dry accents.

He chuckled appreciatively. "No, I don't suppose that you will."

"He knows you are here, then?"

"Yes."

"And has given you carte blanche to use his name?"

"He insisted upon it, in fact."

Cybelline was curious, but when Ferrin offered no explanation, she did not ask for one. "Then he really is the grandson of the Viscountess Bellingham."

"Oh, yes. Did you doubt it?"

"Not really. I could not quite bring myself to believe that the Lowells were part of your scheme."

Ferrin took mild exception to this characterization of his presence in Penwyckham. "I have no scheme, Cybelline."

Now it was Cybelline who proffered the dramatic arch of one eyebrow.

"It's true, though I understand that you cannot credit it. I came here to make your acquaintance, discuss the spear, and learn how I might find Boudicca. As I told you, I thought you were only her friend. I had convinced myself that you must have loaned her the spear."

"Loaned it? An Iceni spear?"

"You would have me believe you could not have been persuaded to lend such a valuable article? Before you assure me that is the case, I feel I must remind you that you showed considerable carelessness for the thing by leaving it behind." He watched her jaw snap shut and knew his point had been made. "Why *did* you leave it?"

"I assure you, it was not done with purpose."

"Truly?"

"Of course it was not!"

He thought her denial perhaps too vehement, but he let it pass. If the truth were otherwise, she was most definitely not prepared to answer for it. It also occurred to him that she might not know the truth of it herself. "Very well. It was not done with purpose."

"Do you think I did not want it back?"

"I don't know. You never inquired after it."

"How could I?"

"Lady Rivendale, mayhap?"

"She did not know I took it. I left the house as a shepherdess." Cybelline noticed that he seemed to expect this answer. His mien became more contemplative, and his lips curved in a way that indicated satisfaction.

"Your aunt plays her cards very close."

"I imagine you do not mean that only in the literal sense."

"She did not give you away," he said. "But it seemed to me that she knew something was not quite as it should be when I asked her about Boudicca."

"I wish you had not involved her."

"She was a link to you, and you were the link to the spear and Boudicca."

"So you told her about them both."

"I did. I am surprised she did not write to you regarding our conversation. I invited her for an evening of dinner and card play in my home. My family was there. So was Mr. Wellsley. You have received some correspondence from her, I believe."

"Yes, but you do not know her at all well if you supposed she would inform me of what transpired that evening. I can believe it was her intention to do so, perhaps several times she even thought of it, but once she puts the pen to paper, it is what is on her mind at the moment that she will write about. Apparently, my lord, neither you nor your discourse made so lasting an impression."

"Perhaps," he said.

Cybelline could hear that he was unconvinced of this last, though modesty—or pride—forbade him from expressly saying so. "Tell me, my lord, did you describe Boudicca to her?"

Ferrin tried to recall what was said. "I believe she asked about the costume."

"And the hair?"

"Whether it was said or not is of no consequence. Everyone knows Boudicca has red hair."

"As did I that evening, and Aunt Georgia knew that very well. She saw it the following morning in spite of my attempts to conceal it from her. I can believe very easily that she has neglected to write of an evening's conversation in your home, but I will never believe she did not comprehend the import of what she heard. Lady Rivendale is no one's fool."

"Of that I have no doubt."

Cybelline nodded faintly, gratified to hear it. She sipped her tea. "It was my intention to ask her to make inquiries about Mr. Wellsley, but I never did."

"Why not?"

"As I reflected on it, it did not seem so very important. I knew who you were. It did not matter who he was."

"And I imagine you did not want to rouse her curiosity."

"That also." Cybelline regarded the biscuits on the tray and wondered if she dared eat one. Her stomach was no longer roiling, but she was uncertain if that would last long. "What are your intentions, my lord?"

"Will you not call me Ferrin?"

"No."

"Then I hope you will not give me up to your servants

by addressing me as 'my lord.' I prefer to be Mr. Wellsley while I am in Penwyckham."

"And I would prefer to be a tea cozy, but that is not what I am, is it?"

Startled, Ferrin blinked. It was a rare occurrence that he was disconcerted in conversation, and he required a moment to form a response. "I had forgotten that you are in possession of so tart a tongue."

"Some would say sharp."

"That does not surprise."

Cybelline set her teacup in the saucer and returned it to the tray. "But have I made my point?" she asked. "You can pretend all you like that you are a gentleman, but you have the manners of a lord."

"I don't believe you mean to compliment me."

"I don't. You cannot help yourself, I suppose. It is bred in the bone, or at least I have always thought so. Sherry, too, can be rather full of himself on occasion. The scoundrels have been known to call him His Nibs."

Ferrin frowned. "They are permitted to address him as such?"

Cybelline tamped down her smile at his reaction. "I would not say that it is permitted but rather that it is done on occasion. I have heard them. And Lily treads firmly upon his toes when he is getting too high in the instep. You don't approve?"

"I cannot say just yet. One wonders about the collapse of civilization."

His arid accents provoked her to laughter. "I think you are far more amused than alarmed," she said. "And *that* is a compliment."

He inclined his head slightly, communicating approval in his most toplofty fashion, then threw back his head and gave a shout of laughter. "You are quite right, of course. I am tolerant of all manner of things until I do not get my way, then I adopt the disagreeable disposition you have mentioned. I am not as certain as you that it would be any different were I only Kit Hollings rather than also the Earl of Ferrin, but I suppose that is what you mean when you say it is bred in the bone. One cannot properly separate the two."

"Then you understand me perfectly."

Ferrin only wished that were true. He did not think he understood her at all. It was still to his advantage not to point this out, as she would seize the high ground soon enough on her own.

"You have not told me your intentions," Cybelline said. "Did you think I had forgotten that I'd asked?"

"I doubt that you forget anything, but I was moved to hope it might be so."

She would not allow herself to be set off course this time, so rather than acknowledging his words, she waited him out.

Ferrin sighed. "I have not given it a great deal of thought."

"You will find it difficult to convince me that you did not come here with some specific plan in mind."

"Yes," he said. "To learn Boudicca's identity, perhaps even to learn where she lives."

"That was your purpose," Cybelline said evenly. "And it is has been accomplished, no matter that I wish it were otherwise. So what is your plan? You have said nothing of why you wanted to find Boudicca. And, pray, do not tell me it was so that you might return the spear. You suspected before you left London that the spear was the property of my late husband. You might have simply had it delivered to my home."

"I considered it. I looked to Lady Rivendale to confirm the spear was yours, and she denied it."

"You showed it to her?"

"No. I described it to her. I also described the gold bracelets and torc Boudicca wore that evening. She claimed you owned none of those items and would not have lent them to a friend if you had."

"I imagine she hardly knew what to make of your inquiries and chose to say less rather than more. Certainly she knew I was in possession of all the things you mentioned."

"I thought the same, though I could not prove it."

"Did you bring the spear with you?"

"No."

Cybelline's smile was mildly mocking. "Then you did not truly care to confirm that it was mine."

"On the contrary. I thought it too valuable to take from my London residence. According to Sir Richard, it is a museum-quality piece. I don't know its worth in terms of money, but I imagined I knew something of its value in terms of history and the sentiment that you might attach to it."

The ache behind Cybelline's eyes returned. She could not speak for the swelling in her throat. Leaning forward, she picked up her teacup and raised it to her lips. She was capable only of sipping it. A mouthful would have choked her.

"Forgive me," Ferrin said. "I have distressed you."

She shook her head and took a steadying breath. Still, her voice was thready and uneven, and she barely recognized it herself. "You demonstrated more consideration for the piece than I did. If I am distressed, then it is on account of my own disregard for it."

"I will see that it is returned to your London home."

"Thank you." Cybelline thought she might have need of the handkerchief again but managed to blink back the hot tears that threatened. She regarded him gravely, finding her bearings again. "And so I still have the same question, my lord: What were your intentions toward Boudicca?"

"It doesn't matter what they were."

"I beg to differ."

Ferrin did not force the argument; he studied her instead. He thought it unlikely that she could know how heartbreakingly lovely she was in this moment. She sat so very still, her shoulders back, her spine unyielding, and yet there was more brittleness in the posture than stamina. The muslin day dress she wore emphasized the gray in her eyes and not the blue. This afternoon, with the translucency of tears coming to the surface, her eyes had what was in common with mist rising from the Thames, not steel that had been forged in hot ovens. Her slim fingers curved around the cup she held as though she craved the warmth more than the sustenance. Her thick, honey-colored hair was loosely swept back from her forehead and tied with a ribbon at her nape. She made simplicity seem elegant and stoicism appear fragile.

"I was going to ask Boudicca to accept my protection," he said at last, matching the solemnity of Cybelline's expression. "You understand what that means, do you not?"

She nodded once. "I understand. I was not aware that you often set up a mistress."

Ferrin realized he would seldom err by depending upon her to speak plainly. "I do not, no."

"I could not determine if it was a practice of all rakes or merely a practice of yours."

"I couldn't say," he told her. "For myself, I find the complications of a mistress too often outweigh the conveniences."

Cybelline considered this. "I imagine even a mistress has expectations of fidelity. It is perhaps too much to demand of a rake."

"That has been my experience," he said wryly.

"And yet you would make this offer to Boudicca?"

"I would have made it," he said, correcting her tense from the present to the past.

"Why?"

"It seemed to me that the complications would be vastly entertaining."

"Oh."

"Indeed." Ferrin finished his tea and set his cup down. "None of it is of any consequence now."

Cybelline's eyes darted toward the open doorway, then back to Ferrin. He was regarding her with something like amusement again, as though he anticipated her saying something untoward now that she had confirmed they were quite alone. It grieved her that she would not disappoint him. "I am wondering why it is of no consequence," she said.

"I am compelled to point out that you are Sheridan's sister."

"Isn't that merely a complication?"

"But not one that is remotely diverting."

"That is where you are wrong. I would be greatly amused to see you face Sherry among the oaks at dawn."

"That is because your thirst for blood is as great as Boudicca's."

"You flatter me."

He chuckled. "I find you to be in every way a singular woman."

"Then mayhap you are not so worldly as you would have society believe. I assure you, I am most unexceptional."

While Ferrin could easily argue with this last, her first observation was uncomfortably close to the mark. He deliberately altered the course of the conversation. "I wonder if you will permit me to offer protection of a different nature?"

Surprised, and not a little wary, Cybelline was only able to give him a most reluctant nod.

"I understand there has been correspondence of late that has disturbed you," he said. Ignoring her sharp intake of air, Ferrin went on. "I would consider it a privilege if you were to take me into your confidence and allow me to offer what assistance I am able."

Cybelline's lips parted, then closed again. A muscle worked in her cheek as she clenched her teeth.

"I see my offer is not welcome."

"It is not an offer. It is interference. I will have the name of the person who shared this with you. Never mind, it can only have been Webb." As she became agitated, Cybelline's teacup rocked in the saucer. She returned it to the tray and stood. "She is under a misapprehension, and it was wrong of her to relate to you what poor observations she has made. I will take up the matter with her, and you should not concern yourself with any of it."

Ferrin knew he was on the point of being dismissed and decided there was little he could lose by making a frontal assault. "Are you being blackmailed?" he asked baldly.

Cybelline's feathered eyebrows rose halfway to her hairline. "Blackmailed? What absurd line of reasoning has led you to put that question to me?"

"Boudicca."

"I don't understand what you mean."

"Is it absurd to wonder if you have used Boudicca before to move among society? You seemed to have made a study of me prior to making my acquaintance. It is not unreasonable to suppose that you have done the same on previous occasions with other men. It appears to me that you make your selections carefully so that you might avoid the complications and enjoy the convenience. You choose a man with morals to match your own impoverished ones."

At her sides, Cybelline's fingers clenched into bloodless fists. "You go too far."

"I have not said enough," he told her, coming to his feet. "If I found you with so little difficulty, it is possible that someone else has done the same. Perhaps you left another artifact behind. Perhaps you said something that revealed yourself. I imagine you asked other men to make the same promise you asked of me, and perhaps you even put all of it into words for them. You wanted discretion, silence, and, above all, anonymity. You could not be so naive that you didn't comprehend you were asking it of men who might easily fail you on all of those counts. The very reasons you chose any of us also made you vulnerable to scandal, to blackmail"—he paused, and when he spoke again his voice had dropped to a husky pitch—"and finally to risk of harm."

Cybelline's chest had constricted, and now she could no longer draw a breath for the tightness. Her nostrils pinched as she tried to take in air. There was darkness at the periphery of her vision, and she would have welcomed fainting if it meant he would be gone when she awakened. She had the presence of mind to realize he would not be so easily moved.

"Sit down," Ferrin said.

Cybelline dropped like a stone into the chair behind her. She felt Ferrin's hand at the back of her neck, pressing her face toward her knees.

"Breathe."

Her body convulsed as she fought for breath. His hand was on her back now, moving up and down along the length of her spine, easing the unnatural tautness of the muscles between her shoulder blades. He dropped beside the chair and brought his mouth close to her ear.

"Shall I give you the breath from my body?"

Uncertain of his meaning, Cybelline turned her face toward his. Her eyes closed as his lips covered hers, and she felt him blow gently into her mouth. The intimacy of it made her liquid. She sensed he was rising to his feet but came late to the understanding that she was being lifted with him. Her body was weightless, buoyed as if in water, and her lungs were filled now so that she could not slip below the surface.

It was a kiss as she had never experienced. He indulged himself in her mouth, taking extravagant pleasure in the taste of her. He sipped her lips, running his tongue along the underside, drawing first one, then the other between his teeth and making her feel the tender bite of his mouth. He drank from her, sucking her tongue into his mouth until it twisted and thrust alongside his. He cupped her face and pressed his lips hungrily again and again to hers, and when she began to sag, he caught her at the small of her back and brought her flush to him. His feasting made her mouth swollen and sensitive, and each time he kissed her there was some exquisite nuance of sensation that she had not felt before.

She clutched the lapels of his frock coat, though there was no need for her to do so. He cradled her against him so securely that she could not have torn herself loose had she wanted to.

She did not want to.

In defiance of reason, she wanted his mouth on hers, his hands at her back, the pressure of his erection against her belly. She wanted him to be the reason she had no breath and the source of getting it back.

Her breasts swelled until they were almost painfully tender. She whimpered in frustration as much as relief when he cupped one in his hand. The fabric of her gown dulled the sensation as he ran his thumb across the nipple. It seemed to her that she would not be close enough to him until he was under her skin.

There was a roar in her ears as she was jerked off her feet and lifted hard against his chest. Eyes closed, she did not think about where he was taking her. She would have been satisfied if he'd borne her to the sofa, the window bench, or all the way to the floor. What he did, though, was press her deeply into the feather tick on her own bed.

He followed her down, the weight of him pleasantly heavy and warm against her. A white winter sun lent its light through a break in the damask drapes. A bar of sunshine slanted across her arm where she'd flung it to one side. She turned her head as he raised his and regarded the beam of light while his fingers began to draw the neckline of her gown off one shoulder. She felt her breast exposed to the cool air first, then to the wet and warm suck of his mouth.

It seemed that the bar of sunlight restrained her, and she realized she rather liked the idea that this might be true. What blame could be attached to her if she was held back and made subject to what he wanted? She did not have to be ruthless in pursuit of her own pleasure, merely willing to accept what he would do to her. And she already knew there was nothing she would not permit him to do.

She arched, exposing the long line of her neck when he rolled her nipple between his teeth and lips. She bit off a cry and tasted blood on the tip of her tongue. He raised his head and took her mouth again, nursing her lips where before he had plundered them.

She stirred under him. He made her restless and anxious with his heavy kisses and hands that would not be still. He lifted himself enough to raise one of her knees. Her gown and shift fell back to her hip before he settled himself between her legs. He laid his palm above her stocking and rubbed the back of her naked thigh all the way to the curve of her bottom. The restive impulse was upon her again, and this time she couldn't move. His thumbnail lightly scored her skin. She felt herself contract inside, closing around an emptiness that he had not yet deigned to fill.

She was breathing hard now, taking sharp, defined sips of air as his hand moved between their bodies. He cupped her mons and slipped one finger inside her. It was when he added the second that her heels dug deeply into the tick, and she arched so violently that she thought she would throw him off.

Tears stung the back of her eyelids. Her moan became a hiccup that she could not quite cut off. Blinking hard,

she stared up at him. There was passion in the darkening
centers of his eyes and the fullness of his lower lip. He
breathed deeply and his nostrils flared. She knew that he
had captured the scent of her. His features were pulled taut
by his self-imposed denial and the anticipation of release,
yet there was nothing hard or savage in his expression.
What she could not have divined was that he not only
wanted her but that he still wanted to protect her.

He was a man at war with himself.

The band of sunlight across Cybelline's forearm had
shifted and now curved around the edge of the mattress.
She lifted her arms and clasped her hands behind his
neck. With the application of very little pressure she bent
his head toward her until their mouths touched, then she
kissed him.

Her body contracted again. Her arms. Her knees. The
muscles of her thighs. And finally, more intimately, she
tightened around his fingers. His soft groan was torn
from him, rising up from the back of his throat so that it
rumbled against her lips. She felt him release her, raise
her gown and shift, then he opened his breeches. She
made no protest as he positioned her as he wanted, pressing back her knees and palming her bottom. Her fingers
curled in the sheet under her.

Cybelline accepted the thrust of his body. More than
that, she pushed back, taking him as deeply as she could.
If he had meant there only to be passion, she was the one
who meant for it to be something more. A thread of vio-
lence wound around each caress, every kiss, and what
might have been lovemaking became vaguely cruel and
punishing.

It satisfied Cybelline to be taken in anger, to have the
stamp of his mouth on her neck and at her breasts, to
have the faint bruising between her thighs, and the taste
of her own blood on her tongue.

He made certain there was pleasure for her, and this

was something else she allowed him to do. It would be her most profoundly felt shame that he could make her know pleasure, and she would wear it like a hair shirt.

He stroked her long and slowly and deeply, and she knew he was gauging her every expression, the movements she could not help and the small sounds she could not hold back.

He did not try to keep her from crying out as she climaxed, rather he stopped her from pressing her fist to her mouth. She surrendered her pleasure to him, and, closing her eyes, she shuddered hard and was still riding the crest as he came.

Chapter Nine

Cybelline pushed at the hem of her gown as Ferrin rolled to one side. He attended to righting his own clothes while she tugged at her neckline to cover her breasts. She was relieved when she felt him rise from the bed, but wary when he merely stood beside it.

When he finally spoke it was with quiet intensity. "Do you despise yourself so much, then?"

Cybelline avoided meeting his gaze. "You cannot imagine."

There was a significant pause before Ferrin answered. "Do not be so certain."

Now Cybelline's eyes darted to his, and what she saw was a look of such ineffable sadness and pain that she turned from it immediately. "Go," she said, laying her forearm across her eyes. The weight of her arm eased the throbbing in her head. "Please go."

Ferrin stood over the bed a moment longer. Nothing in his expression changed. "As you wish."

Cybelline did not know the fullness to which he would take her meaning. She learned when supper was brought to her that he was preparing to quit the Sharpe house.

According to Webb, no one among the staff was pleased to learn of it.

"You could not expect he would stay here forever," Cybelline said. She dutifully uncovered the tray that was delivered to the sitting room, though she had no idea whether she could find appetite enough for Mrs. Minty's roast beef and boiled potatoes. "You can see for yourself that I am well enough. There is no reason that Mr. Wellsley must hover any longer."

Webb shrugged. "I see that you want to be well enough."

Cybelline broke off a piece of bread and dabbed at the gravy on her plate. "What do you mean by that? You seem to believe I am happy to see the last of him."

Webb picked up the blanket that was on the window bench and began to fold it. "Am I mistaken in thinking that's not the way of it?"

"He knows very well that I am grateful for his assistance."

Pausing as she folded, Webb merely regarded her mistress with a knowing mien. She did not have to point out that Cybelline's response was no answer to her question.

"It is not right that Mr. Wellsley should live in my pockets," Cybelline said. She picked up her knife and fork and began to cut her meat. "He must have other things to occupy him."

"He does." Webb lifted the lid on the window bench and placed the blanket inside. "I never knew a gentleman could have so much to occupy his time."

Cybelline told herself that she did not want to know. She managed to get a slice of roast beef all the way to her lips before she gave in to her curiosity. "How so?"

Webb busied herself straightening the drapes at the window. "He's always reading, except that when he's not, he's got this odd look in his eyes, like he's thinking about what he's read, and when he's not got that look, it's because he's making sketches or writing or fiddling with one thing or another. He showed Mr. Kins where to set extra springs on the carriage, and that was because he'd overheard Kins mention to Henley that there'd been a dangerous sway the last time he'd taken it out. That was only this morning."

Stepping back from the drapes, Webb looked them over and nodded, satisfied with her efforts. "I don't think a day's gone by that he hasn't done a bit of tinkering in his workroom."

Cybelline cheeked the potatoes in her mouth so she could speak around them. "He has a workroom?"

"Oh, aye. It's not much, mind you, and was no trouble at all to do for him. Henley set it up in the old wine cellar. Dragged in a chair and table and gave him what tools he asked for. It seemed to suit Mr. Wellsley well enough, leastwise he never indicated it didn't."

"He spent a lot of time there?"

Webb crossed the room to the fireplace and selected the poker. "Better than a fair amount, some would say. Henley told us Mr. Wellsley tinkered in there more than a few evenings long after midnight."

"But what does he do?"

"Can't say exactly. He's closed-mouthed, is Mr. Wellsley." Webb turned thoughtful. "Though I don't think he's building a telescope."

Frowning, Cybelline set down her fork. "What would make you think he was building a telescope? Or rather make you think he's not building one?" Frustrated with her own inability to say what she meant, Cybelline came close to throwing up her hands. "For heaven's sake, Webb, what has a telescope to do with anything?"

Smiling to herself, Webb gave her full attention to the fire. She poked at the logs, rolling one to the back and bringing another forward. "I don't suppose the telescope is of any account since he's not making one, but he has, you know, made one, I mean. He made a present of it to his father."

Cybelline sat back in her chair. It was not Mr. Wellsley whom Webb was really talking about, she reminded herself, but Ferrin. Wellsley had no contact with his father. On this occasion Ferrin had been telling Webb something about himself, not his friend.

"And he made his own compass," Webb went on. "Mr. Henley told me that. Then there's Henley's new sticks, but you know about them. I've heard talk about building a bridge."

"A bridge," Cybelline said a little weakly. "What manner of bridge?"

"One wide enough for a carriage to cross the brook between here and the Pembroke property. It seems there used to be one years ago. Might be that there will be again. Of course it could be that it's only talk." She turned and regarded the supper tray. "Will you not eat more? You can't hope to be fit if you don't eat. Mr. Wellsley's been particular about that, and I agree with him."

"Does the man have any opinion that he keeps to himself? I thought you said he is closemouthed."

"Not concerning your recovery and good health," Webb said. "As to anything else, I couldn't say, though I believe Mr. Wellsley is a deep one."

If Webb had not been watching her so closely, Cybelline's lip would have curled derisively. She sat up and lifted her fork again, spearing a piece of meat with particular relish. "Did he never leave here and go to the village?"

"Not that I recall. He never went back to the cottage, either. What Mr. Lowell didn't bring right off came in drips and drabs over the fortnight."

"Then he had all his possessions here."

"Seems as though he must have. Some things arrived for him at the cottage from London, and Mr. Lowell brought them here as well. Books mostly, from what I could tell. Some instruments, too, though I couldn't say what purpose they serve. Couldn't even properly describe them to you as I've only heard the maids comment about them after they've tidied up the workroom. Oh, he did make a bit of a fuss about that. One of them tossed a piece of glass he still had use for. Mrs. Henley cautioned the maids not to go in there again, and as far as I know, no one has."

A faint crease appeared between Cybelline's brows. Her head ached and there was a peculiar pressure behind her eyes again. She felt as if she might want to cry, though she could not have named the reason this was so. "He does not impress as a scapegrace," she said, giving voice to her confusion. "Do you think he does?"

"No. Oh, no. I would not say he is that. I have to believe we have mistaken his reputation, else someone has been severe in their judgment of his character."

Cybelline nodded slowly. "Then you also observed nothing in his character to determine that he is a rake."

"Mr. Wellsley? A rake?" Webb chuckled. "Goodness, no. What a notion."

"Yes," Cybelline said with rather more calm than she felt. "It is."

Webb returned the poker to its stand. "Has Lady Rivendale indicated he is such?" She hurried to add, "If I might be so free as to inquire."

"I have said nothing to Aunt Georgia about Mr. Wellsley, so she has no reason to mention him." She glanced sharply at Webb. "You have not taken it upon yourself to write her, I hope."

"No! Not after giving you my word I would not. And I would have had no cause to mention Mr. Wellsley."

"I am sorry, Webb," Cybelline said rather stiffly, "but you did tell Mr. Wellsley about the letters, and I did not think you would do that."

"The letters? Did I?" Webb cast her mind back, trying to recall. "I may have. I suppose I did if he says I did."

"He didn't say it was you, but I cannot imagine that it was anyone else. No one else knew I was distressed by them, and that is how he put it to me, that he was aware of some correspondence of late that had disturbed me. Even when I try to have secrets from you, Webb, you see more than you let on. How long have you known?"

Webb set her shoulders firmly and tried not to fidget under her mistress's cool study. "For months now."

"Before we left London?"

"Yes. Months before."

Cybelline's short laugh was humorless. She set her fork down and pushed the tray back. "You said nothing at all about it. Have you told anyone besides Mr. Wellsley? Lady Rivendale, perhaps?"

"No. No, I never said as much to her."

"And not a word to my brother?"

"I've never exchanged more than a half dozen words with his lordship."

"And nothing to his wife?"

"Nothing. I swear it."

Cybelline nodded, believing her. "Have you read the letters, Webb?"

"No."

"I have them all, you know."

"I didn't know."

"Would you like to see them?"

"No, I'm sure I wouldn't."

"No," Cybelline said with something like resignation in her tone. She spoke more to herself than to her maid. "I'm sure you wouldn't, either."

Webb glanced toward the doorway.

Cybelline understood the nature of that glance. Webb wanted to be dismissed but would not ask it for herself. "In a moment, Webb. I'll release you in a moment, and you'll be free to make your farewell to Mr. Wellsley with the rest of the staff. Tell me first, though, if there was any other bit of intelligence that you decided he should know." When her maid looked longingly at the doorway again, Cybelline divined the answer. "Out with it, Webb. There are times I can comprehend your thoughts as well as you comprehend mine. What did you say to him?"

Webb bit the inside of her cheek. "You were very ill," she said in her defense. "And it seemed that what I knew that troubled you could be of import."

"That is your reasoning, but it does not tell me what particulars you related to Wellsley."

"It was only the one other particular. Truly. I mentioned the letters ever so briefly, and then I told him . . ." Her voice trailed off, and she swallowed hard.

"Yes?"

"I told him how you were troubled by dreams."

Cybelline actually felt the color leave her face. Still, she kept her voice steady. "You can know even less about my dreams than about the letters, Webb. What could you have possibly said to him?"

"That you weep at night. That's all, I swear it. Oh, and that I heard a word here and there when you were speaking to her ladyship, and I thought it might be about the dreams."

Cybelline was sufficiently provoked to snap, "Bloody hell, Webb, did the man have a pistol to your head?"

The words hung there in a room that was quite suddenly silent. Webb was clearly shaken, but no more than Cybelline. They shared equally anguished glances, then looked away. Webb pleated her apron with nervous fingers while Cybelline closed her eyes and massaged one of her throbbing temples.

"You can go, Webb," Cybelline said at length. "We will not speak of it again. It's done."

"Yes, ma'am." Webb only narrowly managed to choke out her agreement before fleeing the room.

For a time, Cybelline did not move. She rested her head against her hand and remained that way with her eyes closed and her heart thrumming. Simply because Ferrin knew she wept at night, it did not follow that he knew her dreams. If he gave any thought at all to their content, it was more likely that he supposed she dreamed of Nicholas. It was true, in its way, yet also infinitely more complicated. Neither did Webb know the whole of it. If she had not overheard some part of the discussion with Lady Rivendale, then Webb might have suspected nothing save that Cybelline wept for the loss of her husband. This was also true, and neither was it all she wept for.

Cybelline wondered why she ever supposed she could manage to have secrets from Webb. It was not a thing that could be done successfully. No one knew her better. On the other hand, it shouldn't have mattered what Webb discovered, because discretion and her position dictated that nothing would ever be said. Webb had violated her trust, and she knew it.

Cybelline would not dismiss her, but she might entertain Webb's resignation if it were tendered. She hoped it would not come to that, though she knew to whom she would assign responsibility. Not by any measure was Ferrin blameless. Cybelline could well imagine that he had bullied Webb into telling him what she knew. If he took exception to being named a bully, then at the very least he had used his lord's high-handed manner on her poor maid and arrived at the same end.

Rising from her chair, Cybelline closed the door to the sitting room to secure her privacy before she went to the window bench and knelt in front of it. She lifted the lid and removed the blankets. At the bottom she found the black enameled puzzle box she'd put there upon her arrival at the Sharpe house. It was one of her first items of business, to find a place for the box she'd carried from London. Someone would have to be searching specifically for it to find it, as all of the blankets stored in the chest would never be used. The discoverer of the box might well suppose it held jewelry or coins or bank notes, but that was not the nature of the contents.

The box held only letters.

His letters: Nicholas's correspondence to his mistress.

Her letters: the ones that came anonymously to Cybelline and accused her of murder.

Cybelline turned the box over and carefully slid the cross-hatching of wooden pieces in the exact sequence and pattern that would open the box. The lid was merely for show. The Chinese box, a wedding gift from Nicholas, opened only on one side, and to accomplish that, one had to know how to manipulate the intricate inlay of pieces on the bottom. She smiled now, remembering how surprised he'd been by her determination to do the thing for herself. He'd wanted to offer her hints, but she had given him that certain glance that warned him not to interfere in her attempts to solve the puzzle. Did he mean to deny her the joy of accomplishment? she'd asked him. Nicholas had grinned at her then, understanding perfectly.

Didn't that mean he loved her? She'd thought so at the time. It seemed to her that to be so clearly in agreement must be one of the more critical aspects of love.

He'd also said he loved her. He'd said it often, in fact. She had never considered that he might have been trying to convince himself. Looking back, she didn't think she needed to hear it as often as he needed to say it, but she hadn't known enough to question it then.

If not for the letters, she might never have doubted his sincerity. Even Nicholas's suicide did not make her leap to the conclusion that he hadn't loved her. She'd been too numb to consider any thoughts save that he had abandoned her; later she'd been too angry. Grief had come in time. In the beginning it was for him, but with the arrival of the first letter, she had also grieved for herself.

Turning, Cybelline sat on the floor and rested her back against the bench. She opened the box's side panel and shook it so the contents spilled onto her lap. She'd hoped that her coming to Penwyckham would make the letters stop. The box had little room left in it when she left London, and now it had even less. There had been two more missives since her arrival. Just as in London, they did not come in the same post, but they were addressed to her in the same careful, unsteady hand. One of them held Nicholas's composition inside; the other held the accusation.

As soon as she received the first, she knew she could expect to receive the second. The Sharpe house had not proved to be the sanctuary she was seeking. She had escaped nothing by coming here, neither the letters nor Ferrin.

Quelling this last thought, Cybelline chose one of the missives. It was not entirely a random selection. She could tell by the relative thickness of one to the other which were those penned by her husband and which held only the few words of his mistress.

14 August 1813

My dearest,

    You cannot conceive how it pained me to take my leave so abruptly. I felt as if more should have been said between us, certainly I had more to say. You were angry, though with good cause, and I hold myself responsible for provoking you to that most agitated state.

I wish that you might find some measure of happiness for me, or if that is too presumptuous, then that you might yet forgive me. We have always known that our lives must take mostly a parallel course. Mayhap I am selfish to think that occasionally our paths will cross and that when they do, you will make room for me in your heart and in your bed.

It is a great burden to me that you grieve so. I wish also that you would find another protector, though I do not know that I would bear it half so well as you if I discovered you came to love him as you have always loved me.

My wife (I know you will think me without regard for you for writing of her now) makes my life less difficult in ways I have only begun to comprehend. She has joy of small things that I often fail to notice, though I endeavor to attend more to them, as it gives her pleasure. To whatever degree you hold me in contempt, you must not allow it to touch her. She is an innocent whom I have sorely abused, but selfishly, I am glad of her presence in my life, as I cannot always be in yours.

Always

Cybelline folded her husband's letter carefully. He never put his name to paper. *Always* was his signature. He often closed notes to her in the same manner, though nothing in the content was as intimate or heartfelt.

My dear Mrs. Caldwell,

I will be late this evening. The trial begins tomorrow and I must prepare.

Always

And:

My dear Mrs. Caldwell,

I must beg off from attending you at Lady Hendershot's this evening. I trust your brother will offer his escort when he understands I am on the Crown's business.

Always

Not *My dearest*. Not for her. *My dear Mrs. Caldwell*. And the same signature. She'd teased him about them. Always excuses, she'd called them, and he'd laughed and made it up to her by presenting her with the golden torc he'd discovered on his last trip to Norfolk. If she found joy in small things, she also appreciated the extravagant gesture.

Nicholas made her happy in so many ways, she'd told

herself it was of little consequence that their marriage
bed felt so oddly empty even when he was there. In some
ways she was grateful to his anonymous mistress for
helping her understand why that was. It did not absolve
Cybelline of guilt that she had not been able to please her
husband, but it did offer an explanation as to why he had
not been able to please her.

She tapped one corner of the letter against her chin. He
had written it a little more than a year after they were married. She had one other in her possession that was penned
earlier, but she no longer doubted that there were more.
She imagined how she would feel when she received one
that was written even before their marriage. She could only
believe that such a letter existed. Nicholas was conscien-
tious. He would have told his mistress, and he would have
done so in person first, then poured all of his soul into his
writing.

Cybelline dropped the letter into the box and chose another. This one was from the mistress.

My dear Mrs. Caldwell,

We both know you killed him.

Always

More obscene than the message itself was the way
Nicholas's mistress used his salutation and closing. To
Cybelline it meant that Nicholas had shared the always
excuses he'd penned to the woman he married with the
woman he loved. She had bled a little the first time she'd
realized it. That wound had never healed.

Cybelline chose another.

My dear Mrs. Caldwell,

When will you tell your daughter that you murdered her father?

Always

This one Cybelline closed quickly and pushed back into the box. She gathered a few more and thrust them inside as well. She knew she was punishing herself by taking them out at all. It hadn't been enough that she'd been a whore for Ferrin this afternoon, now she must needs do this as well.

Her hands trembled. She finally stilled them by making a single fist and pressing it against her midriff. She realized she had been right to eat only a little of her supper, because what remained in her stomach was turning over. It passed in time, just as it always did, though she often thought it would be better if she could be sick.

She slowly picked up the remainder of the letters and replaced them in the box. As always before she put it away, she wondered if she should destroy it. The fire blazed hotly thanks to Webb's care. The Chinese puzzle box would burn quickly, and the letters would be reduced to ash. She had imagined doing it any number of times, yet this occasion ended no differently than the others. She put the box away, returned the blankets to the chest, and closed the lid.

If the Sharpe house could offer no sanctuary, where would she go now?

* * *

Most of Christmas Day was celebrated quietly. Cybelline had hoped to entertain the villagers in her home with food and drink, music, and dancing. Now that she was in residence and occupied the largest home in or around the village, such entertainments were as much her duty as her privilege. Until she became bedfast, she had been looking forward to it.

Mrs. Henley called upon Mrs. Meeder to spread the word that there would be no festivities at the Sharpe house. It was a disappointment, Mrs. Meeder told the housekeeper, but not unexpected, as everyone in Penwyckham knew Mrs. Caldwell had been gravely ill. She also reported that there was favorable talk in the village regarding the very fine gentleman Mr. Wellsley. Everyone seemed to know that he had been the model of charity in lending his most excellent assistance to Mrs. Caldwell's full recovery. Upon hearing this from her housekeeper, Cybelline had to chuckle. Her survival had guaranteed that poor Mr. Wellsley's reputation once again would come under some scrutiny. He was making the ascension from paragon to near deity.

Cybelline had prepared small boxes for her staff with money and treats, but it was Ferrin who arrived that evening—without invitation—to pass out the real treasures. She couldn't turn him away, not at Christmas, and when she saw Anna's radiant smile, she knew she would not turn him away on any other day.

Her own welcome was considerably cooler, though polite. She stood when he entered the drawing room and offered the greetings of the season. Ferrin replied in tones that were just as cool and impersonal, and he saved his warmth for Anna.

Watching him, Cybelline was struck again by how very handsome he was. He moved easily, always with purpose and no wasted motion. His eyes were constantly assessing, watchful to a degree that could make one feel either discomfort or attended to. He listened with his entire body and demonstrated more than courteous interest. He leaned forward and engaged the speaker with his direct gaze and the thoughtful tilt of his head. Those eyes, wintry blue and reflective at times, could also be deep pools of light that beckoned one closer. His chin was strong, his features cut with the same broad strokes as his pirate—or privateer—forebears. His smile was a trifle lopsided, which lent it equally well to amusement or scorn.

It was amused now, she saw, as he scolded Anna for trying to reach into his pockets and retrieve the gift he'd promised her. "It's not here," he said. "I left it outside." Over the top of Anna's head he mouthed the word "puppy."

Cybelline was prepared to deliver a scold herself, then stopped and surrendered to what was surely inevitable. She nodded and waited almost as impatiently as Anna for Ferrin to retrieve the present. Anna's squeals brought several servants to the edge of the drawing room, and Cybelline invited them in.

The puppy, a small, black terrier bitch, was a wriggler. She squirmed mightily trying to evade Anna's grasping hands and even made a few attempts at nipping, but Anna was more tenacious, and she managed to capture the dog and hold it to her chest like one of her dolls.

Cybelline watched the proceedings with some trepidation. She noticed that Ferrin, too, appeared ready to lend a hand if Anna could not quiet the puppy. In the end, there was much mutual nuzzling, and Anna made another conquest.

"What will you name it, darling?" asked Cybelline.

Anna looked at Ferrin. Clearly, she had not considered this. "No name?"

Ferrin shook his head. "I have left the naming to you. She's a girl, though, so you should consider that when you christen her."

Anna glanced around the room, looking for inspiration. She found it when her eyes alighted on the greenery strung along the mantelpiece. "Holly," she announced. "Name is Holly."

"That is an excellent name," Cybelline said. To Ferrin and the others she said, "Tomorrow it is likely to be something else. If it is still her name in three days, it will be Holly always."

There was general agreement that this was so, and those present took delight in Anna's fascination with her pet. When Holly tired of Anna's attention and wriggled her way behind the drinks cabinet, Anna crawled onto her mother's lap and offered her own belly for rubbing. Laughing, Cybelline obliged, then agreed to Ferrin's request to assemble all the staff in the drawing room so that he might distribute his presents. Mr. Henley was dispatched to bring them all forward.

Cybelline owned that she was as curious as anyone when Ferrin stepped outside again to retrieve the gifts. He carried in a large burlap sack and set it on the floor beside Cybelline. She was relieved to see that nothing inside it appeared to be moving. One animal inside the house was all she was prepared to accept.

The first drawstring pouch that he pulled out of the bag was for Mrs. Henley. The housekeeper marveled at finding a small magnifying glass inside. It was attached to a blue silk cord, and she held it up for the assembly to see. "So you can wear it around your neck," Ferrin explained, "and have it close at hand when you want to read your Bible."

There was a pair of sharpened shears for Webb's sewing basket and a compass for Mr. Henley. The maids received combs for their hair that were admired for the clip that kept them securely in place. Mr. Kins was the recipient of a lantern that Ferrin promised would extinguish itself if it tipped on its side. "So you won't worry that one of your animals will kick it over and start a fire." Ferrin had others exactly like it for the stable lads. The footman received a grooming kit with a razor like the one he'd admired in Ferrin's possession.

"You can split a hair with it," the footman announced, prepared to pluck one from his head to demonstrate until Ferrin stayed his hand. Sheepishly, he added, "But it takes a remarkably unsteady hand to nick a throat."

Nanny Baker showed more animation than was her usual mein as she thanked Ferrin for the unique metal bookmarks he'd given her, and Mrs. Minty declared herself the most fortunate of women to receive a box of recipes, every one of them translated from their original French into the King's English.

There were gifts for those who worked at the Sharpe house but who were in Penwyckham with their families, and finally there was one last present, and it was meant for Cybelline.

She was embarrassed to accept it, but Ferrin insisted. With so many looking on, she would have seemed churlish to refuse. The drawstring bag she opened had a match and striker inside it. She held it up, a question in her eyes.

"Come," he said. "Everyone, get your coats and hats and come outside. Mr. Lowell will have made everything ready by now."

Cybelline was startled to realize that poor Mr. Lowell had been out of doors so long, but when she saw him he tipped his hat and gave her a nod, which taken together was the warmest of greetings. Hefting Anna in her arms, Cybelline came to stand on the lip of the small porch and waited for Ferrin's instruction. He asked for the match and striker back, then went to join Mr. Lowell in the center of the curved drive.

The servants spilled off the porch but didn't go far. A murmur went through their tightly huddled group as everyone speculated on what Mr. Wellsley had planned. Cybelline didn't participate in the conjecture. She felt so very young of a sudden, full of anticipation and almost giddy with hope. She gave Anna a squeeze and endeavored to demonstrate more patience for the proceedings than her squirming daughter did.

The thin blanket of snow and a half moon provided enough contrast and light for Cybelline to see Ferrin hunker down and strike the match. She glimpsed a dark, slender cylinder half as long as his forearm poking out of the ground. Ferrin set the fire at his fingertips to it, then stood back.

"Oh, Anna," Cybelline whispered, "what a treat we shall have tonight."

The Roman candle whistled as it rose in the air. Like everyone watching, Cybelline tipped her head back to try to make out the arc of its ascent. She held her breath in expectation of what it would bring before the fall.

Its explosion rained stars above her head. They sparkled and shimmered, dancing gracefully as they dropped from the sky. Before they were quite gone, another shrill whistle cut the awed silence all around her. This time the stars were bright green, lighter and more brilliant than emeralds. They spun end over end in their descent to the ground.

Cybelline smiled at her daughter's *oooh* of appreciation and raised her own voice in a like fashion when the next firework was released. Ruby stars burst forth like the petals of a rose after a nourishing rain. Pinwheels of light spun with dizzying speed in their race to make it back to Earth before they burned themselves out.

Pyrotechnic displays by their very nature were ephemeral, but Cybelline knew this one would remain with her long after the last spark was extinguished. She would be able to recall the crispness of the evening air, the pungent scents of fresh pine and acrid smoke, the precise pitch of the whistling fireworks and Anna's squeals, the radiance and clarity of the light. This was a memory to be treasured, she thought, one that she might bring to mind when darkness threatened her vision and her future.

When it was over and the applause finally ended, Cybelline remained behind on the porch, giving Anna to Nanny to carry inside. She waited until all the servants had filed into the house before she stepped down and crossed the drive to where Ferrin and Mr. Lowell were collecting the detritus of the fireworks.

"We'll be taking our leave shortly," Ferrin said as Mr. Lowell conscientiously moved out of hearing range.

Cybelline nodded. It was on the tip of her tongue to invite him in for warm cider and mince tarts, but she stayed the urge and merely thanked him instead. She wished that she could infuse her voice with just a small measure of the intensity of her feelings, but even to her own ears her delivery was stiff and perfunctory.

"You're welcome," Ferrin said.

"Anna has never seen fireworks before." If she could not speak for herself, Cybelline thought, then perhaps she could speak for her daughter. "She was properly awed."

"It was a success, then."

Ferrin's laconic response did not seem to be in want of a reply, so Cybelline only nodded in agreement.

"You should go back inside," Ferrin said. "It is too cold for you to linger."

She acknowledged this, but she didn't move away. "I thought you would return to London for Christmas. Your family must miss you."

"I suspect that's so."

"Perhaps by the new year . . ." Uncertain if she intended a question or a comment, Cybelline's voice simply trailed off.

"Perhaps."

She felt unaccountably sad of a sudden. Tears threatened, and she was grateful for the chill that seemed to press them back. "Then . . ." She paused, wondering what she might say if she could not say it with proper feeling.

"Then in the event I do not see you again, I wish you a safe journey."

"Thank you."

Cybelline pressed her lips together, nodded once, and turned to leave.

"Mrs. Caldwell?"

She stopped and glanced back at him. "Yes?"

"I arranged for the spear to be returned to your home in London. I wanted you to know that it had been done."

Unable to find the words because she scarcely knew how she felt, Cybelline nodded again, jerkily this time, then hurried off in the direction of the house.

Lady Rivendale's correspondence that detailed her evening at Lord Ferrin's card table finally arrived the day following Penwyckham's new year celebration. Cybelline smiled as she read her aunt's account. There was a great deal more said about her skillful card play that night than was mentioned about the tenor of the conversation.

The countess did, however, provide some interesting descriptions of her companions at the table. Mr. Porter Wellsley—and Lady Rivendale confirmed his relation to her friend the Viscountess Bellingham—had a perfectly agreeable countenance and was possessed of a cordial manner and even temperament. His card play, though, was unexceptional, and it had fallen to the countess to make their bids.

Mr. Restell Gardner was handsome beyond what was good for a gentleman of his means and manner, her aunt wrote, but he was in every way an amusing companion. His competitive nature made him an excellent foil at whist, and she thought she enjoyed playing more because he was her opponent rather than her partner.

Lady Rivendale saved her observations about Lord Ferrin for last:

He is not what he seems to be, though I have never been able to ascertain whether that favors him or presents a liability. You will know yourself from attending his stepsister's masquerade that he is a most gracious and congenial host. I find him to be as unfailingly considerate of his guests as he is of his family. I imagine you have heard that he is a great favorite with young ladies and their mamas. (This is understandable when one takes into account the perfectly vulgar amount I have heard in regard to his income, though one cannot help but notice he is almost as handsomely favored as his stepbrother Mr. Gardner.) Ferrin has a fearsome intellect, I have observed, *and is excellent at cards whether he is one's partner or opponent. I had the greatest pleasure fencing with him, as he put me in mind of your dear brother.*

Imagining the conversational thrusts and parries that had taken place that night, Cybelline's amusement surfaced. She suspected there had been enough bloodletting that even Dr. Epping would have approved.

As Cybelline read on, she came at last to her aunt's recounting of Ferrin's questions about Boudicca. Lady Rivendale made no accusations or posed any questions of her own in the correspondence, but it was clear to Cybelline that no point had been missed. Her aunt knew quite well that she had attended the masque not as a shepherdess but as Boudicca.

It appears to me, my dearest Cybelline, that your friend has been successful in securing the interest of a most curious gentleman. It stretches the imagination to suppose he will not wish to seek her out. It has occurred—most belatedly from your perspective, I am sure—that I have been remiss in bringing this to your attention. You will forgive me, of course, as I forgive you for certain peculiar lapses in your own memory.

Cybelline was gratified that no one was present to observe the flush that colored her cheeks. Lady Rivendale's rebuke was rather gentle, but there was no mistake that it was meant to upbraid her for being much less than forthcoming regarding the masquerade.

Knowing the reproach was well deserved, Cybelline could do naught but sigh in acceptance. She regarded her aunt's expansive closing and signature with fondness, then her eyes dropped to the postscript.

If it should come to your attention (but only by a most reliable source) that Mr. Wellsley and Miss Wynetta Gardner mean to become affianced, you will inform me. I have placed a discreet wager to that end and hope to collect a perfectly vulgar sum myself for my prescience.

Cybelline laughed loud enough at this last to attract the attention of her daughter, who was playing with Holly in the bedchamber. Anna came running into the sitting room, the terrier at her heels, and launched herself like a Roman candle at the window bench were Cybelline was sitting.

"Are you being good to Holly?"

Anna nodded, though she swung her stockinged feet up quickly so Holly could not nip at her toes.

Cybelline set her letter aside and pulled Anna onto her lap. Holly ran back and forth in front of the bench, leaping at intervals as she tried to reach the seat. "I think Holly wants one of these piggies," she said, tugging on Anna's littlest toe. "The one that goes wee, wee, wee—"

"All the way home!"

Anna's giggle never failed to lift Cybelline's spirits. She glanced out the window. The sky was cloudless, and the winter sun seemed warm as it pressed its light through the glass. Cybelline estimated several hours of daylight remained. That presented sufficient opportunity for what she wanted to do. She bent her head and whispered against the perfectly shaped pink shell of her daughter's ear. "How would you like to go with Mama to visit Misterlee?"

Ferrin carefully trimmed the end of the wire he was holding and threaded it into the bottom of a glass cylinder. He was on the point of affixing the wire when he heard the snuffling of a horse at the front of the cottage. Sighing, he set aside his work on the table and prepared to give Mrs. Lowell his most polar look when she stomped her way through the front door, then he would have a word with Mr. Lowell.

Mrs. Lowell had assured him she would be gone for all of the afternoon visiting her married daughter in Bell's

Folly. Mr. Lowell had indicated that he would see that she stayed away much longer, using physical force if it should come to that. At least that was Ferrin's conclusion, though he freely admitted he had not yet mastered the shades of meaning attached to Mr. Lowell's various grunts.

Prepared as he was for Mrs. Lowell's entrance, a crease appeared between his eyebrows when he was greeted by a knock instead. He pushed back his chair from the table and rose to open the door.

Cybelline stood on the path directly in front of the cottage with Anna in her arms. Her mount was tethered to a sapling. "Have we come at a poor time?"

"What?" Ferrin shook his head and wondered if he looked as unsettled as he felt. A lock of dark hair fell forward over his brow, and he raked it back somewhat apprehensively. "No. Oh, no. It is just unexpected, that is all." He stepped aside. "Please, won't you come in?"

As Cybelline started across the threshold, Anna extended her arms to Ferrin. He looked to Cybelline for permission to take her daughter.

"She will be devastated if you do not put her upon your shoulders, my lord." She realized only when Ferrin darted a look from her to Anna that she had misspoken. "I mean, Mr. Wellsley," she said quickly. "Anna will be happy for your attention."

"Then she shall have it." He took the little girl up and closed the door behind Cybelline. "You will want to know, I think, that Mr. and Mrs. Lowell have absented themselves. They have gone to visit their daughter and left only a short time ago. I actually thought some mishap had caused them to return when I heard your horse outside."

"Oh, I hadn't given a thought to them being gone." She paused in the act of removing her bonnet. "Perhaps this is not—"

"If it is a matter of a chaperone, then Anna can fill the position admirably."

"A chaperone is rather a quaint notion in Penwyck-ham," Cybelline said. "It is just that I imagine you have little enough time to yourself here. There is a contraption on the table that would seem to indicate we have disturbed your work."

Ferrin shrugged, dislodging Anna from his shoulder so that he could catch her again on her descent. "One more time," he said when she begged him prettily not to put her down.

Cybelline smiled as she set her bonnet aside and began to remove her gloves. Ferrin was perfectly helpless in the face of Anna's coquettish demands. When Cybelline finished taking off her pelisse, she made to rescue her host. "I must get her out of her coat, else she will become overheated."

Ferrin gave her a grateful look over the top of Anna's head. He pulled out a chair at the table with the toe of his boot and allowed Anna to stand on the seat while Cybelline untied the ribbons on her bonnet and removed her coat and mittens.

"Does your contraption have a name?" Cybelline asked, pointing with her chin toward the cylinder and wire on the table.

"It is a variation on a voltaic pile, or it will be when I am finished. Do you know what that is?"

"I have heard of such, but I've never seen one before. It has something to do with electricity, I believe."

"Very good. Lightning in a bottle, or so I am attempting. The glass has insulating properties and will permit me to carry the battery even when the current is running though it. By alternating copper and zinc disks separated by pads soaked in brine, I will be able to create an electrical current. The wires at the bottom, when touched together at their ends, will produce a spark." His crooked smile was slightly self-conscious. "There, I have succeeded in boring you. Forgive me."

"No, not at all. It is fascinating." She observed that his skepticism mingled with hopefulness. "Will you show us?"

"It is not quite finished; you will have to allow me a moment."

"Certainly. Perhaps I might put the kettle on for tea." Cybelline saw that he was prepared to apologize yet again for what he felt certain were his poor manners. She had never observed him so discomposed. Gone was his easy manner and sureness of expression. She held up her hand, staying him. "It is no trouble at all and the least that I might do for imposing upon you. Indeed, you are gracious to invite us in. I hope you will continue your work. Anna will attend me."

By the time Cybelline and Anna had prepared the tea, Ferrin was ready to demonstrate his battery. The air crackled as he touched the wires together, and the spark made Anna jump and reach for her mother, then promptly insist that he do it again. Chuckling, he obliged her.

"What is the application?" Cybelline asked.

"How practical you are, Mrs. Caldwell. I fear you have no romantic streak at all. Is it not enough that it is merely fascinating?" Before she could defend herself or take exception to his words, he went on. "I suppose the applications are as few or as many as society will tolerate. I might have used it myself to light the fuses for the pyrotechnics. The wind and wet would have been of no consequence, but the disks had not yet arrived from London." He shrugged. "Electricity also has the power to separate compounds to their individual components, so being able to apply the current in such a controlled fashion will contribute greatly to other experimentation."

"You do such experimentation?"

"On occasion."

"Though my aunt makes no accusation of fraud, she warns me that you are not what you seem to be. I am inclined to believe she is right once again."

Ferrin set the wire leads on the tabletop and regarded

Cybelline with the fascination he'd previously reserved for the voltaic pile. "Warns you? That is rather more intriguing than not. Am I to suppose that you have received a letter from her?"

"Yes, only today. It's why I've come. Mr. Henley mentioned in passing this morning that you were still in residence at the cottage. Until I had it from him, I wasn't at all certain that was the case. I brought the letter. I do not believe Aunt Georgia will be seriously put out with me if I share it with you."

"But she will have an objection."

"She will pretend to. It is not the same thing at all."

Ferrin nodded, understanding. "I am familiar with the ruse. My own mother practices such subterfuge upon occasion. She moves us about as if we are pieces on a chessboard, then absolves herself of all responsibility for it."

"Then you know there is nothing for—" Cybelline broke off as her daughter's high-pitched wail of distress charged the room with more electricity than the voltaic pile.

Chapter Ten

When Cybelline returned from putting Anna down for her nap, Ferrin was sitting by the fire reading Lady Rivendale's recent correspondence. He looked up as Cybelline reached the bottom of the stairs. "Is she sleeping?"

"As deeply as if she were drugged. She cried herself out, I think."

He set the letter on his lap. "I am not certain I can satisfactorily express how sorry I am that she was hurt."

"But she was not hurt, my lord. She was startled, certainly, and shocked, most literally, but there has been no lasting injury." Cybelline's gentle smile underscored her reassurance. "In any event, it was not your fault. I was sitting at the table also and did not observe Anna picking up the wires. My daughter and I should apologize to you for the distress we've caused. In fact, we do apologize, and I thank you most particularly for your forbearance and the use of the Lowells' bedchamber for my daughter's nap."

Because Ferrin looked as if the weight of the entire voltaic pile was still settled on his shoulders, Cybelline sought to distract him. "Have you finished reading Aunt Georgia's letter?"

He shook his head. "I am to the part where she is describing her intelligent card play in detail. It is incredible that she recalls the hands so well. I am glad she was my partner for most of the evening, and I now understand perfectly how Restell and I were defeated when she took Wellsley to her side."

"Pray, do not tell me she cheated." When she saw Ferrin's startled look, the smile that had hovered around her mouth deepened. "She does, you know, though to my knowledge she has never done so when it mattered. Certainly not when there is an important wager on the table. It is a game she plays with Sherry. She cheats, and he tries to catch her out. The scoundrels have been brought into the fold, I'm afraid, so you must never play cards at Granville Hall."

"Unless I am prepared to be a better cheat," he said dryly.

"Precisely." Cybelline took the chair opposite him, glancing at her aunt's missive. "Please, go on. You will be vastly entertained, I believe."

Ferrin picked up the letter and continued reading. His grin became more pronounced in time. "Your aunt has a certain felicity of expression. She finds Wellsley to possess an agreeable countenance, while I have told him that his face does not stop clocks. I think he would prefer Lady Rivendale's remarks."

Cybelline watched him chuckle as he read what her aunt had to say about his brother, then fall silent as he was apprised at last of her views of him. When he looked up, she could not divine what he was thinking.

"She says I am not as favored in my looks as Restell," he said. "I do not think that is a fair observation. She saw him largely in profile, while I was directly across from her for most of the evening. Restell has a noble profile, but when he is seen from the front, I have always thought his eyes were a tad too close together. You saw him at the masquerade. The Viking, remember? What is your opinion?"

Cybelline stared at him a long moment, wondering

how she might respond. It was only when she was on the verge of speaking that she caught the twitch of Ferrin's lips. "Oh, that was very bad of you, my lord. You made me believe you were offended, and I was so certain you would find it amusing. I was afraid I had mistaken the matter."

Ferrin's grin resurfaced. "It does no good to be offended by the truth. Restell is greatly favored. I most particularly like her description of my annual living as perfectly vulgar. It is. I am accounted by many to have very deep pockets, though my father did his best to make me a pauper." He settled back in the chair, his head tilted at a thoughtful angle. "Tell me, do you think when she remarks that I am a curious gentleman, her meaning is that I am odd and eccentric, or that I have an inquisitive nature?"

"Is the answer of great consequence to you?"

"Do you mean will I take exception to your answer?"

"Yes."

He considered that. "No, I don't suppose I will, though I am interested—even curious, you might say—as to how you view the thing."

A smile edged Cybelline's lips. "You mistake Aunt Georgia when you suppose she means one or the other. She means both."

"So I am odd *and* prying. That is your perspective also?"

She laughed. "I say you are singular and am done with it."

"Clever." His eyes saluted her before he returned his attention to the letter. He read on, remarking, "She gets a little of her own back, I see. She comprehended quite well from our conversation that you were Boudicca. I notice, too, that she does not inquire as to the why of it."

Uncomfortable, Cybelline's eyes darted away. "No, she doesn't."

"I suppose it is never wise to ask questions when one truly doesn't want to know the answers."

"I believe that is her thinking, yes." Cybelline could have added that she also hoped it was his. She waited, aware that she was holding her breath in anticipation of his question. When it did not come, she exhaled slowly and silently, trying not to call attention to her relief as he read on. She knew when he arrived at her aunt's post-script because he gave a shout of laughter.

In deference to Anna sleeping above stairs, Ferrin made an effort to compose himself and lower his voice. He shook his head in admiration. "Your dear aunt is a considerable piece of work."

"I like to think she is a piece of considerable work. It is an important distinction."

He smiled. "It certainly is. So she has made a wager that Wellsley and my sister will become betrothed. That is most interesting. I wonder if she based her thinking on her observations of that particular evening or whether she has seen the pair of them about. I sincerely hope it is the former. Wellsley will surely be in Dutch with his grandmother if it becomes known that he is still in town."

"Then you are not concerned that a *tendre* is perhaps developing between the two of them?"

"A *tendre* hardly describes how Wellsley feels, though you will understand that I cannot disclose the particulars. He was deep in his cups as he confessed all, and it would be very poor form for me to repeat every word of his devotion. In truth, I only suspect that it is Netta that he loves. He would not reveal as much to me, but I observed the very same as Lady Rivendale."

"Then you would countenance the match?"

"Of course. Have I not established to your satisfaction, indeed, to all of Penwyckham, that the man is a paragon?"

Cybelline could not help but be diverted. "You have."

"Well, there you have it. It will be a good match for both of them." Ferrin watched Cybelline try to make sense of it. She was clearly curious but reluctant to put forth the question. "You will not ask, will you?"

"It is as you said before. I'm uncertain if I want to know the answer." She regarded his expression, closed to every inkling of his thoughts save wry amusement. "And you will not offer an explanation."

"Not if you do not ask for it."

"Then it is a stalemate."

"So it seems."

They matched stares for several long seconds before Cybelline looked away. While she found his eyes to be impenetrable, she imagined her own revealed her soul.

"Why are you here, Cybelline?"

It was the husky, intimate nuance to Ferrin's voice that brought her attention sharply around again. "You know why. I brought the letter."

"So you did, but that also begs the question: Why?"

"I wanted you to know that Aunt Georgia had only recently written to me. It seemed that you did not entirely believe me when we spoke of it before. I didn't like it that you thought I might be lying."

"And my opinion is important to you?"

"No," she said reflexively. Her cheeks pinkened as she realized that in her desire to be less vulnerable she had spoken without thinking. Watching her as closely as he did, he knew it, too. There was precious little that he missed. Feeling cornered, Cybelline lifted her chin. "That is, your opinion is not entirely unimportant."

One corner of his mouth twitched. "That is something, at least." Rather than pinning her back with his cool glance, this time he used silence to wait her out.

"I had no liking for how things were left between us," she said at last. When he offered no comment, she continued. "I could not properly express how your gifts touched me. It seemed wrong that I said so little when your gesture meant so much. And when I thought . . ."

She paused, collecting herself. "When I thought that you would leave Penwyckham without knowing the truth of that, it made me . . . well, it made me sad that I hadn't the courage to say so."

Cybelline's faint smile was self-conscious. "I don't know that I could have said it yet if you did not provoke me to it. I suppose I hoped you'd understand without hearing it."

"Sometimes it is better to hear it, better yet to hear yourself say it."

She nodded slowly. He had gotten to the very heart of it. She had indeed needed to hear herself say these things aloud. "Yes," she said. "That's true."

"I wonder if you will allow me to say something?"

This time Cybelline did not respond reflexively. Curiosity and wariness mingled, and she wondered which would prompt the better response. "Of course," she said finally. "You must speak freely."

"That is perhaps more license than you will wish you had given me, but I shall not abuse your generosity. I have been thinking that we might call a truce, you and I. I know, we are not at war, but I believe we have been engaged in a skirmish, if not an outright battle. Has it seemed so to you?"

Cybelline studied her hands in her lap. "I had not considered it in such a light," she said quietly, "but there is that aspect."

"From the outset, I would say."

She nodded, pressing the tips of her fingers together. "I have provoked you."

"You have been provocative. It seems a shade different."

Cybelline watched her fingertips turn white. "Yes, it does."

"Will you not look at me?"

She slowly lifted her face and returned his regard. Searching his features, Cybelline could find no censure there, no accusation, nor pity. Yet there was something, for he had not shuttered his expression to her this time, and what she thought she saw was hope. "There is no retreating," she said. "Or at least it does not seem so."

"I am not in expectation of your surrender," he said. "And you must not expect mine. There is no method by which we can undo what has already passed between us. A truce means we agree to cease hostilities and consider how we intend to go on. I think it is the true reason you came today."

Was it? Cybelline realized she wanted to believe he had correctly divined her motives. "I would like to think you are right."

"I'm always right. It's my most annoying trait, I'm told." When Cybelline's mouth curved upward, Ferrin said, "Do you think I'm making it up?"

"Oh, no, my lord. I know for a fact that among all your annoying traits, being right is far and away the most galling."

Ferrin's own smile was wry. "Perhaps I did not adequately explain the part about ceasing hostilities."

"No, you explained it well enough. I have not the hang of it yet. It will require some time, I think, and a great deal of patience on your part, especially if you mean to bait me."

He laughed. "Just so. Is it to be a truce, then?"

"Yes," she said. "Yes, it is."

"Good." He set Lady Rivendale's letter aside. "Will you have more tea?" When Cybelline declined, he asked, "All is well with your brother and his family?"

"Yes. I had a letter from Lily just after Christmas. At the time she composed it, she was in anticipation of a peaceful celebration, although how such a thing is possible with the scoundrels underfoot is more difficult to imagine. Lily is invariably optimistic, but I forgive her for it."

"You would not describe yourself in the same way?"

"No. There was a time I confused naivete for optimism, but I understand the distinction now. I am neither."

"You are rather severe in your outlook, then."

She shrugged. "Perhaps I have become so."

"Life lessons?"

"Is there any other teacher?" she asked. "I imagined that a rake would possess a jaded, skeptical disposition, but that is not the case at all, is it?"

"Are you speaking of me or of rakes as a particular variety of *Homo sapiens*?"

"Is there a difference?"

Raising one dark eyebrow, he gave her a stern, knowing look. "I believe you know the answer to that."

Cybelline sighed. He would force her to face the truth she had been denying herself. "You are not a rake at all, are you?"

"No."

"But you have cultivated that reputation and encouraged people to believe it. I am not wrong about that."

"No, you're not wrong."

Her brow knit as she frowned deeply. "It seems a queer sort of fraud to perpetuate on society."

"It does, doesn't it? Sometimes the path of least resistance is to live down to the expectations of others, the *ton* in particular, rather than to fly in the face of them. I have been advised by my own mother, who means well enough and loves me quite to distraction, that I have a lamentable tendency to be bookish and boring. She could accept bookish, I think, but it is unpardonable that I am tedious company."

The vertical crease between Cybelline's eyebrows became more pronounced. "It does not seem that you can have understood her meaning."

"I assure you, she has been clear on that account. And she's right, you know. Left to my own devices I would be closeted in my library or laboratory. It does not matter whether I am in London or at my country home. I enjoy being similarly occupied in either place."

"But why is that not acceptable? You are to be much

admired for your experimentation and improvements. It seems to me there are many who would applaud your efforts and seek to learn from you. Is your mother averse to you receiving the approbation of a grateful society?"

"You will understand once I have told you the whole of it." Ferrin leaned back comfortably in his chair and crossed his long legs at the ankles. "Mother is averse to society learning how the family has acquired that perfectly vulgar sum of money your aunt mentions."

"But surely that is no secret. You told me at the masquerade, do you not recall?"

"I remember. I told you about Captain Christopher David Hollings, the privateer and first Earl of Ferrin. That was all perfectly true. What I did not mention is that every Hollings after him squandered some portion of the wealth he amassed. By the time my own profligate sire came into his inheritance there was little enough of it left to support his gaming. He married my mother when he was better than a decade older than I am now, and she was but fifteen."

Ferrin was conscious of having Cybelline's full attention. Her frown had eased, but the cast of her features remained sober, and she was regarding him with those splendid blue-gray eyes that now held both curiosity and compassion.

He made a steeple of his fingers and rested his chin on it for a moment as he considered how to continue his explanation. "Mother brought a substantial dowry into the marriage. She was the oldest daughter of a baron who'd had a recent reversal of bad fortune. He was desirous of her making a good marriage, hoping it would provide seed money for his own gaming, so he wagered his winnings on his daughter captivating the fifth Earl of Ferrin. She did, but the true state of my father's financial affairs did not become known until months after the marriage when my grandfather applied to him for funds. I have been told that Grandfather was so furious that he had been gulled, he actually challenged my father."

Cybelline's eyes widened. "It is beyond belief. Never say one of them killed the other."

"My father demonstrated a modicum of good sense at this juncture and refused to accept the challenge. To escape his creditors my grandfather booked passage to America for his wife, his three remaining daughters, and his horse."

"His horse?"

"Yes. An Arabian that my grandfather entered in stakes races, which were an exceedingly popular form of entertainment." He grinned as Cybelline's lips parted in something like surprise and reluctant admiration. "He won many times. That is, my grandfather won. The Arabian was a mare, I'm told. Grandfather amassed enough winnings to live comfortably, see his three daughters settled, and enjoy some success in the state legislature of the Commonwealth of Pennsylvania."

"Incredible."

"It is, isn't it? He never returned to England and offered no financial support, not even in secret, to my mother, but he maintained regular correspondence with her until he died. He outlived my own father, which I have to believe satisfied him so completely that it hastened his own passing."

"You mean he had nothing to live for after your father died?"

"No, I mean he imbibed so freely celebrating the demise of the fifth earl that he got himself caught under the wheels of a passing carriage as he staggered home."

Cybelline's hand flew to her mouth. "But that is awful."

"It is no good, Cybelline, I can see that you are hard pressed not to laugh."

"Yes, but it is shock that makes it so, and I know it is very wrong of me."

Ferrin did not feel the same urge to compose himself and was quite open in his amusement. "My grandmother, who is the one who communicated the details of her husband's passing to my mother, died some years back. I never knew her except through her letters. My aunts have never returned to England, so there is an entire branch of the family tree that is America's problem now."

Cybelline had been in the process of lowering her hand, and now she brought it quickly back to her mouth as suppressed laughter became a hiccup.

Ferrin rose and brought a cup of tea for her. "This will help if you take care not to choke."

Thanking him, Cybelline gratefully accepted the tea. "Your grandfather is not the source of your family's wealth, then."

"No, as I mentioned, he made enough to live comfortably but did not settle any of it on my parents." Ferrin added a log to the fire, gave it a poke, then returned to his seat. "Society was not aware of the declining family fortune. There were still lands in abundance and the rents from them were substantial. My father had to work very hard to empty the coffers, but he was nothing if not dedicated."

This last was said without any trace of bitterness, merely as a statement of fact. "My mother, who values the look of things above practical considerations, was determined to maintain appearances. It is not clear to me that she ever understood how much Father lost to bad investments, gaming hells, and the occasional mistress. Her own society demanded entertainments and fine clothes, patronage of the arts and support of popular charities. Her devotion to these things was the equal of my father's attachment to his own interests."

Ferrin caught Cybelline's slightly bemused expression and stopped his recitation to make an inquiry of her thoughts. "You perhaps think I am too harsh a critic of my parents and should not speak so frankly."

"Pardon?" She belatedly realized that he was in expectation of a reply. "Oh, no. That is not at all what I am thinking. I am wondering if you are quite certain these people are in fact your common sires?" The inappropriateness of this remark was not borne home to her until she heard it aloud. An apology came quickly to her lips only to be silenced by the roar of Ferrin's laughter. Cybelline could do naught but stare and wait him out.

Ferrin's self-possession was hard-won. Each time he was on the point of composure, Cybelline's perfect, pithy observance would tweak his humor again. "My mother has often entertained the very same question," he said when he could speak. "But she also assures me she was present at my birth and that my paternity is not in doubt."

"So she recognizes you are an anomaly."

"An aberration, but I like your description better."

Cybelline was no longer disposed to feel kindly toward Lady Gardner, but she did not voice this to Ferrin. He did not seem to find his mother's remarks in any way exceptional. "How old were you when you became earl?"

"Fifteen. Although I had not yet reached the age at which I might legally manage the estate, my mother simply could not. There were solicitors to direct the trust, but she relied on me to advise her. Eventually the solicitors dealt with me. It is difficult to say what she really understood about the financial ruin we were facing and what she simply refused to understand. I did not press this subject with her. I knew what must be done, and her comprehension of the matter was of no account."

Cybelline warmed her hands around her teacup. "What did you do?"

"I was tinkering with a printing machine at the time and found a way to improve the speed at which the type might be set. It involved some simple modifications to the blocks that allowed them to be arranged and exchanged more quickly, then I added a compound to the ink that gave the print more clarity and allowed for a greater number of copies with the same amount of ink."

"Of course." Cybelline would have clapped her hands together if she had not been holding the cup. "Oh, but that is splendid. You applied for a patent."

"Two," he said, holding up a like number of fingers. "One for the type and the other for the ink. The solicitors arranged a demonstration with the London *Gazette* and a group of investors." His smile was faint now and self-effacing. "It was a success."

"A very great success, I should imagine, if you are accounted to be richer than Croesus."

"Yes, well, there have been other patents since then."

"Five? A dozen? Pray, do not be modest. It is a most excellent achievement."

"I believe the count stands at one hundred eighteen."

A rush of air left Cybelline's lungs. "Oh my." She set the cup aside before she dropped it.

"They are not equally lucrative," he hastened to tell her. "Some have not found their worth, but one is always hopeful."

"If one is an optimist."

"Precisely."

"But why are you not known for these things that you have done? Why do you not—" She stopped as her mind finally turned the key to this peculiar lock. "Why, you are in trade."

He nodded. "A cit. There, I have said it. Mother prefers that I take the Lord's name in vain."

Cybelline gave him a narrow look, unsure whether she could believe him. "I think you are having me on, my lord."

"Only a little. My mother is of the firm opinion that it is acceptable for one's fortune to be made on the industry of others: the tenant farmers; the ship masters and tea merchants with whom one invests; the piracy of one's forebears. Wagering on the outcome of a horse race, a boxing match, or a cockfight is also perfectly acceptable for a gentleman, though she does not hold with wagering on the outcome of a duel and believes ladies should place bets only in a most discreet manner."

Ferrin paused, allowing Cybelline opportunity to take this all in and compare it to her own experience. "You know she is not alone in her thinking. The *ton* admires the diligence of the commoner who contributes to their comfort. It arouses comment and praise when a clergyman makes a discovery because of his odd passion for science or a glassmaker perfects a lens because he has had a happy accident while grinding his glass."

He uncrossed his ankles and sat up. "Society does not yet know what to make of someone like me. If my interests and contributions were political in nature, they would be unexceptional. Even my tinkering might be considered only eccentric if I did not seek to profit from my efforts. That is what appears to be unacceptable."

Cybelline nodded slowly. She was familiar with the attitude he described. "It seems wholly unfair."

Ferrin shrugged. "I have never found it helpful to think in terms of the fairness of a thing. It is what it is. I have enjoyed a great many rights because I was born to privilege. That is not fair, either. There is always tit for tat, action and reaction." He smiled a little then and regarded Cybelline frankly. "Opposites and attraction."

"You are being deliberately provocative." Because Ferrin's look put her to a blush, Cybelline acknowledged her confrontation was not entirely effectual.

"I was. Forgive me."

Cybelline noted there was nothing in his tone to indicate he was sorry for it. His roguish manner was not in all ways a fraud. "How is it that you came upon the idea that you must become a rake?"

"Pose as one," he said. "Not become one, although it is sometimes a fine line that separates the faker from the fact." Rising, Ferrin crossed the room to a small, round table where the decanter of whisky was kept. He poured himself a drink. "It was not so much a plan that was designed and executed but a misapprehension that was never corrected. I told you that it is often easier not to resist society's expectations. That is what I did. Being descended of libertines and gamers on both sides of the family, and having no enthusiasm for politics, it seemed the obvious road to take to protect my real interests."

He sipped his drink. "As it happened, I was caught in a . . . well, let us call it a compromising situation. She was a friend of my mother's. I was the innocent. The catching out was done by her husband, and he chose to believe that his lady was the injured party. As she made no attempt to disabuse him of that notion, I was cast in the role of the seducer. I cannot honestly say that it was honor that kept me from relating the truth of the matter. Guilt and a giddy afterglow were the culprits."

Ferrin raised his glass in mock salute. "That is how a rake's reputation is made, Cybelline. Managing it requires some effort but is not without reward."

She simply shook her head. "It is incredible."

He finished his drink and set down the glass. "Mother remarried when I was seventeen. Sir Geoffrey is very good to me, but his interests *are* political, and he is the first to admit he has no head for investments. He has always depended upon me to advise him as I did my mother before."

"Then he does not frequent the gaming hells."

"No, he frequents the Parliament." He added dryly, "You will collect there is not much difference."

"You are too harsh."

"Perhaps. I do admire him. And he does me the immense favor of taking Mother in hand."

"But you have assumed financial responsibility for

your family," Cybelline said. "That is what Aunt Georgia meant in her letter, is it not?"

"Yes, I imagine it is. My mother is happy to paint me as a generous scoundrel. She would not like it if people thought me cruel or callous. It's a narrow path that I walk." He returned to his chair but sat on the arm, not the cushion, and folded his arms against his chest. "The twins, Sir Geoffrey's oldest children by his first wife, have made successful marriages and require little in the way of support from me. If I am right that Wynetta is the young woman who's captured Wellsley's eye, then it will be another coup. Wellsley is perfectly capable of providing for my stepsister. My sisters Hannah and Portia are years away from making matches, so that is for the future. Restell is the one complicating my life at present."

"You do not count Mr. Wellsley and Miss Wynetta as a complication?"

"No. They are an amusement." He added significantly, "Neither do I count you."

"It is so difficult to know whether to be affronted or relieved." Cybelline raised her hand, staying his reply. "How is Mr. Gardner a complication?"

"Restell has conceived the idea to fashion himself a life like mine, or rather as he supposes mine to be."

"Surely he knows of your inventions and accomplishments."

"He does. But he views my mind as a well that will never go dry, freeing him to imitate that part of my life he believes is enormously fascinating. I am not yet certain how to rein him in. He has not shown the least interest in tempering his pursuits."

"Perhaps if he thought you were tempering your own."

"What do you mean?"

"It seems to me that you might perpetuate another fraud since you excel at that sort of thing."

The cast of Ferrin's features was wry. "It is so difficult

to know whether to be affronted or relieved," he said. "Tell me what you mean."

"If you were to marry, for instance, it might influence Mr. Gardner to consider a different course."

"You are the second person to suggest that my marrying could be the solution to a problem."

"Oh?"

"Wellsley said the same when we were yet in London. He believes that his friendship with me will put him in a better light with his grandmama if I am married."

"That is an interesting perspective."

"He was foxed at the time. I do not know what accounts for your suggestion of the same. It is unnatural."

Cybelline realized she was enjoying herself immensely. "Perhaps it is. But I was suggesting a humbug, not a real marriage."

"It seems like a further complication."

"Hmm. You may be right."

"Thank you."

"A betrothal would be just the thing. More easily arranged and more easily ended."

"Are you certain you do not know Wellsley? It might be that you are well suited."

She regarded Ferrin in a more serious vein. "Why are you not married, my lord?"

"It has always seemed like something I could ill afford."

"You cannot be speaking of your financial obligations."

"No. But I imagine I would have to surrender the things that give me pleasure and purpose."

Cybelline glanced toward the voltaic pile on the table. "Your experiments? Oh, surely not."

"Would you tolerate a husband who spends hours in his library and absents himself in the middle of supper because he must record his observations?"

It was a long time before Cybelline answered. "I did

once," she said quietly, gravely. "I cannot say if I would do so again."

Ferrin realized he had unwittingly exposed a wound. "I apologize. I quite forgot that Mr. Caldwell also made a study of things."

She nodded. "It is all right. I do not mind talking about it."

Ferrin suspected it was truer that Cybelline thought she should not mind. He vowed to tread carefully here. "Did he make a study only of artifacts?"

"That was his primary interest. And law, of course. You know my husband was a barrister, do you not?"

"Sir Richard Settle brought that to my attention, yes."

"Ah, yes. Sir Richard. The professor seemed to think a man could have but a single passion and encouraged Nicholas to choose one over the other. My husband could not do it. He loved both." Hearing herself, Cybelline realized it was the same in Nicholas's more private life. Had she known about her husband's mistress she would have put the same choice to him. Could he have picked one over the other? she wondered. Perhaps he had loved her after a fashion and would not have been able to choose.

A chill slipped under her skin and she shivered. Cybelline knew she did not want to be loved like that. She was selfish enough to want to occupy the whole of her husband's romantic heart.

"You're cold?" asked Ferrin. He made to go the fire again, but Cybelline stopped him.

"No, it's nothing. The odd shiver. Do not trouble yourself." In spite of her words, she shivered again.

This time when Ferrin got to his feet he put himself directly in front of her. Without asking permission to do so, he placed the back of his hand against her forehead, then her cheek. His touch lingered in spite of his intention for it to be otherwise.

"I told you it is nothing." Cybelline's skin tingled under his fingertips. She did not ask him to remove his hand.

How was it possible that he could evoke such a response from her? The merest brush with him arrested her heart. She glanced upward and saw the dark centers of his eyes were wider than before. She suspected it was the same for her.

"You feel it, don't you, Cybelline?"

She did not ask him to explain. She simply nodded.

He took one of her hands in each of his and raised her up. "It is like completing a circuit."

Cybelline remembered the shock Anna had felt when she touched together the leads of Ferrin's voltaic pile. It was what Cybelline felt now. "Electricity," she said softly.

"Yes."

She wanted to wail. She closed her eyes instead and allowed herself to experience the current under her skin, the raised charge that slipped along her spine and lifted the downy hairs at the nape of her neck.

His mouth was gentle on hers, the tug of his lips infinitely soft. Opposites. Attraction. His words came back to her as he nudged her lips apart. The kiss was long and slow and deep, and when he raised his head she felt herself being pulled toward him. She started to come upon tiptoe.

Realizing what she was about, Cybelline dropped back to her heels. She opened her eyes and searched his face. Desire was stamped on his features in small ways: the heaviness of his eyelids; the slight flaring of his nostrils; the muscle that worked in his jaw. His eyes, though, were the singular feature that communicated his need. Still dark and wide at the center, they were also thoroughly alert and calculating, the eyes of a hungry predator who understood the value of patience.

Unable to move, Cybelline found her voice. "Anna is—"

"Sleeping."

She swallowed. "I did not come here for—"

"I know," he said.

Cybelline felt his fingers tighten where they laced with hers. It lasted only an instant, as though he anticipated she might bolt, then thought better of restraining her from doing so. It was this willingness to let her go that kept her precisely where she was.

She asked, "Why have you not left Penwyckham?"

"How can you not know?" Ferrin smiled faintly, shaking his head. "But you do not, do you? I can see that you don't." He raised one of her hands and brought it to his chest. "I want to make things right between us. I don't know what that means entirely, or precisely what it entails, but I know one aspect is that we must be lovers again, and it most especially cannot be because you wish to punish yourself. I would have you let me take you to my bed this time and give you joy of it. I know you have had pleasure, but you have not had joy. I am not certain you know the difference."

Cybelline was quite certain she did not. What he was proposing frightened her, and he seemed to know that, too. This time when his fingers tightened around hers, she had the sense of one being reassured, not restrained.

The nature of this man was better known to her now, and that had been his doing. She considered all that he'd told her this afternoon and understood it had been done of a purpose, not as a prelude to taking her to his bed— or not only that, she amended—but as a sign of good faith and proof that he meant to trust her. Ferrin was not invulnerable. He'd allowed her to know that, to see where his shield was battered and soft, where a direct blow might flatten him. Yet he stood there still, wanting her, but wanting her permission more.

"Yes," she whispered. "Show me."

He nodded, releasing one of her hands but not the other. Turning, he led her toward the stairs. "Go on," he said. "I will follow."

Cybelline raised the hem of her gown and started up the

narrow steps, conscious that he was watching her. As she turned in the stairwell she heard him move away from the bottom of the steps. She could not imagine what he was doing until she heard the sound of the front door being barred. A sensible precaution, she supposed, against the early return of the Lowells. It made her smile.

At the top of the stairs she stopped and listened at Anna's door. It was not enough for her that she could hear nothing. She had to know that her child slept. Cybelline opened the door just enough to angle her view to Anna on the bed. Just as quietly, she closed it again and moved on.

Not knowing quite what to do with herself in Ferrin's room, Cybelline moved to the window and drew the curtains closed. She was absently smoothing their folds when she head Ferrin enter. Her hand stilled, and she turned.

He was carrying a stack of logs across his forearms. She hurried toward him and relieved him of two. Until he laid the fire she'd been unaware of the chill in the room. When she would have stepped closer to the flames, he caught her elbow and applied the gentlest pressure to turn her toward him.

Seeing Cybelline's sliver of a smile, Ferrin asked, "What amuses you?"

"I was thinking you must be an excellent rider." Her smile deepened when she saw his confusion. "It is the way you nudge me in one direction or another. I always end up precisely where you want me."

Ferrin's eyes darted toward the bed, then back to her. "Not yet." He brushed aside a tendril of hair that lay across her cheek. "You observed that Anna is sleeping?"

"Yes." She realized what he had not quite said. "You observed the same?"

"Yes."

She was glad he was not insensible to her daughter's

presence in the next room. "She sleeps soundly," Cybelline said. "Still, I would not want to risk waking her."

Ferrin placed a kiss on her forehead. "Then I shall endeavor not to make you scream."

She went a little weak in the knees then and might have even moaned, but she wasn't certain if the sound came from her or the updraft in the fireplace. When she saw his knowing smile, she knew that it hadn't been the wind.

His fingers found one tail of the ribbon in her hair and tugged. The knot came apart easily. He let the ribbon slip through his hand before threading his fingers in her hair. Even without benefit of the late afternoon light, her silky hair was like honey filtered by sunshine. He parted it at her back and brought it forward over her shoulders, sifting through the heavy waves with his fingertips.

She shivered. He did not mistake it for anything to do with a chill. "Will you turn around?" he asked. She did. The part he'd made in her hair gave him access to the back of her gown. He unfastened the satin belt that lent her gown its empire waist and allowed it to join the hair ribbon on the floor. "Raise your arms."

Cybelline obliged, taking his direction as if there were nothing at all peculiar about him playing the lady's maid. She felt his fingers gathering in the folds of her gown at her waist and hip, then lifting it more slowly than Webb had ever done. It was only at the end, when she might have been smothered by the bombazine that he quickly pulled it out of the way. When his hands did not return to her immediately, she glanced over her shoulder. Ferrin was laying the gown carefully over the back of a chair.

"You said you would endeavor not to make me scream," she told him, watching him take his time to smooth the fabric much as she had done with the curtains.

He feigned curiosity, but his eyes were knowing. "Oh? Do you want to?" Abandoning the gown, he stepped behind her again and placed his hands at the back of her neck. Her head immediately swiveled around and drooped forward to expose the length of her nape. He used his thumbs to massage the cords of tension there and at her shoulders. He kissed her just above the knob of her spine, then higher, then his hands were making fists in her muslin petticoat, and he was raising it just as he had her gown.

He did not give it the same care but let it join the ribbon and belt. "I think I might indulge in a tantrum myself," he said, eyeing her back-laced corselet. "Unless you have a knife at the ready to split this thing open."

In spite of her liquid limbs and thudding heart, Cybelline learned that she retained the wherewithal to laugh. "You do not like being thwarted."

"I certainly do not. And I cannot recall giving you any reason to think that I do." He plucked at the lacings. Unlike the ribbon and the belt, they held fast. His subsequent attempt to pull the laces only tightened the knot. "Let us agree you will not wear one of these again."

"All right." When her easy capitulation seemed to give him pause, she said, "I do not like to be thwarted, either."

That motivated him to inspiration. "A moment," he said, leaving her side to disappear into the adjoining dressing room. When he returned, he was carrying the razor from his shaving kit. He held it up to show her. The finely honed blade gleamed orange in the firelight. "Don't move."

Cybelline did not require this caution. She recalled the footman who had wanted to demonstrate the razor's efficiency by splitting a hair plucked from his own head. She stood very still and waited. There was the smallest sound—*sssnit*—then the absence of pressure around her midriff and under her breasts. She did not move even when she heard him set the thing aside on the mantelpiece, nor did she move when he pulled the lacings free of the eyelets.

"You can breathe," he said, removing the corselet.

It was true in every sense. Cybelline filled her lungs. "Better?"

She nodded. When he tossed the corselet into the fire, she gave a start but did not protest. "Infinitely better."

Ferrin's arms circled her from behind. He nuzzled her hair with his chin. The muslin shift she still wore was a flimsy barrier at best. He could feel the heat of her skin through the fabric. "Will you come to the bed with me?"

His voice, husky and low, and so very close to her ear that she could feel the moist warmth of his breath, made Cybelline know the powerful ache of wanting. "Yes," she whispered. "Yes." She thought he might lift her in his arms as he had done before and carry her to the bed, but he was more clever than that, she realized, and more devious. Taking her to his bed would not be accomplished without her permission, and while she had never denied him, and certainly had initiated their first coupling, she understood that he wanted something different from her now.

We must be lovers again, he'd said, *and it most especially cannot be because you wish to punish yourself.*

Cybelline placed her hand in his and led him toward the bed. "Shall I undress you?"

"Will you?"

She'd had little enough experience with it. Nicholas had always come to bed in his nightshirt. The only time she'd touched a man's breeches to unfasten the flies had been with this man, and he had been a pirate. "Yes," she said. "Will I need the razor?"

Cybelline had to place her hand over his mouth as he prepared to laugh. "I did not think you would find the prospect so diverting."

Ferrin removed her hand. "You have mistaken amusement for alarm." He drew her wrist downward until her palm lay squarely over his groin. "I am but half the man I was a moment ago."

Since he was still of a prodigious size, she was glad to hear it and told him so.

This time there was no mistaking that it was laughter that rumbled in his chest. He did not mind that Cybelline threw her arms around him and clamped her mouth over his to smother the sound. When she finally drew back, they were both breathless. They were also smiling a little drunkenly.

Cybelline undid the small cloth-covered buttons of his waistcoat and helped him shrug out of it. When she would have given it the same due care that he had shown for her gown, he plucked it from her hands and tossed it on the chest at the foot of the bed.

"What happened to action and reaction?" she asked. His low growl made her suppose that Newton's laws had no place in the bedroom. "Very well." She loosened his stock and unwound it, then threw it off to one side so that it fluttered like a streamer before it fell to the floor. "Your linen next?" she asked. "Or the breeches?"

"The boots."

"Of course." She indicated the bed and waited for him to sit, then she raised one of his legs and worked the boot free. The second one proved more difficult. She thought she heard him chuckle. "Is there a simpler way to do it?"

"Without using the razor, you mean?"

"Do not tempt me, my lord."

"You only have to ask me."

She released his foot and straightened, arms akimbo. "Will you be so very good as to remove your boot?"

Ferrin raised his booted ankle to the knee of the other leg and pulled the boot off. More tellingly, he let it thud to the floor. "Now the breeches, I think."

Cybelline did not miss a beat. "Will you be so very good as to remove your breeches?"

"Saucy wench. Come here." Ferrin caught her wrist before she could dance away and pulled her between his splayed legs. He drew her hand to the buttons of his breeches and waited, though he was sensible enough not to dare her.

Cybelline's eyes dropped to where her hand lay over his heavy, straining erection. She was aware that he was watching her face, not her fingers, and she wished she were in better control of the color that was pinkening her complexion.

"Butter might not melt in your mouth," Ferrin said, "but I could boil water for tea on your forehead."

That was when she leaped at him.

Chapter Eleven

Cybelline could not miss that Ferrin welcomed her assault. He obliged her by falling backward on the bed and taking her weight on top of him. He did not try to escape when she planted kisses at the corner of his mouth, his jaw, and at the sensitive spot just below his ear, or even when her teeth caught his earlobe and nibbled.

She raised her head just enough to see him clearly. "You are not resisting, my lord."

"That is because I know the futility of it. It is you, madam, who is the superior force."

"I believe I like that." Cybelline kissed him on the mouth. "Do you know you are not entirely comfortable to lie upon? Mayhap if you—"

She was given no opportunity to complete her suggestion. Ferrin rolled, taking her with him, and when they were at the center of the bed, the only force she applied was the one of attraction. Ferrin had her wrists at the level of her head and was giving her throat his undivided attention.

"That tickles," she said when his mouth settled at the curve of her neck and shoulder. She wriggled, trying to avoid the little bursts of air that he was blowing against her skin. She stopped when she realized he was completely satisfied with her efforts to escape. "Oh, that is very bad of you," she whispered. She tried to lie still, but what he was doing really did tickle and in moments she was attempting to escape again.

Made breathless by her efforts, her staccato laughter gave sound to Ferrin's volley of kisses. "You must stop," she told him. "Please. I tell you, I cannot breathe."

He lifted his head to gauge her sincerity. She looked too innocent for his tastes. "I have one term you must satisfy before I'll permit you to go."

"State it quickly, then."

"My name," he said. "I want to hear you say my name."

She blinked, surprised, then offered up a smile that was slight and slightly wicked. "Wellsley. Porter Wellsley."

Ferrin was not proof against her sly cleverness. Grinning, he released her wrists and turned onto his back. Cybelline raised herself on one elbow and stretched out alongside him. She laid her free hand on his chest.

"Ferrin," she said. "Is it enough? Shall I call you Christopher? Kit?"

"My family calls me Kit. My friends call me Ferrin. I can think of no one who has ever called me Christopher."

"Then that is what I shall call you. Do you mind?" She leaned toward him and brushed his cheek with her lips. "Christopher." Cybelline walked her fingers from the center of his chest to the waistband of his breeches. She felt him suck in his breath, leaving her room enough to tease him with the tentative foray of her fingertips. When she caught the fabric of his linen in her fist and began to tug it free, she heard him groan softly, though whether in disappointment that she had not set her sights lower or in anticipation that she would return, Cybelline could not be sure.

She instructed him to raise his hands, and he willingly complied. She hoisted herself to a sitting position at his side and helped him out of the shirt, then gave it a toss over her shoulder toward the foot of the bed.

"You are staring," Ferrin said.

Cybelline nodded absently.

"You are still staring."

Reluctantly, Cybelline lifted her gaze from his naked chest to his face. Her regard remained frank, but there was a certain reverence in her tone. "It is because by every measure that is known to me, you are an extraordinarily beautiful man." A faint smile curved her lips as his complexion turned ruddy. Leaning forward, she kissed him sweetly on the mouth. "So you *can* be put to a blush," she said, sitting back again. "I have often wondered."

"I had not thought so, but you have the knack for putting me off my stride."

Cybelline wondered if he knew how often he did the same to her. She reached out and carefully brushed back a lock of hair that lay against his forehead. Her fingertips strayed to his temple, and she held his eyes with hers. "If I were wearing Boudicca's mask," she said quietly, "I would torment you with a promising smile and tease you about your stride. But I am Cybelline, and that does not come so easily to me. I was sincere when I said you are a beautiful man, and I meant that in every way that it can be meant." She cupped his jaw in her palm, and her thumb touched the corner of his mouth. "I thought you should know." Bending, Cybelline kissed him again, this time with passion more keenly felt than before.

Her lips parted his; her tongue touched the ridge of his teeth. She tasted a hint of the whisky he'd had earlier and the salty sweet tang that was peculiar to him. She kissed him deeply and softly, sharply and kindly, and knew a response in this man that was equal to her own.

Ferrin caught Cybelline's face in his hands and applied pressure that was both gentle and insistent to make her go still. "I can taste your tears," he whispered against her mouth. "I meant that this should be different."

"And it is," she said on the same thread of sound. "You cannot imagine how different."

She lifted her head, and it was then that Ferrin saw it was not merely a sheen of tears that lent her eyes luster. Here was radiance, as clear and brilliant as light could be, and he understood what it was to know the face of joy.

Ferrin slipped his hand through her hair and cupped the back of her head, drawing her down. "I am come undone." Profoundly humbled, thoroughly aroused, he slanted his mouth across hers. Urgency and wanting defined the kiss, and the need to possess her was so deep-felt that he feared for them both.

He grasped handfuls of her shift and began to raise it. She tore at the buttons on his breeches. He held up one corner of the blanket before it was hopelessly tangled around them and invited her inside. She made the same invitation a moment later. The covers crested and broke like wavelets coming ashore as they removed their drawers and stockings. Breathing hard, they flattened their naked bodies against each other.

Ferrin accepted the brunt of their combined force, lying back and pulling Cybelline on top. He palmed the rounds of her bottom and fit her snugly against him. He learned immediately it was not possible for her to be still; she rode up on him, rubbing the twin points of her breasts against his chest. Her lips found the curve of his neck, and she kissed him, drawing his skin into her mouth, laving it with her tongue. He knew she felt the rise and fall of his chest and the moment his breath caught.

He stroked the back of her thighs, urging them apart. He listened to the cadence of her breathing change. She made herself open to him and slowly, deliberately, took him inside her. The restraint she exercised made Ferrin think she meant to kill him, and he told her so. Her low laughter was not encouraging.

Cybelline found herself flat on her back, her knees

raised around Ferrin's hips and his cock settled deeply inside her. She simply contracted around him: her arms, her knees, her thighs, and even more tightly where she held him most intimately.

Ferrin demonstrated caution and control equal to Cybelline's own on his next thrust. When she accused him of seeking revenge, he merely smiled.

Laughter was eventually their undoing. Hers first, then his. They surrendered control for spontaneity, execution for abandon, and were made breathless by discovery.

He learned that she liked his mouth on her curve of her shoulder. She found that by touching the base of his spine just so, she could make him draw in a sharp breath. Sifting her hair with his fingertips seemed to dissolve her bones, but a flick of his tongue across her nipple snapped her to attention. She realized that by gently scoring the arrow of dark hair from his navel to his groin with her fingernail, she could make him pledge to be her slave.

The very air in the room was charged. Their bodies rubbed and rocked, came together hard, then stilled. Their rhythm changed as they tried to draw out the pleasure past what they thought they could bear. It would be too soon that it was over, then not soon enough.

She met his thrusts and shared his heat. Current flowed and friction created tiny sparks just below the surface of her skin. He felt the same skittering along his spine and down the backs of his thighs. Tension pulled their limbs taut, and they rose and fell on the strength of the contractions.

Each time Cybelline felt her breath catch at the back of her throat, she thought it would be the last. She wasn't certain she could be made to climb so high, yet Ferrin urged her on, and the pleasure became sharper and more keenly felt with each step. She kept going because he was always there, supporting and encouraging, and when he had to be, demanding.

She closed her eyes and imagined the pyrotechnics of

Christmas Day, then she became her own Roman candle. She was both the source and the recipient of a shower of sparkling light. Twisting and spinning, she felt herself falling from an unimaginable height, weightless and almost without substance, accelerating in her descent.

And yet there was no landing, no abrupt, hard fall to Earth. She was simply tumbling, then she was not. He cradled her, and in time, she cradled him. The light and lightness faded, but the memory lingered more deeply than what she could see in her mind's eye. It resided in her skin, on the tip of her tongue, in the very breath she drew, and finally in the thrumming of her heart.

"No," she said when he made to leave her. "Not yet." Embarrassed by her need, Cybelline's eyes darted away. "I have no right."

Ferrin followed her glance, caught it, and brought her splendid blue-gray eyes back to him. "You do," he said. "Of course you do." He supported his weight so that she would not take all of it, then after a time had passed, he slowly turned onto his back and brought her with him. He withdrew but kept her close at his side. Her head rested comfortably in the crook of his shoulder, and she hitched one leg to lie along the length of his. Ferrin wondered how aware she was of laying claim to him in this easy manner.

Cybelline glanced up and saw the last vestige of his smile before it disappeared. "What were you thinking?"

"That it is no hardship to be a rock when you are the limpet."

She looked down at herself and realized she was clinging to him in precisely the manner he described. "You are certain it is no hardship?"

"If I had pockets," he said, "I would invite you to live in them."

"What an absurd notion."

"Not if I kept my pockets in the wardrobe."

Cybelline gave him a smart pinch, surprising herself as much as she surprised him. She was already forming an apology when he put a finger to her lips and halted her.

"Do you think I want your regrets?" he asked. "I don't. Not at all. You are not so shy about tweaking me outside of bed; I do not mind if you tweak me in it. In fact, I think I prefer it." He let his finger fall away from her lips and used it to lift her chin so that he might see her better. "You don't know what to make of that, do you?"

She shook her head. "It seems that we are perhaps too comfortable."

He noticed that she didn't move. "Is that unacceptable?"

"I don't know. This is outside my experience."

"Mine also."

Cybelline frowned. "But you have had mistresses."

"And you have had a husband."

"That is different."

"In some respects, but comfort is comfort, and I am saying I have not known this ease of feeling with any woman under my protection."

Cybelline said nothing. She tried to recall if she *had* felt this ease with Nicholas. It troubled her that she could not answer with certainty. Was it the passage of time that made her less sure, or had the letters shaded her thinking so that she questioned every aspect of what her marriage had been?

Ferrin gave her shoulders a light squeeze. "It is not always advisable to conduct an inquiry. I have had mistresses enough to know that."

"Braggart." But she said it without rancor.

Ferrin felt a gentle stirring against his chest. It was enough disturbance to rouse him from slumber but not enough to push him to alertness. An unusual torpor made his limbs feel pleasantly heavy. He was put in mind of sinking slowly to the bottom of a lake, bubbles of air rising as he drifted down. Time stretched endlessly before him, and the water was dark and warm and embracing.

It was with the greatest reluctance that he opened one eye—and immediately had cause to wish he hadn't. The weight on his chest was quite real. He estimated it to be twenty-five pounds and some thirty-two inches long. It answered—when the mood was upon it—to the name of Anna.

"Bloody, bloody hell." This softly spoken epithet did not move Anna to rouse herself. Ferrin glanced sideways and saw that it also had not roused her mother. "Cybelline?" She was lying on her side facing him, her knees drawn toward her chest. One hand rested beneath her head, but the other was stretched out under the blanket toward him. He could feel her fingertips resting against his naked hip.

Naked. He had the sense not to swear aloud this time. Lifting his head, he looked down at the silky red-gold cap of Anna's hair. His breath made the fluff flutter, but she didn't seem to sense the movement. Turning sideways, he regarded Cybelline again. He could imagine that there might come a time when finding himself abed with these particular females would bring him a sense of enormous well-being. What it filled him with now was something akin to dread.

It was not for himself that he minded. Indeed, he did not mind at all. Rather it was anticipation of Cybelline's reaction that provoked the peculiar tightening in his chest. Anna's twenty-five pounds felt more than twice that now.

"Cybelline?" He saw her wrinkle her nose and was encouraged. Reaching for her hand under the blanket, he gave her fingers a careful squeeze.

"Mmm?" She stretched sleepily, then was still.

"Wake up." He glanced at Anna to make certain she hadn't heard him. "Cybelline!"

She stared at him owlishly.

Ferrin knew the exact moment Cybelline woke. Her blue-gray eyes lost their smoky appeal and became like flint. It was not precisely an accusation that she shot in his direction, but neither was it promising.

Cybelline dragged the sheet to her shoulders and tucked it under her arms as she sat up. She patted down the blankets, searching for her shift, and found it tangled with her stockings at the foot of the bed. Kicking out several times, she managed to toss it high enough in the air to make a successful grab for it without losing the sheet.

In other circumstances—ones that did not include a child sleeping on his chest—Ferrin would have felt free to comment on the acrobatics. Setting his jaw, he resisted the urge.

Cybelline eased into her shift, eying Anna all the while. Once modestly attired, she slid off the bed and began quietly gathering her clothes.

When Ferrin realized she meant to dress herself before she removed Anna, he nearly groaned. "Will you not take her now?" he whispered.

"She is perfectly comfortable there."

"But I am not."

"If I move her and she wakes, one of us should be properly clothed."

"My vote is that it should be me."

Cybelline picked up his shirt, walked to his side of the bed, and placed it in his hand. "Very well." Turning her back on him, she carried her own clothes to the chair in front of the fireplace and began to dress.

Ferrin stared at his linen, wondering how he might manage to put it on without jostling Anna to wakefulness. Bunching it in his hands, he slipped it over his head and cautiously worked his arms into it. The bulk of the shirt lay uncomfortably around his throat and shoulders like the yoke on an ox. That picture did not cheer him.

Using a great deal of care, Ferrin began to pull the hem of the shirt downward, working it in tiny increments between his body and Anna's. It would have been easier had Anna situated herself on top of the sheet and blankets, but the room's chill had driven her to burrow under them and warm herself against the furnace that was his chest.

He glanced in Cybelline's direction to see if she was observing his progress. She was, but he noticed that nothing about his predicament or his solution to it disposed her to humor. "I did not carry her in here," he said.

"I was not aware I accused you of such." Cybelline sat down while she pulled on her stockings. Under her breath, she added, "You did not lock the door."

"There is no lock."

Cybelline made no reply to this. One stocking dangled from her fingertips as she bent forward and rested her head in her hands. She ignored Ferrin's cautious use of her name and said nothing when he inquired if she was all right.

Ferrin searched for some sign that she was weeping and saw no evidence of it. The slope of her shoulders and the stillness of her posture spoke to her discouragement and anxieties. He continued to tug on his shirt and was finally able to ease it completely under Anna. Cradling her bottom and the back of her head, Ferrin sat up and put his legs over the side of the bed.

"I'm taking her back to the other room," he said. He paused long enough to know that Cybelline was not going to object, then he carried Anna out. He made certain the bed was warm enough, then laid her down and tucked the covers around her. Anna's long lashes fluttered once before she smiled vaguely and inserted her thumb in her mouth. Ferrin waited to see if she would wake, but Anna merely turned over.

By the time Ferrin returned to his own bedchamber, Cybelline was dressed and busying herself straightening the bedcovers. "She's still sleeping," he said. Cybelline didn't pause in her work or acknowledge that she'd heard him. He closed the door quietly behind him and stood there a moment, wondering if he would be required to block her exit so they could speak frankly. "Leave that, Cybelline, and look at me."

Cybelline's back stiffened, but she stopped tugging on the quilt and pivoted. Her rigid carriage and implacable expression did not invite conversation.

Ferrin sighed. "I am heartily sorry that happened, but there is no reason to suppose the sky is falling. Anna is unlikely to remember climbing into our bed. And even if she does, what sense will she make of it?"

"You have such a breadth of experience with children, do you?" She did not pause long enough to allow him to answer. "It matters not a whit whether my daughter will remember coming into this room. I will remember. She might have gone anywhere, done anything. Or did you think I only cared that she wandered in here while we were abed? That is the very least of it."

"I don't believe you." Ferrin's glacial gaze dropped to Cybelline's side, where one hand clenched into a tight fist. "What you say is true: She might have gone anywhere. But as best as I can determine, she didn't. She came looking for her mother and found her here—in my bed—and that is what rankles and what you are not prepared to forgive. Admit what you fear most, Cybelline. It is not simply what Anna will recall or repeat to others, it is what you will have to do to make it right."

"Some things cannot be made right."

"This is not one of them."

"I won't marry you."

"Your refusal is in want of a proposal. I do not recall making one."

Cybelline's mouth flattened, and she drew in a sharp breath through her nose. Her posture remained unyielding.

Ferrin raked back his hair. "Is it me you object to?" he asked finally. "Or is it the prospect of marriage that you find so abhorrent?"

"Why must it be one or the other? Why cannot it be both?"

"Is it, Cybelline? Is it both?" He was not surprised when she remained silent. His slight smile held no humor. "I am coming late to the realization that you are skilled at skirting even the direct question. Perhaps it is just as well. I am no longer certain I want to know the answer, and more important, whether it matters. I have no doubt that should circumstances conspire against you, you will do what is necessary for Anna's sake, if not for your own."

Her struggle for composure, he observed, was an inward one. None of it showed on her face. She remained dry-eyed and unblinking, and her breathing was steady. It was her very stillness that hinted at the depth of her distress. Ferrin stepped aside, giving her a clear path to the door. "Go on," he said quietly. "Go to your daughter."

Cybelline fled.

The activity at the Sharpe house increased tenfold over the course of the next four weeks. Cybelline hired craftsmen from Penwyckham and nearby hamlets to begin the restoration of the house in earnest. Listening carefully to the advice of her laborers, Cybelline approved every detail of the work. She learned about framing and joists and plasterwork and mortar. From her study of the paintings in the house, she was able to chose colors and fabrics that were reminiscent of the Sharpe house in its grander days. The rooms that Lady Beatrice Sharpe largely had occupied in her later years were brightened with white wainscoting and more cheerful appointments. Cybelline insisted on stripping, sanding, and staining the pedestal that held Beatrice's heavy family Bible. This was accomplished under the watchful eye of the carpenter, who was moved to comment a dozen times over that he had never seen the like before.

If anyone on her staff thought it peculiar that she demonstrated such a fever of interest in the house, no one broached the subject with her. There was the odd moment when she caught Webb looking at her as if she meant to say something, but the maid always held her tongue and could not be drawn out. Cybelline acknowledged to herself that she did not make a serious effort to learn what Webb was thinking. It seemed the wiser course to avoid disagreements that would test their fragile peace.

Ferrin did not distance himself from the Sharpe house. He was a regular, if not daily, visitor. In the beginning, Cybelline stopped what she was doing to sit with him in the drawing room and engage in polite, though not particularly warm, conversation. After almost a week of entertaining in this manner, she decided not to disrupt her activity and invited him to join her wherever she was working.

It was not her intent to offend him; however, Cybelline concluded that if her invitation discouraged his visits as her cool discourse had not, she would not be consumed by regret. Since Ferrin was in every way amenable to her suggestion, and more than a little amused by it, she wasn't presented with the opportunity to determine if she was perhaps lying to herself.

Ferrin's patience unnerved her. She was not unaware of his purpose in appearing as often as he did, but she believed he would lose interest in her as his most recent experiment. At the end of a fortnight she was moved by frustration to finally say as much. He considered this at length, then allowed that she might be right.

She did not experience the sense of satisfaction she'd anticipated.

Just as he had done during her illness and convalescence, he made himself useful. It was diabolical, really, the way he presented himself at just the right time. She found herself turning to him simply because he was always there. He never offered a suggestion when one was not requested, and he never refused her his best judgment when she was in need of it.

Cybelline noticed that he seldom arrived empty-handed. Sometimes he carried clever tools for her laborers that made their tasks easier; sometimes he came with a trinket for Anna. Most often he brought a book and read to her while she worked on some stationary project that confined her to a single room.

At night she fell asleep still hearing his voice. It was maddening.

In a very short time, all of Penwyckham knew that Mr. Wellsley was courting her. Had anyone inquired, she would have described his suit as more in the way of laying siege. She considered sending for the Iceni spear.

Ferrin spent part of each visit with Anna. Cybelline did not discourage him, but she often found herself figuratively holding her breath, waiting for the moment Anna would disingenuously announce that she wanted to take her nap with Masterlee and Mama again. The disclosure would cause a scandal only if it was said in front of others, but since there were always people moving about, it seemed unlikely that it would not be overheard.

As days, then weeks, passed, her daughter's silence gave Cybelline hope that a nine days' wonder and a hasty marriage could be averted. Like Anna, she and Ferrin did not discuss what had happened at the Pembroke cottage. If Anna's silence was predicated on her inability to recall the incident or assign it any import, Cybelline knew the same could not be said for her and his lordship.

Although no words on the subject were exchanged, the looks they traded were telling. More than once Cybelline felt her breath seize because Ferrin's glance sliced through her defenses. Whether she glared back or feigned indifference, he only ever showed amusement.

Because of that faintly secretive and uneven smile, he was completely recognizable to her as the man she dreamed about each night.

Desperate for distraction, Cybelline contemplated inviting the scoundrels to the Sharpe house. Pinch, Dash, and Midge excelled at drawing attention to themselves even when their intention was the opposite. The respite they could provide was reason enough to have them underfoot, but Cybelline's concern that such an invitation would be met with suspicion by her brother and Lily kept her from extending it.

Distraction, when it came, was unwelcome.

The post arrived on a Tuesday afternoon. As she was instructed to do, Mrs. Henley set the letters on the tray in the entrance hall and went to inform Cybelline of the delivery. When the housekeeper returned for the tray, she discovered Ferrin standing near the front door, in the act of removing his hat and coat.

She hurried over to take his outerwear. "Oh, and I'm sure I didn't hear you at the door, Mr. Wellsley. It is good that you do not stand on ceremony, else you would be standing in the cold." Mrs. Henley took his gloves and laid them over the greatcoat. "Have you ever known a winter to be so bitter?"

"Not many," he said, though he was not speaking strictly of the season. The chill that often greeted him inside the Sharpe house was in every way a match for the weather outside of it. While Ferrin expected there would be a thaw in the weeks to come, he was not nearly as certain he could anticipate the same from Cybelline. "What task is occupying Mrs. Caldwell today?"

"Sewing. The fabric for the new drapes in the drawing room arrived today. Mrs. Caldwell's working in her sitting room." Her eyes fell on the book he was cradling in the crook of his arm. "Is it still *Pride and Prejudice*, Mr. Wellsley?"

He shook his head. "We finished that. This is something of an entirely different nature. An amusing story: *Rip van Winkle*."

Mrs. Henley frowned. "Aren't you served better by a romance?"

"Do you think so? I confess, I was afraid of comparisons to another formidable gentleman in the mold of Mr. Darcy. I think Mr. van Winkle will not cast me in too poor a light."

"Very clever," Mrs. Henley said approvingly. "Shall I announce you?"

"I'll announce myself. The sitting room, you said?"

"Yes. And if you do not mind, it will be such a favor if you'd take the post to her. I was on that very mission when you arrived."

"Certainly." He picked up the letters without examining them and slid them inside his book, then he took to the stairs.

Cybelline was not successful at tempering her heartbeat. It had begun to race the moment she heard Ferrin's familiar tread. Since he was capable of approaching almost soundlessly, she could only suppose that he wanted her to know he was coming. She was better at schooling her features than she was at moderating her pulse. When he appeared in the doorway, her polite smile was fixed.

"Good afternoon," Ferrin said. "I told Mrs. Henley that I would announce myself."

"And so you did. I heard your approach while you were yet on the stairs." It was only after the words were out that she realized she had given something away. He might well conclude that she had come to know his step, even that she was in anticipation of it. He confirmed this with the lift of a single dark eyebrow. Cybelline quickly returned her attention to the fabric lying across her lap.

Ferrin did not have to restrain his grin, as she was studiously avoiding him. He crossed the room to stand in front of her. "This is for the drawing room?" he asked, gesturing to the material bunched all around her on the window seat.

"Yes. Mr. Foster delivered it himself this morning."

"Did he? He must set great store by your patronage."

She glanced up. "I can't say if that is so. I believe he has developed sincere feelings for Miss Webb."

"I see." He had had an inkling that such might be the case. "I seem to recall Mrs. Meeder informing Mrs. Lowell that it was so."

Cybelline chuckled. "It is difficult to imagine what weather conditions would have to exist to deter Mrs. Meeder from making her rounds. She is more reliable than the post."

"Ah. You have reminded me." He opened the book he was holding and removed the pair of letters. "Mrs. Henley asked me to bring these to you." Ferrin extended the letters to Cybelline without glancing at them. He had already made a study of the pair once he was away from Mrs. Henley's watchful eye, and now his attention was all for Cybelline's response. He could have been observing only half so well and not have missed the color draining from her face.

"Will you put them on the table?" she asked, not deigning to take them. "I will read them later when my hands aren't otherwise occupied."

Ferrin decided to press a little. "Mayhap you would allow me to read them to you."

"No!" Then more softly, as she composed herself, she said, "No, thank you. I can never know what Aunt Georgia might be moved to write. It is perhaps better that I read them first."

It was not a bad recovery, Ferrin thought, though he could not give her full marks for it. He knew too much to be fooled. "Cybelline," he said gently, holding up the letters, "I have read your aunt's correspondence and am familiar with her penmanship. These are not from her." Before she could offer another lie, he stopped her. "And do not say they are from your brother, your sister-in-law, or any of the scoundrels. Neither envelope has been franked by Sheridan."

Agitated, Cybelline nearly pricked her finger as she stabbed her needle into the fabric. "You must think you are very clever, my lord. I wonder that you have not already informed me who they *are* from."

"Do not tempt me, Cybelline. I resisted the urge to read one written by the same hand as this pair before, and I brought you these straightaway without trying to divine their content. I would rather you explain why they upset you, but I cannot promise I won't be moved to read them if you do not."

Cybelline stopped plying her needle and looked up at him. "What do you mean, you resisted the urge before? When did you—"

He interrupted her. "The evening Webb summoned me to assist her," he said. "There was a tray at your bedside with letters on it. Your maid had already informed me that you had been troubled of late by certain correspondence, and when I was alone I made a cursory examination of your post." Ferrin watched Cybelline's jaw come together tightly and thought he knew the bent of her mind. "Miss Webb is not at fault here. She did as she thought best and is more responsible for saving your life than I am. If she revealed rather more than you wish she had, then your reckoning must be with me, for surely I placed her in a position where her loyalty was compromised by her fear."

Cybelline exhaled slowly. "I know," she said quietly. "I blamed Webb. It was badly done of me."

"Yes, it was."

She accepted his censure as her due and offered no defense.

Ferrin set the book aside and drew her attention back to the letters. "Will you tell me about these, Cybelline? Are they from a creditor? A solicitor? Have they something to do with Anna or your late husband's estate?"

"No. None of that."

"Am I to guess, then? I will, you know. I will arrive at the truth of the thing eventually. I always do."

"Persistence is another of your annoying traits, I have found."

"It is accounted to be so, yes."

A shadow of a smile crossed her features and left a grave countenance in its wake. "Is it so important that you know this particular truth?"

"Yes," he said. "I think it is."

"Why?"

"Because it seems to me there should not be so great a secret as this in a marriage."

Both of Cybelline's eyebrows lifted. "Marriage? You are speaking generally, is that correct?"

"I was speaking of our marriage most specifically, though it is a principle that deserves wider application."

Neither of Cybelline's eyebrows lowered even a fraction. "You are quite mad."

He shrugged. "But you are intrigued, are you not?"

"I am stunned."

Ferrin shook his head. "I doubt that. You have been in anticipation of a proposal every day since you visited Pembroke cottage. Set your mind at ease. It will not be today. Perhaps not even tomorrow, though one can never tell."

"But Anna has said nothing."

"True."

Cybelline's voice lowered to a whisper. "And I am not carrying your child."

He sighed. "That is a disappointment, but it presents us with the opportunity to put marriage and childbirth in the proper order." He held out the letters a second time. "As to this correspondence, I believe the time is upon us for you to tell me the whole of it."

"And make you think I welcome your proposal?"

"A proposal is inevitable, Cybelline, whether you welcome it or not."

Cybelline held his eyes for a long time to judge his truthfulness. She was forced to acquit him of any pretense and wondered that her own heart did not lodge permanently in her throat. With some difficulty, she swallowed, then asked, "What do you want to know?"

Ferrin placed both letters in her outstretched hand. "Who wrote these?"

"That is more difficult to answer than you might credit." She moved the fabric to one end of the window bench and regarded the letters again after she held one in each hand. "As you've noted, they are both addressed by the same person," she told Ferrin. "But this one"—she raised her right hand— "most likely contains correspondence from my husband."

"I'm not certain I follow. Your husband writes to you?"

"That is easily the most absurd utterance I have ever heard you make."

"The same also occurred to me." He used his fingers to rake his hair. "You will explain yourself, I hope, else I will be forced to repeat it."

Cybelline returned the envelope to him. "Go on. You may open it. All will be made clear."

Ferrin hesitated only a moment. He accepted the letter, opened it, and began to read. "It is dated 12 March three years ago." He heard Cybelline's sharp intake of breath and glanced at her. "You know this letter?"

"I can guess at the content. That is the day my pregnancy was confirmed, and I shared the happy news with Nicholas."

"He was pleased?"

"I thought so. The letter will tell you more, I think. Does it begin, 'My dearest'?"

"Yes."

She nodded. "Then it is indeed from Nicholas."

Ferrin glanced at the letter again but did not try to read it. Words stood out: *my heart, most joyful news, my agreeable and accommodating wife, a wish fulfilled.*

"You are discomfited," Cybelline said, watching him. "And you were so certain you wished to know the content."

"It is a love letter."

"Yes."

"You will want to read it yourself," he said. "It was meant for you." Ferrin thought Cybelline's rueful smile communicated a greater depth of sadness than was her practice to reveal. It made him look more closely at the letter, then read it to himself in its entirety.

My dearest,

My heart is full. The most joyful news has been made known to me, and there is no one with whom I would share it before you. I hope you will find it cause to celebrate rather than grieve. I have never made a secret of my desire for a child. I have longed for this outcome in my marriage, and it has finally come to pass. My agreeable and accommodating wife is enceinte. I am to be a father at last, my love. You know it is a wish fulfilled, and eventually one I hope we will share. I cannot say that it matters at all if she will bear a son or daughter, but that I look forward to the day with great excitement.

You will comprehend the consequences for us. We will have more opportunity to be together, not less, as my wife is almost certain to engage herself in raising our child. It is because she was abandoned by her own parents, I think, that she will want to give her undivided attention to the babe, no matter that it is not the popular thing to do. I am satisfied, however, that she will be a most excellent mother and that our child will want for nothing nor be spoilt by excess. You must see that she is most suited to this purpose and acknowledge at last that I have chosen well. She will be able to do what we cannot, my dearest, and for that she will have my gratitude.

Pray, do not forget that it is you who owns my heart.

Always

Cybelline nearly recoiled from the icy hardness of Ferrin's expression as he looked up. She saw his fingers begin to curl around the letter, and she stood quickly to stay his hand. "It is mine," she said. "Not meant for me when it was written, but mine now. I beg you not to destroy it."

Ferrin allowed her to take the letter before his fingers

closed in a tight fist. "Bloody hell," he said softly. "Why would you want to keep it?"

Tears came to her eyes. "I don't know." Her gaze was drawn to the letter and the words swam in front of her: *longed for this outcome, abandoned, most suited, always.* A tear splashed the paper, and she swiped at it, then knuckled her eyes. "I have never known," she whispered brokenly. "But I have them all."

Ferrin took her gently by the shoulders. "How many?"

She shrugged as if it were of no import. "A dozen, I think. Perhaps this makes a dozen. I am not certain."

"Who knows about them?"

"You." Cybelline gathered the frayed edges of her composure as if it were a tangible thing and could be wrapped about her. "Do not pity me, my lord. I would find that to be most objectionable."

"I'm sure you would." He let his arms slide from her shoulders to her elbows, then fall away. "What of the other letter?"

Cybelline had forgotten she still held it. "I think you will like this even less. I know I do."

He took it but did not immediately open it. "Is it from her?"

"I have always supposed so."

My dear Mrs. Caldwell,

Will Anna love you still when she learns the truth? Murder is not easily forgiven nor forgotten. I know it well.

Always

Ferrin used his fingertip to break the wax seal. He unfolded the letter and read aloud:

Ferrin caught Cybelline before her knees buckled and encouraged her to sit. "I take it they are not all like this."

She shook her head and tried to draw breath. Panic welled up inside her, and she thought she would be sick. She realized she must have looked ill as well, for Ferrin brought a basin from the dressing room and positioned it just above her lap. Several minutes passed before she knew she could safely push it out of the way.

"Are you certain?" he asked, eying the empty basin and then her pale face. "It's no trouble to hold it."

"Take it."

Ferrin was impressed enough with the firmness of her response that he put it aside. "You have not examined Mr. Caldwell's letter yet. Do you wish me to read it to you?"

"No." She smoothed it open on her lap before she raised it. Her hand shook slightly as her eyes moved across and down the paper. When she was finished, she thrust it at Ferrin. "It makes her letter all the more vile. I do not think I am mistaken that she means to threaten me."

"It is my sense of the thing also." Ferrin folded both letters and dropped them in the basin. "Is there anyone you suspect of having been your husband's mistress?"

"You must understand that I did not suspect he had a mistress. I learned of it only after he died and one of his letters was delivered to me. It was followed shortly by one from her. Until this afternoon, that has always been the pattern. A letter that he penned, followed several days later by one from her. I have never received them together. I can only suppose it is because we are so far from London and the post is not always certain here. One letter caught up to the other."

"May I see the others?" When she hesitated, Ferrin did not press. His silence seemed to decide her.

"Very well, but I cannot sit here while you examine

them. I believe I will take a walk. It will help to clear my head."

Ferrin nodded and stood when she indicated that he should do so. He watched her open the bench lid and dig deep into the bottom. She removed a Chinese puzzle box and placed it in his hands.

"Do you know how to open it?"

"At another time I would be intrigued. Just now, I would sooner smash the thing than discover its secret."

Cybelline took the box back long enough to open it, then she quit the room without a last glance in Ferrin's direction.

He came upon her later standing at the site where he meant to build a footbridge some day. She appeared to be impervious to the cold. The chinchilla collar of her pelisse was turned up so the fur brushed her cheeks, and she stood at an angle against the gusting wind.

"When Mrs. Henley told me you had not returned to the house, I became concerned. If it is peace that you want, I will leave you to it."

She shook her head. "No, don't go. I have had enough of my own company. I am also humbled to discover that I prefer yours." She tilted her head back to look up at him. "That surprises you."

"Yes, but that you would admit as much surprises me more."

"It is the same for me." She turned away again, facing the frozen brook. She strained to hear the rush of water under the ice but she could not make out the sound. Except for the occasional rising wind, the stillness of winter had settled everywhere. "You read all of it?"

"Yes."

Her breath was made visible by the cold air. "It was lowering to learn my husband kept a mistress, but worse still to discover how much feeling he had for her and how tepid were his feelings for me. I know there is a certain acceptance by society for a husband and his mistress, but I do not think I would have been able to feign indifference or ignore it. It's true that women are often asked to do such things, and many comply, yet I believe I might have been moved to divorce him." She glanced at Ferrin to gauge his reaction. "A scandalous solution, is it not?"

"Some would say so, yes."

"Would you?"

"It is a solution. Whether it is scandalous is better left for the wags to decide. They attend to the gossip, especially if they are self-righteous and in want of keeping their own transgressions secret."

She smiled faintly at this observation. "There is an irony there, my lord, for you make your vices public and keep your virtues secret."

"It has never caused me to lose a night's sleep," he said.

"You are very different from Nicholas in that way."

"I hope in other ways as well."

Cybelline ignored that. "My husband's sleep was often disturbed. He worried that his restlessness would keep me awake. Sometimes it did, though I do not recall complaining. From time to time he put forth the idea of separate bedrooms, but I did not want that. He indulged me until I told him I was with child, then he insisted on another bedroom for himself. He said he was afraid he would hurt me with his fitful sleep, but after Anna was born he never moved back."

She blushed a little and self-consciously fiddled with the raised collar of her pelisse. She did not look at Ferrin. "Sometimes I went to him. He did not turn me away, though I wished on occasion that he would. It was never comfortable between us when he did not come to me first. Eventually I stopped seeking him out and learned that I could wait."

Cybelline hugged herself. "I loved him, you know. You must never think that I did not love him. He was kind and generous, charming and clever. He was a good companion everywhere save in our bed, and I was prepared to take the responsibility for that. To discover he had a mistress hurt deeply, but it was the discovery that he loved her so well that I thought would kill me."

She raised her face to Ferrin and regarded him frankly. "My husband died by his own hand, my lord, but were he in front of me as you are now, he would die by mine."

Ferrin nodded slowly, taking this in. "You are telling me this for a reason, I collect."

Her anxious eyes searched his face. "I must have fidelity."

"It is the same for me." He waited, wondering if she would say more. When she did not, he asked, "And love, Cybelline? What of that?"

"I do not trust my own heart. You cannot expect that I will trust yours."

"I see." He opened his arms to her and was encouraged that she came into his embrace without hesitation. "A proposal is still inevitable, you know."

Turned as she was, her head resting lightly against his shoulder, Cybelline was glad he could not see her bittersweet smile.

Chapter Twelve

The scoundrels were reciting Byron, of all things, when Sherry entered the schoolroom. The trio rolled their eyes in unison but were unaffected by the interruption and made no mistake in their phrasing or meter.

Sherry crossed the room to his wife's side. She was sitting at her desk, reading from the book of poetry as the boys recited. She absently offered her cheek for his kiss and he obliged, grinning. Apparently Lord Byron's work did not excite the blood when recounted by three young ruffians who wished themselves elsewhere.

When they finished, Sherry nodded approvingly. "Well done, sirs. It was a noble effort. Someday you will say those words with a passion that will impress the ladies."

"Oh, I 'ope not," Pinch said, frowning deeply, his dark eyes keen with worry. "Don't want a lady that goes swoony for poetry."

Sherry glanced at Lily. "Swoony?"

She shrugged helplessly.

Chuckling, Sherry said, "And you, Dash? Will you like to make the ladies go swoony?"

Always a bit restless, Dash's knee bounced under his desk. He pushed back an errant lock of flaxen hair. "Would they be pretty ladies?"

Sherry regarded his young ward thoughtfully. At twelve, the boy was showing very clear signs of the strikingly handsome man he would become. "I suspect so, Dash. You might not even be required to know Byron."

"That's all right, then," Dash said. "I'd rather know pirates."

"Sherry!" Lily admonished him as he gave a shout of laughter. She threw up her hands when he sobered and winked at the boys.

"Midge?" Sherry caught one of Lily's hands and set it against his thigh as he hitched his hip on her desk. "Swoony ladies?"

Still the smallest of the scoundrels, Midge had to move forward in his chair for his feet to touch the floor. "I don't know," he said. His deep blue eyes were thoughtful. "I'm learning that the ladies make me a bit swoony. Can't be a good thing if we're all dropping to floor like sash flies."

"No, indeed," Sherry said carefully. He felt Lily's fingernails pressing deeply into his leg as she bought composure with his pound of flesh. "Perhaps the romantic poets are not for you, Midge."

"That's what I'm thinking, sir."

"Good man." He tilted his head in the direction of the door. "Go on. I would have a word with my wife now." He was not astonished in the least, or even offended, when they looked to Lily for approval. This room was her domain.

"Do not go far," she told them.

The boys' effort to exit with a modicum of reserve had Sherry and Lily rolling their eyes this time. As soon as they were out of sight in the hallway, they abandoned restraint in favor of a foot race.

"Perhaps they did not understand what you meant by not going far," Sherry said. The scoundrels' footsteps were already a mere echo.

"I am confident that you will collect them for me." At

Sherry's frown, she added. "Think of it as hide-and-seek. You enjoy a good game of it now and again."

"I like it better when you are hiding and I am seeking."

She gave him a butter-would-not-melt smile, released his thigh, and reminded him, "You have interrupted my lessons."

"I know. Really, Lily. Byron?"

"It will not damage them permanently, Sherry, and mayhap they will even come to appreciate it."

He regarded her curiously. "Do you go a bit swoony when I read Byron to you?"

"I drop like a sash fly."

Sherry laughed. "That is a picture, is it not?" He reached inside his frock coat and withdrew a letter. "Here is the reason I have come. Once again I've had the most curious correspondence from Cybelline. Will you read it?"

"If you like." She accepted the letter after he unfolded it. Cybelline's missive was not long, and Lily read it quickly once, then more slowly. She comprehended perfectly why Sherry had not waited to bring it to her attention. "Do you know this Mr. Wellsley?" she asked, lowering the letter and raising her eyes to her husband. "I do not, but you will agree that it is always to be desired."

Sherry nodded. Lily's past made her cautious of meeting people, especially London gentlemen. The prospect of an introduction always filled her with dread, and Sherry was conscious of this. It also did not follow that simply because she was unfamiliar with Wellsley's name, that she was therefore unfamiliar with Mr. Wellsley. "I met him once, I believe, if it is the same fellow of whom Cybelline writes. Ferrin made the introduction. It's been an age, though. I cannot well recall the look of him. I imagine he is completely unexceptional. No hump or missing parts, I am sure of that."

This last comment teased a small smile from Lily, but it faded quickly. "And Ferrin? Who is he?"

Sherry understood that Lily must have all the information. "The Earl of Ferrin. An acquaintance of some years, though we rarely shared the same company. He is rumored to be something of a rake." He saw that gave Lily immediate pause. "That reputation necessarily separated us. You know well that I have never craved the attention of the *ton*."

"What is this Mr. Wellsley's reputation?"

"I don't know that I've ever heard, but he is more than an acquaintance to Ferrin. Fast friends, I should think. You will have to put your own construction on what that might mean, but I caution you against painting Ferrin and Wellsley with the same brush."

"Do you suppose your sister knows Wellsley is fast friend to a rake?"

"I couldn't say."

"But you'll tell her, won't you?" Lily asked anxiously. "Then she can decide if it is important."

"If you think it's best."

"I do. Knowing is always better than ignorance." Lily glanced at the letter again. "She writes that they will arrive at the end of the month. Do you think he means to seek your approval for a match?"

"I am only certain that Cybelline will not." A crease appeared between his eyebrows as he considered the whole of his sister's correspondence. "I wish she were not so damnably vague, but you are interpreting her missive in the same manner I am. Can you tell if she is in love?"

Lily shook her head. "Perhaps we are making too much of the fact that she has invited Mr. Wellsley to travel with her, or the fact that she is coming to Granville at all. We should not forget how much she loved Nicholas. That he killed himself was a betrayal. She might not want to risk loving so deeply again."

"No, I understand, but I do not like to think of Cybelline

as a partner in a marriage of convenience. She should know joy. Is it wrong for me to want that for her?"

"Of course not, but it's what she wants for herself that will matter." Lily found his hand and threaded her fingers through his. "We shall see what that is, I suppose, when she arrives." She picked up the letter with her free hand and gave it a last look. "Now, please tell me what business Cybelline can possibly have with Sir Richard Settle that she must delay her trip until the end of the month?"

Cybelline invited Sir Richard to sit as she poured tea. The former don at Cambridge chose the wing chair opposite hers. She noticed that he sat rather more correctly than other men of her acquaintance. He did not show the least inclination to stretch his legs or push himself forward in a casual recline. His manner was invariably correct and unfailingly courteous, and it hinted at a superiority of self that never failed to set Cybelline's teeth on edge.

The tightness in her jaw was not helped by the notion that he seemed to expect that his extensive accomplishments allowed him to indulge in a certain arrogance of expression. Nicholas had never been entirely in accord with her assessment of Sir Richard, though he was moved to say once that the professor was impatient with anyone who could not be persuaded to agree with him. Cybelline thought that made Sir Richard unattractively narrow-minded, but Nicholas said it meant only that he did not suffer fools.

When she'd asked if she was such a fool, Nicholas had merely laughed and called her a nuncheon for thinking it. She supposed that answered her question.

As unattractive as Cybelline found Sir Richard's narrow-minded scholarship, she had never denied to herself that he was an attractive man. As he was of an age with Lady Rivendale, Cybelline had wondered from time to time if her aunt would consider him an acceptable suitor. Along with his shock of thick brown hair and equally dark eyes, he possessed even features that were shaped by a fine hand. Although she was certain Sir Richard was handsome enough for Aunt Georgia's tastes, she finally decided his manner might be off-putting to her as well. When she raised this with Nicholas, he'd been in complete agreement.

Sir Richard thanked her politely when she passed him a cup of tea, but he refused the tiny sandwiches she'd had Mrs. Minty prepare. Cybelline set the plate back on the table between them.

"I am very glad you were able to come so far to discuss this matter with me," she said. "It has been a terrible inconvenience for you, I'm afraid, and I would have you know how much it is appreciated."

"It is inconvenient, as you say, but what is one to do?"

"Your accommodations are satisfactory, I hope."

"Satisfactory, yes. The room faces east, I believe, and will receive the morning sun."

"That's right."

He sighed. "No matter. I shall draw the bed curtains."

"I can have you put in another bedchamber if you like." She thought of Ferrin's windowless workroom and wondered if it might not suit.

"No. I shall not stay above a few days. Long enough to conduct our business and rest for the return to London. I will stop in Cambridgeshire on my journey home, so that is something to look forward to."

Cybelline nodded graciously, but she was still contemplating the workroom as a bedchamber. She watched Sir Richard cast his eyes about the room as though searching for something on which he might comment favorably. Apparently finding nothing, he remained silent and sipped his tea.

"I was not certain you received my initial inquiry," she said, "your reply was so long in coming."

"I had other matters to occupy me."

"I understand." She could hear boredom edging his tone. His features, too, were drawn in a weary mien. "I did not mean to imply that you had been remiss or uninterested." Cybelline managed to imply both those things simply by raising them. She experienced a small measure of satisfaction as Sir Richard uncrossed his legs, then crossed them again, this time to the other side. It is what passed for discomfort, and she was unashamed of provoking it. "You have expressed interest in my late husband's collection," she said. "As I mentioned in my first correspondence, I am desirous of parting with some of the pieces."

"You do not want to give them to the Royal Society?"

"You are welcome to make a gift of them if you wish. You are a member, are you not?"

"Of course."

"My husband was not."

"Your husband was a barrister, not a man of science."

"He was both," she said, "but we can agree to disagree."

"Have you considered Nicholas's wishes?"

"I have. He admired you and considered it an honor that you assisted him in his study. I cannot think of another living gentleman that he respected more. He did not speak of judges on the high court with such reverence, and my husband loved the law. I believe he would want you to have them."

"At a price."

Cybelline did not think she mistook the mockery in his tone, but she ignored it. "That is my decision. I would see that Anna is well provided for. I *know* my husband wanted that."

"I'm sure." Sir Richard took another sip of tea. "Let us discuss the pieces, then. I am familiar with the ones you listed in your letter. The Iceni shield is of particular interest."

"It was a favorite piece."

"Nicholas almost gave it to the museum, is that right?"

She nodded. "He parted with one of lesser quality but could not bring himself to turn over the one I am offering you. I think it had as much to do with the discovery of the shield as with the condition of the piece itself."

"Do you know how he discovered it?"

"He was traipsing through a ruin in Norfolk and struck his toe on it." She smiled faintly, recalling Nicholas's account. "He told me he tripped and stumbled about before crashing to his knees. There were stones all around, and he thought that's what he'd caught with his boot. You know from your long association that it was like him to be certain of a thing before he moved on. He went back to see what had caused his fall and found one small sliver of the shield rising above the ground like a fingernail moon."

Sir Richard set his empty cup on the table.

"Will you have more?" asked Cybelline.

"No, thank you." He took a sandwich instead. "There were several pieces you did not mention. The gold torc, for instance. You do not wish to sell it?"

"No."

"And the bracelets?"

"No. Nicholas gave them to me."

"I see. So you are willing to part with what was his but not what is yours."

"That's correct."

"And the spear?"

"I haven't decided. You may make an offer, but I do not know if I wish to sell it."

"Then the spear is in your possession again?"

"Yes."

His eyes narrowed faintly. "You are not surprised that I know you didn't have it for a time."

"No. Lord Ferrin told me that he went to you to learn

about it. That hardly surprises, given your expertise in these artifacts. He told me he was your student at Cambridge." Cybelline watched Sir Richard smile with what appeared to be genuine pleasure. It deepened the faint creases at the corners of his eyes and mouth, yet stripped away a decade from his age. She could not help staring at him, fascinated by the change.

"Ferrin was not my student," he said. "He was everyone's. Do you know him well?"

"I know his reputation," Cybelline said.

"Then you might not credit that he was a student such as few of us have had the privilege to tutor. He has failed to realize his potential, but his intellect remains quite fierce, I believe. It is his interests that have changed."

Cybelline felt herself come under Sir Richard's more thoughtful regard. She was made vaguely uncomfortable by it.

"How did Ferrin come to have the spear in his possession?"

"He didn't tell you?"

"I wouldn't ask otherwise, would I?"

"I carried it to a masquerade at his home and left it behind." Telling the truth had certain rewards, she realized. Sir Richard's supercilious expression was not in evidence when he was choking on his sandwich. She poured a second cup of tea for him. "Since I was in costume, his lordship did not know to whom the spear belonged."

"But you did not claim it immediately."

"No. I was preparing to leave London. The spear was not uppermost on my mind, though I can appreciate if you think it should have been. It was returned to me after I arrived in Penwyckham."

"It is here, then?"

"No. I wasn't clear, was I? I have it from his lordship that it was returned to my London home."

"Has he made an offer for it?"

"No. I had not considered that he might. Does he collect artifacts?"

"As a dilettante only. It is a minor collection. We discussed it when he brought the spear for me to examine."

"I hadn't realized." That was another truth. "Do you think he would be interested in the spear?"

"If he has not already said as much, then I doubt it."

Cybelline nodded. "It's not important. As I said, I am not certain I want to part with it."

"I understand. I trust you will permit me to reconsider what offer I might make for the pieces. I'd hoped you would entertain adding the torc and the bracelets. As this is not the case, I will require this evening to review my figures. Regardless, my offer is dependent upon a final appraisal of the items."

"Of course. I believe I wrote that you were welcome to look at them before you set out for Penwyckham. I instructed my housekeeper to make the pieces available to you."

"It is the appraisal that I make before taking them into my possession that matters. You must not take offense, Mrs. Caldwell. I am always so careful. I have discovered there is considerable fraud in the acquisition of artifacts and relics."

"I take no offense," she said coolly. "My husband shared your opinion."

"Naturally."

Cybelline rose. "Supper is at seven. I hope you will dine with me, but I will understand if you wish to retire to your room and remain there."

Sir Richard came to his feet also. "I shall look forward to dining with you, Mrs. Caldwell, but I will retire to my room until then."

It was after midnight when Cybelline awoke and knew with certainty that she was no longer alone. "Anna?" It would not be the first time her daughter had slipped out of the nursery and come looking for her. Nanny Baker slept too soundly to deter her. "Anna? Is it you?"

Cybelline pushed herself upright as a dark figure much too substantial to be her daughter passed in front of the doorway to her sitting room. "Sir Richard?"

"No, but shall I ask him to attend you?"

Cybelline snatched a pillow from behind her back and threw it at Ferrin. Since it didn't hit the floor and he didn't give up any sound of distress, she imagined he'd caught the thing easily. "What are you doing here?"

"Satisfying my curiosity." He pitched the pillow back at her. The firelight was sufficient for him to find a chair with no difficulty. He picked it up and moved it to Cybelline's bedside, then he lighted a candle, dropped a kiss on Cybelline's slightly open mouth, and sat down. Tipping the chair back on its two rear legs, he set his feet against the bed rail.

"Your curiosity will kill you."

"That's cats."

Cybelline tucked the pillow behind the small of her back and made herself comfortable. "I suppose you want to know the particulars of my conversation with Sir Richard."

"Unless you are prepared to explain the particulars of electrodynamics." He held up his hands, surrendering, when she looked as if she was prepared to upend his chair. "Did Sir Richard make an offer?"

"Not yet. He was disappointed that I was not willing to sell him either the torc or the bracelets. He is also interested in the spear, I think."

Ferrin did not comment on this last, though his eyebrows lifted a fraction. "I wish I might have joined you."

"I should have allowed you to do so just for the pleasure of listening to you explain how you came to be Mr. Wellsley. You could not hope to keep it from him, not with Mrs. Henley most assuredly announcing you as such."

"There is that." He folded his arms in front of him. "Are you quite certain you want to sell the pieces, Cybelline?"

"Yes. I considered it long before I left London, but I wasn't ready. I had to leave them behind to appreciate what a burden they had become. The torc and bracelets will be Anna's someday, and with what the other pieces bring I will establish a trust for her."

"Do you think I won't provide for Anna?"

"No, I know you will, but Nicholas also provided for her, and she should know that. It will be important to her."

"Your parents provided for you?"

She frowned, but her features cleared as she understood what prompted his question. "You are referring to Nicholas's letter, the one in which he wrote that my parents abandoned me. It's not true. They were killed in a fire that destroyed the inn where they were passing the night. They were on their way to visit Sherry at Eton. I grieved for them, but I never felt abandoned. Aunt Georgia made certain I didn't, and yes, they provided for me."

Cybelline drew up her knees and hugged them. Her features were set thoughtfully. "Nicholas spoke very little of his own parents. He was raised by his grandfather, and he died shortly after we were married. It had not occurred to me before, but perhaps he was thinking more of himself than he was of me."

Ferrin had wondered the same. Nicholas Caldwell remained something of a puzzle to him, and Ferrin knew himself to be like a dog with a bone when he was presented with a puzzle. "How long will Sir Richard be staying?"

"A few days only. He knows I am leaving for Granville Hall at week's end. I believe he intends to visit his old haunts at Cambridge before returning to London." Cybelline brushed the underside of her chin with her knuckles. "I have been wondering why he no longer teaches. Do you know?"

Ferrin shook his head. "I have never inquired. It's been more than three years, I think."

"Five years and six months." When Ferrin looked surprised that she would know with such confidence, she said, "I recall it because it occurred only a few weeks after my betrothal. Nicholas had gone off to investigate a ruin in Essex and went to Cambridge afterward to show Sir Richard his find. That's when he learned Sir Richard was no longer there. I remember Nicholas was distressed because he had no one to help him authenticate the artifact. He spent considerable time poring over old manuscripts, looking for information about the shield he found. It was his first attempt at doing the research all on his own, so he was particularly eager to get it right. Between his preparing for trial and learning about the shield, I do not think I saw Nicholas more than a few hours at a time for weeks."

Cybelline's smile was a trifle sheepish. "So, when you wonder that I recall Sir Richard leaving his teaching post, it is because it proved to be a great inconvenience to me."

Ferrin grinned. "Is that not how we all remember as much as we do, by the impact disparate events have on our lives?"

"It is good of you to paint it with that brush, but I cannot dismiss that selfishness and jealousy helped engrave it in my memory. I wonder if it is not the reason I have never held Sir Richard in the same esteem as did Nicholas. It is small of me, I know, but it was a relief to have our business concluded and supper done, and I was thankful to leave Sir Richard to his port and pipe and take myself off to the nursery." She regarded Ferrin frankly. "Do you find his character in any way objectionable, my lord?"

"I have spent little enough time in his company outside the lecture hall. He is the foremost authority in his field here in Britain, and he studied relics in Egypt before all things

Egyptian were made popular by Napoleon's advance into the country. He writes frequently for the journals and has done extensive research on rock striations. I understand this assists him in identifying the probable age of certain artifacts."

"Those are impressive credentials. But what of his character?"

"Apart from his regrettable tendency to employ his intellect to belittle others, you mean?"

"Apart from that," Cybelline said wryly.

"Then I suppose he is no more or less objectionable than most people of my acquaintance. I confess, his character is not of particular interest to me. His achievements are."

"That was Nicholas's argument also." Cybelline sighed. "In the end, I suppose it is neither here nor there. I do not expect to have dealings with him again after this business is done. Do you think he will give me a fair price for the artifacts?"

Ferrin's mouth pulled to one side as he considered her question. "I have no reason to think he will not make an honorable offer, but I imagine much depends on what he believes you know about the value of the pieces."

"I know a good deal more than he is likely to credit. It is my opinion that he does not entirely respect a woman's capacity for independent thought. If he were uneducated, his notions about women and their capabilities would be quaint, but because he is a man of learning, his views are dangerous." Cybelline saw Ferrin's lips twitch. "What? You do not agree?"

"It is a thorny subject, and it is late."

"Coward."

"I freely admit it."

"Oh, very well." Cybelline pulled her hair forward over her shoulder and began to loosely plait it. "He speaks very highly of you, you know. He says you were every professor's favorite pupil."

"A gross exaggeration."

"I don't think he is given to those. He also seemed disappointed that you have not lived up to your intellectual promise."

Ferrin chuckled. "If he knew about my patents, he would call me a tinker and dismiss my work out of hand. He would not look favorably upon the manner in which I've applied science. It is precisely the sort of endeavor for which he has no regard."

"He was not favorably impressed with your licentious behavior, either."

"You will have to trust me. Like my mother, he would be less impressed with the fact that I am in trade."

"I believe you. It is exactly that sort of thinking that I find so distressing."

"We are returned to that, are we?"

"Would you prefer to discuss the impending interview with my brother?"

"God, no."

"Careful. You almost tipped the chair."

Ferrin saw she was not trying to temper her amusement. "You know, he might well call me out."

"Call you out? Oh, I doubt that. I don't think you should expect that Sherry will make any sort of formal challenge." She waited just long enough to see a shadow of relief pass over his features, then told him, "He'll shoot you where you stand."

In a single, fluid motion, Ferrin set his chair down on all four of its legs, dropped his heels from the bed rail, and rose to his feet. "You enjoyed that a little too much, I'm thinking." Leaning over her, Ferrin kissed Cybelline hard on the mouth. She was a bit breathless when he drew back, but he was smiling with perfect satisfaction. He returned to the chair, propped his heels on the rail again, and resumed teetering on the two back legs. "I am credited to be a decent shot myself."

"I am very glad to hear it."

Ferrin was tempted to kiss her again. She served up considerable sauce with her cool tone and prim demeanor. "Sheridan has always impressed me as someone not given to acting hastily. I believe I can depend upon him to give me a fair hearing. It will be a bit of a shock, I suppose, when I arrive instead of Wellsley, but when he understands that I have never deceived you, it will all be made right."

"You are very confident."

He shrugged, then collected himself as the chair wobbled. "I find that men are infinitely more willing to engage in reasoned discourse than—"

Cybelline arched one eyebrow and waited.

"Well, than monkeys or magpies."

She nodded approvingly. "Impressive. You do very well in extracting your foot from your mouth."

He snorted softly.

Smiling to herself, Cybelline smoothed the blanket lying across her knees. "Do you mean to stay the night?"

"No." He did not ask if she would allow it. That was implied in her question. "I merely wanted to know that you were all of a piece."

"Why did you think I wouldn't be?"

Ferrin cast her a look of patent disbelief. "Let us say that you conceal some things more successfully than others. I know that you asked Sir Richard to come here, but I think you hoped he would not accept your invitation. You may have even regretted extending it."

Cybelline's long sigh confirmed Ferrin's thinking. "I did not invite him here at the outset. I encouraged him to visit my London residence and make an appraisal. I was quite willing to conduct our business through correspondence, and it occurred to me that having the matter set in writing was better than a gentleman's agreement. When he finally did reply, I decided I would not be inconvenienced by him and offered him the opportunity to discuss the purchase here. I admit to some surprise when he accepted. Do you regret that his arrival keeps us from Granville?"

"I regret that his arrival keeps us apart. I am not in so very great a hurry to renew my acquaintance with your brother."

She chuckled. "Sherry is everything reasonable. You must not anticipate that he will make it difficult for us to marry—in the event there is a proposal, you understand."

"I understand."

She waited, and when he remained silent, watching her with faintly mocking eyes, she said, "Well, it seems there will not be one this evening."

"Disappointed?"

"As if I would admit to such," she said in prim accents.

Ferrin set his chair down and leaned forward, resting his forearms on his knees. "How did you choose me, Cybelline?"

She blinked. "Pardon?"

"How did you choose me? At the masquerade, I mean. Was I a deliberate selection or a chance one? If Wellsley had stepped away from the card table before I did and taken you in hand, would you still have suggested seduction?"

Cybelline wondered if their positions were reversed if she would have the courage to pose the same question. "I imagine you have given considerable thought to whether you are prepared to hear whatever I might say."

He nodded. "As long as it's the truth."

"I will give you that," she said quietly. "The first time I saw you was not at your sister's presentation. It was months earlier, in June. You were standing outside your gentleman's club, conversing with two young women. One of them was tugging on your sleeve very coyly, while the other was mounting her own coquettish assault. You appeared to be quite entertained by their antics—at least for a time.

"I was seldom gone from my home, so it *was* the merest chance that I spied you that day, but because you were oddly familiar to me, I asked my companion if she knew you. She did, and she proceeded to regale me with every bit of gossip she'd ever heard about you. I also observed that your conversation with the young women took some sort of unpleasant turn, and you left them abruptly—with considerable coldness, in fact—and sought the certain sanctuary of your club. The young women looked as if they'd been set adrift. One called after you quite plaintively. I thought she might begin to cry. It seemed to me that everything my friend was telling me about your character was borne out by what I had witnessed."

Ferrin's mouth curled to one side, and he shook his head slowly as disbelief warred with amusement. "So you had some knowledge that I was a spoiler of young women, is that it?"

"Yes." Cybelline had the grace to flush. "What I did not understand then was that you spoiled those two women in a very particular fashion."

"Oh?"

"They were your sisters: Mrs. Branson and Miss Wynetta."

"I see. Your companion neglected to mention that."

"I don't know if she was aware of it, either. She never suggested to me that she was acquainted with you, only your reputation. You must take responsibility for that, my lord. Her notions were precisely what you meant to foster."

"Hoist by my own petard," Ferrin said. "Very well. When did you discover the women you saw me with that day were my sisters?"

"At the masquerade. It made me wonder if I was mistaken in my other beliefs about you. I engaged you in conversation about rakes and libertines, and you confirmed to me that you were such a person."

"Bloody hell," Ferrin said under his breath.

Cybelline simply nodded, then her eyes darted away as she continued the more difficult part of her explanation. "I could not have approached just any gentleman. He had to be a man without exacting scruples, one who would welcome an evening's diversion and make no further demands. Certainly he should be the sort of man who would not trouble himself with inquiries afterward. It seemed rather more right than not that it should be you. You had the look of the man who'd been coming to my bed for months, the one I tried to pretend was my husband, but was not."

"Your dreams," Ferrin said, more to himself than to her. His eyes narrowed slightly as he regarded her averted face. "Look at me, Cybelline. You dreamed of me?"

She turned, forcing herself to meet his eyes. "Not precisely of you. Not at first . . . someone like you . . . then after I saw you on the street . . ." Cybelline took a steadying breath. "After I saw you, yes, it was you in my dreams."

"I see. And I made love to you?"

"Not always." Her eyes darted away again. "But often."

"Did it make you afraid?"

"Sometimes. Sometimes it made me sad."

Ferrin nodded. "You had begun to receive the letters from your husband's mistress by then, is that right?"

"Yes. The first one arrived on the day that would have marked the fifth anniversary of our marriage. I must believe it was purposely done. Ten days earlier was the anniversary of Nicholas's death. I have often wondered if it was that that prompted his mistress to send the first letter." She shrugged. "I don't suppose that it matters."

"No," Ferrin said quietly. "I don't suppose that it does."

Cybelline impatiently swiped at unwelcome tears. Composure was hard-won, but when she began to speak, it was in a matter-of-fact tone that distanced herself from the actions she was explaining. "That I attended the masquerade at all was certainly Aunt Georgia's doing. She brought the affair to my attention when she received her invitation. As she was encouraged to bring a guest, she decided that I should be the one to accompany her. I was not in the least interested, you understand. It was just this sort of thing that I took great pains to avoid."

"I imagine Lady Rivendale was insistent."

"She was, but I still could have said no. It was when I realized that the invitation was initiated by you that I began to waver. I wanted to meet you, and I could not conceive that another opportunity would present itself. I am not speaking euphemistically when I say that I desired to make your acquaintance. An introduction was all I wanted. I thought I would be able to dismiss you then."

Cybelline touched her fingertips to her temple and massaged lightly as an ache began to form behind her eyes. "I cannot say precisely when my thinking changed, only that it did. Certainly it happened before my arrival at the masquerade. All my preparations were in aid of seducing you."

"Am I permitted to be flattered?"

She discovered she had the wherewithal to smile. "Only a little. Please recall that I was trying to cut you from my life."

"You were trying to cut me from your dreams. There is a distinction there that I think you failed to recognize. In point of fact, you invited me into your life." Standing, he motioned to her to move toward the center of the bed. When she complied, he made himself comfortable in the place she'd occupied, leaning back against the bedhead and stretching his long legs in front of him. He extended one arm to the side, curving it around Cybelline's shoulders and drawing her closer. "It never fails to astonish how well we fit," he said. "Lean your head back here . . . against my shoulder. That's right. Close your eyes." He began to massage her temples in the manner she had been doing and was rewarded with her heartfelt sigh of contentment. "Better?"

"Mmmm."

He smiled. "Do not become too much at your ease. I would have the rest of your story."

"You are fiendish, my lord." She felt his fingers pause. "Christopher," she said softly. "You are a fiend, Christopher."

"Much better." He resumed his gentle massage. "Tell me how the shepherdess with the green ribbons became Boudicca."

"I discovered that Aunt Georgia had no intention of escorting me to the masquerade. I overheard her tell the dressmaker that she would not be requiring a costume of her own, then confide that she was certain she would not be feeling at all the thing that evening. It was all in support of pushing me out of the nest. She was fearful that I was too often alone. She was also worried that I still grieved so deeply for Nicholas. It's understandable since I told her nothing about the letters nor shared any of the bitterness in my heart.

"When I realized she meant for me to go alone, I considered not attending at all. It came to me slowly, though, that I could enjoy anonymity that her presence would have denied me. That is how Boudicca was conceived. Webb and I made the costume. The torc, bracelets, and spear were already in my possession."

"The mask?"

"No. I owned nothing like that. I had it made for the occasion."

Ferrin's fingers strayed to her hair. "And this?"

"Henna."

"You told me at the masquerade you chose Boudicca for her ruthlessness. Was that true?"

"You cannot doubt it. She was not at all a convenient choice."

"So the shepherdess could not have proposed seduction."

"I don't think so, no. In spite of how it must have appeared to you, that proposal did not come easily to the warrior queen, either."

"It seemed you were more often tempted to use your spear."

She smiled a bit drowsily. "That's true."

Ferrin chuckled and kissed the crown of her head. "There never was a friend wearing the shepherdess costume?"

"No. I left my home wearing it and returned in the same fashion, but I was only ever Boudicca at the masquerade."

"Did you accomplish what you set out to do, Cybelline? Did our anonymous coupling in the servants' stairwell remove me from your dreams?"

She flinched a little at this description of their encounter, yet she acknowledged that it was mostly accurate. "It was not entirely anonymous," she said. "I knew who you were."

"You knew my name, my title, and something about my reputation, but you did not know me."

"No, you're right, I didn't. And no, it did not remove you from my dreams."

"You left London to put distance between us."

"I knew I was leaving London before I attended the masquerade. My departure did not hinge on the outcome of our introduction, or even on whether we met at all. I meant to leave because the letters had not stopped, but I would be less than honest if I did not admit that shame compelled me to make a more hasty departure."

"Shame, Cybelline? Do you really mean that?"

"Guilt, then. A guilty pleasure. I had to escape." She felt his hands move to her shoulders to stop the abrupt flow of tension there. In moments she was boneless. "But as you pointed out, there was a distinction that I failed to recognize, and you indeed came into my life. The anonymity I thought I enjoyed was only ever an illusion."

"You left the spear behind. What was I supposed to make of that?"

"I don't know. I hardly know what to make of it myself. I don't think I did it intentionally, but I'm not as confident of that as I was before. It seems a bit too disingenuous."

"Do you sometimes still wish I had not found you?"

Cybelline did not answer immediately. Instead, she was thoughtful, considering the question carefully. "Sometimes? No, not even sometimes. It seems right somehow." She paused, lifting her head and glancing back at him, then said significantly, "It seems inevitable."

Ferrin merely smiled.

"You understand, do you not, that 'inevitable' means incapable of being avoided?"

"I believe I'm familiar with the meaning."

"You are maddening, do you know that?"

"I'm learning that *you* think so."

She turned back and settled comfortably against him again. "I think I did not mind so much if you found Boudicca, but that could not happen, of course. It was only ever possible that you could find me."

"Are you so very different from her? I'm not so sure you are. I think adopting the look of her merely emphasized certain aspects of your character."

"The slattern aspect, you mean."

"I mean nothing of the kind. Boudicca was hardly a whore, and neither are you. Can you not suppose that a woman's rage is but one facet of her passion? I thought that's what I saw in you that night . . . what I still see from time to time."

Cybelline frowned. "Is it your intention to unsettle me? Because that is what you've done. It is not always necessary to share your observations, you know."

"I think it is, at least on this count. I'm not afraid of your passion, Cybelline."

"And you think I am?"

"Oh, yes. I know you are."

"You are daring me to show you otherwise."

"Indeed."

Cybelline removed herself from Ferrin's embrace, turned, then gave him a hard shove from the side that made him teeter on the edge of the bed. It only required that she extend a foot to push him over. She was happy to put the dainty appendage to such good use. The bedside table almost toppled as he went overboard. She lurched, catching it with her fingertips before the candle fell and carefully set it right. Sprawled forward as she was, Cybelline simply peered over the bed and looked down at Ferrin. He was sitting on the floor, listing to one side as he rubbed his posterior. And to prove his point that he was not afraid of her passion, even of that aspect that was anger, he was grinning at her.

Cybelline's heart lurched just as she had. She was painfully aware that she would not be able to catch it. Still, she threw out a hand reflexively only to have it immediately taken up by Ferrin. She did not resist. It was fitting, she supposed, that he should have both her heart and her hand.

Sitting up, she made a show of helping him to his feet. He could have easily brought her down on top of him had that been his desire. Instead, he came up in a fluid motion and allowed himself to be pulled onto the bed.

"You made a great noise," she whispered, turning on her side to face him. Her knees bumped his. "I shouldn't wonder that someone will come to investigate."

"Then it's a good thing I locked the outer door."

"So in spite of what you said earlier, you knew it would come to this."

He shook his head. "I'm not prescient, but I am an optimist."

Cybelline inched closer and caught his mouth with

hers. "You make me hopeful. I cannot tell if I am more or less afraid because of it, only that I don't mind so much."

Ferrin's fingers curled around her loosely plaited hair and deftly unwound it. He let it slide over his hand, then gathered it up in his palm as though weighing its silky mass. He kissed her slowly and deeply, using his hand in her hair to keep her still. The movement of her mouth over his was warm and sweet, and the teasing forays of her tongue quickened his heartbeat until he knew a dull roar in his ears.

It was she who was maddening now, and he told her so. He was not surprised when her low laughter held a hint of wickedness, and she repeated his own words to him: "I'm learning that *you* think so."

She helped him out of his frock coat and stock and required no encouragement to unbutton his waistcoat and lift his shirt away from his trousers. Ferrin's breath caught as her hands moved under his shirt. He would not have objected if they'd slipped under his skin.

It was like that anyway. She moved over him and seemed to burrow inside. First there was the way her lips caught his earlobe and her teeth worried it, then there was her sultry breath at the nape of his neck. She seemed to glide across his chest, but it was only her fingertips that marched from his navel to his throat and left a trail of prickly heat behind. When she did the same with her mouth, the trail only got hotter.

She cupped his erection through his trousers and massaged it much as he had done with her neck and shoulders. Her fondling made him want to grab her wrist and force pressure into her palm. Instead, she found what he needed on her own, gauging the strength of her caress by the sounds that escaped the back of his throat. She listened to him in a way no woman had before. Her touch was light when he could bear her teasing and firm when he could not. She seemed to know precisely when to stop her carnal assault and when to resume it. There was no artifice, no faked interest. She was openly curious, perhaps as much about her own power as she was about his response, and Ferrin knew himself grateful to be the subject of her inquiry.

She released the buttons on his flies and drew him out. He had to set his jaw when she took him in hand and began to stroke him along the length of his shaft. Her fingers squeezed around him, mimicking the contractions of her body when he was deep inside her.

And when she made to take him most intimately between her lips, Ferrin held his breath in anticipation of the hot and humid suck of her mouth, then he gave in to it.

Chapter Thirteen

Cybelline was late coming to breakfast. Sir Richard had already served himself from the sideboard. She greeted him and began to investigate what dishes Mrs. Minty had prepared for their guest's pleasure. She choose coddled eggs, sweet sausage, and two triangles of toast with orange marmalade, then joined Sir Richard at the table.

He was reading from a London paper that was several days old but only recently delivered to the Sharpe house. He set it down to come to his feet as Cybelline was seated by the footman. "I wasn't certain if you would take your breakfast with your daughter," he said, returning to his chair.

"It's often my habit to sit with her in the nursery, but I slept later than I intended." The words came coolly to her lips, but it was heat that she felt everywhere else. When she breathed deeply she caught Ferrin's scent on her skin even though she'd bathed this morning. She did not dare close her eyes for long, sure she would see him as he'd been last night, hovering over her, taking her breast in his mouth, then marking a damp path from her throat to her navel with his lips and tongue, then dipping lower still until he tasted the wetness between her thighs.

"Is something wrong?" Sir Richard asked.

Cybelline blinked, flushing a little as she realized that in spite of her best intentions she had not been attending to her guest. She observed that Sir Richard was watching her with narrowed eyes and a stamp of vague disapproval on his mouth. "No, nothing's wrong. I am feeling very well, in fact."

"You appear somewhat flushed."

"Do I?" She put a hand to one cheek. "Mayhap it is because I overslept. And you, Sir Richard? Did you pass the night comfortably?"

"I did, yes. I read until quite late. Thank you for permitting me to take a book from your library."

"It's hardly a library," she said. "But I'm gratified to learn that you found something of interest."

"Indeed. A number of titles intrigued me. I chose *Pride and Prejudice*."

"Really?" She was pleased to discover her voice did not quaver. The book belonged to Ferrin, not her. She wondered what other books or journals he might have left behind. She hoped that Berzelius's *Theory of Chemical Proportions and the Chemical Action of Electricity* was not one of them. "Is that not an odd choice?"

"Why do you think so?"

Cybelline knew she was being baited, so she replied carefully. "I would have thought the society of so many women would not recommend itself to you. Mrs. Bennet, in particular, is a twit."

"She is, but I find much to admire about Mr. Darcy."

"As do I." Cybelline cut her sausage and speared one bite. "I believe I will walk after breakfast. Will you join me?"

"No, thank you. I am prepared to make my offer, Mrs. Caldwell, and not press upon your hospitality longer than necessary."

"Oh, but it is no trouble to have you here." The wonder of it was, she thought, that she did not choke on those words. "Surely, you do not mean to leave today when you have only just arrived."

"Tomorrow," he said, "I will be sufficiently rested to make the journey to Cambridge. My driver assures it will be the same for the horses, and the carriage is in good order." He lifted his coffee cup and drank before he went on. "Again, I must caution you that my offer is not final until I have appraised the pieces, but I am prepared to offer you one thousand pounds. If you will include the spear, my offer is three hundred more."

Cybelline did not hesitate, nor did she try to put her refusal delicately. "No. That is unacceptable. I have it from my husband's own journal that you once appraised the shield at a thousand pounds. I had hoped that you would not think me such a great fool that I did not have some idea of the worth of the collection, but apparently that is not the case. You will have to do better, Sir Richard. Your offer does not make me think you are truly interested."

A wash of crimson color rose higher than Sir Richard's intricately folded neckcloth. "Are you clever, Mrs. Caldwell? Or merely sly?"

Cybelline did not dignify the question with an answer. She lifted a triangle of toast to her lips and bit gently. The marmalade lay pleasantly on her tongue; the sweet and slightly tart taste of it reminded her of Ferrin's kisses. She would have orange marmalade at every breakfast from this point forward, she decided, and was very pleased with herself for thinking of it.

Twin muscles jumped in Sir Richard's cheeks as he ground his teeth together. "Your late husband thought you were clever," he said. "It has always been my opinion that you are cunning."

It had never occurred to Cybelline that Nicholas might have discussed her with Sir Richard. She wondered if she could trust Sir Richard to be telling her the truth. Such behavior seemed out of character for her husband. "I am certain you each had your reasons for thinking so," she said evenly. "Frankly, your good opinion is of no import. It is your offer that must come up to snuff."

Sir Richard smiled thinly. There was no evidence of humor in the line of his mouth. "I have always had it in my mind that you do not care for me, Mrs. Caldwell, and it seems I am correct. I have asked myself what offense I gave you; I even put the question to your husband. Was there an offense? A slight? Or is it that I remind you of someone who has given such? Your husband had no answer for me, and I find myself at a loss to explain it."

"You disrespect me," she said. "And you have always done so. I can say it no plainer than that. If I required more proof, your offer supplied it." Cybelline's chin came up, and she did not avert her gaze. She refused to be moved from her own table. Indeed, she was hungrier now than when she had joined him. She took a bite of her coddled eggs and chewed with evident pleasure.

Sir Richard set down his coffee cup and picked up the paper. "You will excuse me, Mrs. Caldwell. There are matters to which I must attend."

Cybelline nodded politely, hoping that one of the matters involved recalculating his offer. When he was gone from the room, she smiled to herself, well satisfied with the outcome of the exchange.

Ferrin dismounted as soon as he saw Cybelline walking through the woods toward him. "Have you lost your bearings?" He pointed to the northeast. "The Sharpe house is that way."

"I know precisely where I am. I found you, didn't I?" She stood on tiptoe and kissed him on the mouth. His laughter made his lips vibrate and tickled hers. She dropped to her heels and pressed her forehead against his shoulder. "I didn't hear you leave this morning. I wish you had waked me."

He cupped her chin with his forefinger and lifted it. "I do not think the explosion from a Roman candle could have roused you. It was still dark when I left, and no one saw me go."

"Sir Richard is leaving tomorrow. We will be able to leave for Granville the following day."

"If you like." He slipped his arm through Cybelline's. "This way. We'll not be disturbed." He dropped Newton's reins and let him trail behind. "Sir Richard's offer was acceptable, then?"

"Not at all. It was insulting." Cybelline repeated the exchange she'd had with Sir Richard. "Really, he put me out of all patience with him. I don't know if he'll make a second offer, but if he does, it is certain to be more agreeable than the first. I told him I had Nicholas's journals. My husband kept meticulous records of his discoveries."

"So that's how you knew their worth."

She nodded. "He even noted which items were appraised by Sir Richard, and I have it here." She tapped her head.

"Clever."

"Yes," she said, smiling up at him. "I am."

Ferrin veered off the path suddenly and took Cybelline with him. He backed her against a tree trunk and kissed her hard.

Her arms lifted around his neck, and she kissed him back. The chinchilla collar of her pelisse framed their faces and warmed their cheeks. Ferrin unfastened her coat and slipped his hands inside, pressing them against the small of her back. He brought her as flush to his body as their heavy clothes would allow and held her there.

Last night seemed so long ago, and yet every spark that was fired came from that same fuse. The intensity of the heat between them had not cooled even a few degrees. When they were able to break away, it was their breathless, slightly embarrassed laughter that still bound them together.

"Oh my," Cybelline whispered.

"Indeed."

"Mayhap it was not a good idea for me to come this way."

"It was an excellent idea." He stepped back and began to fasten her pelisse. "Come, I will let you continue your walk unmolested. Unless you are provocative, of course, then I cannot answer for what will happen."

Amused, Cybelline simply shook her head and allowed Ferrin to take her arm again. They chose a route that took them toward the brook, then they followed its meandering path. Behind them, Ferrin's mount made snuffling noises and occasionally thrust his nose hard at Ferrin or Cybelline to move them along, but mostly he was content to follow in the persistent manner of a loyal, but very large, hound.

"You never told me how you entered my home last night," Cybelline said. "I know the doors are not often barred or locked as they are in London, but I am imagining that you were not so bold as to simply walk in the front door."

"I can be that bold," he said, "but not that slow-witted."

"The distinction is important?"

"I think so."

"Very well. Impress me."

"I walked in the tradesman's entrance."

Cybelline chuckled. "My, that is inventive."

He shrugged. "Your rose trellis is all rotting wood, and there was nowhere to set a pulley that might have easily lifted me. I never mastered stilts. I did want to reach you alive, so that necessarily narrowed my options."

"Thank goodness. Sir Richard mentioned that he read quite late. *Pride and Prejudice,* if you can credit it. Could you tell if he was still up?"

"No. But I didn't go near his room. I used the stairs at

the rear. Before you inquire, the Lowells were also undisturbed by my going and coming." Ferrin's steps slowed then stopped. He brought Cybelline up short as well. "What did you say he was reading?"

"*Pride and Prejudice.*"

"A book he brought? You don't own a copy of that."

"No. I gave him permission to take what he liked from the small collection of novels in the study. He made a point to comment that the room hardly deserved description as a library."

"Then it was my book that he read."

"I assume so. I didn't realize you'd left it behind."

"I allowed Nanny Baker to borrow it. She must have put it with the others to keep it out of Anna's reach."

"At least it was not one of your scientific journals. That would have been difficult to explain."

"So Sir Richard did not ask why my name was scrawled inside the book, because that would have been difficult to explain as well."

Cybelline stared at him.

"You didn't know, did you?"

She shook her head. "You read the book to me. I never looked at it. Are you certain you put your name inside? Perhaps you are thinking of some other book."

"I mark all my books in the same manner."

"You are meticulous, then."

He smiled a little because she made it sound like a character flaw. "Yes. It has seldom been a problem."

"I didn't mean . . . oh, it doesn't matter." Even to her own ears, Cybelline sounded impatient and out of sorts. "If he inquires, some explanation will occur to me."

"Will you consider the truth?"

"What do you mean?"

"Mr. Lowell returned from Penwyckham this morning with several letters for me. My mother writes that Wynetta is in the first full throes of love, or else . . . let me think how she phrased it . . . yes, or else 'the girl is silly beyond what can be imagined or properly tolerated.'"

"I suppose we must hope that it's love."

"Netta will only ever be marginally less silly."

Cybelline smiled because Ferrin said it with such obvious affection that there was no sting to his words. "Does your mother say that it is Mr. Wellsley who has captured her heart?"

"No. She mentions several gentlemen but thinks none of them can account for Netta's mood of late. That suggests to me that Wellsley may indeed have made an impression on my sister. Such courtship as they've had would have been conducted in secret. Even my mother thinks Wellsley's retired to the country. She writes to me at Fairfield and my steward sends the letters on."

"It seems like an elaborate and thoroughly unnecessary deception."

"I believe I explained that Wellsley was foxed at the time it was conceived."

"I understand, but what accounts for your part in it?"

"Friendship and a desire to be gone from London."

"Of course."

"And Boudicca."

"And Boudicca," Cybelline repeated softly, warm of a sudden. "Have you written to Mr. Wellsley that you found her?"

"No. I wrote at length about making your acquaintance instead."

Cybelline nodded, grateful for his discretion. "Are you telling me that you are sufficiently encouraged by Lady Gardner's correspondence that I might tell Sir Richard you are here in Penwyckham?"

"I am never encouraged by my mother's letters, though I am invariably diverted. It is Wellsley's correspondence that I depend upon for information. I see you are doubtful, but it is only when he's in his cups that his thinking takes an unfortunate turn toward farce. He writes that he proposed to his young lady and that she has accepted his offer of marriage."

"But is his intended your sister?"

"I certainly hope so. I do not like to think she's gotten so silly over anyone less worthy than Wellsley. He planned to speak to her father soon, so I suspect he's already had the interview by now."

Cybelline frowned. "I thought he was waiting for you to marry. Wasn't the idea of all this that you should leap first? It seemed to me that Mr. Wellsley wanted to polish his reputation by repairing yours."

"That was the gist of it, but as I have already acknowledged to him that a proposal here is not only inevitable, but also imminent, it seems he has decided to storm the gates."

Cybelline's attention was caught by one particular word. "Imminent?" she asked. "Can I trust that you know the meaning of this word also?"

"Ready to take place," he said.

Once again Cybelline waited expectantly.

Ferrin shook his head. "You are confusing 'imminent' with 'immediate.'"

She sighed. "Perfectly maddening."

Ferrin was satisfied that it was more of an endearment than an accusation. "You understand that I am counting on Wellsley's discretion, but I also know my mother. When she realizes that Wellsley has been in town paying suit to Wynetta in secret, she is certain to corner him as to my whereabouts."

"Why will she think you are anywhere but at Fairfield?"

He regarded her with disbelief. "Do you know when Anna has been up to some trick?"

"Naturally. She cannot—" Cybelline stopped herself and gave him a sheepish smile. "Oh, I see what you mean."

"Wellsley will not do well under my mother's gimlet

eye. If he's cornered, I suspect it will require only a few minutes to have it all from him."

"Then we are found out."

"Or soon will be."

"Lady Gardner will seek out Aunt Georgia."

"It seems likely. And the Viscountess Bellingham will not be excluded. It is her grandson, after all."

"It will be a triumvirate such as society has not known since the Roman empire."

Ferrin chuckled appreciatively. "I could not have explained it better."

"They will not descend upon us here, will they?" A thread of anxiety crept into her voice. "I don't think I should like that."

"No, they won't travel so far, not when they know we'll return eventually and they can chide me at their leisure. You will be guilty only by association."

"That is hardly comforting."

Ferrin caught Cybelline's chin. "You are the innocent, remember. I am the rake. This is one Gordian knot that will unravel of its own accord."

"Not if we do not reach my brother before Aunt Georgia does. There are things I must say to Sherry. I do not like to think he will receive correspondence from Aunt Georgia before we arrive. There can be no supposing what construction she will place on such things as she learns, except that she will take full credit if what she hears is to her liking. Remember, she is the one person who knows I was Boudicca at the masquerade."

"So she does. Perhaps I am too hopeful about the Gordian knot unraveling."

"I think it's fair to say it will become tighter first." Cybelline began walking again. "Do you think there will be a scandal?"

"I imagine that depends on the Gardner-Rivendale-

Bellingham triumvirate. They have considerable influence, but a proposal will calm their nerves."

"That is my opinion also."

"Then we are of like minds."

She nodded but was not encouraged when Ferrin offered nothing more substantial to prove it. "Wellsley has stolen a march on us," she said, casting about for an explanation for his reticence. "I suppose it is only right that he should enjoy the admiration of his set for making so excellent a match." Her brow furrowed. "You are quite certain your stepfather will allow the marriage?"

"Quite certain. Wellsley would know it as well if he was not so besotted with Wynetta."

"I thought you said his thinking is compromised only when he is deep in his cups."

"Doesn't being in love have all the same qualities as intoxication? The poets write as if that were so. It is certainly my observation."

"But not your experience," Cybelline said quietly after a moment had passed.

"Why do you say that?"

"You are always remarkably clearheaded."

"Do you think so?"

"Yes, or at least you have always been so with me." Her cheeks reddened as she realized the meaning he might attach to her words. "That sounded presumptuous, did it not? I did not mean that you should think or behave differently because you are in love with me." Her flush deepened. "No, that is not quite what I intended to say, either. I meant that I do not expect you to be in love with me, or even that you should show it in some particular way. I believe that's what I meant, though I might be mistaken on the whole of it." Frustrated, Cybelline pivoted and looked up at him. He was regarding her with such gravity that she knew he was but a heartbeat away from roaring with laughter. "Do you have any idea what I'm trying to say?"

"No. It was a muddle from one end to the other."

Cybelline made a dismissive sound deep in her throat, then gave Ferrin her back and walked on. She preferred to pretend it was the brook she heard chortling behind her.

Ferrin did not attempt to catch up to her until he had composed himself. "Will you be taking both of your carriages to Granville?"

"No. Webb will remain behind, as I believe Mr. Foster might be encouraged by my absence to make an offer."

"You have some inkling of it, then?"

"She accompanied me to Mr. Foster's shop several days ago. I saw how things were. He, at sixes and sevens. She, perpetually pink in the cheeks."

"Intoxication."

Cybelline nodded. "I will take Becky Potter with me. She can assist me with Anna on the journey and act as my personal maid once we've arrived."

"Nanny Baker?"

"She will also remain behind, though she protested my decision. She simply does not travel well, and I know that Anna will be in the equally good hands of Rosie's nurse. The scoundrels will also attend to her, and they are extraordinarily patient. You will be jealous of the attention she heaps on them."

He smiled. "I expect I will."

Cybelline ducked under one of the low, skeletal branches blocking her path while Ferrin lifted another out of the way. "We've spoken very little of Anna," she said. "Sherry will want to know that you mean to be a proper father to her."

"I understand. Do you have any questions in that regard?"

She did not have to think about it. "No. None. I know you hold her in deep affection and will do right by her."

"Cybelline." He said her name in a gently chiding fashion. "I love her, and I hope I will do much more than right by her."

When the path cleared again, Cybelline let her gloved hand be taken in Ferrin's. "It doesn't matter that she's another man's daughter?"

"I think you have forgotten my family. Most of the *ton* doesn't know that Restell is my stepbrother. Imogene and I have more interests in common than she and her twin. Wynetta is a changeling, so there is no accounting for her, and young Hannah and Portia are dervishes who show regrettable signs they will tread at least lightly in her footsteps."

Cybelline glanced sideways at him. She could not deny what she heard in his voice. "You love them all."

"Sometimes to the point of intoxication." He squeezed her hand. "It is like that with Anna."

Cybelline said nothing. Tears threatened, and she blinked them back, offering up a watery smile instead. She experienced the same ache in her chest as she had last night, the one that was caused not by loneliness or longing but by such a surfeit of love that she could barely contain it.

Ferrin stopped and drew her into his embrace. "You are a watering pot," he said with gentle humor.

Cybelline meant to take exception to this, but her scornful sniff was more in the way of a sniffle. Sighing, she searched for her handkerchief, then accepted the one Ferrin gave her. She could not find it in herself to be offended by the low, rumbling laughter that vibrated his chest.

"You are benefiting from my wealth of experience with emotional females, you know."

"Oh?" Cybelline looked up at him, vaguely suspicious of his bravado. "Because you carry a handkerchief? I hadn't realized."

"Because I carry an *extra* handkerchief. Go on, you can keep it. I purchase them by the gross."

Cybelline tried to determine what she might believe, but the expression Ferrin showed her was perfectly serious. "I suppose that you've had to be prepared on any number of occasions to manage a woman's tears. A handkerchief is practically a calling card for a rake."

"More practical, anyway."

In spite of her wish to appear unaffected, Cybelline felt herself stiffen. "I see."

Ferrin shook his head. "I don't think you do. The emotional females in my life are my mother, my sisters, my sister-in-law, and Mrs. Lancaster."

"Who is Mrs. Lancaster?"

"The cook at Fairfield."

"Oh."

"Indeed." He held her loosely, threading his fingers behind her back. "I don't have a mistress, Cybelline. I haven't for some time."

It seemed incredible to her, but she believed him. Quickly, before her courage failed her, she asked, "When I approached you at the masquerade, what did you think?"

"That I was the most fortunate man in all of England."

"No," she said, shaking her head. "Please do not make light of me. I am prepared to hear the truth."

"I don't lie to you, Cybelline. I may not have told you everything, but I don't lie. It's important you know that."

"Then tell me everything."

He said nothing for a moment, searching his mind for the memories of that November evening. "I thought you were dangerous. If not to me—though I wasn't entirely certain of that—then at least to yourself. I thought you had selected me at random, that I might have been anyone. I can admit that I was flattered by your attention, but I feared for you as well. If I turned your extraordinary offer down, I didn't know what you might be moved to do next. It was most assuredly self-serving, but I trusted myself to deal fairly with you. I was not so confident of others."

"Not even Mr. Wellsley?"

Ferrin touched his forehead to hers and whispered, "I believe I explained it was self-serving."

Cybelline felt her breath catch in anticipation of his kiss. When he raised his head without brushing her lips, disappointment warred with frustration. She found it difficult to grasp the threads of their conversation. He seemed to be waiting her out, as composed as she was disquieted.

"Did you wonder if I was a whore?" she asked.

"No. No common one, at least. It occurred to me that you might be a courtesan, but that was when I was wondering if you intended some trap for me."

"Why would I do that?"

"All sorts of reasons came to my mind. Few of them made sense."

"You accused me of having a brother or father or cousin waiting to call you out."

Ferrin did not miss her oversight. "You did not mention a husband."

"Didn't I?" She bit her lip. "No, I suppose I didn't."

"Wasn't he the reason you were there?"

"No, not the way you mean. Not entirely. It wasn't revenge. What sense would that make? At best, it would be a hollow victory. Nicholas is dead." Cybelline's throat thickened; her voice dropped to a husky pitch. She plunged ahead with her explanation because she believed it must finally be said, not because she wanted to say it. "It's truer that I wanted to get something of my own back."

"And that's not revenge?"

"No. Not when that something I wanted was a part of me. That I set out to meet you . . . that I suggested a seduction . . . that I had it in my mind that you must needs be a rake . . . all of it was in aid of experiencing my own base satisfaction. You named your own actions that night as self-serving, but they hardly qualify as such when compared to my own. I wanted my own selfish pleasure . . ." Her voice was a mere thread of sound now. "And I no longer wanted to find it alone."

Ferrin cupped the side of Cybelline's face when she would have looked away. "Delicately put," he said, "and still the most frank admission I have ever known. You humble me, Cybelline, and you honor me."

She frowned a little. "Perhaps you did not understand what I was saying."

"I understood quite well." He bent his head and kissed her softly on the lips. "And I approve of your curiosity. I could not very well do otherwise, could I? It was an experiment of sorts."

Cybelline was much less certain of that. "You are good to want to see my behavior in that light, but we both know it was beyond the pale. You cannot deny that you thought so. You have said as much to me."

"A judgment I made without facts. It was not well done of me." The wind whipped a lock of Cybelline's hair across her cheek, and Ferrin tucked it behind her ear. "I can regret what I said but not what you did. How can I? We might never have met. That was not inevitable."

"Wasn't it? I have wondered, you know. Sometimes it seems to me that we could not have avoided each other."

One of Ferrin's dark eyebrows kicked up. The look in his eyes was significant and knowing. "You are making it difficult for me to return you to the Sharpe house unmolested."

"Am I?"

He pulled her closer and let her feel the answer pressing hard between them.

Cybelline slipped her arms around him again. "That is very good to know," she said softly, resting her head against his shoulder. "Very good to know."

* * *

Pinch, Dash, and Midge ran out to meet the carriage as soon as Mr. Kins turned into the drive. Excitement had them trading friendly shoves as they each sought to be at the front of their impromptu receiving line. They exchanged places several times before the carriage finally came to a halt. At the last moment Midge surged ahead only to be brought up short when Pinch caught him by the hair and yanked.

"Bloody 'ell, Pinch! Let go!"

Pinch released his grip so suddenly that Midge fell on his backside. "Serves you right!"

Dash took the opportunity afforded by this altercation to circle them both and set himself within inches of the carriage door.

Ferrin looked away from the window and glanced at Cybelline. "These three can be none other than the scoundrels."

She nodding, sighing. "The one with his nose pressed to the door is Dash. Midge is on the ground, and that's Pinch standing over him." She held Anna up to the window. "Wave to your favorite young gentlemen, darling."

Anna tried to launch herself off Cybelline's lap to get to the boys. Her happy laughter filled the carriage, and she beat her small fists against the glass. This was the cue for the scoundrels to take turns jumping up and down so their faces appeared framed by the window.

Ferrin noticed that Anna was highly entertained by their antics; Cybelline, only marginally less so. He realized he was smiling as well. Their exuberance was almost as contagious as Anna's laughter.

Mr. Kins shooed the boys out of the way and opened the door. Servants were hurrying from the house to assist with the valises and trunks, their approach infinitely more dignified than the scoundrels' had been. Grooms rounded the drive from the stable and prepared to take the horses and carriage.

Anna grew shy as soon as she was confronted by the welcoming party. She buried her face in Cybelline's fur collar and refused to allow anyone to take her. Cybelline returned to her seat until Ferrin exited, then she pried Anna's fingers loose and handed her down. Anna clung with equal tenacity to the capes of Ferrin's greatcoat and steadfastly ignored all attempts to get her to go to someone else. Even Becky Potter, the maid Cybelline brought along to assist her, was unsuccessful at cajoling Anna from Ferrin's arms.

"She's fine where she is," Ferrin said. "Let her be."

Cybelline smiled to herself as everyone stepped back, even the scoundrels. There was no mistaking either Ferrin's protectiveness or his command. She accepted the hand Mr. Kins extended to her and carefully stepped down. She did not try to take Anna back. "I am not fooled," she said in a whispered aside to Ferrin. "You are thinking Sherry will not shoot if you are carrying his niece."

Ferrin did not even pretend to be offended. "If there is something wrong with my strategy, tell me quickly, because I believe I see your brother now."

The grandeur of Granville Hall faded into the background the moment Cybelline spied her brother. He stood on the lip of the uppermost step, framed by the wide entrance. He was a dark, stoic figure against the hall's ochre stones, seemingly impervious to the chill wind that blew up from the lake and across the dormant, terraced gardens. Wearing neither coat nor hat, he nevertheless stood perfectly still while his hair was whipped about and his trousers beat a tattoo against his legs.

His arms had not quite begun to lift to welcome her when Cybelline started her charge toward him. Sherry rocked back on his heels as she threw herself at him. Feeling something desperate, something needy in her embrace, he held her just as tightly and was thrown back in time to the first moment he'd seen Cybelline after learning their parents were dead. It had been an embrace such as this one that held them upright, each leaning against the other, each making a shelter for their hearts.

"I am so very glad you've come," he said quietly. "It's been too long."

"I know. For me as well."

Above her head Sherry observed the activity around the carriage. With almost preternatural calm, he said, "The gentleman holding Anna . . . that is not Wellsley."

She sighed. "You won't shoot him, will you?"

"What an absurd notion." He loosened the embrace and regarded Cybelline closely. "Will I want to?"

A faintly guilty smile crossed her face. "I think you might, yes."

"Why? What have you done, Cybelline?"

Bracing her hands on Sherry's shoulders, Cybelline stood on tiptoe and whispered in his ear.

Sherry listened to her confession, nodded slowly, then said, "I think I should like to hear his explanation for it."

Cybelline dropped back on her heels. "Yes," she said. "That would be the prudent thing to do."

The prudent thing to do, Sherry knew from experience, was rarely easily accomplished. He had to cool his heels while Cybelline and Ferrin were shown to their rooms, Anna was made comfortable in the nursery, the scoundrels were taken in hand, and his own wife was apprised of the true identity of their guest. Lily was all for immediate confrontation and divulging his sister's confession only increased her wariness.

Still, Lily was gracious when she was introduced to Ferrin, and there was no awkwardness when she smoothly suggested an activity in the schoolroom that would take her and Cybelline away.

"Whisky?" Sherry asked when he and Ferrin were alone in the library. "Brandy?"

"Whisky," Ferrin said.

Neither man spoke while Sherry poured the drinks. The silence was not uncomfortable, merely long. Ferrin did not insult his host by offering inconsequential observations about the weather, Granville Hall, or the journey from Penwyckham. He waited for Sherry to make the overture.

Sherry handed Ferrin a tumbler with three generous fingers of whisky. Ferrin regarded his glass with a skeptical eye. "In vino veritas?"

"Precisely." He raised his glass in a mock salute. "Truth from you, comfort for me. Will you sit?"

Nodding, Ferrin chose the sofa set at an angle before the fireplace. He was not surprised when Sherry remained standing. Had their situations been reversed, he also would have chosen the high ground beside the green-veined marble mantelpiece.

Sherry rolled his tumbler between his palms. "I informed my sister that you are not Wellsley," he said. "That I am permitting you to make an explanation now is because she already knew, otherwise . . ." Sherry did not underscore the unspoken threat with a helpless shrug or a hard, significant look. His silence was sufficiently powerful.

"I understand," Ferrin said. "I have four sisters of my own." He sipped from his glass, considering how he might best begin. He had purposely not dwelled on the explanation he would make, knowing that a practiced account might be interpreted as a well-rehearsed lie. As he thought about it now, it seemed to him that Sherry had given him the best possible opening. "In fact, the circumstances surrounding my introduction to Mrs. Caldwell have everything to do with one of my sisters. Her name is Wynetta, and she is . . ."

Beginning with the masquerade, Ferrin made his presentation of the facts as objectively as he could. Of necessity, there were details he omitted, but they were the ones that would have compromised Cybelline and prompted Sherry to seek redress. As he believed Sherry eventually could be made to embrace reason, Ferrin was far less concerned about a challenge being issued than he was about compromising Cybelline in her brother's eyes.

Sherry listened without interruption, though Ferrin was fairly certain this was done of a purpose. His host seemed bent on hearing the whole of it once; the interrogation would begin presently. There were any number of points that Sherry would be well within his rights to question, Ferrin thought, especially the particulars regarding his reputation. To Ferrin's own ears his explanation sounded suspect. Since Sherry's expression gave nothing away, Ferrin could only imagine what significance was being placed on these revelations. Ferrin concluded his explanation with a brief account of the last correspondence he'd had from Wellsley, then sat back and awaited Sherry's questions.

Sherry set his tumbler on the mantelpiece. He'd taken very little drink and did not fail to notice that Ferrin's glass was similarly full. "It seems neither of us depend on drink for truth or comfort," he said. "Though I will admit that your description of Wellsley's impoverished thinking while deep in his cups helped stay my hand."

Ferrin nodded. "It has had considerable influence on me also."

"I imagine so," Sherry said, dryly, "since you were sufficiently moved by his suspect logic to fall in with his scheme."

"I own that after several hours of drinking in his company, his scheming seemed to have a certain brilliance, but I had already determined to search for Boudicca before I met up with Wellsley at the club. That I was encouraged to fall in with his plans had as much to do with being his friend of long standing as it did with serving my own purpose."

Sherry's dark eyes narrowed slightly. "Yes, well, let us speak of your purpose. I believe the less said regarding your intentions toward Boudicca, the better. Do you agree?"

"I do, yes."

"Good." Sherry picked up his drink and pushed away from the fireplace. He sat in a leather wing chair across from Ferrin. "What is it that you think you know about my sister? Please, be frank."

This question was not at all what Ferrin expected, but he fully appreciated the challenge inherent in it. He would be judged not only for the breadth of his assessment but also for its honesty. "She is not Boudicca," Ferrin said, "but not so unlike the woman I imagine Boudicca might have been. I have said as much to her." Ferrin paused, smiling faintly at the memory. "She didn't agree, though I don't believe modesty prevented it. She is not so confident as she once was."

"That presumes rather a lot, don't you think? You've known Cybelline but a few short months."

Ferrin nodded. "By any measure we understand you will always have known your sister longer than I, but it does not follow that I can never come to know her as well. Not better, perhaps, but differently. I have glimpsed her self-possession, and I have seen it falter. It is still her instinct to bring her chin up, but it wobbles just so. She will stare down a problem, then look away because her eyes well with tears. She no longer trusts her judgment and often as not chooses the wrong battle. Where she might have welcomed confrontation, she now avoids it—even runs from it if she's allowed." Ferrin held

Sherry's dark stare a long moment before he added, "I don't allow her."

Sherry drew a deep breath, then exhaled slowly. "It wasn't her idea to come to Granville, was it?"

"No. It was mine." He sipped his drink. "I did not have to convince her. She saw the sense of it quickly enough."

"But she wouldn't have suggested it."

"No, I don't believe she would have."

Sherry nodded and lifted his glass. His large swallow eliminated one full finger of whisky. "Cybelline used to enjoying managing me. Did you know that?"

"No, but I suspect that it was because you allowed her to."

"Perhaps. I am not always certain. She was wed at nineteen and believed her status as a married woman gave her even more license than before. It did not pain me overmuch, so I didn't often complain. What pains me now is that I ever expressed any displeasure. She has no well-intentioned advice for me these days. In point of fact, I would welcome even her most ill-considered opinions."

"I take it your own marriage does not account for the change in her."

"No, not entirely."

"Then the substantial change occurred after Caldwell's suicide."

"Yes," Sherry said. "She has spoken to you about it?"

Ferrin made a careful reply. "Not of the particulars of that day."

Sherry put down his glass and rested his elbows on the arms of his chair. He threaded his fingers in front of him and lightly tapped his thumbs together. "She found him. She had only just left the house when it happened. I have to believe that was deliberate on his part and meant to be considerate of her. I think he intended for the servants to take care of the blood and brains before she returned. He did not anticipate her forgetting a package that she meant to take back to the dressmaker's.

She had left it in his study when she went in earlier to tell him she was leaving."

"Then he didn't wait long to set the pistol to his head."

"No. Cybelline had not gone even half the block. She didn't hear the shot, but the servants did. They were crowded around the door to the study when she walked back in. There was an attempt to dissuade her from entering the room, but you were right when you said her first instinct is to put her chin up."

Sherry set his jaw a moment before he continued. "I spoke to the butler later and learned that my sister did not faint, did not cry out, did not shed a tear. She went to where her husband had fallen beside his desk and knelt, then she took his bloody head in her hands and cradled him in her lap. She was in precisely that position when I arrived within the hour. Her countenance was devoid of all expression, her complexion was as pale as salt, and in spite of the heat of the day, she trembled from a chill that ran bone deep. Had I not been in London at the time, I believe she would have remained just so until I came."

Sherry's voice took on a husky tenor. "Or been lost to me if I had not." He collected himself and went on. "I do not think I have all of her back yet, though today has given me some hope that it might still happen."

"You will never have all of her back, Sheridan."

"No?"

Ferrin shook his head. "I am learning I am too selfish to permit it."

Sherry did not raise an eyebrow, but his look was considering nonetheless. "Good for you," he said at last. "Very good for you."

"I told Mrs. Caldwell that you would be reasonable."

Sherry shrugged. "Cybelline asked me not to shoot you. It is fortunate for you that I still enjoy indulging my sister."

"Indeed," Ferrin said. "It is possible I will give you and

Mrs. Caldwell cause to regret it. There are matters I am honor bound to bring to your attention."

"Cybelline knows this?"

"No."

"Then you're not about to discuss an offer of marriage, are you?"

"No."

"I see." Sherry's thumbs stopped their rhythmic tapping. "Or rather I don't, but I feel certain you are about to explain."

Nodding, Ferrin leaned forward. His eyes were grave. "Just after the first anniversary of Caldwell's suicide, your sister received a letter that Caldwell had written to someone else long before his death."

"A letter describing his intentions to kill himself, you mean?"

"No. Not at all. It was a romantic correspondence."

Sherry became very still. "To whom?"

"A mistress. That is the construction that Cybelline has placed on it, and there is every good reason to do so."

"Bloody hell."

"Yes, well, that is not even the worst of it. Another letter followed, this one composed by a different hand. It was brief and very much to the point. The author accused Mrs. Caldwell of murdering her husband."

Sherry did not visibly react. "The mistress?"

"One would think so."

"You've seen these letters?"

"Yes. But there are many more than the two I've mentioned. She has close to a score of them now. Almost twenty of Nicholas's letters and an equal number that name her a murderess."

"Why didn't she come to me before this?"

Ferrin's reply was candid. "She's not coming to you now. I am. She will not thank me, no matter that some part of her understands the necessity of telling you. It is my opinion the letters from the mistress are more threatening of late. They are not so straightforward that I can divine the exact nature of the threat, but there is one there. The most recent letters have mentioned Anna."

Sherry's nostril's flared as he sucked in a breath. "Are the letters here?"

"I don't know. I think it's likely that she packed them, but you will understand that I am not privy to that. The maid she brought will be of no help. Your sister did not trust Webb with them, so she certainly would not allow this girl to secure them for her."

"Where is Webb? I didn't see her hovering about."

"Left behind."

"That is unusual."

"Done of a purpose, I suspect. Mrs. Caldwell will tell you it is because she expects Webb to receive an offer of marriage directly and does not want her own affairs to stand in the way. That is not untrue, but it is not the entire truth."

"And what is the explanation that you think satisfies?"

"There are two that I have been considering. The first is that your sister does not want Webb close enough to be questioned by you."

"That explanation supposes that you and I will be having this very conversation," Sherry said. "What is the other?"

"The other is that Mrs. Caldwell suspects that Sarah Webb was her husband's mistress."

Chapter Fourteen

"Webb?" Sherry asked, clearly incredulous. "That is the single most difficult thing you've asked me to believe, Ferrin. I can see you are perfectly serious, but you are also wrong."

"I didn't say that I believe it," Ferrin said, "only that I suspect Mrs. Caldwell does."

"Then you have sadly misinterpreted the bent of Cybelline's mind. Webb has been with her since . . . well, it seems as though it's been forever. I cannot comprehend what would bring Cybelline to the conclusion that her maid was her husband's mistress."

Ferrin ticked off the reasons. "Caldwell's correspondence indicates there is some impediment that keeps him and his mistress from marrying. The impediment might very well be a social inequality. He writes of desiring to be a father. Webb could not very well give birth beneath your sister's nose. And finally, the letters followed Mrs. Caldwell to Penwyckham. I will not be at all surprised if one arrives here shortly. Again, Webb is privy to all of your sister's plans."

"You told me that Cybelline's recovery from her illness was largely due to Webb's interference."

"That's right. And Webb is also the one who told me that

Mrs. Caldwell was disturbed by some letters she'd received. I would have no knowledge of them if Webb had not confided in me, but I believe that your sister viewed sharing that confidence as a betrayal. She is wondering still in what other manner Webb might have betrayed her trust."

Sherry said nothing for several moments as he attempted to absorb this new intelligence. "You said Cybelline did not argue when you suggested coming here."

"That's right."

"Do you think that's because she wanted to remove herself from Webb?"

"It would be more to that point that she wanted to remove Anna."

"So we are returned to that. The threat against my niece."

Ferrin nodded. "Again, do not imagine that I share your sister's conclusions regarding Webb. I have not discussed this with her, so I cannot be certain it is truly her thinking on the matter, but the letters are quite real, as is her fear. She is searching for an explanation that fits the facts as she understands them, and her judgment is compromised by her lack of information." Quietly intent, he added, "As is mine."

"Is that why you've come? You think I know something?"

"Do you?"

Sherry's dark glance was sharp. "Your judgment is also compromised," he said after a moment. "Else you would not pose your question as an accusation."

Ferrin did not blink, nor did he back down. "I have to believe you made a study of Caldwell's prospects and background when you began to suspect that he and your sister would become betrothed. I did it for Imogene when she was affianced to Mr. Branson, and if I discover that Wellsley is not Netta's intended, I will do it again. Imogene would be righteously angry if she knew, so I have never told her. She would reason I did not trust her estimation of her fiancé's character, not that I didn't trust her fiancé."

"That is splitting hairs, is it not?"

"Not to Imogene, and I suspect, not to your sister. She is very firm that a woman's thinking must be respected. I doubt that is a recent opinion."

Sherry sighed. "No, you are in the right of there."

"And am I right about the rest? You did have Caldwell investigated, did you not?"

"I did. Twice. Once when he was courting Cybelline, and again following his suicide. You will not be happy to learn that I discovered no evidence of a mistress. That surely would have revealed itself."

"Mrs. Caldwell says—"

Sherry raised his hand, stopping Ferrin. "Has she given you leave to call her by her Christian name?"

"Yes." Ferrin could not recall that he'd ever asked permission, but the wiser course here was not to make too fine a point of it.

"Then you may do so with me."

Ferrin inclined his head slightly, acknowledging the privilege, and went on. "Cybelline told me that her husband spoke little of his own parents. A grandfather raised him, I believe."

"That's right, though I would not presume he took much interest in Nicholas. Nicholas went to Harrow very early and remained there. I have the impression that he did not often return home."

"At holiday? Summer?"

"No, not even then. I believe it was Nicholas's choice. He told me once that the reason he studied law was that one of the headmasters encouraged him early on to do so. He spoke quite fondly of this teacher's interest in him. Given a choice between going home to a grandfather for whom he had little affection and remaining at school with a headmaster who inspired him, the decision was an easy one."

"He was a good student?"

"Excellent at his studies. A prefect when he was older. The usual rows and dustups with fellow classmates. My study into his background did not dwell on his school days, you understand. What I'm telling you now, I learned in the course of conversations with him after he and Cybelline were married. In comparing stories, I'd have to allow that I caused considerably more trouble at Eton than he ever thought of at Harrow."

"That's because the Harrow lads have no imagination."

"True."

"Where did he study law?"

"Oxford."

"Then his grandfather was comfortably set."

"A bit more than comfortable. Shipping and lucrative investments in the China trade."

"Cybelline said that his grandfather died around the time they were married. Did Caldwell inherit?"

Ferrin shook his head. "Nicholas was named in his grandfather's will, but he did not receive the lion's share. That went to Cambridge."

"Cambridge? His grandfather made a gift?"

"A substantial one. Nicholas and his grandfather shared one interest in common: artifacts. The collection went to the Royal Society. The money to continue the study and develop it went to Cambridge."

"Sir Richard Settle."

"You know him?"

Ferrin explained his acquaintance with Settle and Cybelline's recent business with the former don. "Did he benefit in any way from the contribution?"

"Not that I am aware. I am not certain of the order of events, but it is my recollection that Settle left Cambridge before Caldwell's grandfather died. Mayhap he was instrumental in soliciting the donation, though I couldn't say. What is your interest?"

"I'm not sure," Ferrin admitted. "I find your sister's antipathy toward him interesting, I suppose, perhaps because the origins are not clear to me." He waved it aside. "I can agree with her that Settle is not the most amiable of gentlemen."

"My thoughts also. I met him a few times because of Caldwell's association with him. Cybelline once invited me to dine at her home when Settle was a guest. She at least was able to excuse herself following the meal. I was subjected to a rather lengthy recounting of a discovery Settle and Nicholas made together. A shield, I think, though that is of no import. What is, is that I persuaded my sister never to ask me to dine again with Settle in attendance."

Ferrin leaned against the back of the sofa and pressed his thumb and forefinger to the bridge of his nose. He closed his eyes briefly, thinking. "Why do you think Caldwell killed himself?" he asked at last.

"I don't know."

"No creditors? Gaming debts?"

"No. Cybelline managed the finances. She says there was nothing like that, and he made provisions for her. It would have permitted her to live in modest comfort for several years, more if she was frugal. Of course, Cybelline has her own inheritance, so Nicholas did not need to provide for her financial well-being, only her emotional one."

"If that was his true intent, then it's been undone by his mistress." Ferrin could only shake his head. "How did Cybelline's inheritance not come under his control?"

"Caldwell petitioned for exception on her behalf. I don't know the details of how it was accomplished, but he managed the thing. I can own that I admired him for it. He was adamant that she understand that he was no fortune hunter." Sherry reached for his drink and knocked back another swallow. "He was in every way a model husband."

Ferrin said nothing.

Sherry found the silence telling. His dark eyes narrowed. "Now you are the one who knows something. What is it?"

"Precisely what you know. He had a mistress. If that is the model, then the *ton* has become too tolerant. *We* have become too tolerant."

Sherry nodded slowly. "Does Cybelline blame herself?"

"Sometimes. Less now than when she was yet in London."

"Your influence?"

"I do not count myself as having much sway over your sister's thinking, but it's my opinion that she's angrier at Caldwell now than she is unhappy with herself. The letters seem to indicate that Caldwell married Cybelline in order to father a legitimate child. I believe he grew to love her but that it paled in the face of the feelings he had for this other woman."

It was what Sherry believed as well. "I want to see these letters."

"I understand, but I don't know if Cybelline will permit you to read them or even if they're here."

"I will ask her, of course, so you must be prepared for her opposition of feeling when she realizes I know about them. I suspect she will refuse me."

"And then?"

"If they're here, I shall read them."

"But how will you find them? They might be anywhere."

Sherry arched one eyebrow and regarded Ferrin consideringly. "I believe you've met the scoundrels."

"Well?" Lily demanded when she saw her husband at last was coming to bed. "I do not like being kept in the dark, Sherry. That was the most uncomfortable supper I have ever experienced in this house, and afterward . . . in the music room . . . I despaired that we would find any topic that would engage a conversation. Even your turn at the pianoforte was uninspired."

Sherry did not turn back the covers. He sat on the edge of the bed and loosened his stock. "Cybelline is out of all patience with me."

"That was clear enough. She did not exchange more than a dozen words with you."

"That is because we had words in private."

"Did you tell Ferrin his suit wasn't welcome?"

"The subject never came up."

"Never came up? But Cybelline told me that a proposal was imminent."

"Mayhap it is, but he's not proposing to me now, is he?"

Lily's brows rose in tandem. "You are adopting a tone I do not care for, my lord."

Sherry raked back his hair and drew in a calming breath. "I apologize." He saw that Lily was not particularly mollified. "I will explain all of it, but tell me something first. Has Cybelline ever confided in you that her marriage was not as it should be?"

Lily's reply was cautious. "What do you mean?"

"I mean did she tell you something was amiss, perhaps something . . ." His voice trailed off, and he shook his head. "No, I don't suppose it matters now."

Extending her hand, Lily laid her fingers over Sherry's arm. "Something intimate? Something about her relations with Nicholas?"

Startled, he glanced sideways at Lily. "Yes. Exactly that."

Lily sucked in her bottom lip and worried it gently as she considered her response. "Were you aware that while Cybelline was carrying Anna, she and Nicholas often slept apart?"

"No, but that is not unusual." He frowned. "Is it?"

"I have no idea. You did not leave my bed." She observed him thinking on that, then she said, "And afterward, when Cybelline was ready to resume her—" Lily stopped because Sherry's sensibilities were being tested mightily. "You understand, do you not?"

"Perfectly."

"Well, Nicholas did not visit her often. She asked me about it, but I couldn't advise her."

"I see."

"Do you? His neglect hurt her, Sherry, and she could not divine the reason for it. Frankly, neither could I. Nicholas was completely attentive to her outside of the bedroom."

"He had a mistress." Sherry told her everything then, and when he was done he simply held her, or perhaps it was that she held him. There were many things about being married to Lily that he no longer questioned. They just were.

Still dressed, he lay back when she released him and cradled his head in his palms. She curled against him and was quiet. He could sense her waiting, trying to anticipate the turn of his mind.

"Do you think he loves her, Lily?"

"Ferrin?"

"Yes."

"I thought Nicholas loved her. I don't want to make a judgment about someone else's heart. I know what's in mine. That's enough."

He smiled. "I was thinking the same." He lifted his head to kiss the crown of hers. "Do you think they're intimate?"

"Sherry. You really do not want to speculate."

"I'm not. I put the question to you."

"Then I do not want to speculate." Lily was not proof against the silence that followed. She sighed. "You can make of it what you will, but I gave his lordship the suite of rooms across the hall from Cybelline."

Sherry gave Lily's shoulders an affectionate squeeze. "That's just as well. Unless they are extraordinarily careless they will not be caught out."

"My thought exactly."

* * *

Cybelline looked up and down the hall before she marched across it and opened Ferrin's door. He did not look up as she entered, nor when she closed the door with more force than was required. He was sitting in front of the fireplace with his legs stretched before him and his feet resting on a stool. A book lay unopened on his lap, and he appeared to be in deep contemplation, oblivious to her entrance.

"I know you are not sleeping," she said as she approached him.

"A fair observation, as my eyes are open."

"Then you were ignoring me."

"Not possible. You haven't made the least attempt to be quiet. I could hear you before you left your room. It occurred to me that I could expect a visit." He looked up at her. "And here you are."

"Do you never tire of being right?"

"Do you never tire of being predictable?"

Cybelline's mouth opened, then closed. She dropped slowly in the chair behind her and absently tugged on the belt of her robe. "Am I?" she asked quietly. "I hadn't realized. That does not bode well for us, does it?" She mocked herself with a short, humorless laugh. "You will not want a wife who bores you."

"God, no."

She nodded. "I suppose it is better to know that at the outset."

"Indeed."

Cybelline stopped tugging on her belt and untied it. She only had to shrug once before the robe slipped off her bare shoulder and revealed the high, white curve of one breast. She watched the center of Ferrin's eyes darken as his lashes lowered to half-mast. Her smile was a trifle smug. "I know that look, my lord. Do you never tire of being predictable?"

He suppressed his laughter but not his deeply appreciative grin. "No, not about this. And you will thank me for it."

"Perhaps later." She covered her shoulder, removed the temptation of her breast, and cinched the belt tightly. "First, there is the matter of your conversation with my brother. I did not give you leave to tell him about the letters, Ferrin. That was for me to do."

"I don't disagree, but as you have avoided it from the very first, I was compelled to disclose it myself."

"Compelled? In what way were you compelled?"

"By honor. By concern. By obligation." He pushed the stool aside and sat up. "There is your welfare to consider. And Anna's. The letters come more frequently of late. I know you realize it. You must also be aware of the increasingly threatening tone. I fully anticipate the arrival of more letters while we're at Granville, and I will not be at all surprised if the first one is delivered within a few days. Tell me you have not already considered it."

Cybelline could not. As she looked down at her hands, the admission came reluctantly. "I have been dreading it. This woman—Nicholas's mistress—she seems to know where I will be almost before I do."

"I know. And if a letter arrives shortly, we will perhaps know something more about her than we do now. I believe there are not many people privy to your decision to depart for Granville."

"No. Very few on my staff know that I am not returning to London."

"So even though you recognized the necessity of certain precautions, you still elected to keep your brother ignorant of your fears. It isn't fair to him, Cybelline, and you shouldn't expect that I will follow your lead when I think you're mistaken."

Bracing herself not to flinch from Ferrin's implacable stare, Cybelline glanced up. What she found instead was compassion. "He wants to read the letters," she told him. "That is too much. He must be made to see that. You shouldn't have told him I brought them here."

"I didn't. I told him I didn't know if you had them."

"Then he tricked me. I did not think I could be so easily caught. It is just the sort of thing he did to me when we were children."

"Then you didn't agree to allow him to read the letters."

"No. And do you know what he did? He threatened me with the scoundrels. I will tell Lily, of course, and she will put a stop to that nonsense. She doesn't hold with using the boys as bloodhounds."

Ferrin's lips twitched. "No, I suppose she doesn't. Can they really find the letters?"

"Given time, they can find anything. I cannot hope to hide the letters well enough to prevent that end, and there are too many to hide on my person—not that they would be safe there, either."

"Really?"

Because Ferrin was still wearing his evening clothes, Cybelline asked him how many handkerchiefs he was carrying.

"Two," he said.

"Show me."

He reached for one, then the other, and each time he came away with nothing. Impressed, he asked, "When did they do it?"

"I think it was when they came to the music room to bid us goodnight. They crowded around you while Sherry and Lily were at the piano. It's the rum-hustle. I've seen them do it before, and something is invariably missing at the end of it. They'll return your handkerchieves. Indeed, they may already be in your chest of drawers. The boys only do it to keep their hand in."

"A literal truth, it seems," he said dryly, putting the book aside. He shifted, leaned forward slightly, and regarded her with more gravity of expression. "Do you not think some compromise is in order, Cybelline? You have convinced me that the scoundrels will find the letters if your brother requests it of them, and I am convinced that Lady Sheridan will want to put a stop to it. Do you really want to be at the center of the controversy? Could you not find from among all the letters in your possession a few to show to Sheridan?"

"Not Nicholas's letters," Cybelline said. The heat of humiliation flushed her cheeks. "Please, Christopher, I cannot."

Ferrin nodded. It was all he could do not to reach for her, but if he touched her now he would give into her, and this was a battle that he could not allow her to win. "Very well, then the letters from his mistress. Share those. Allow your brother to make his own assessment."

Cybelline was long in answering. She stared at her hands and nodded once.

Releasing a breath he hardly knew he was holding, Ferrin leaned across the distance separating them and took Cybelline by the wrist. It required only the gentlest persuasion to bring her out of her chair and into his.

"This doesn't mean I've forgiven you."

Ferrin fingered the satin collar of her robe. "You came to my room wearing nothing but you under here. I remain hopeful that you mean to forgive me eventually."

"I don't like being bullied."

"I thought I was advancing a solution."

"It's bullying when you take my brother into your confidence to get your own way."

"My own way? What way is that exactly?"

"You are determined to protect me."

"Yes," he said. "I am. Anna, too. Do you have some objection?"

"Only to the bullying. The rest I find rather comforting." She slipped one arm around his neck and leaned in to kiss his cheek. "I was unconscionably ill-mannered at supper."

"And afterward. Don't forget about afterward."

"I played the pianoforte with all the feeling Sherry lacked."

"You pounded the keys."

"I was angry."

"And now?"

"I am never angry with Sherry for long. It's not possible."

"I understand that you'll make amends with your brother, but I think you can appreciate the nature of my own interest is more selfish."

Cybelline's mouth hovered above his. She could feel the warmth of his breath against her lips. "You were right to be hopeful." She kissed him, lightly at first, just enough to savor the taste of him, then gradually increased the pressure when the mere taste no longer could satisfy. He returned her kiss with a fullness of passion that made her breathless and weightless and insensible.

She found herself lying under him on the bed with no clear recollection of ever having left the chair. Certainly her feet had not touched the ground. Her robe was open, and he was pressing kisses along the line of her collarbone. She could feel the damp edge of his tongue make a tracing across her skin. He moved lower, then lower still, and suckled her breast, worrying the darkening rose nipple between his lips and teeth. It puckered to the hardness of a pearl, and he attended to it as if he held the jewel itself.

When he rose, her hands slipped under his frock coat and she helped him shrug out of it. His loosened stock unfolded easily. She held one tail in each hand and used them like reins to draw his head down to hers. She kissed the corner of his mouth, his jaw, and then just below his ear before tossing the stock to one side. He caught it midair, and before she understood the meaning of his wicked smile, he had it wrapped loosely about her wrists and was drawing them over her head.

"What is that in aid of?" She did not recognize her own husky whisper.

"Trust," he said. He fixed the linen tails to the bedhead, then rolled away to remove his clothes.

Cybelline twisted a bit, trying to free herself, but the stock actually tightened. She stopped immediately and stared at his naked back. She heard one boot drop to the floor, watched him shift slightly, then heard the other. "I shall scream."

"Eventually."

She blinked. Her next breath came more raggedly. She continued to stare at him as he stood and stripped out of his remaining garments. When he turned to face her she simply couldn't breathe at all.

"I think I'll choose to be flattered," he said. He sat down again at the level of her waist, then bent to kiss her. "You know we fit. We always have."

Still uncertain, she nodded slowly while searching his face.

"Part your lips."

Surprise did it for her.

His mouth covered hers. He wet her lips with his tongue, then plunged deeper, past the ridge of her teeth to draw on hers. It was a long, leisurely kiss, deeply satisfying, and he lifted his head only when he heard the whimper at the back of her throat. "You see? Our mouths fit."

Cybelline closed her eyes.

"Oh, no," he said. "Watch me."

She felt his fingertips on the soft inner side of her elbow and instinctively tried to turned her head toward his touch.

Ferrin shook his head. "No, look at me." He lifted his

hand until her eyes were on him, then began again, graz
ing her elbow and the underside of her extended arm. He
scored her skin with his nail just under her shoulder and
traced the bottom curve of her breast. His thumb flicked
her nipple and then he cupped her breast in his palm. "We
fit here."

Cybelline arched slightly, pushing herself into his
palm. She frowned, unsettled, when he pulled back and
bid her watch him again. She tried to relax, to think of
anything but what he was doing to her, but that was no
possible. His eyes never strayed from hers, while his fingers made an exquisitely torturous route from her breas
to her hip. She clearly saw his desire and his denial. She
imagined herself mirrored in the black center of his eyes.
His expression was unyielding, yet she yielded to him.
The taut planes of his face gave him the sharp, severe
look of an ascetic, yet his touch could not have been
more tender.

She tried to close her eyes when he grazed her thigh.
He only had to lift his hand to make her attend him again
She felt him follow the curve of her leg as far as her knee
then pause.

"Lift it."

Cybelline drew up her knee. The movement made her
feel the dampness between her thighs. He meant to touch
her there. She watched his nostrils flare and knew he'
had the scent of her sex. The whole of her stilled in anticipation of his touch. He smiled instead.

Frustrated, she tugged at her bonds. She was not looking at him the moment his hand slipped between her legs.
Her entire body went rigid with the intense pleasure of
the pressure he applied. Her heels dug into the mattress
and her hips lifted. He moved his fingers between the
folds of damp flesh and stroked her. She was reaching the
crest so quickly that she couldn't catch her breath.

He removed his hand.

Cybelline collapsed. When she tried to bring her legs together and satisfy the need that he would not, he stopped her by holding one knee. "Please," she whispered. "Release me."

"Release you?" He bent his head again so that his mouth was at her ear. "Or give you release?"

"Yes." She heard him laugh softly, deeply, his breath hot against her cheek. The sound of it seemed to steal under her skin, made her feel tender and raw and tingling. When he raised his head she couldn't look away. She could tell he was gauging her response, studying her breathing, the pulse in her neck, the flutter of her eyelashes. She tried to do the same, to anticipate when he would touch her, but he surprised her again, and she thought her skin could not possibly contain the intensity of sensation.

She contracted around the two fingers he pushed inside her. Her hips rocked as he withdrew and thrust and . . . paused. He poised her on the edge of pleasure again and again until every one of her senses was finely honed. The scent of him filled her nostrils. She could still taste him on her lips. There was a gentle roar in her ears that sounded very much like the thrumming of her own heart, though it might have been his. She saw nothing beyond him and felt nothing so deeply as the exquisite tug-of-war between pleasure and pain.

"We fit here," he said.

She nodded, then cried out softly as he left her a second time. Before she could comprehend the loss, he was moving to lie between her open thighs. He reached above her head and loosened the binding on her wrists. She immediately snaked her arms around him and sunk her nails into his back.

"And here," he told her.

Cybelline held her breath. He entered her with a carefully measured stroke. It was only when he was fully seated inside her that she allowed herself to breathe again. That first unhurried expulsion of air was part sigh, part moan, and all of it about her satisfaction.

When he began to move, she joined him, her body a counterpoint to his. She raised her legs and pressed her heels into the backs of his thighs. Her fingertips made a trail to the base of his spine, held there, then went lower, following the curve of his buttocks.

She knew the headiness of her own power when he groaned deeply, then made his next thrust harder. She teased him with low, husky laughter until he trapped it in her throat with his grinding kiss and she returned his heat. One tail of the linen stock was still wrapped around her wrist. She caught the other end and drew it up his back to keep him close. It was his low laughter that taunted her now, and the sound of it was enough to trip the first shiver of pleasure.

She tried to hold back, ride the crest until he was ready as well, but he urged her on, and she was helpless in the face of what he wanted for her. She screamed a little then.

For Ferrin, it was a promise fulfilled. He absorbed her shudders first, then her cry. Their cadence changed, quickened. He felt her body's pulse and the rushing of his own blood. She never entirely abandoned him for her own pleasure; every one of her responses brought him closer to crisis, and when it was upon him he simply let it be.

He lay heavily on her a moment, then carefully lifted himself and rolled onto his back. Cybelline slowly came up on one elbow and regarded his profile. His lips were parted, and his breathing was soft, though faintly uneven. His eyes were closed. A lock of hair had fallen across his brow. When she made to push it back he caught her wrist and brought her hand to his mouth. He held it there, folded in both of his hands, and pressed his lips to her knuckles.

With his own hands clasped around hers, it seemed to Cybelline that he'd made her part of a prayer. It was not only his kiss that he pressed to her fingers, but also words so softly spoken that his mouth simply moved around them.

Why had she ever doubted that she could trust this man's heart?

She watched him set her fist near the center of his chest. Her fingers splayed open, and she could feel his heartbeat under her palm. She leaned into him and kissed his shoulder.

"I love you, you know," she said.

"I know."

His acknowledgment made Cybelline smile. He'd made the admission softly, not arrogantly. It was a matter of fact, something as obvious to him as a flower turning to follow the sun's path or the constancy of the North Star.

"There is something else," she told him.

"Hmmm."

"I trust that you love me as well."

Opening his eyes, Ferrin turned his head just enough to make a study of her face. He wanted to remember her always as she was in this moment, perfectly composed, without fear or wariness, accepting at last what he'd known almost from beginning as his own truth. He saw that understanding now in the serenity of her smile and in the steadiness of her gaze. Her splendid blue-gray eyes did not dart away from his, and her smile never faltered. A wash of pink color tinted her cheeks. No line appeared between her eyebrows.

She showed him contentment, not expectation, and he held that close to his heart as her most intimate offering.

"I do love you," he said, squeezing her hand. "I wasn't certain you would ever allow me to confess it."

"I never stopped you."

He merely cocked an eyebrow at her.

"Oh, very well. I did not invite you to say so. Is that better?"

"It will do." Releasing her hand, he unwound his stock from her wrist and let it slip over the side of the bed. They shifted together, wrestling with the tangled covers until they were under them.

Cybelline remained turned on her side. She watched the play of candlelight on Ferrin's three-quarter profile. He was amused by her study, but he didn't turn away from it. "I told my brother I love you," she said after a moment. "Ah, you did not expect that, did you?"

"No."

"Then I am not entirely predictable."

"Bloody hell, no."

She nodded, satisfied. "Good. That remark stung a bit."

He glanced at her. "Have I apologized for it?"

"No, but then I haven't apologized for giving you cause to say it." She kissed the corner of his mouth. "I should not have asked you if you never tired of being right. That was not well done of me. I meant to provoke you." She saw him start to respond with his own regrets, and she stopped him. "Enough has already been said."

Ferrin did not agree immediately, but gauged her sincerity first. "All right. As you wish." He felt her leg slide over his as she turned in to him. He slipped one hand under the blanket and absently caressed her hip and thigh. "When did you make your confession to Sheridan?" he asked.

"Upon our arrival. You were still standing beside the carriage."

"So that is what you whispered in his ear."

She nodded. "Does it seem odd to you that I could admit to Sherry what I could not say to you?"

"You did not have to trust him to be anything but discreet, and I assume you learned long ago you could depend on your brother for that. He's never betrayed you."

"No," she said softly. "But neither have you."

"I think I did." His hand continued to make a gentle sweep of her thigh. "The moment I began looking for Boudicca . . . that was a betrayal. I cannot even make amends for it, because I have no regrets."

"And I'm glad of it. I have none of my own." She swept back a heavy fall of hair that lay over her shoulder. "Will you marry me, Christopher? If I go to my brother and tell him that I very much want you for my husband, will you have me? I find that being your lover is satisfying after a fashion"—she adopted his wicked smile when his own expression turned wry— "but I am persuaded that being your wife will be infinitely better."

"If you are persuaded, I would be a fool to argue."

"Then you will marry me?"

"Of course."

"But why was there never a proposal?"

"There was," he said. "You just made it. Did I not say it was inevitable?"

Cybelline turned suddenly so that she lay fully on top of him. "Do you mean you've been waiting all this time for *me* to make it?"

"Well, yes."

"But you've known for weeks that I would accept yours."

"And I was very glad of it." He grinned up at her. "It gave me hope that you could be brought around to just this end."

"You manipulated me."

"I gave you time to learn the bent of your own mind."

She snorted lightly. "What I am learning is the twisted disposition of yours. You will have to answer for tying my hands."

"As always, I am optimistic."

Cybelline laughed. "Do you know, my lord? So am I."

* * *

Anna clapped her hands together as Ferrin entered the nursery. "Up!" she demanded. She abandoned her mother at the tea table and tipped over her little chair in her haste to reach him. "Up, Misterlee!"

Ferrin's glance at Cybelline was a shade guilty. "I suppose she will have to learn to call me something else." He bent, swept her up, and launched her into the air. She fairly screamed her delight. "Goodness, poppet, you sound more like your mother every day."

"Ferrin!" Cybelline quickly looked around to see if Rose's nurse had heard the exchange. The woman's attention seemed to be all for her young charge and the pink bottom she was liberally dusting with cornstarch. Nevertheless, Cybelline flushed deeply and glared at Ferrin.

He merely grinned and launched Anna again.

Suspicious of his mood, especially that he seemed impervious to her admonishment, Cybelline came to her feet and set her hands on her hips. "What have you done, my lord?"

"I took the liberty of speaking to your brother."

"You did?" Her militant stance dissolved. "Already? But he has not yet had his breakfast."

"What does that signify? Neither have I."

"I was going to speak to him afterward."

"I'm certain he'll be glad of it, but regarding the matter you broached with me last night, well, there are some things that are better discussed first between gentlemen." Giving Cybelline his back, he carried Anna into the hallway and out of hearing of Nurse Pinter. When he turned, Cybelline was standing toe to toe with him, just as he'd known she would be. He set Anna on his shoulder, then proceeded to back Cybelline against the wall and kiss her thoroughly. It was Anna's small fist yanking on his hair that made him end it.

Amused by Anna's jealousy and having no pity for Ferrin, Cybelline let her daughter pluck a few strands before she rescued him. She lifted Anna from Ferrin's shoulder and set her on the floor, then gave her a gentle push in the direction of the nursery. Anna attached herself to Ferrin's leg instead.

Neither Ferrin nor Cybelline tried to pry her loose.

"Did you think I wouldn't go to him?" Cybelline asked.

"No, I was afraid you would." He brushed her cheek with his fingertips. "I needed to present myself to your brother, Cybelline, and make my intentions clear. There is a proper manner for doing such things, and I found myself unwilling to abandon it. You are worthy of that respect, and frankly, so am I."

She smoothed the lapel of his black wool frock coat. "Thank you for honoring both of us. It is the sort of thing that does not go unnoticed by Sherry."

"That was also my sense."

"He was receptive?"

"He indicated he would be if you are also agreeable."

"Then that is what I will tell him after he's broken his fast." She watched Ferrin pat Anna's hair as her daughter chewed on his nankeen breeches. Shaking her head, she bent down and removed the fabric from between Anna's pearly teeth. There was a bit of protest, but that subsided when Cybelline picked her up. "If you did not meet in the breakfast room, then where did you find Sherry so early?"

"At the stable. I invited myself to ride with him."

"Of course you did." She sighed. "That was clever."

"I don't know. He saw through to my purpose almost at once."

Cybelline's eyes danced. "Sherry is clever, too."

The final missive that Cybelline gave her brother he read at a glance. Watching him, she repeated the words to herself:

My dear Mrs. Caldwell,

When will you tell your daughter that you murdered her father?

Always

Setting it down on his desk, Sherry took a moment to compose himself before he addressed Cybelline. "I wish you had come to me immediately."

She did not look away. "I understand, but I am not as certain as Ferrin that I should be here now."

"Thank God he has sense enough for the both of you."

"It does not surprise that you think so, but I would like to know what either of you think can be done."

"We will find her, of course, and end it."

"Yes, well, I wish you luck with it. I have racked my brain for something that will make her reveal herself to me and have nothing but the occasional headache to show for it."

"Then you've never considered Webb."

Cybelline sat back in her chair as if she'd been pushed. Consternation etched a tiny vertical crease between her eyebrows. "I don't . . . that is, it wouldn't be proper to speculate . . . I can't . . ." Impatient with herself, she took the offensive. "Where did you come by such a peculiar notion? No, don't answer. I can imagine. *He* told you so."

"If by *he* you mean the man who only a few hours ago declared himself, then yes, *he* would be the one." Sherry paused long enough to stack the letters and square off their corners. "Apparently *he* would also be in the right of it."

"That man is unnatural."

Sherry's eyebrows lifted. "I hope you do not mean that. I am finding I rather like his company."

"That is because he does not pluck the thoughts from your head the way he does mine."

"No, Lily does that. You and I are rather predictable, you know."

Cybelline came very close to throwing something at him. The fact that the only thing within reach was a porcelain bowl that Lily admired kept her from acting on the thought.

"Calm yourself, Cyb, and pray, do not throw that bowl at my head."

What she did was throw up her hands. "Yes," she said. "I have entertained the thought that my husband's mistress was my maid." Pushing herself out of the chair, she walked to the window and stared out. Patches of snow dotted the lawn and there were still mounds of it in the shade of the hedgerow. "It doesn't make sense to me precisely. Webb was with me years before I met Nicholas. I cannot imagine how they might have had an opportunity to become acquainted except through me, yet neither can I dismiss the notion. I tell myself that it is unfair to her— and it is—but when I look about for someone to take her place, I invariably return to her. You cannot imagine how I despise myself for thinking it."

"Perhaps I can," Sherry said quietly. He did not elaborate. "Ferrin says there is someone in Penwyckham who seems to have a romantic interest in Webb."

She nodded. "Mr. Foster. He is a decent man. Very kind."

"And if she marries him, you hope the letters will stop."

"It occurred to me."

Sherry shook his head, but Cybelline was still turned away toward the window and didn't see. He picked up the letter opener on his desk and balanced it between the index finger of each hand while he considered what must be done. "I believe we will have to cast a wider net, Cybelline. There is something that we have failed to recognize that will explain the whole of it. We must discover what it is. Where is Ferrin?"

Cybelline glanced in Sherry's direction. "In the schoolroom. Lily entreated him to make a voltaic pile for the scoundrels. We shall be fortunate if no one is struck by lightning."

"That would be impressive."

She sighed. "It is."

He tempered his chuckle behind a polite cough. It seemed to him that she was speaking of electricity of a different sort, but there were things a brother could not properly ask. "I'll send Wolfe for him. I think Ferrin should be here."

"Very well, though I don't know what any of us can contribute by further discussion."

Sherry didn't challenge her thinking. He rang for the butler and requested Ferrin's presence. Wolfe nodded and handed him the morning post on a silver tray, then disappeared. Sherry left the doors open and returned to his desk. He idly sifted through the letters as he set the tray down. His fingers paused when he had gone halfway.

"Sherry?" Cybelline's heart lodged in her throat as soon as she saw him hesitate. "It's from her, isn't it?" He didn't have to say anything; she knew she was right. "Let me see it, Sherry. Do not open it."

He began to remove it, and that was when he saw there was a second one addressed by the same hand. "There are two." Cybelline was already at his side and reaching for them. She had them in her grasp before he could think better of it. He laid one hand over her wrist and entreated her, "Read them here, Cybelline. Please don't leave."

"Wounded animals are allowed privacy to lick their wounds. Would you deny me that?"

Sherry could say nothing for a moment. The ache he felt for her warred with his anger toward Nicholas and his mistress. "No," he said finally. "Go on. You can take them in the gallery. Ferrin and I will be waiting when you are ready."

She nodded once, clutched the letters against her breast, and fled the room.

Sherry was splashing whisky into a tumbler when Ferrin arrived. "Before you judge me harshly, you should know that two more letters came. Cybelline's in the gallery reading them now. Perhaps she is right about Webb."

Shaking his head, Ferrin closed the pocket doors behind him. "It might be better if she were," he said. "I was on my way to find you when your butler met me. I have learned the identity of Nicholas Caldwell's mistress."

Sherry paused in lifting his drink to his lips. "You learned it?"

Ferrin nodded. "Only minutes ago."

"But I thought you were in the schoolroom?"

"I was."

"Then how . . . ?"

"In the oddest manner possible. The scoundrels told me."

Chapter Fifteen

Cybelline chose an upholstered bench in the corner of the gallery farthest from the doors. The distance was quite purposeful. Although she hoped no one would intrude upon her, she nevertheless prepared for it. The few moments it would take for a visitor to find her would give her some small opportunity to compose herself. It was not her own pride that dictated that she should do so, but concern for Ferrin and Sherry. She understood they were moving toward a course of action with unforeseen consequences; she did not want to hasten them toward that end.

The gallery at Granville was much larger than the one she'd toured in Ferrin's London home. There were no pirates in the Grantham family tree, though she thought the bloodline might be improved for it. Portraits of her own parents flanked one of the great fireplaces. Her father's parents also were here, and the Viscount Sheridan before him. Sherry's portrait was not yet finished, but then he was not a patient subject. The oil he'd commissioned of Lily hung in the music room where he could look at her while he played the pianoforte.

Cybelline's gaze drifted to the opposite end of the gallery, where her experienced eyes found the panel in the wainscoting and wall that could be turned aside to reveal a passageway. She and Sherry had discovered three such hidden staircases at Granville Hall. The scoundrels located another. The passages were a necessity in a time when those who found favor with their sovereign also could lose it at a whim. The intrigues at court meant that sanctuary needed to be established in the country.

Cybelline wondered how long it had been since anyone had used the gallery passage. She was almost certain the scoundrels hid in it now and again. It was the sort of dark, secret place that Sherry's wards could not possibly avoid, regardless of how often they'd been admonished to do so. It was hardly fair to scold them when she and Sherry had not been able to resist the lure, either.

This passage led to the wine cellar below, to the adjoining music room, and to a bedchamber and drawing room on the upper floors of the hall. It did not provide a route out of the manor, but it led to areas where exits were accessible, and Cybelline could admit to herself it was a temptation to find one of them now.

Her eyes strayed to the letters in her hand. She held them steadily and separated them to judge their weight and thickness, then chose the heavier one—the one she knew Nicholas would have written.

Unfolding it carefully, she smoothed it open in her lap. The date immediately captured her attention, and she sharply sucked in a breath. Here was proof at last that Nicholas had been involved with another woman well in advance of their betrothal. She had always suspected it was so, but the confirmation still stung.

15 *January 1812*

My dearest,
I am a coward. I do not make this admission

lightly, and certainly not to excuse my behavior. You have asked many times of late what manner of thoughts troubled me, and I have always dismissed your concern. You cannot know how deeply I regret that. So often it came to my mind to tell you, and I most selfishly allowed each opportunity to pass. Thus, my cowardice. I could not bear witness to your despair.

There is no manner in which I might put this before you that will ease my conscience or your pain. It must be communicated forthrightly: I have met the young woman I hope to marry.

It does not follow that this must significantly alter what exists between us. That is not at all my desire, though I will understand if you do not agree. You have avoided just this end, but I find I cannot. You have always known that my advancement at law is dependent on the observation of certain social conventions. Perhaps you will think me without feeling for admitting this, but I can state unequivocally that the opposite is true.

My passion for the law is no greater than my passion for you, yet you might suspect that I am making a choice that does not favor you. That is also not true. My marriage will change our circumstances only if you permit it to come between us. I believe it will grant us opportunities that were denied to us before. Pray, do not think me naive. I have thought of little else for months, and trust that I have considered all of the consequences of my decision.

I do not hold out hope that you will find much to recommend Miss Grantham. She is wholly unexceptional, though from my perspective it makes her quite perfect. Her bloodlines are blue enough to suit (her brother is the Viscount Sheridan), and she is modestly pretty.

She is an independent thinker and holds remarkably firm opinions. She is perhaps too free sharing them, but I can forgive her outspoken manner as I am often entertained by her enthusiasm. An important personage in her life is Lady Rivendale, a dreadful woman with more means than social graces, but she is popular with the *ton* for her eccentricities.

Miss Grantham has a clever mind and does not chatter. As is not often seen in one so young, she is surprisingly restful company, which I desire. She is sensible in her concerns and does not indulge in whims and fancies. I believe she will have me if I am earnest, but not desperate, in my attentions.

I am one of several gentlemen expressing interest, and I may not win her hand, but it remains my hope to do so.

I pray that you will not cut me from your life, though you have every right. You must see that Miss Grantham, though pleasant and suitably accomplished, does not engage my passion. My heart is still yours.

Always

The letter slipped through Cybelline's nerveless fingers and drifted to the floor. She sat there quietly for several long minutes, and when the numbness passed, the odd emotion that came to the forefront was relief.

Nicholas's mistress was not Webb. Cybelline could acknowledge at last just how much she had feared having that suspicion confirmed, and guilt that she had ever entertained the thought quickly followed. She knew the measure of peace she'd finally made with Nicholas's faithlessness would have vanished in the face of learning of Webb's betrayal. Now she had cause to wonder which would have been more deeply felt at this juncture, the perfidy of her husband or her maid.

Sighing, Cybelline bent and picked up Nicholas's letter to exchange it for the one that was sure to be from his mistress. She doubted she could adequately prepare herself. Still, she took a deep breath and released it slowly before opening the letter. She read it in a single glance.

My dear Mrs. Caldwell,

You do not deserve to be happy.

Always

Cybelline did not hear her own gasp for the blood pounding in her ears. Fainting might well have been a blessing, but she learned that willing that end did not bring the thing about. She simply sat with her hands folded tightly around the crumpled letter and waited for the searing pain in her chest to pass so she could draw another breath.

When she knew she could stand without faltering, she drew on her resolve to exit the gallery.

Sherry tapped the tip of the letter opener against the edge of his desk. For a few moments the rhythmic drumming was all that could be heard in the library. Neither man looked at the other. Sherry watched the blur of motion that his tapping created. Ferrin stood much as Cybelline had earlier, staring out the window with his arms folded across his chest.

"It's a fantastic notion," Sherry said finally.

Ferrin simply nodded.

Sherry sat up and tossed the letter opener aside. "What are your thoughts on telling Cybelline?"

Turning slowly away from the window, Ferrin regarded Sherry with a slight frown. "What do you mean?"

"Should she be told or not?"

"It never occurred to me that she should *not* be told. You have some doubts, I collect."

"Not as many as you might think; I simply would like to consider the consequences."

"I understand, but from my perspective there is only one consequence of import: keeping my promise to your sister to deal honestly with her. Even if she never discovered the truth on her own, I would know that I'd held it from her."

"You don't know that you've discovered any truth at all," Sherry said. "It is at best a theory."

Ferrin nodded. "Still, I would remind you that I did not formulate the theory to fit the facts, rather the facts fit my theory. How does Cybelline benefit by not being told?"

"She will not be hurt more deeply than she's already been."

"Can you not imagine that she might experience some measure of relief?"

"Relief? I don't see how that can be her reaction."

"It is as I said yesterday: I know your sister differently than you do. I think she will be relieved to learn not all of her judgments have been without foundation. Cybelline has had certain knowledge at her fingertips that she simply could not make sense of because of a single mistaken premise. In her place, I'd want to know that."

Sherry's brow furrowed. "You can appreciate that I want to protect her."

"I want that also. Knowledge can do that; ignorance cannot."

"My wife would say the same." He rose from his chair. "I do not even disagree, it's only because Cybelline will always be my younger sister that I find this so bloody difficult. As you wish, we will tell her your suspicions and allow her to decide her own feelings about them."

"Not both of us," Ferrin said. "I will tell her."

Sherry started to protest, then caught himself. After a moment, he inclined his head and agreed to this also.

Ferrin understood the concession that was being made. Sherry was relinquishing the role of protector. Ferrin did not make the mistake of supposing that Sherry would not take it up again if the outcome was not to his liking, but that he was willing to surrender it, even briefly, was an act of profound trust.

"She is in the gallery?" asked Ferrin.

"Yes." He glanced at the clock on the mantelpiece. "I thought she would have returned by now."

"It's just as well that I go to her."

"Of course." Sherry joined Ferrin at the doors and parted them. "You will seek me out afterward?"

"As soon as she gives me leave to do so." Ferrin observed this seemed to satisfy Sherry. He laid his hand firmly on Sherry's shoulder, squeezed once, then he slipped through the doors and crossed the hall to the gallery.

Pinch sourly regarded the cards he was dealt. "I don't like the looks o' this," he said, casting a suspicious glance in Midge's direction. "Did you deal from the bottom, Midge?"

"I say, Pinch, that's unkind of you."

"I say, Midge, you ain't answered the question."

Dash looked up, his eyes darting right, then left. "Is it to be a row or cards? If it's to be a row, I'm leaving."

"Bad hand, eh?" Pinch said.

Dash shrugged, unwilling to be provoked into taking sides. "I promised Anna I'd let her play with my soldiers."

"She won't remember," Midge told him. "And she'll just put them in 'er mouth. That's what she does."

"Doesn't matter. I promised." He started to study his hand again when a movement in his peripheral vision caught his attention. He swiveled in his chair to face the wall on his left and immediately observed the widening of a vertical crack in the wainscoting. "We have a guest, lads," he said, jerking his chin in the direction of the hidden panel. "Just see if we don't."

Pinch and Midge turned to observe what was toward

just as Cybelline slipped between the wall and the panel. Their astonishment mirrored hers.

Dash set down his cards and jumped to his feet to help her close the door. "You gave us a start, Mrs. Caldwell. It's been a spell since anyone used this passage." He stopped, considered his words, and amended them. "Well, since anyone was *allowed* to use this passage."

Cybelline brushed off her shawl and muslin day dress. A few cobwebs clung stubbornly to her bare forearms. Dash gallantly offered her a handkerchief. Cybelline took it and thanked him, then gave him a wry look when she saw the embroidered initials. "I'll return this to Lord Ferrin." She tucked one corner under the satin belt that defined her bodice. "Do you have another?"

"No." Dash had the grace to look sheepish. "Pinch's got it."

Cybelline held out her hand. Pinch dutifully came forward and gave it over. "And Midge? What did you take?"

"Had a compass but I thought it might cause a stir if I was to keep it. I put it back."

"In his pocket, I hope."

"Oh, yes, ma'am. Right away."

Cybelline merely shook her head. It required considerable effort to be stern with them. "I thought you boys were in the schoolroom."

"We were," Dash said. "His lordship showed us how to build a voltic pile."

"Voltaic," Cybelline corrected absently.

"And magnets," Pinch added. "Don't forget about the magnets."

"That's right," Dash told her. "We were stacking magnets. Great fun, that. Midge and me pretended to be magnets. Repelling, don't you know. Cause we're alike. Interesting, I'm thinking, but then his lordship left suddenly, so Lady Sherry gave us leave to do the same."

"I see." Cybelline didn't see at all, but she felt compelled to murmur something, as Dash clearly expected a reply. She wished she had said more because the brief silence that followed was the opportunity the scoundrels were seeking to pose some questions of their own.

"Why'd you use the passage?" Midge asked. "Something wrong with the main staircase?"

"Ain't precisely safe, Mrs. Caldwell." Pinch shifted his weight from one foot to the other. "That's why we're not allowed to use it, you know."

Dash went directly to the heart of the matter. "Who are you trying to hide from?"

Cybelline forced a short laugh. "Goodness, aren't you all curious? I hope you show Lord Ferrin this aspect of your character, as he's certain to appreciate it ever so much more than I am."

The scoundrels exchanged uncertain glances. Pinch was the first to look guilty. "She means we overstepped ourselves," he said. "At least I think that's what she means." He lifted his eyes to Cybelline, looking for confirmation.

"That's right, Master Pinch." Her smile communicated forgiveness. "If you will excuse me, lads, I am all for a brisk walk this afternoon." She saw their hopeful faces and shook her head ruefully. "Later," she promised. "I'll take you with me when I go out with Anna. The princess always likes to have her knights around her."

"But the queen wishes to be alone," Dash said in lofty accents.

"Very much alone," Cybelline said. Her look encompassed all three of the scoundrels. "I am depending upon you to make it so."

The afternoon sky was becoming overcast, a circumstance that suited Cybelline's mood perfectly. The white winter sun was not able to find a break in the clouds, and a blue-gray shadow flickered on the horizon. Cybelline glanced over her shoulder once on her way to the lake.

Granville Hall looked bleak to her of a sudden, not welcoming. When she arrived, she'd had the familiar sense of returning home, of being embraced by the house in much the same way she'd been embraced by her brother. That perception of the hall as a sanctuary had vanished—worse, she was gripped by the notion that her presence within its walls made it unsafe for others.

You do not deserve to be happy. Those words cut her to the quick. She had found happiness, not only with Ferrin and her daughter, but also with herself. There was no mistaking the intent was to steal it away from her, and it was not difficult to imagine the surest way to do it would be to strike out at those she loved. She could bear it if she was the target, but not if she was made to stand by and watch injury done to others.

Cybelline lowered her head against the chill wind off the lake and tugged on the sleeves of her pelisse. She followed the path along the bank, noting how worn it had become since the arrival of the scoundrels two years ago. The boys and Sherry spent a great deal of time fishing and racing sailboats under halcyon summer skies, and in the winter they skated on the frozen lake.

Somewhere behind her she heard the playful shouting and laughter of the scoundrels. She smiled to herself. It had been too much to hope that they would not follow. Turning, she looked for them and was surprised to see the distance she had traveled from the hall. She could just make out the figures of the boys hurrying down the path through the terraced garden. All three of them were carrying kites almost as tall they were, while they dragged each kite's absurdly long rag tail behind them.

So they weren't intent on following her, she realized, but had come out on their own for a bit of fun. On the rise behind them she saw Lily appear with a bundle in her arms that had to be Rose, then a moment later Becky came into view with Anna tugging on her hand.

Cybelline was tempted to join them. The echo of their laughter was like the seductive call of the sirens. She resisted only because her own dark mood would not serve them well.

She quickly removed herself from the path and slipped into a stand of trees where she could not easily be seen. She stayed there to watch the scoundrels launch their kites, then moved through the trees toward the road on the opposite side. The trio of colorfully decorated kites eventually rose high enough to clear the treetops, and she could mark their flight from the road.

Cybelline walked with no particular destination in mind. The Granville estate extended for miles, and the nearest village was beyond that. There was an inn on the outskirts of the village run by a friendly hosteler, but Cybelline did not think she wanted to go so far without a companion. In the end, she simply placed one foot in front of the other, content to press on without design.

Lost in thought—or the absence of it—Cybelline heard the hoofbeats approaching her from behind only as she felt their vibration. She stopped but did not turn.

Ferrin reined in his gelding as he came abreast of Cybelline. When she glanced up at him, then continued walking, he did the same. "Your brother says I should not offer you a ride even if you blister your feet."

Cybelline nodded. "That sounds like Sherry."

"I told him you would not want to ride after I blistered your backside."

She glanced up at him and judged by the set of his jaw that it was no idle threat. "What did Sherry say?"

"He said only that I should remove my glove first."

"Oh." She faced forward, chin high, but her step faltered a little. "I needed to be alone."

"It seems to me that Granville Hall is of a sufficient size to allow for that. There was no need to use hidden passages and engage the scoundrels in helping you escape."

"They did not help me."

"They did not offer that they'd seen you until Lady Sheridan lent her influence to the interrogation."

"Then I am sorry for that. It was certainly not my intent that they should be in trouble."

Ferrin's gaze lifted to the low-lying blue-gray clouds off to his left and the three brightly colored kites dipping and swaying in the wind. "They are not in trouble, Cybelline. You are."

She also glanced at the kites but said nothing.

"Do you have the letters?" he asked.

She nodded.

He sighed when she did not produce them. "May I see them?"

Cybelline paused long enough to fish them out from under her pelisse. She also found the two handkerchieves she'd attached to her belt earlier and gave those over as well.

Ferrin stared at the handkerchieves with reluctant admiration before tucking them away. "I shudder to think how they will make use of their talent when they grow to manhood."

"I believe they propose to be pirates, so it suits admirably."

"Yes," he said dryly, "it does." He held up Newton and dismounted, then handed the reins to Cybelline. When she regarded them as if he'd given her twin snakes, he said, "To keep him from wandering off while I read." He did not know how to interpret the look she gave him, so he ignored it and opened the thicker of the two letters. He read quickly, without comment, though his mouth was grimly set. The second letter required only a moment's attention.

Ferrin pocketed both, then took up the leading strings. "Onward?" he asked. "Or back to the hall?" When Cybelline simply stood there, seemingly unable to make this decision on her own, he realized she had finally reached the end of her tether. "We'll walk on a bit."

Nodding, she fell in step beside him.

"Why didn't you leave the gallery by the usual route?" he asked after a time.

"For the obvious reason that I hoped to avoid a confrontation. Sherry does not appreciate how difficult it is to face him."

"I think he does. I am here alone, after all."

"I'd wager it was at your insistence."

He shrugged. "I did not have to threaten him."

That raised Cybelline's small smile. "How did you find me?"

"The view from the north turret is panoramic. Once we knew you'd left the hall by one of the least used exits and gone for a walk alone, Sherry suggested I look for you from that vantage point. I saw you just before you disappeared into the wood."

"I was trying to avoid the party of kite flyers. They were a bit too gay for my mood."

"You do not deserve to be happy, is that it?"

She looked at him askance, startled. The manner in which he said those words placed a different construction upon them, as if she were the one denying herself happiness. Uncertain of what meaning she should assign them now, she said, "It seems wrong, I suppose."

"You are so wise to the ways of the scoundrels, yet you do not see when the rum-hustle is being used to steal your own heart."

"I've been afraid for Anna," she said. "And now for you as well."

"I know. It is reasonable to suppose we've been found out."

"Do you think I shouldn't be concerned?"

"About me? No. About Anna? I'm not certain. But I know you should be concerned for yourself. If you think you do not deserve to be happy, Cybelline, then you will not be happy. It is as simple and as complicated as that."

Cybelline glanced skyward. The kites still bobbed and

weaved above the treetops. It was nothing short of astonishing that the boys hadn't tangled the rag tails or their twine and brought the things crashing into the boughs. The kites soared and dipped, then rose again, finding a new current of air to lift them higher than before. The tails fluttered and curled, and beyond the trees, out of line of her sight, she imagined each boy holding tenaciously to his string and Anna begging for a turn at the same.

Her own heart soared. She reached for Ferrin and tucked her arm in his as her heels lifted momentarily off the ground. "Let's find them," she said. "How long has it been since you flew a kite?"

"More years than I care to contemplate." He was not proof against the smile she turned on him. Other matters could wait. "This way. There looks to be a break in the trees."

Cybelline was on the point of stepping off the road when Ferrin drew her back. She looked down, thinking he meant for her to watch her step, but there was nothing there. Her eyes darted to his, then to the direction of his skyward gaze. The kites—all three—were suddenly flying erratically. Cybelline could tell by the tails and the distance between the kites that the strings had not tangled. One of the kites took a sudden turn and dipped downward. When it didn't recover from its plummet, she knew that no one was holding the string any longer. A second kite flew higher, its path taking it directly over the trees. There was no hand at the end of that string, either, she realized, else there would have been a collision with the boughs. The third kite floated toward them, bouncing on the upsweep of air, then taking a dive in their direction.

She ran ahead to pick it up. "What do you suppose happened?" She put the kite under one arm and began to pull on the string, winding it as she followed its trail.

Ferrin did not answer. He mounted Newton and came alongside Cybelline. "Leave it." His tone brooked no argument. "Give me your hand."

What she saw in his face would have panicked her minutes earlier; now the effect was one of transcendent calm. She dropped the kite and helped him swing her into position behind him. Without having to be instructed to do so, she slid her arms around his waist and held on. Cybelline pressed her cheek to his back and closed her eyes as Newton fairly flew through the wood at Ferrin's urging. The hood of her pelisse fell back, and her knot of hair lost its moorings, slipping free of the anchoring pins so that it whipped about like a streamer of ribbons.

The diagonal course that Ferrin cut should have led them out into the open some fifty yards closer to the hall than the scoundrels. Instead, it put them almost directly into their path. If Pinch, Dash, and Midge had been able to run any faster, the horse would have charged into their midst.

"Hold!"

The boys ground to a stop as quickly as Ferrin's mount. They did not wait to be asked for an explanation for their mad run toward the hall. They plunged into it simultaneously, like a poorly rehearsed Greek chorus.

Neither Ferrin nor Cybelline could make any sense of what was being said, but there was no mistaking the fear in the boys' eyes. They danced in place, waving their arms and pointing toward the hall, then to the wood, then to the sky. Newton began to dance nervously.

Ferrin thrust one gloved hand forward and called a halt to the scoundrels' excited jabbering before their expansive gestures caused his mount to bolt. "Who's been hurt?" he demanded, attending to the one word he understood in the midst of all the others.

Cybelline tapped him on the back and pointed to where Lily was coming over a small rise with Rose hitched on her hip. She was using her free hand to wave the group over to her.

"It's Becky," Dash said. "Becky went down straightaway. She couldn't hold on."

"She tried!" Pinch told them, his breath heaving. "We all did!"

Midge started to fidget again. "It 'appened so fast! As quick as that." He snapped his fingers to underscore his point.

Cybelline's chest tightened as Ferrin tugged on the strings and set the gelding off in Lily's direction. She glanced behind her and saw the boys had abandoned their run to the house in favor of following. It seemed clear they had been running for help.

For Becky? Cybelline wondered. Or Anna?

They caught up to Lily quickly. Her face was pale. She held Rose protectively against her. The infant was fretting, absorbing her mother's anxieties as her own.

"Lily?" Cybelline's eyes darted around until they settled on Becky's slim figure on the ground, folded awkwardly against the trunk of a pine tree. Her daughter was not in sight. "Where's Anna?" she asked sharply. "What's happened to Anna?"

"I don't know. The rider . . . he went directly for her." Tears welled in her eyes. She patted Rose on the back, her agitation making the attention less soothing than was her intent. "He came out of the woods. Did you see him? He had to have gone toward the road. We had no chance to fight him off. When we realized his purpose, Becky tried to protect Anna. She was like a ferret bent on climbing his arm, but he shook her off. She went under his horse, and he trampled her when he fled. He has Anna, Cybelline! He took Anna!"

Ferrin rounded on Cybelline. "Off!"

The command was scarcely necessary. Cybelline was already slipping to the ground. The weight that she felt in her chest almost dropped her to her knees. "Find her! You will find her!"

He nodded abruptly, then followed the direction of

Lily's extended arm as if he were following his own compass needle and charged back into the wood.

Cybelline watched him go. Her entire body trembled, but she remained standing. "Did you recognize him?"

Lily shook her head. "No. I never saw his face." She stepped closer to Cybelline as the boys crowded around. "Are you going to faint?"

"No. No, I'm not." Drawing a steadying breath, she parted the scoundrels and began walking toward Becky. "How badly is she hurt?"

"I think her arm is broken. She wouldn't allow me to touch it, so I can't be sure."

Cybelline knelt beside the young girl. In spite of the cold, there were beads of perspiration dotting Becky's upper lip and brow. "Lady Sheridan tells me you fought hard, Becky. I'm grateful for that."

Becky sobbed abruptly, then was quiet. She did not look in her mistress's direction but simply held her arm as protectively to her chest as Lily held Rose.

"No one blames you," Cybelline told her gently. "His lordship will bring Anna back . You'll see. Let me examine your arm, Becky. Please. Will you permit to do that?" She glanced at Pinch. "You must run back to the hall and fetch Sherry. Tell him what's happened and explain that he should send someone for the surgeon. Ask him to have the servants bring a litter for Becky. I don't think she can walk." She lifted the hem of Becky's gown a few inches and revealed a blood-stained petticoat and stocking. There was already swelling above her scuffed leather boot.

Pinch turned to go and the other boys made to follow. Cybelline called Dash and Midge back. "Only one," she said firmly. "Three of you together cannot be understood, and Sherry must be made to come quickly."

Lily asked Dash and Midge to take turns holding Rose while she helped Cybelline attend to Becky. Rose stopped whimpering as soon as she was placed in Dash's arms. At another time Lily would have found humor in Rose's defection. Now she accepted it without comment and knelt beside Cybelline.

"Stretch your leg," Lily instructed Becky, "and rest your heel in my lap. That will help keep the swelling down." She helped the girl ease her leg forward, then guided it carefully onto her lap. "Did you know Anna's abductor? I've explained to Cybelline that I didn't see his face, but you were closer. Could you identify him?"

"No." Her voice was barely audible. Both women leaned closer to hear her. "The muffler covered most of his face. I tried to pull it off, but he struck me down. I feared he'd drop Anna. What if she'd gone under the horse instead of me?"

That prospect made Cybelline shudder. "You were very brave, Becky. Nanny Baker could not have done more than you, and we know how dear Anna is to her."

"Oh, aye, ma'am. She loves the little one like she was her own."

No, Cybelline thought, it wasn't possible that anyone loved Anna as she did. The loss not only tugged at her heart, it tugged at her womb. She did not comment, though, and busied herself brushing back Becky's dark red hair where it was matted to her cheek and brow. The girl's skin was clammy and colorless. She glanced sideways at Lily, concerned, but addressed the maid. "Where else are you hurt?"

"There's a fiercesome pain in my ribs, ma'am."

"Let's take a peek, shall we?" Cybelline said calmly. "I'll just push your cloak aside and . . ."

Ferrin had been able to follow the trail of Anna's abductor through the wood, but when he reached the crossroads three miles distant of Granville Hall, the route he should take was no longer obvious. He knew in which direction Westin-on-the-Narrows lay and where he would find the inn. The path to the east was unknown to him, but he suspected it bordered Sheridan's property and was an unlikely route for his quarry to take. Reasoning that the village was another place to avoid, Ferrin urged his mount to the southwest toward the inn and London.

He rode hard. In the few places where the road was dry, small eddies of dust rose up behind him. More often there were water-filled ruts to be avoided and thin patches of crusted snow that caused even the sure-footed Newton to slip.

He saw evidence again that a horse had recently covered the same ground, but it was impossible to know if he was drawing nearer to his prey or an innocent traveler desiring respite at the inn. He charged ahead, certain only that he had to find Anna, that here was a loss from which Cybelline might recover but would never heal.

Ferrin's eyes were drawn toward the curve in the road up ahead. A tree had fallen across it and lay angled like a rail against the crumbling stone wall on the other side. Ferrin gave his horse permission to fly, leaned forward, and prepared to make the jump. He came as close as he'd ever done to losing his seat when he caught sight of Anna out of the corner of his eye. Her downy red-gold hair was lifted away from her small face so that it formed an angel's halo about her head. Sitting calmly atop the wall, she was amusing herself by swinging her legs up and down and banging her heels against the stone.

Ferrin pulled up on the reins after he cleared the obstacle and sharply turned his mount to face her. "Anna?"

She immediately burst into tears.

He came abreast of the wall, leaned over, and scooped her up. She came without protest, even lifting her arms at the last moment to help him reach her. He cradled her against his chest, and she buried her face under one of the capes of his greatcoat. He rubbed her back and spoke soothingly, calming her fears even as his own remained jangled.

Above Anna's head, Ferrin surveyed the countryside as far as he could see. There was no sign of the mysterious rider, though he observed there were any number of places where the man could be hidden. Farther down the road the stone wall was high enough to conceal horse and rider behind it, especially if the rider lay low or dismounted altogether. Another stand of trees dense enough to embrace darkness only a few feet from their edge could also obscure the abductor.

Ferrin knew the man was close by, most likely observing Anna's rescue. He could only theorize that he had gained so much ground during his pursuit that the other rider believed he was in imminent danger of being run to earth. A choice had to be made: risk capture with Anna, perhaps hurting her in the chase, or leave her safely behind and make good on his escape.

Ferrin uncovered Anna's head and gave her a thorough examination. Her sobs had devolved into jerky little hiccups that were able to squeeze the occasional tear from her dewy eyes. "We shall have to do something about the nose," Ferrin told her. "Before it runs away."

She sniffed inelegantly.

"Yes, well, that is one way, poppet, but I seem to have several handkerchieves about my person this morning. You are welcome to use one or all of them." He reached into his pocket and fished one out. Anna tried to hide her face from it, but he persevered. "Blow. Harder." When she was cleaned up to his satisfaction, he thrust the handkerchief away and guided his mount carefully around the trunk end of the fallen tree. This required climbing part of the rocky incline that had no longer been able to support the roots and heavy trunk. Stones tumbled and slipped, but Newton managed the course without stumbling and unseating his riders.

"We're for home," Ferrin told Anna. If he'd had someone to take her, he would have continued his pursuit, but because Anna's safety was paramount it dictated that he return to Granville Hall and Cybelline. Glancing up at the sky, he saw ominously dark clouds approaching from the west. He judged that it was probably not cold enough to snow. That left him with the strong suspicion that he and Anna were going to be caught in a thunderstorm long before they reached shelter.

Ferrin remained vigilant. With Anna comfortably curled against him and warmly protected inside his greatcoat, he was free to look around in the event he was being followed. He observed nothing that led him to that conclusion, yet he couldn't shrug off the sensation that his progress was being marked. Although he had great respect for facts as they applied to his scientific work, indeed, to any circumstance, he also had learned not to dismiss intuition. The perceptions that made his fingertips tingle and the hair on the back of his neck stand up long ago had proven their value as precursors to discovery.

It was reasonable to suppose that Anna's presence was protecting him. Though Ferrin did not intend that she should be used as a shield, any threat against his own person threatened her as well. The one truth that appeared irrefutable was that Anna's abductor had not wished any harm to come to her and that given the opportunity to take her safely away, another attempt would be made to do so.

A second glance at the darkening skies assured Ferrin that a storm was imminent. Lightning flashed on the horizon, and minutes later thunder rumbled overhead. Something colorful flashed below the lowering clouds, making Ferrin blink, then fix his gaze on the object.

When he realized what it was, he could only shake his head at the folly of it. He peeled back his greatcoat enough to give Anna a glimpse of the same patch of sky that he was studying. "Look, Anna! There! Do you see the kite? It belongs to one of your friends." Under his breath, he added, "Obviously the one with the least gray matter in his upperworks."

Ferrin pressed his heels into the gelding's flanks, pushing him to increase the pace. He could only imagine in what manner Cybelline and Lily were occupied that neither one of them saw that one of the kites had been recovered and was now being flown by someone's sure hand on the ground. He acknowledged that Cybelline might not have understood the danger, but Lily had been present when he had demonstrated the voltaic pile to the boys and told them the tale of Benjamin Franklin, the kite, the key, and the lightning storm.

"Bloody hell," Ferrin said softly. Apparently soothed by his tone, Anna snuggled closer. He closed his greatcoat around her again and pressed on. Now that Anna was safe, he set his sights on the kite and making a timely rescue of whichever scoundrel was holding the string.

"You take Rose," Dash said. "I want to fly the kite."

Since Midge had been the one to climb a tree to retrieve it, untangle the tail, and run hard into the wind to send it flying, he was understandably reluctant to surrender it in exchange for a mewling infant. He glanced up from the lake toward the tree line where Lily and Cybelline were still kneeling at Becky's side and tending to her injuries.

"All right," he said with little grace, "but we should move away from the lake. We'll be in Dutch with her ladyship if we're caught out this close to the water with Rosie."

"I'm not going to drop her," Dash insisted.

"I *know* that. *She* doesn't." Midge tugged on the ball of string cupped in his hands as the kite dipped. He skillfully helped it find another air current to lift it again and began walking toward the open field at the far end of the lake. "Come on." He released more string and this time the skeleton key he'd attached before he left the hall was finally visible. It dangled from a loose knot in the twine. "It's too bad Pinch isn't here for this," Midge said. "Always likes to be part of an experiment, Pinch does."

Midge turned then and walked backward for a bit, squinting in the direction of the hall. "They're coming now." He jerked his chin toward the gardens. "His lordship's at the front of things."

Dash also turned. He counted five servants and Pinch following in Lord Sheridan's wake. Another of the grooms was riding out to the road to fetch the surgeon from the village. Hefting Rose in his arms again, he glanced worriedly toward the trees. "Do you think she's badly 'urt? The maid, I mean."

"I expect so," Midge said. "That 'orse was a brute."

"The rider, too."

Midge nodded. "Should have done more myself, I'm thinking. Leapt up on the back of him, perhaps. Or thrown myself at his leg from the other side. Becky's a right'un, though. She held on. Ain't no one can say she didn't give it 'er all."

Dash hurried to catch up to Midge. "I was thinking the same." A rumble of thunder shook the ground under him. "I say, what's that?"

Midge pointed off to his left. "Bit of thunder, I expect. There was a bolt of lightning over that way a little while ago."

"I should take Rose back to her mum," Dash said, glancing around. "Or at least give her to one of the grooms when they get here."

Midge agreed. "Pipkin will take her."

Dash took off, cutting a diagonal toward the trees and arriving at Lily's side only slightly out of breath. "His lordship's on his way," he told her. "And he has grooms with him." His eyes darted toward Becky. She scarcely seemed to be breathing. "Is she going to be all right?"

Lily didn't answer his question. She gestured vaguely to the side and issued a brisk order. "Stand over there, Dash."

Dash stepped away quickly. He heard Lily and Cybelline speak in hushed tones that were unintelligible to him. Giving them his back, he waited for the arrival of Sherry and his entourage. Two of the grooms carried a litter between them. Pipkin, the senior carriage driver, and Mr. Kennerly, the master of the stable, arrived just behind them. Pinch and Mr. Penn, the groundskeeper, brought up the rear.

Dash thrust Rose into Mr. Pipkin's arms before the older man had an opportunity to consider what he was being given. "Lady Sherry doesn't want me standing about," Dash reported by way of explaining himself. He waved to Pinch to join him, then he turned and ran off to tell Midge what he'd seen.

Midge relinquished the kite in exchange for information. "I remember when Ned Craven served up a proper beating to Ol' Fitzhugh," he said. "Does she look like that?"

"Worse." Dash kept an eye on the kite but glanced from time to time at his companions. "I fear for her."

Pinch nodded. "I saw the same as you, Dash, and his lordship looked grim."

"What's to be done for Anna, then?" asked Midge. "Lord Ferrin set out all alone. What chance does he have of bringing her back?"

"I don't know," Dash said, "but Mrs. Caldwell seems to think he will."

"I expect she can't let herself think otherwise." Pinch drew on wisdom learned from living on the mean and squalid streets of Holborn. The others, his boon companions for more than half his life, were of a similar mind. "Mayhap we should go to the road to look for him. You never know but that we can lend a hand."

Midge was all for it, but Dash glanced doubtfully at the kite. "I can't take it through the woods."

"We'll tie it to a tree branch at the edge. Look! The wind's blowing hard enough to keep it aloft. Just see if it doesn't. And if what Lord Ferrin says is true, then if lightning strikes, it will fell the tree, not you."

Dash allowed that this was an excellent point and wondered why he had not thought of it himself. He was not so certain Pinch would have come up with the idea if they all still had their kites and keys. "Very well. Let's find a place to tie it down."

They struck off for the wood and did not have to look long for a branch they could reach by putting Dash on Pinch's shoulders. With the kite secured, they set off through the trees for the road, crashing through the underbrush so loudly they startled deer and a family of rabbits. In contrast, Ferrin's approach on horseback was infinitely more quiet.

He came upon the scoundrels so suddenly they actually teetered up on their toes as they stopped. Cocking an eyebrow at them, he made a circling motion with his index finger then pointed behind them, indicating they should return from whence they came.

Except to set down on their heels, they didn't move. They asked some version of the same question at the same time.

Ferrin answered them by opening his greatcoat and revealing Anna's chubby little body clinging to him. She turned, saw the boys, and smiled beatifically.

The scoundrels clambered closer, making the horse shy. Ferrin steadied Newton and cautioned the boys to step back. "I see you've abandoned the kite," he said. "A very good decision."

"Tied it to a tree," Dash said.

"Tell me, does it have a key attached to the string?" All three of them nodded, and Ferrin could only shake his head. "I'm the one who has learned a lesson today," he told them. "Come on, we should move on. A storm's coming, and we have a little girl who very much wants to see her mother."

The boys led the way back, their exuberant cries announcing Anna's return long before they broke through to the clearing. Cybelline was already headed toward them at a run, her hair flying, her skirts raised almost to her knees. Ferrin dismounted before she collided with his horse and took her under his wing in exactly the same manner he'd taken Anna.

He folded both of his women into a single embrace and allowed them to weep and laugh and talk in a nonsensical fashion until the intensity of the emotions they shared simply wore them out.

Standing on tiptoe, Cybelline pressed kisses to Ferrin's face just as she had Anna's. "I never doubted," she whispered against his throat. "Never once. I knew you wouldn't come back without her, and I knew you'd come back."

The enormity of the trust she had placed in him left Ferrin quite without words. He swallowed hard and held on. Looking past Cybelline, he saw that Becky was being carried away on a litter. She was surrounded by a phalanx of servants who bore her like Roman soldiers carrying the Caesar. Sheridan and Lily followed the solemn group, but after a few steps, Sherry turned, put two fingers to his lips and whistled shrilly for the scoundrels to join them. They trotted off, glancing back wistfully from time to time at the kite they were forced to leave behind.

Grateful for these moments alone, and appreciative of Sherry's confidence, Ferrin drew Cybelline back a little so he could assure himself she was all of a piece. "Becky's injuries?" he asked finally, searching her face. The gravity of the maid's injuries was immediately apparent to him. "I'm sorry, Cybelline."

"You're not to blame."

"I didn't find him," he told her. "I can't be certain who it was who took Anna, but I believe I know who arranged it."

"Nicholas's mistress," Cybelline said.

"In a manner of speaking, yes."

Taking Anna into her own arms, Cybelline stepped back. "I don't understand what that means."

The rider at the edge of the wood judged it safe to finally make his presence known. "My dear Mrs. Caldwell," he said in crisp accents. "I think I can explain."

Chapter Sixteen

Cybelline instinctively took a step backward; she drew Anna closer to her breast. Ferrin immediately stepped sideways to partially block her and Anna from the intruder's view. The pistol aimed at them did not waver.

The rider dismounted but remained in the shadowed edge of the wood where he could not be seen by any of the party making their way back to the hall. When Cybelline glanced in the direction of the house she saw that the servants were already beginning the climb through the terraced gardens. Sherry and Lily still followed behind, but the scoundrels were making a race of it to the front door.

"I must caution you against summoning help, Mrs. Caldwell."

Cybelline's head snapped around as she realized how transparent her thoughts had been. The muffler that covered the lower half of the man's face made his speech less distinct and somehow more menacing. It did not, however, conceal his identity from her.

Sir Richard Settle's carefully correct manner and carriage had always been his calling card.

Cybelline did not shy away from his dark, piercing regard. "I wonder that you find a pistol necessary. It suggests you are not so confident of your superiority as you would have me believe."

Sir Richard tugged on his muffler until his chin was raised above it. He did not address Cybelline but made his remarks to Ferrin instead. "Do you find her cleverness appealing, Ferrin? For myself, I do not."

Ferrin made no reply. As a test of the other man's patience, it was successful. Sir Richard jerked the pistol so that it was clearly pointed at Ferrin's chest and no longer aimed just past his shoulder at Cybelline.

"Nicholas found her entertaining," Sir Richard said. His tone remained relaxed, conversational, but his grip on the pistol tightened. "I wonder if you do not find her the same."

Ferrin shrugged. At his side his fingers brushed Cybelline's pelisse. He caught a fold and pulled on it without drawing Sir Richard's attention to the movement. Cybelline responded by sidling a bit closer, making herself and her daughter even less of a target.

Sir Richard's horse pawed the ground nervously when lightning flashed overhead. "Easy, Titan." He held the reins firmly until the rolling thunder had passed, then he looped the reins around the slim trunk of a beech and pulled them to make a loose knot.

Ferrin's own mount was similarly distressed by the approaching storm. Newton swung his head and nudged Ferrin's shoulder.

"Send him here," Sir Richard said. He jerked the pistol to punctuate his order when Ferrin was slow to obey.

Ferrin gave Newton a sharp rap on his hindquarters and sent him off. The gelding wandered close to Sir Richard and the shelter of the trees, but another jagged bolt of lightning had him veering away sharply and heading in the direction of the stable. Ferrin lifted his hands helplessly, indicating he was not responsible.

Sir Richard's mouth thinned. With his free hand he

motioned Ferrin and Cybelline to join him under the trees just as the first fat droplets of rain began to fall. When neither of them deigned to move, he steadied his aim on Ferrin, although his message was for Cybelline. "I will shoot him. I doubt anyone at the manor will hear or, if they do, will think it is naught but thunder. You won't get away, not with Anna, not with his lordship lying at your feet."

A raindrop fell on Cybelline's cheek. Another caught her lashes. She wiped them away impatiently, unwilling to allow Sir Richard to mistake them for tears. Without waiting to take her cue from Ferrin, Cybelline stepped outside his protective stance and began walking toward her late husband's lover.

Ferrin did not allow Cybelline to get in front of him, rather he fell into step beside her. He watched Sir Richard carefully during his approach, waiting to see if the man would shift the direction of his aim to Cybelline. He didn't. It seemed to Ferrin that Sir Richard had finally set his strategy after determining that Ferrin was indeed the more serious threat. This was completely to Ferrin's liking. The extent to which Sir Richard underestimated Cybelline's resolve and resourcefulness would surely be their advantage.

Cybelline sheltered her daughter's head with her hand. In spite of this effort, a few raindrops splashed Anna's face. With the eagerness of a fledgling bird, Anna squirmed and tried to catch more in her open mouth. Cybelline removed her hand as they reached the edge of wood and a canopy of pine boughs lent them protection. She shifted Anna to her hip. A clap of thunder encouraged her daughter to hold on tightly.

Sir Richard retreated the few steps necessary to ensure he maintained a safe distance from Ferrin. "You did not seem particularly surprised when I revealed myself," he said to Cybelline. "Or is it that you are so adept at concealment?"

"It is odd that you should speak of concealment," she said calmly. "I suspect it has always been a practice of yours."

"Always."

"And Nicholas's practice as well."

"Can you doubt it?" asked Sir Richard. "He hid behind you, did he not? Your woman's skirts made a chameleon of him, hiding him in plain sight. So few of us have the eyes to see it, though. Did you?"

Cybelline answered honestly. "No. No, I didn't."

Sir Richard nodded slowly, thoughtfully. "It worried Nicholas, you know. Your animus toward me gave him pause. He wondered if you did not suspect our relationship."

"I couldn't suspect what I could not conceive," she said. "But I will tell you that my dislike for you had little enough to do with my husband. You earned my enmity entirely on your own merit." Out of the corner of her eye she thought she saw Ferrin smile. Sir Richard, she observed, was unamused, and she took an indecent amount of pleasure from it. "I have noted, however, that you kept Nicholas from being invited to join the Royal Society. It gives me cause to wonder how well you loved him. It has always seemed to me that you were pleased with his accomplishments as long as they did not overshadow your own. I have invariably found it difficult to think of you in any way except as a small man."

Sir Richard's nostrils flared at the insult. "His accomplishments? He had none that were not at my urging. I was the one who mentored and encouraged him. Nicholas had no direction until he allowed me to shepherd him, and he was grateful for my guidance."

Ferrin drew Sir Richard's attention to himself again by posing a question of his own. "Was it you who suggested that Mr. Caldwell should pursue law?"

Sir Richard's eyes narrowed slightly. "It was."

"Then you knew him at Harrow." Ferrin saw his comment caused Sir Richard a moment's concern. There was the slightest hesitation before he answered by nodding his head. Ferrin went on. "You were his professor there."

"Yes," Sir Richard said. "For a while. I went to Cambridge then."

"But Caldwell didn't follow."

"No. He decided against it."

"That must have rankled. It cannot be easy for the shepherd who's lost his sheep."

Sir Richard merely shrugged. The pistol didn't move.

"When did you realize you were no longer so influential in Caldwell's life? When he announced his intention to marry? Or was it earlier, when he arranged for his grandfather to make a substantial gift to Cambridge in his will with the proviso that you leave your post there?" This time Ferrin saw a muscle jump in Sir Richard's lean cheek and knew that his intuitive leap had hit the mark. "I thought that you exercised considerable control over him, but I know now he was every bit your equal in this regard."

Sir Richard glanced at Cybelline again. "He loved me that much," he told her. "He could not bear it that I would be at Cambridge while he remained in London."

"With me," Cybelline said softly. "While he remained in London with me." A brilliant flash of lightning made the very air around her crackle. Anna was becoming heavy on her hip, but Cybelline would not set her down. "He made a choice that you've never been able to accept."

"Which choice is that?" he demanded. His words were almost drowned out by the rolling thunder. Rain was beginning to saturate the pine boughs. Droplets slipped through the canopy and spattered his hat and the capes of his greatcoat. "The one he made to stay with you or the one he made to leave us both?"

That took Cybelline's breath, but she recovered quickly.

"I was thinking of Anna," she said. "Nicholas chose to father a child. That is what you could not accept."

"On the contrary. Anna is the reason I'm here. Do you not yet comprehend that you were merely a brood mare? She is in every way more my daughter than yours. From the very first I've made her care my responsibility, and Nicholas indulged me."

In the eerie light of another lightning strike, Cybelline's face was perfectly white. She held her ground even while it shook under her. Anna began to fret and Cybelline gave her a small bounce on her hip. "Do you imagine I'm going to give her to you?"

"I imagine you will, yes."

Ferrin was not certain he would be permitted to draw another breath. Sir Richard had the pistol's hammer cocked and seemed bent on proving to Cybelline that he did not make threats of no account. Watching him, Ferrin had no more time to prepare for what happened than Sir Richard did, but his reaction was quicker when Cybelline gave Anna a second bounce. While it seemed as though she meant only to shift Anna to the other hip, what she did instead was toss her high into the boughs, then make no move to catch her. It was Ferrin who plucked Anna out of the air. That action stayed Sir Richard's hand and gave Cybelline the moment she needed to throw herself at him.

The force of her charge was not enough to push Sir Richard off his feet, but it did make him stumble into his horse. His pistol fired and the shot creased Titan's flank, making the animal rear up and swing his head mightily. The loosely tied reins slipped free of the beech, and Titan tore away and headed deep into the thicket. Lightning struck again, this time close enough for Cybelline to feel every hair at the back of her neck stand at attention. She fought Sir Richard for the spent pistol, clawing at his arm when he would have brought the weapon down on her head. Thunder masked his wounded animal cry as Cybelline bit through his leather glove to the fleshy ball of his thumb. He flung her aside hard enough to make her fall to her knees on the muddy ground but dropped the pistol in the same motion.

Useless as a firing weapon, the pistol nevertheless could batter a skull. When Sir Richard stooped to pick it up, Ferrin kicked it out of the way, then brought up his knee. He clipped Sir Richard in the jaw with enough force to make bone crack and drive his upper teeth into his gum. Screaming, Sir Richard fell backward and sprawled on the ground. His hat tumbled to one side. Rain diluted the blood seeping from his crushed mouth so that it ran past his cheeks into his hair and finally into the mud under his head. He raised himself up as far as his elbows before Ferrin planted a foot firmly in the middle of his chest and flattened him again.

Cybelline stood, shook off the rain that matted her fur collar to her face, then calmly bent to retrieve the pistol. She gave it to Ferrin. Anna was crying in earnest now, but Cybelline refused Ferrin's offer to take her. Instead, she circled around and stepped out into the open, where the rain beat hard against her.

"Cybelline?" Ferrin watched her go. She didn't even acknowledge that he called after her. She didn't turn in the direction of the hall but hurried away from it. He glanced down at Sir Richard, who remained quite still beneath his boot. Not trusting that he would remain that way, Ferrin removed his foot to prevent being upended with Anna in his arms and took a step back. He stuck the pistol into the waistband of his breeches. "I'm not certain Mrs. Caldwell realizes you threatened her husband with exposure. You meant to ruin him. Ruin her and Anna as well."

Sir Richard's eyes opened, and he stared darkly at Ferrin. He had to support his jaw in one hand to speak plainly. "You can't know that."

"True, I don't. But it's accurate, isn't it? That's why he killed himself. He loved you, certainly, but he loved Anna more. You knew he would never leave her mother. Whatever promises he made to you, whatever his assurances, you saw that he no longer was capable of keeping his word. He meant to cut you from his life to protect Anna. Perhaps he did not say as much to you, but you suspected it. I've read his letters; I know that he was trying to convince himself that nothing would be changed by his marriage and fatherhood. You knew everything would be different, and in time, so would he."

"She killed him."

Ferrin opened his greatcoat and moved Anna protectively inside. She stopped weeping and nestled against his chest just as she had done earlier. With her face hidden, Ferrin felt free to grind his heel into the soft underside of Sir Richard's outstretched arm. "One would think you would exercise more caution in your speech," he said pleasantly. Ferrin removed his foot only when he elicited a surrendering groan from his captive. "I should very much like to hear what you had in mind for Anna. That is not entirely clear to me."

Sir Richard did not answer. He folded his injured arm against his chest and continued to nurse his jaw with the other.

Ferrin nudged Sir Richard's knee with the toe of his boot. As a warning of where he intended to strike next, it was sufficient to loosen Sir Richard's swollen tongue.

"Meant her no harm," he said.

"I know that. You would not have left Anna on the wall for me to find if you'd intended to harm her." Ferrin expected some confirmation from Sir Richard, not a subtle shift in the man's dark stare. It roused his curiosity. "You did not abandon her," he said slowly, working out the puzzle. "There was someone else. It was your accomplice who left her." This time it was the slight lift of Sir Richard's eyebrows that confirmed Ferrin's suspicions.

Ferrin immediately took another step back to remove himself from Sir Richard's reach. Lightning crackled the air again and momentarily limned the skeletal tree branches with searing white light. Under his coat, Anna's small hands curled tightly around the throat of his shirt. Making a circle where he stood, Ferrin made careful note of his surroundings again before he returned his attention to Sir Richard.

"Who is he?" Ferrin asked. "I will have the name of the man helping you."

"Will you?"

Ferrin did not allow himself to be baited by Sir Richard's dry, disdainful tone. He nodded. The movement caused water collecting on the brim of his hat to cascade over the edge and drum the ground with more force than the falling rain. "I think you will give him up when you consider the alternative."

"The alternative?"

"Pain." He noticed this seemed to give Sir Richard pause. "Do not mistake my resolve. I can inflict a great deal of pain. You will welcome the briefest moments of respite; you will beg me to be merciful. And when you realize that I will show you no kindness, you will pray to your savior for death." Ferrin fell silent when he judged that Sir Richard's complexion was sufficiently pale. He allowed Sir Richard a few moments to think and called out for Cybelline. That she had gone off alone disturbed him, but that she had not already returned gave him good reason to be alarmed. The certain knowledge that Sir Richard had not acted entirely on his own lent him new awareness of the danger she faced.

Ferrin called for Cybelline again. Thunder stole his voice. When it passed, he cupped one hand around his mouth and made a third attempt to draw her attention.

Out of the corner of his eye he watched Sir Richard rise up on his elbows and look toward the clearing. Ferrin knew well that it might be a trick to distract him, but he could not risk that it wasn't. He pivoted on his heel, ducking the water-laden pine boughs, and darted a glance in the same direction as Sir Richard.

Cybelline stood just ten yards into the clearing. She was no longer alone. Her figure was made more fragile by the rain that pressed her pelisse to her slender frame and the breadth and height of the horse and rider at her side.

The distance was not so great, nor the curtain of rain so dense, as to prevent Ferrin from seeing the rider was not Sherry. This did not surprise. From the moment he turned to follow Sir Richard's telling glance, Ferrin had prepared himself to discover the presence of the accomplice, even to discover that Cybelline was being forced to accompany him, so his first look confirmed his expectations.

A second, more thorough, look revealed that his expectations had been set far too low. He had been as guilty of underestimating his warrior queen as Sir Richard. Cybelline was not accompanying the horse and rider, rather they were accompanying her. She held the leading strings, and the rider—most astonishingly—held fast to the string of a kite.

Rain beat against the kite, but a gust of wind lifted it. The rider's hands were raised at the same time, and Ferrin saw clearly that Cybelline's captive was not simply flying the kite. He was bound to it.

He looked back over his shoulder and saw that Sir Richard was attempting to get to his feet. "Drop the reins," Ferrin called to Cybelline, waving her closer. "Come! Take Anna!"

Cybelline let the reins fall and ran to Ferrin. "Is she all right?"

"Of course." Now that Cybelline was beside him and out of immediate danger, he realized that nothing was so urgent that he could not draw her close and hold her for a long moment. He let her take Anna out from under his coat, then he turned and slipped under the boughs to haul back Sir Richard.

Ferrin caught up to Sir Richard before the man had gone twenty feet. He had to duck when Sir Richard turned suddenly and struck out with his fist. Ferrin took a glancing blow to his shoulder but didn't lose his footing. He responded with a hard right punch that landed solidly against Sir Richard's midriff. While Sir Richard was trying to recover from that driving fist, Ferrin delivered a second blow with his left, clipping Sir Richard on his unprotected cracked jaw and breaking it.

Sir Richard's howl of pain coincided with another lightning strike, this one giving a supernatural brilliance to the heavy underbelly of dark clouds. Ferrin anticipated thunder, not the high-pitched, keening cry that followed the strike. Fearing for Cybelline and Anna, Ferrin ran back to where he'd left them. The thunder, when it came, was powerful enough to vibrate the entire wood.

Ferrin drew abreast of Cybelline and saw that she and Anna were uninjured. The cry had not come from her. He followed the direction she pointed even as she turned away from it. Ferrin saw the horse first. The animal was tearing across the clearing toward the lake. Spooked by the lightning, he seemed determined to outrun the storm, and with no rider to rein him in, there was a greater chance that he would injure himself than win the race against the wind and rain.

Ferrin's gaze was drawn next to the kite lying at an oddly pitched angle in the high grass. Partially obscured by the colorful fabric and rag tail was the fallen rider. When he didn't stir, Ferrin began to suspect that he'd not merely been thrown when his horse bolted.

Glancing skyward, Ferrin ticked off the time between strikes. He felt Cybelline try to hold him back, but he shook her off and ran into the clearing. He hunkered down and quickly tossed the kite aside. Sir Richard's partner was lying facedown in the grass. The smell of burnt wool and flesh, the acrid scent of singed hair, firmly set Ferrin's impression of what had taken place.

He touched the man's shoulder, shook it, then slipped two fingers under the muffler to press against his neck. The pulse he detected was faint, so faint he was not entirely certain he hadn't imagined it. He rolled the man over and tore at the muffler.

Astonishment set him back on his heels.

"Bloody hell." He closed his eyes a moment and rubbed the bridge of his nose with his thumb and forefinger. Rain dripped from the brim of his hat. A rivulet of water slipped under his coat and worked its way down his back. He shivered slightly, then slowly got to his feet. "Bloody, bloody hell."

He *had* imagined the pulse. The eyes that returned his stare had no consciousness behind them. Perhaps there had never been any conscience either. It no longer mattered.

There was nothing he could do.

Several long minutes passed before Ferrin realized the storm was moving on and that Cybelline had come to stand beside him. She held Anna's head cupped in her hand to prevent her from seeing the body. He would have liked to have protected Cybelline in the same manner. A sideways glance at her grim expression assured him she would not have permitted it.

"Did you know?" he asked.

"No."

He put his arm around her shoulders and turned her once again to the sheltering wood. The rain was falling more gently now but every drop had an icy edge. In spite of that, they didn't hurry. Ferrin took Anna from Cybelline and pointed to the hall where Sherry was leading another group of servants through the gardens toward them. The scoundrels ran alongside, easily keeping pace with his horse.

Ferrin knew he would have to stop the boys before they reached the kite, but he did nothing to impede Sir Richard's halting progress across the field. Neither he nor Cybelline paused when he limped past them. There was nowhere for him to go except to the body, and when Ferrin glanced back, Sir Richard had dropped to his knees beside it.

"Who do you suppose she was to him?" he asked.

Cybelline could only shake her head.

The question they shared was answered as Sir Richard Settle clutched Nanny Baker in his arms and cried out mournfully for the loss of his sister.

The music room at Granville Hall was unusually quiet. Sherry sat on the bench at the pianoforte but with his back to the instrument. In a half recline, he rested his elbows on the lid covering the keys while his long legs stretched before him. He appeared to be contemplating the toe of his boots.

Lily had chosen a straight-back chair beside the candelabra. She had an embroidery hoop in one hand and a needle and floss in the other. She had yet to make a single stitch, though from time to time she plucked one out.

Ferrin and Cybelline shared the chaise longue. His hand lay lightly over hers. Occasionally his thumb would make a pass across the back of her hand. Like Sherry, he seemed to be contemplating the toe of his boots. Cybelline's attention was for the corner of the room where Anna was stacking blocks. The scoundrels had already been sent to bed, but Cybelline was not yet prepared to allow Anna out of her sight.

It did not matter that the danger had passed, that Sir Richard was in the custody of the authorities or that

Nanny Baker's body had been removed for burial. What mattered to Cybelline was that she could see her child. No one objected. Cybelline noticed that when her companions were not staring at their feet—or in Lily's case, her hoop—they were stealing glances at Anna, assuring themselves of her presence.

In truth, Anna was perhaps the least affected by the events of the day. From her perspective, she'd had an adventure. Every cautious question that Cybelline put to her was answered in a way that supported that view, and no one pressed her for more information than she was prepared to give at the outset. As best as Cybelline could determine, the thunderstorm seemed to have made a larger impression on Anna than either her abduction or the confrontation with Sir Richard in the wood. There was nothing for it but to wait for time to tell.

The attention of everyone in the music room was drawn to the door when the butler appeared. Wolfe inclined his head and addressed Sherry. "You asked to be informed if there was a change in Miss Potter's condition."

Uncertain what he was about to hear, Sherry rose from the piano bench and indicated to Wolfe that they should step out into the hall. He reappeared a few minutes later and shut the door quietly behind him. "It is good news," he said. "Miss Potter is alert again and able to recall her name. She has taken a light repast, which apparently did her no harm. She also recollects how she came by her injuries and most particularly asked after Miss Anna."

Out of the corner of her eye, Cybelline observed Anna lifting her head, alert to the sound of her name. When no one fussed over her, she simply went back to the blocks. Anna's perfectly self-centered world raised Cybelline's small smile. She squeezed Ferrin's hand, reassured in equal measure by her daughter's calm and Sherry's report.

"Good news, indeed," Cybelline said softly. "I confess,

after Dr. Meacham explained her condition to me, I feared she would not fully recover her senses."

Lily dabbed at her eyes with one corner of the fabric lying across her lap, then smiled apologetically. "My thoughts also. She was a long time having her arm set and even longer under his knife. When she remembered nothing that had transpired earlier, then not even her own name or where she was, it occurred to me that the surgeon's cure had rendered her feebleminded."

Sherry went to Lily's side, touching her cheek gently before he placed his hand on the back of her chair. He addressed Cybelline and Ferrin. "Miss Potter will require a lengthy convalescence, and there is no question of moving her. I hope you know you are welcome to remain at Granville Hall as long as you like, but you should be confident that Miss Potter will be well looked after and not plan your own departure around her ability to travel. In time she can join you or she might consider taking a position here at the hall. Rosie's nurse is up to the task of tending to an infant, but Potter has demonstrated a tenacity that Lily and I believe will serve our daughter in good stead."

Cybelline nudged Ferrin with her elbow. "Do you see, my lord, he is trying to steal her from me. He puffs the thing up, but that is the gist of it. Deny it, Sherry. I dare you."

"I cannot, but it was Lady Sheridan who proposed the idea to me."

"Sherry!" Lily gave him a disapproving look. "Lord Ferrin is not so well acquainted with your rather odd sense of humor as I am. He will think you are quite serious."

"I am," Sherry said.

Watching the play between Sherry and his wife, Ferrin's lips twitched. He glanced at Cybelline and saw she was also holding a smile in check. Given all that had taken place this day, it was perhaps still too soon for outright laughter, but it would surely be forthcoming. Ferrin believed that boded well for the future.

Cybelline's eyes followed her brother as he returned to the bench. "Let us agree that Becky shall have choices and leave it at that."

Sherry arched an eyebrow at her. "That is impressively fair-minded of you."

"I intend to bribe her, of course."

"Have you forgotten? I'm accounted to be as rich as Croesus."

"Ferrin's richer."

Sherry glanced at Ferrin, looking for confirmation.

Wincing slightly, Ferrin nevertheless agreed. "I'm afraid so."

Cybelline's satisfied smile was so cat-in-the-cream that it moved Sherry to laughter. When he cut himself off abruptly, the silence that followed was uncomfortable.

Cybelline looked over at Anna, saw her daughter was paying them no heed, and said quietly, "I think we should speak of it. Of all of it. Avoiding the discussion is painful, at least I find it so."

Lily stabbed her needle into the fabric stretched taut in the hoop and set the whole of it aside. She also turned briefly in Anna's direction. "I agree with Cybelline."

When Sherry and Ferrin said nothing, Cybelline plunged ahead. "I should like to know what charges will be leveled against Sir Richard. Sherry, you and Ferrin spoke at length to the men who came here."

Seeing that Cybelline meant to have her answers, Sherry reluctantly obliged. "The attempts at abduction and murder will be the most grievous charges. There are the harassing letters also, although their existence will not be made public, just as the entire nature of his association with Nicholas will not be revealed. I believe we can depend upon the discretion of the authorities, and Sir Richard understands the benefits of remaining silent in certain matters. There is little chance any of it will become fodder for endless gossip." He continued to watch Cybelline closely. "You are relieved?"

"Yes, of course . . . for all of our sakes." Cybelline regarded her folded hands a moment, then her brother. A measure of color returned to her face. "Thank you. You had no small influence there."

"On the contrary, Sir Richard was cooperative almost from the outset and made a complete confession of every one of his actions."

"A confession?" Cybelline was immediately wary. "I cannot not imagine it. He is entirely too arrogant." She slipped her fingers free of Ferrin's and considered him suspiciously. "I detect your fine hand, my lord. What did you say to him to provoke a confession?"

"I said very little, actually."

Cybelline did not waver in her suspicious regard.

Ferrin chose his words carefully. "The demonstration was persuasive on its own."

"Demonstration?"

"Yes. Of Berzelius's work. Perhaps you recall that I was studying his *Theory of Chemical Proportions and the Chemical Action of Electricity*."

What Cybelline recalled was the jolt Anna had received touching the leads of Ferrin's voltaic pile. Her eyes widened. "You attached him to a voltaic pile?"

"No. I merely threatened to."

Before Cybelline could make a response, Sherry interjected a broader explanation. "It was effective, though some might say badly done of us. Sir Richard was susceptible to Ferrin's suggestion, having witnessed a more powerful display of the same when his sister was struck down. Ferrin had only to show that he could create a similar charge and Sir Richard found his voice."

Lily's glance swiveled from her husband back to Ferrin, then came to rest on Cybelline. "They are not remorseful," she said, "and I cannot say that I am properly appalled by their methods. Indeed, it is difficult not to applaud them."

"Sir Richard is no innocent," Sherry said when Cybelline remained silent. "His confession means there will be no public trial."

"I understand," Cybelline said. "It is rather more than I expected to hear. As you say, Sir Richard is no innocent." She quietly reached for Ferrin's hand again and threaded her fingers through his. "What is to be done about me?"

"You?" Ferrin asked. "What do you mean?"

"In regard to Sir Richard's sister." With Anna present, it was not possible to speak of the woman as Nanny Baker. "When I left you with Sir Richard, I meant only to retrieve the twine that was securing the kite so we might restrain him. Coming upon the horse and rider was quite unexpected, but surprise was my advantage this time. I caused the horse to rear by poking it with a stick. I couldn't unseat the rider, but she hit her head hard on a heavy branch, and I had time enough to retrieve the kite and bind her hands. Afterward I led her out into the open. That is where she was finally thrown when her horse bolted, and that is when . . ." She fell silent a moment, remembering. Her head came up, and she said quite frankly, "It is understood, is it not, that I am responsible for her death?"

"What is understood," Ferrin said, "is that you apprehended Sir Richard's accomplice and used what means were available to secure her after capture. The lightning strike was a phenomenon of nature."

"It was providence," Lily said.

Sherry smiled at the certainty in his wife's tone and inclined his head, deferring to her judgment, then responded to his sister. "No responsibility has been attached to you, Cybelline. If that were the case, where would it end? Should Pinch, Midge, and Dash be made accountable because they put keys on the kites? Mayhap I should hold Ferrin's feet to the fire for telling them the story of Franklin's discovery. Is Lily culpable? She did not observe what the scoundrels had done to their kites, and she underestimated the speed of the approaching storm."

Ferrin's thumb lightly brushed the back of Cybelline's hand. "You acted to protect your child. No one faults you."

Cybelline worried the inside of her bottom lip. "It is all such a turmoil of feeling. I am not remorseful, yet I am guilty. I didn't recognize her beneath her man's outerwear and muffler, but I do not like to think on what I would have done if I had. I doubt I would have led her so calmly back to the clearing."

"She betrayed you," Lily said quietly.

"Nicholas betrayed me. He hired that woman to care for our daughter. He allowed Sir Richard to believe he had certain privileges of parenthood."

Ferrin recalled Sir Richard's taunt to Cybelline: *Do you not yet comprehend that you were merely a brood mare? She is in every way more my daughter than yours. From the very first I've made her care my responsibility, and Nicholas indulged me.* Ferrin said nothing as the ache in Cybelline's heart gave rise to anger.

"It was at Nicholas's urging that I hired her. I mistook his interest in the applicants as further proof of his thoughtful attention. Attention? What he did was encourage me to take a spy into my home. I do not fault the care she gave my daughter, but we know that her most excellent oversight had another purpose. I believe it was always in Sir Richard's mind to take my daughter from me, and Nicholas humored him."

Ferrin shook his head slightly. "I am less certain than you how much your husband supported Sir Richard's imaginings. Sir Richard turned on Nicholas. He threatened to publicly reveal their affair."

"He told you this?"

"Yes."

"He wouldn't have done it."

"I don't think so, either, but that doesn't mean he didn't convince Nicholas. We can only guess at what provoked Sir Richard to make the threat. It might not have been any one thing, but it is likely that Anna figured largely in whatever brought it about."

Hearing her name, Anna noisily scattered the blocks as she scrambled to her feet. She skirted Lily's chair, stepping carefully over the basket of floss and material on the floor, and went to her mother. She climbed onto the chaise in the space that Ferrin and Cybelline made for her between them. With little urging, she let herself be cradled in the crook of Ferrin's arm.

Cybelline brushed back a lock of hair that lay against Anna's temple so that it curled around her ear. Almost absently she asked, "Did Sir Richard confess to the letters?"

It was Sherry who answered. "Yes. As you might suspect, his sister assisted in their delivery."

"I have seen his handwriting many times. It is vastly different than those notes he penned."

"A minor subterfuge. He used his left hand to record his accusations and address the missives. That is why each letter seemed so painstakingly formed. He told us that he did not correspond with his sister but that she wrote regularly to him. It was learning of the interests of a certain Mr. Wellsley that alarmed him enough to make him leave London for Penwyckham."

"Then he was never interested in the artifacts."

"It would be truer to say that his interest was not entirely feigned," said Ferrin. "He did not want to pay for what he believed was always meant to be his. The shield, for instance, was a discovery he and your husband made together. The collection gave him a reason to visit you and determine what threat Mr. Wellsley's attentions were to his own plans. His sister did not know I was Ferrin, but if you will recall, both she and Sir Richard saw—"

"The book," Cybelline said softly. "*Pride and Prejudice.* They saw your name on the bookplate."

"That's right. She did not know the significance of it when I lent her the book, but one cannot accuse Sir Richard of being a slow top. He was able to gather enough information about Mr. Wellsley from his sister to reliably confirm that we were one and the same."

A small crease appeared between Cybelline's eyebrows as she considered this. "It explains why he was not at all surprised to see you in the wood. I do not even think I comprehended it at the time." She darted a sideways look at Ferrin. "And you knew who he was, even before he revealed himself. How?"

Ferrin glanced at Sherry, who nodded once, indicating he should explain. "The scoundrels pointed it out to me."

This bit of intelligence brought Lily to a forward position in her chair. She spoke before Cybelline could. "The scoundrels? How is that possible? They know nothing at all of Sir Richard Settle."

Sherry admonished his wife gently. "Allow Ferrin to explain, dearest, and I promise you will be as astonished as I was."

Lily settled an accusing glance on her husband for making her wait to hear something he already knew.

Unnoticed by either her brother or her sister-in-law, Cybelline tugged on Ferrin's sleeve, urging him to account for himself quickly.

"It's true the lads do not know Sir Richard, but they know about magnets," Ferrin told Lily. "Do you recall what happened during the science lesson when I was teaching them about attracting and repelling forces?"

"Indeed, I do," Lily said. "I thought I would have to restrain Midge and Dash before they hurt each other. They were . . . oh, I see . . . well, yes, I suppose they did lead you to . . . how extraordinary."

"Well, I *don't* see," Cybelline said. "I was not there, was I?"

Ferrin tamped down his smile. "Midge and Dash decided they would demonstrate the repelling forces by bumping chests into each other. They were like roosters strutting about, puffing themselves up, then"—he brought his hands sharply together and let them fly apart—"they prattled on about how they—"

"How they were alike," Cybelline said softly as comprehension came to her. "Two boys, of course. Yes, they told me when I ran into them after I left the gallery. I didn't understand then, but it opened your eyes to a new possibility, didn't it?"

"Yes."

"And you understood what it meant."

He shrugged. "Where human beings are concerned, the forces that act on attraction are not so easily understood."

A faint smile lifted the corners of Cybelline's mouth. "He is being modest," she told her brother and Lily. "He knows everything. It is really a very serious fault of his."

Sherry looked to his wife. "Why do you never make such pretty compliments on my behalf?"

"Because your most serious fault is not that you know everything, but that you think you do."

"Oh, Sherry," Cybelline said, "you deserved that. You know you did."

"Indeed." He gave Lily a wry look. "At least my sister knows what I know."

Lily held her retort as Anna yawned widely. Her smile was immediately indulgent. "I think someone is telling us she is quite ready for bed."

Cybelline looked down at her daughter. "Is that right, darling? Shall I take you upstairs?" The surest sign that Anna was prepared to go was the lack of protest as Cybelline got to her feet. She bent to pick up her daughter, and Anna held out her arms. "Goodness, you are a sleepyhead." Cybelline straightened and hefted Anna against her breast and shoulder. "Say goodnight, then we're off to your bed."

"Your bed," Anna said.

"You want to sleep with me tonight?"

Anna nodded. "And Misterlee." Turning her head sideways, she flung out a hand in Ferrin's direction. "Come!" she ordered imperiously. "We sleep in the same bed. Like your house."

Anna's disclosure hung heavily in the air. For a long—very long—moment, there was only silence.

Sherry held up his hand, palm out, forestalling Cybelline's explanation. "It is as Lily says," he told his sister. "I only *think* I know everything. It will be better, I believe, if this last revelation remains in that uncertain realm."

Lily left her chair and went to her husband's side. She laid a hand on his shoulder. "I am never so in love with you as when you step down from your high horse." She bent to kiss him on the mouth. Behind her back she waved Ferrin, Cybelline and Anna off, encouraging them to make their escape.

They were slipping out the door when Sherry broke the kiss long enough to call after them. "I should very much like to learn in the morning that a wedding date has been set."

"Soon," Cybelline said, pulling Ferrin across the threshold. "It will be soon."

Ferrin closed the door behind them. He bent his head toward Cybelline and whispered, "It will be sooner."

She never doubted that in this, too, he would be proven right.

Epilogue

The bride was radiant. Everyone in attendance would remark later that her feet did not quite touch the ground on her way to the altar. The groom, they would say, seemed unaware of anyone in the crowded church save for his bride, and that was exactly as it should be.

Were there ever two people so in love? the wags asked.

Cybelline had the question posed to her several times. Ferrin also had the same query put to him. No, they assured the family, friends, and guests, they certainly had never seen the like before, and did it not strain the bounds of propriety the way they looked at each other? Then Ferrin and Cybelline would exchange that very same propriety-straining glance.

Lady Rivendale witnessed such an exchange and left her circle of friends to deliver a scold. "Oh, that is very bad of both of you," she said. "Poor Mrs. Palmer does not even realize you were having her on. You must save your wit for someone who is at least conscious of it."

"Or who is at least conscious," Ferrin said in wry accents.

"My lord!" Cybelline tugged on the cuff of Ferrin's black frock coat. "Have a care. You will be overheard."

Lady Rivendale brought up her fan quickly. It hid her smile and softened her laughter. She required a moment to compose herself. "You must realize, Cybelline, that your husband can say or do almost nothing that will place him beyond the pale, and you have only yourself to blame."

"I cannot imagine how that came to be," said Cybelline. She leaned toward her aunt as though to impart a confidence. Her look of mischief was all for her husband. "He has faults, you know."

Ferrin grinned. "Your spirited defense of my character never fails to move me."

Lady Rivendale used her closed fan to give Cybelline a lightly reproving tap on the wrist. "You have reformed the rake, my dear, so it is useless to speak of his faults. He no longer has any that merit comment. Indeed, everyone agrees he is a paragon."

Cybelline laughed when she saw Ferrin was disconcerted. "What is it, my lord? You object to being named such?"

"Reformed rakes are notoriously dull."

"Also high in the instep," Cybelline said. "Do not forget they are high in the instep."

Lady Rivendale offered her own observation of the species. "And they are completely tiresome in their devotion to family."

Ferrin sighed. His glance in Cybelline's direction was faintly accusing. "You must allow that Aunt Georgia is right: You have only yourself to blame."

She stepped closer to him and wound her arm around his. "It is only proper that society finally acknowledges the gentleman you have always been. I do not mind accepting responsibility for that, but in private, if you wish to play the rogue, I would not mind that, either."

Lady Rivendale's eyes darted between the pair. Of a

sudden, she felt a need to fan herself. Tongue firmly in cheek, she asked, "La! Have there ever been two people so much in love?"

Laughing, Cybelline and Ferrin pointed as one to the bride and groom.

Lady Rivendale looked over her shoulder to where Wynetta and Wellsley stood not ten feet distant. Enrapt, they were oblivious to her scrutiny. "Well, of course, *they* are, but the ink is barely dry on their license, while I have it in my mind that you have been wed these past three months."

"And a sennight," Cybelline said. "Three months and a sennight."

"She has also become astonishingly dull," Lady Rivendale told Ferrin. "You deserve each other."

He bent and kissed her cheek. "You flatter me."

Lady Rivendale made a dramatic surrender, throwing up her hands when Cybelline and Ferrin playfully regarded each other with perfectly adoring glances. "You will excuse me, won't you?" she asked dryly. "I am for finding Sherry and Lily. They are no longer wholly absorbed in each other."

"They were absorbed in Lady Bellingham's gardens when last I saw them," Ferrin told her.

"Ducking into the maze," Cybelline said.

"Then I shall find Lady Bellingham. She will have a great deal to say about her grandson, the reformed scapegrace." Ignoring their laughter, she turned on her heel and slipped easily among the guests extending best wishes to the newlyweds.

Watching her go, Cybelline was moved to say, "She is immensely fond of you, my lord."

"I have that sense," he said. "Frankly, I quake at the thought of disappointing her."

"Indeed. That is the power she wields."

"It is a diabolic strategem."

Cybelline nodded. "Sherry and I have always thought so. You know, don't you, that she has claimed full responsibility for bringing us together? She can even make a claim that she had a hand in your sister and Mr. Wellsley exchanging vows today. Her friends are so impressed by her success that they have taken to petitioning her for advice." She saw Ferrin's eyes widen a fraction. "Alarming, is it not?"

"'Alarming' hardly describes it."

"Just so."

"You don't think we'll be expected to attend all the weddings she arranges, do you?"

Cybelline chuckled as Ferrin's concern became clear. "No, my lord, not if we flee London for the country."

Ferrin's relief was so patent that it bordered on the comical. "That is very good news."

"There is one wedding I must insist that we witness," she told him.

"Oh?"

"Miss Webb and Mr. Foster. You cannot have forgotten. They will wed in Penwyckham next month."

"That is entirely agreeable. I have a workroom at the Sharpe house."

"My, but you are dull."

"It is proper that we lend our consequence to the nuptials."

"Terribly high in the instep also."

He leaned toward her and whispered, "I have it in my mind that when Anna goes down for her afternoon nap, you and I will retire to our own room."

She feigned a yawn. "And completely tiresome in your devotion to your family."

His appreciative chuckle was cut short as he saw his mother and stepfather approaching from the left, his youngest sisters making a frontal assault, and Restell and the twins working their way through the throng on the right. Straightening, he gently turned Cybelline in the direction of the open French doors and the garden beyond. "Quickly," he said, "before they set upon us."

Cybelline stared at him, holding her ground as his family swarmed closer.

"Devoted in my attentions," he said, "not defective in my reasoning. They will not allow us to escape."

"I know." Her smile was brilliant. "Isn't it wonderful?"

It was quite late when they arrived home. Lady Gardner had prevailed upon them to remain long after Wynetta and Wellsley had departed. Lady Rivendale and Wellsley's grandmother also stayed. Laughter was the order of the evening as each of them shared their perspective on Wellsley's rather unorthodox pursuit of Wynetta's hand. In truth, because so much of the courting had been conducted in secret, none of them knew the whole of it, but no one hesitated to go on as if they were privy to every particular.

Recalling the evening, Cybelline smiled to herself. She dismissed her maid and stepped out of the dressing room wearing a sleeveless batiste chemise. She absently fingered the lace-trimmed neckline as she walked to her side of the bed. "Do you know, Christopher, I believe Lady Bellingham pronounced Mr. Wellsley a scapegrace no fewer than four times tonight. I am not certain if he has benefited overmuch from your ascension to paragon, at least not in his grandmother's eyes."

"I made it to be six times that she said it, but it might be that I started counting while we were yet at the wedding supper. Lady Bellingham is getting on in years. It occurred to me tonight that she does not always remember his name."

"The woman is as sharp as a soldier turned out in regimental dress. It must be an endearment after all."

Ferrin held up the covers for Cybelline. "That is probably

the case. What is important is that she gave her blessing to the marriage."

"Which it appears she would have done had he explained that his attentions were fixed on your sister."

"Not everyone can be as straightforward or confident as Boudicca."

"True." She edged closer, warmed by the place he made for her beside him. "It was a lovely wedding, I thought. And it was not possible for Wynetta to radiate more happiness. Wellsley was struck dumb."

"I tried to warn him."

"You did?"

"I felt I must. The very same happened to me."

"You never told me that."

"That is the very essence of being struck dumb," he said. "I have only now found the words."

Cybelline raised herself up just enough to kiss him on the mouth. "I think we can depend upon Anna to sleep through the night now that Becky has returned to us."

"Anna always sleeps through the night, yet somehow she manages to find her way here."

"That is because you insisted we should make the nursery across the hall. It is not very challenging for her."

Ferrin's smile was a trifle sheepish. "Then it must be that I sleep better knowing where she is."

Cybelline understood that well enough. She made her own confession. "As comfortable as I find it in your arms, I sleep better knowing Sir Richard Settle is half a world away."

"Nicely put, though he may not be so far as that. By my reckoning, the transport ship will not reach Sydney for at least another fortnight, and that is if the seas are calm and the winds kind. Given Sir Richard's presence on board *Wayfarer*, I would say that neither is likely."

"Did you actually plot the course?"

"No." He pretended to be offended by the question. "I

would not waste gray matter on such a trivial endeavor."
Ferrin sifted Cybelline's silky, honey-colored hair through
his fingers. After a moment, he admitted, "I acquired the
information from a ship's master."

That earned him another kiss, this one considerably
more lengthy than the last.

"What was that in aid of?" he asked when she lifted
her head.

"Thoroughness. I am saluting yours with my own."

He tipped his head, caught her lips with his, then rolled
so that she was under him. She lifted her hands and
placed them at the back of his neck. Her fingers flicked
the dark, curling hair at his nape, then walked down the
length of his spine, following the path of his shiver.

He said her name softly, first against her mouth, then
against her ear. His voice tripped a like response in her.
She stirred in his arms, stretching, rising, reaching. It was
precisely what he had been imagining all day, each time
he looked in Cybelline's direction, each time someone
asked him if there'd ever been two people so in love. He'd
thought of her like this, in his arms, her knees drawing up
on either side of his hips, her soft chemise being lifted
slowly to the level of her waist. He'd imagined coming to
her just as he was now, her hand guiding him, her body
inviting him, then giving her such pleasure in the
moment that he could not help but fall into it himself.

"Reforming a rake has much to recommend it," she
said when they were quiet again and their breathing had
calmed.

"That is my perspective also."

She smiled sleepily. "Of course it is."

Ferrin turned on his side and plumped the pillow beneath his head. He rested his hand lightly on Cybelline's
hip and watched her eyelids grow heavy. The candle in
the dish at their bedside sputtered, then extinguished
itself. It took some time for his eyes to adjust to the

darkness. By then her faintly swollen lips were parted
and she was sleeping.

Moonlight slipped through a break in the curtains. As
she was turned away from the window, a deep shadow
fell across the upper half of Cybelline's face. It startled
Ferrin to see her now as she had been that night at the
masquerade, mysteriously concealed by the hammered
gold mask.

The shadow moved on, the moment passed, but the
memory lingered. In time he slept, and when Boudicca
came to him, he accepted it as the most natural course of
events. She was all fiery hair and brilliant raiment, her
spear standing tall at her side. The golden torc at her throat
was the source of the brilliant light cupping her face. Her
proud bearing warned him that she would give him no
quarter.

Ferrin asked for none.

As he'd known from the outset, surrendering to a
queen had much to recommend it.

ABOUT THE AUTHOR

Jo Goodman lives with her family in Colliers, West Virginia. She is currently working on her newest Zebra historical romance, once again set in the Regency period. Look for it in 2007! Jo loves hearing from readers, and you may write to her c/o Zebra Books. Please include a self-addressed stamped envelope if you would like a response. Or you can visit her website at www.jogoodman.com.

<u>BOOK YOUR PLACE ON OUR WEBSITE</u>
<u>AND MAKE THE</u>
<u>READING CONNECTION!</u>

We've created a customized website just for our very special readers, where you can get the inside scoop on everything that's going on with Zebra, Pinnacle and Kensington books.

When you come online, you'll have the exciting opportunity to:

- View covers of upcoming books
- Read sample chapters
- Learn about our future publishing schedule (listed by publication month *and author*)
- Find out when your favorite authors will be visiting a city near you
- Search for and order backlist books from our online catalog
- Check out author bios and background information
- Send e-mail to your favorite authors
- Meet the Kensington staff online
- Join us in weekly chats with authors, readers and other guests
- Get writing guidelines
- AND MUCH MORE!

**Visit our website at
http://www.kensingtonbooks.com**

More Historical Romance From
Jo Ann Ferguson